THE GOVERNESS

broadview editions
series editor: L.W. Conolly

THE GOVERNESS; OR, THE LITTLE FEMALE ACADEMY

Sarah Fielding

edited by Candace Ward

broadview editions

Library and Archives Canada Cataloguing in Publication

Fielding, Sarah, 1710-1768.
⠀⠀The governess, or, The little female academy / Sarah Fielding ; edited by Candace Ward.

(Broadview editions)
ISBN 1-55111-412-7

⠀⠀I. Ward, Candace II. Title. III. Title: Little female academy. IV. Series.

PR3459.F3G69 2005⠀⠀⠀⠀823'.6⠀⠀⠀⠀⠀C2005-903118-2

Broadview Editions

The Broadview Editions series represents the ever-changing canon of literature by bringing together texts long regarded as classics with valuable lesser-known works.

Advisory editor for this volume: Kathryn Prince

Broadview Press Ltd. is an independent, international publishing house, incorporated in 1985. Broadview believes in shared ownership, both with its employees and with the general public; since the year 2000 Broadview shares have traded publicly on the Toronto Venture Exchange under the symbol BDP.

We welcome comments and suggestions regarding any aspect of our publications–please feel free to contact us at the addresses below or at broadview@broadviewpress.com / www.broadviewpress.com

North America
PO Box 1243, Peterborough, Ontario, Canada K9J 7H5
Tel: (705) 743-8990; Fax: (705) 743-8353
email: customerservice@broadviewpress.com
PO Box 1015, 3576 California Road, Orchard Park, NY, USA 14127

UK, Ireland, and continental Europe
NBN Plymbridge
Estover Road
Plymouth PL6 7PY UK
Tel: 44 (0) 1752 202 301
Fax: 44 (0) 1752 202 331
Fax Order Line: 44 (0) 1752 202 333
Customer Service: cservs@nbnplymbridge.com
Orders: orders@nbnplymbridge.com

Australia and New Zealand
UNIREPS, University of New South Wales
Sydney, NSW, 2052
Australia
Tel: 61 2 9664 0999; Fax: 61 2 9664 5420
email: info.press@unsw.edu.au

PRINTED IN CANADA

FSC

Mixed Sources
Product group from well-managed
forests and other controlled sources

Cert no. SW-COC-003438
www.fsc.org
©1996 Forest Stewardship Council

Contents

Acknowledgements

First, I would like to thank Julia Gaunce, Leonard Conolly, and the Broadview editorial team for their support of this project. I would also like to acknowledge the advice and encouragement of Jan Susina, Ron Fortune, and Susan Kim at Illinois State University. Thanks also to Linda Bree for sharing her enthusiasm for Sarah Fielding. I'm grateful to Madeline Gibson at the University of Illinois at Urbana-Champaign for her assistance and good humor, and to Rita Smith, Curator of the Baldwin Library of Historical Children's Literature, George A. Smathers Libraries at the University of Florida, for help in locating Mrs. Sherwood's *The Governess*. And last but not least, heartfelt thanks to Matthew Kopka for his patience and invaluable editorial advice.

In Memorium: Carrie Frances Wagner, 1961–2005, friend and teacher.

Introduction

Sarah Fielding's Life

After almost two centuries of obscurity, the works of Sarah Fielding, including *The Governess; or, The Little Female Academy* (1749), have recaptured the attention of literary critics. Fielding's novels, literary criticism, translations, and experimental writings evidence a deep intelligence, which, like that of many of her female contemporaries, operated under cover of a self-deprecating modesty. The full scope of Fielding's particular genius has also been overshadowed by her brother Henry Fielding's literary reputation, both in eighteenth-century criticism and that of more recent years. In fact, much of what we know about Sarah Fielding's life and writings was initially recorded as a supplement to Henry's biography.

Although the dearth of information about Fielding is frustrating, it's not surprising given the tendency in eighteenth-century British culture to define women relationally, as daughters, sisters, wives, and mothers. The two latter relationships did not apply to Fielding as she never married or had children. Had she fulfilled either of these roles, which, according to contemporary wisdom, was the only real chance a woman had for happiness, she would most likely not have published, or at least not to the extent that she did. As Fielding herself claimed in the preface to her first novel, *The Adventures of David Simple* (1744), "Perhaps the best Excuse that can be made for a Woman's venturing to write at all, is that which has really produced this Book: Distress in her Circumstances: which she could not so well remove by any other Means in her Power."[1] This attitude was shared by many women of the period, among them, as Linda Bree points out, Lady Mary Wortley Montagu, a distant relative of Fielding. Montagu "heartily pit[ied] her [Fielding], constrained by her circumstances to seek her bread by a method I do not doubt she despises."[2]

---

1   *The Adventures of David Simple* and *Volume the Last*, ed. Peter Sabor (Lexington: UP of Kentucky, 1998), 3.

2   Qtd. in Linda Bree, *Sarah Fielding* (New York: Twayne, 1996), 9.

The circumstances alluded to by Fielding and Montagu were the consequence of Fielding's position as a gentlewoman with no wealth of her own and no father or husband to provide for her financial security. Fielding's precarious position as an adult represented a departure from the life she had been accustomed to in early childhood. Her mother, *née* Sarah Gould, was the daughter of a wealthy lawyer and magistrate, Sir Henry Gould, and Lady Sarah Davidge Gould. In 1706 when their daughter married Edmund Fielding, a soldier who had served in France and Lisbon, her parents disapproved, even though his family connections included the Earls of Denbigh and Desmond. Perhaps the Goulds foresaw that aristocratic connections did not translate into economic solvency: their son-in-law was a soldier and thus subject to the fortunes (or misfortunes) of war and military patronage; moreover, he was not a good economist. Sir Henry, then, determined to provide for his daughter and grandchildren and, in 1710, the year that Sarah was born, arranged for the purchase of a small farm in East Stour, Dorset.

The farmhouse in East Stour would prove a mixed blessing for the Fieldings. For the first seven and a half years of her life, Sarah (the third daughter and one of seven children)[1] enjoyed the pleasant and privileged life typical of a wealthy county family, their house staffed by servants, including a governess for the girls' education. For a time after Sir Henry's death in 1710, Lady Gould lived with the Fieldings and no doubt influenced the way the household was run. As for Edmund, he had been put on half-pay in 1712 and was transforming himself from a soldier into a gentleman-farmer. This transformation was interrupted in April 1718 by the death of Sarah's mother. Edmund left for London soon after, leaving his children in the care of their maternal great-aunt, Katherine Cottington.

The following year Edmund, having received a colonel's appointment, remarried Anne Blanchfield Rapha and brought her to East Stour in 1719. Sarah's new stepmother was the widow of an Italian Roman Catholic with two daughters of her own, both

---

[1] Henry was born in 1707; Catharine in 1708; Ursula in 1709; Anne in 1713 (d. 1716); Beatrice in 1714; and Edmund in 1716.

of whom were receiving convent educations abroad.[1] Neither Colonel Fielding's marriage nor his new wife's Catholicism sat well with Lady Gould and Mrs. Cottington, and relations between Edmund and his in-laws—which had never been smooth—worsened with the new household arrangements. Edmund found it so uncomfortable that he and his wife returned to London. He did not, however, take his children with him. Instead Edmund decided that Henry was to go to Eton to prepare for a university education, and that the three older girls (Catharine, Ursula, and Sarah) were to be enrolled in Mrs. Rookes's boarding school in Salisbury, where Lady Gould had moved in 1720.

As for Lady Gould, she had always been suspicious of Edmund's handling of the East Stour property, the rents of which Sir Henry had always intended for the care of his daughter and grandchildren. In February 1721 she filed suit against her son-in-law in hopes of retaining custody of the children and guaranteeing the farm income for their exclusive use. By all accounts, the lawsuit—based on Lady Gould's assertions that Colonel Fielding and his wife neglected and mistreated the children—was bitter and especially devastating for Sarah and her brothers and sisters. Whether or not the allegations were true, intimate details of the family life were aired in public, and the antagonisms between the two parties must have colored the children's perception of adult life. Certainly in Fielding's writings (including *The Governess*) there are a number of wicked stepmothers and weak and/or negligent fathers.

One of the most dramatic of these portrayals appears in *The Adventures of David Simple*. In that text, Camilla and Valentine, brother and sister, lose their mother. Soon after their father remarries and his new wife does all she can to alienate her husband from his children. Jealous of the influence that Camilla and Valentine might retain over their father, Livia confides to him that their "remarkable Fondness" for one another is based on an incestuous relationship. The father believes her and banishes his

---

[1] Sarah gained six stepbrothers from this marriage. Her stepbrother Sir John Fielding (b. 1721) was a Middlesex magistrate who provided Sarah Fielding with financial assistance later in her life (Martin C. Battestin and Clive T. Probyn, eds. *The Correspondence of Henry and Sarah Fielding* [Oxford: Clarendon P, 1993], 21). Sir John is also credited, along with Henry, with establishing the Bow Street Runners, London's first police force.

children.[1] Although incest was a common theme in eighteenth-century fiction, the inclusion of sibling incest in Fielding's text has attracted critical attention, not least because of her close relationship with Henry. (Henry's first novel *Joseph Andrews*, written two years before *David Simple*, also deals with incest.) One of Henry's biographers, Martin Battestin, suggests that Sarah's and Henry's fascination with this theme arose from their memories of the lawsuit between Edmund Fielding and Lady Gould. According to the court records, a family maid testified that Henry, at the time aged 12, "was guilty of committing some indecent actions with his Sister Beatrice," then aged 4.[2] The testimony does not reveal what those indecent actions were, nor is it clear how much credence was given to the report. What is clear—evidenced by the numerous close relationships between sisters and brothers in Fielding's fiction—is that she understood the significance and fragility of such close ties, especially for economically dependent women. As Jenny Peace's mother explains to her in *The Governess*, "[R]emember how much [your] Brother's superior Strength might assist in his being [your] Protector; and ... in return ... use [your] utmost Endeavours to oblige him; and ... then [you] should be mutual Assistants to each other throughout Life" (p. 64 of this edition).[3] Mutual assistance between brother and sister was even more crucial in the absence of a strong father figure.

That Edmund Fielding was not a model father—he was never able to provide financial security for his children, and was committed, the year before his death in 1741, to debtor's prison—was reflected in the outcome of the lawsuit, which was finally settled in Lady Gould's favor in 1722. The close of the court case also marks the close of the public records that provide details of Sarah Fielding's early family life. Biographers are fairly certain

---

1   As Martin Battestin points out, there is another accusation of sibling incest in the "History of Anna Boleyn," which has been attributed to Sarah and which appears in Henry's *A Journey from This World into the Next* (*Miscellanies* 1743): "I [Anne Boleyn] was brought to my trial, and to blacken me the more, accused of conversing criminally with my own Brother, whom indeed I loved extremely well, but never looked on him in any other Light than as my Friend" ("Henry Fielding, Sarah Fielding, and 'the dreadful Sin of Incest,'" *Novel: A Forum on Fiction* 13.1 [Fall 1979]: 8).

2   Qtd. in Battestin, "Henry Fielding ... Incest" 13.

3   All page references to *The Governess* will refer to this edition.

that she continued her education in Mrs. Rookes's boarding school, spent holidays with Lady Gould, and lived with her grandmother in Salisbury after leaving Mrs. Rookes's. As Linda Bree observes, Salisbury during the 1720s and 1730s, the period of Fielding's adolescence and early adulthood, was "a lively city of about 7,000 inhabitants."[1] The friendships that Fielding made during her adolescence lasted throughout her life. She and Jane Collier, for example, remained best friends long after they had left Salisbury. They lived together in London for several years and collaborated on a number of literary projects, including the experimental text *The Cry* (1754). Jane's brother Arthur tutored Sarah in Greek and Latin; and James Harris, one of the eighteenth century's most respected classical scholars, helped her with her translation of Xenophon's *Memoirs of Socrates* (1762).

In 1733, when Sarah was 23, Lady Gould died. Biographers speculate that Sarah and her sisters continued to live in Salisbury for a time. However, for the next ten years of Fielding's life, very little is known for certain about her activities. Battestin suggests that Sarah, along with Henry, Catharine, Ursula, and Beatrice, returned to East Stour to live after the death of their grandmother. If that is true, the arrangement only lasted until 1739, when the farm was sold: the property that Sir Henry had intended for the financial security of his grandchildren ultimately provided each with under £300. That same year, Catharine, the eldest of the Fielding sisters, inherited her Aunt Katherine Cottington's estate and moved to Westminster. Sarah likely went with Catharine and her other sisters to live there, too, possibly until late in 1744. In November of 1744, Henry's first wife Charlotte died, and most accounts suggest that Sarah moved in to his house in Old Boswell Court, near Lincoln's Inn Fields in London. When Henry remarried in 1747, Sarah rejoined her sisters.

Like Sarah, none of the Fielding sisters married. There are several possible reasons for this. First, as Bree points out, although the Fieldings were allied to the aristocracy, during the sisters' marriageable years they lacked dowries large enough to attract husbands from the same social class. (At the time Catharine

---

[1]   Bree 5.

inherited her aunt's estate, she was 31—in eighteenth-century terms, well into spinsterhood.) Also, they were acutely aware of the inequities of eighteenth-century marriage laws and the dependent status to which married women were reduced. Sarah, for one, considered marriage for financial gain tantamount to selling oneself: in *The History of the Countess of Dellwyn* (1759), when Mr. Lucum tries to persuade his daughter Charlotte to marry the wealthy but decrepit nobleman Lord Dellwyn, she insists she would rather "submit to any State of Life, than to shine in the highest Sphere on such Terms; she called it Prostitution, and heroically defied all such Temptations."[1]

There is no evidence that any of the Fielding sisters faced such "temptations," but surviving correspondence does suggest they lived together harmoniously. Writing to a family friend, Ursula described what might have been a typical scene from the life of the Fielding "sisterhood": "Kitty [Catharine] is at work, Sally [Sarah] is puzzling about it and about it.[2] Bea [Beatrice] playing on her fiddle, and Patty [Ursula] scribbling."[3] The image of a group of women comfortably engaged in intellectual and artistic pursuits—a grown-up version of the little female academy sketched in *The Governess*—contrasts sharply with contemporary images of fretful, dissatisfied spinsters. Arthur Collier reported that all the Fielding sisters "had Parts above the common Run: one of the Girls—*Bee* Fielding ... had an exquisite hand upon the harpsichord, and was otherwise finely accomplished, but Sally was the Scholar."[4] The Fieldings's close-knit sisterhood, however, ended tragically in the summer of 1750, with Catharine's death. Ursula died soon after in December, and Beatrice died in January 1751.

---

[1] *The History of the Countess of Dellwyn*, Book I, chapter 3 <http://www.blackmask.com/books64c/countdelldex.htm>. Charlotte does not keep her resolution, however, and eventually marries Lord Dellwyn.

[2] Linda Bree points out that Sarah's "puzzling about it and about it" is an allusion to Alexander Pope's *Dunciad*, in which he satirizes the Goddess of Dulness's false pedantry: "For thee we dim the eyes and stuff the head/ With all such reading as was never read/ For thee explain a thing till all men doubt it/ And write about it, Goddess, and about it" (4.250–52; qtd. in Bree 12).

[3] *Correspondence* 182.

[4] *Thraliana, the Diary of Mrs. Hester Lynch Thrale (Later Mrs. Piozzi), 1776–1809.* 2 vols., 2nd ed., ed. Katharine C. Balderston (Oxford: Clarendon P, 1951), 1.78–79.

Battestin suggests that Fielding's sisters died during one of the outbreaks of jail fever (typhus) that plagued London throughout the eighteenth century.[1] However they died, the loss must have been devastating for Fielding.

At some point in 1751, Fielding joined Jane Collier in lodgings in Westminster. Fielding and Collier, as mentioned above, had been close friends since adolescence. This friendship extended to literary endeavors, and some of the most interesting work attributed to Fielding (e.g., *The Cry*, 1754) and to Collier (*Essay on the Art of Ingeniously Tormenting*, 1753) bears the mark of their collaboration. The two women were by this time friends with novelist and printer Samuel Richardson, who referred to them as his honorary daughters, and to Fielding as his "much-esteemed Sally Fielding."[2] They often visited him and his family, and Sarah appears to have been especially touched by the warmth of these visits. Writing to Richardson from Bath, she described the happiness she had found under his roof: "To live in a family where there is but one heart, and as many good strong heads as persons, and to have a place in that enlarged single heart, is such a state of happiness as I cannot hear of without feeling the utmost pleasure."[3]

By the 1750s, Fielding's position as a writer was firmly established. Although she never attained celebrity status—she did not have the extroverted nature for that—her works garnered the respect and admiration of many of the most famous personalities of the day, including Samuel Johnson, the actor-manager-playwright David Garrick, and novelist Frances Sheridan. Fielding's health, however, was not as sound as her literary reputation. In 1754, she moved to Bath, the famous spa town that she had been visiting on a regular basis, hoping that permanent residence there would rejuvenate her health. About the same time Henry, also suffering ill health, left London for Portugal, hoping to benefit from the change of climate. He died only a few months later, however, in Lisbon, at the age of 47. Yet another blow came for Fielding with the death of Jane Collier the summer following Henry's death.

---

[1] Martin C. Battestin, *Henry Fielding: A Life* (London: Routledge, 1989), 506–07.
[2] *Correspondence* 131.
[3] *Correspondence* 130.

Despite her personal losses, Fielding continued to publish through 1762. But although her writing provided some income, it was never enough to secure her economic independence. According to Peter Sabor, Fielding spent the last years of her life as "a gentlewoman in severely reduced circumstances."[1] Nevertheless, Fielding's poverty was "genteel": so long as she had friends and relatives to whom she could apply for assistance, she was never destitute.[2] Certainly Fielding retained many of her old friendships and established new connections in Bath. She was never overly fond of "society," preferring to live quietly, but she had formed close friendships with a group of women whose intellectual and artistic accomplishments complemented her own. According to Bree, by 1762, the year she published her last work, a translation of Xenophon's *Memoirs of Socrates*, Fielding had become increasingly dependent on this female circle, whose members included the classical scholar Elizabeth Carter and novelist Sarah Scott. These women were fond of Fielding and became in a sense her guardians, providing financial assistance when needed and watching after her as her health deteriorated.[3] Sometime in 1766 Fielding left her cottage in Walcot, the Bath suburb she had lived in since 1760, and joined Scott in Bath; at one point there was talk of Fielding joining the female utopia that Scott and Lady Barbara Montagu were planning in Hitcham, Buckinghamshire (modeled on the female community in Scott's novel *Millenium Hall*). In the end, however, Fielding's failing health prevented this move.[4]

---

1 Sabor xvii.

2 *Correspondence* xxxix.

3 The exact nature of Sarah Fielding's health problems is not known. From her surviving letters, however, it seems that her health as an adult was never robust, and that sickness sometimes interfered with her writing. Referring to the publication of her last work, *Xenophon's Memoirs of Socrates*, for example, Fielding wrote that she had "been so much confined with Illness since the beginning of Spring as has put me backward in my Translation" (*Correspondence* 156).

4 In a letter outlining this scheme, Montagu wrote to Scott about the possibility of Fielding joining them: "I am sorry poor Fielding has but a small chance to have her sun set so pleasantly as it wd do at Hitcham. I imagine she would be vastly happy there ... I could not enjoy Hitcham if it were to cost that good Woman all her happiness, & whatever deprived her of you [Scott] wd do so; therefore she must not be left out." Apparently, Montagu and Scott were planning to take care of the expenses necessary for Fielding to join the society, but without her knowledge: "... we can cheat her as to knowledge of ye expence & let her imagine her present income equal

Fielding died on April 9, 1768, at the age of 57, with her friends Scott and Montagu at her side. Dr. John Hoadley, a friend since Fielding's Salisbury days, erected a tablet in her memory in Bath Abby, the inscription of which gives a hint of what others thought of her. Her writings, Hoadley claimed, would be remembered as "Incentives to Virtue and Honour to her Sex," but Fielding's "unaffected Manners, candid Mind,/ ... benevolent Heart, and Soul resign'd" were more praiseworthy "than all she knew or thought." Unlike Hoadley, twenty-first-century readers have found that "all [Fielding] knew or thought"—as embodied in her writings—stands as an impressive monument to this extraordinary woman. Her literary reputation, recovered from the obscurity of the nineteenth and early twentieth centuries, has now been revived, and thanks to those critics and scholars who have helped rescue Fielding's works from neglect, her place in the development of eighteenth-century prose has become clear.

Sarah Fielding's Literary Career

In order to more fully appreciate Sarah Fielding's literary career, it is useful to examine her position in one of the eighteenth century's most important literary rivalries, that between Samuel Richardson and Fielding's older brother Henry. This rivalry was much more than a contest between literary personalities. According to Michael McKeon, it "signaled the climax" of the "origins of the English novel," and, in effect, determined the direction this emergent literary form would take over the next century.[1] Although McKeon excludes Sarah Fielding from his consideration of the oftentimes contentious relationship between Richardson, Henry Fielding, and their various allies, her writings express the moral and theoretical concerns that fueled debates about the social role of the novel and its potential to influence readers' behaviors. Rather than being tangential to the

---

to it ... it can never be pleasant to one as ill provided with money as Fielding to think about it, & feel a dependance upon another for what humanly speaking, she ought to have of her own" (qtd. in *Correspondence* xxxvii).

[1] Michael McKeon, *Origins of the English Novel, 1600–1740* (Baltimore, MD: Johns Hopkins UP, 1987), 410.

Richardson/Fielding rivalry, as some literary historians have viewed them, Sarah Fielding's works are central to understanding the origins and development of the English novel.

Many of the concerns revolving around prose fiction at mid-century, and of which Sarah Fielding was well aware, were expressed in the critical responses to Richardson's first novel, *Pamela; or Virtue Rewarded* (1742), a didactic epistolary novel that provoked immediate and intense responses from its readers. *Pamela* tells the story of a lower-class servant who successfully defends her virtue against the various plottings of her master, Mr. B——. Despite Mr. B——'s stratagems (which include kidnapping and attempted rape after Pamela rejects proposals to become his mistress), Pamela perseveres; ultimately, she is "rewarded" by marriage to her would-be rapist. Although *Pamela* was extremely popular, many moralists and writers, including Henry Fielding, thought the sexuality in the novel gratuitous. The anonymous author of *Pamela Censur'd*, for example, felt that Richardson's novel, *"under the Specious Pretence of Cultivating the Principles of Virtue in the Minds of the Youth of both Sexes,"* actually conveyed *"the MOST ARTFUL and ALLURING AMOROUS IDEAS"* to its readers.[1] Indeed, the scenes between Mr. B—— and Pamela were perceived by many critics as so much erotica, and they considered Mr. B——'s plots and plans as a primer for seduction, a text that actually "instruct[ed] the weak head and the corrupt heart in the methods how to proceed to their gratification."[2] On the other hand, Richardson's fans, including Sarah Fielding and many other women, felt the novel celebrated female virtue and empowered virtuous women.

Most participants in the *Pamela* controversy agreed that the purpose of the novel was didactic. Opinions diverged, however, about *how* to achieve that end: were lessons in virtue best imparted by depicting exemplary characters (like Richardson's Pamela Andrews and Clarissa Harlowe) or by drawing "natural" characters that exhibited both virtue and vice (like Henry Fielding's Joseph Andrews and Tom Jones)? The trouble with exemplary

---

[1] Qtd. in McKeon 411.
[2] Ibid.

characters, some complained, was that they seemed too good to be true; writers who drew characters "from the life," on the other hand, too often made vice more attractive than virtue.[1] Henry Fielding's so-called realistic depiction of mixed characters, according to his detractors, was nothing more than a sign of his own immorality. "Poor Fielding!" Richardson wrote, "I could not help telling his sister [Sarah], that I was equally surprised at and concerned for his continued lowness.... [I]t is beyond my conception, that a man of family, and who had some learning, and who really is a writer, should descend so excessively low, in all his pieces. Who can care for any of his People?"[2] According to Richardson and his followers, there should be no doubt in the reader's mind that characters held up for their emulation were virtuous.

The emphasis on virtue and the novelist's duty to cultivate virtue in the minds of his or her readers held particular relevance for women readers and writers. Indeed, at mid-century, virtue was becoming increasingly identified with women, who were often seen as incapable of the kind of vicious behavior sometimes displayed by men. Sentimental novels—narratives that frequently depicted the suffering of innocent females at the hands of men—reflected and facilitated this gendering process and, indeed, contributed to the "feminization" of the novel during the genre's formative years. Most critics agree that Sarah Fielding's fiction belongs to this sentimental tradition. Like Richardson's, her writings consistently engage with women's concerns: their behavior, their sexuality, and their education. In this sense, her position in the Fielding/Richardson controversy seems one of alliance with Richardson, with whom she had become friends after the publication of her first novel, *The Adventures of David Simple* (1744). So close were their artistic conceptions of the novel that Fielding publicly (though anonymously) defended Richardson's second novel in her *Remarks on Clarissa* (1749), which will be discussed below (see Appendix C for excerpts from this work).

---

[1]   In *The Governess*, Fielding points out that writers who failed to deliver a proper moral are "guilty of one of the worst of Evils; namely, That he has cloathed Vice in so beautiful a Dress, that, instead of deterring, it will allure and draw into its Snares the young and tender Mind" (p. 156).

[2]   Qtd. in McKeon 417.

Fielding's friendship with Richardson, however, did not diminish her admiration and respect for her brother's work. Throughout her publishing career, which outlasted Henry's by eight years, she held up his novels and plays as models of good writing. Moreover, during Henry's lifetime, they enjoyed a highly collaborative relationship. In fact, the earliest writings attributed to Sarah are found in Henry's works. The first is the letter from Leonora to Horatio, which appears in the "History of Leonora" in Book II, chapter 4 of *Joseph Andrews*, Henry's satiric response to *Pamela*. This brief letter, Henry writes in a footnote, "was written by a young Lady," and though Sarah Fielding is not named, most critics agree that the letter is hers. The second piece, "The History of Anna Boleyn," appears as the last chapter in *A Journey from This World to the Next*, and features the story of Henry VIII's second queen, told by her after her death. Speaking in his guise of editor, Henry claims that this first-person narrative was included among a set of old papers discovered by a bookseller. It "is ... writ in a Woman's Hand," he says, "And tho' the Observations in it are, I think, as excellent as any in the whole Volume, there seems to be a Difference in Style between this and the preceding Chapters; and as it is the Character of a Woman which is related, I am inclined to fancy it was really written by one of that Sex."[1]

The stylistic differences that Henry points out, and that he associates with sexual difference, are ultimately tied to Sarah's position in the Richardson/Fielding rivalry. For even though the inclusion of Sarah's writings in his works demonstrates Henry's recognition and encouragement of her literary talents, he nevertheless sees her writing as different. This difference becomes more marked in Sarah's subsequent writings, but can be seen in the thematic concerns of these early pieces, concerns that are central to the

---

[1] Henry Fielding, *Miscellanies*, vol. 2., ed. Bertrand A. Goldgar and Hugh Amory (Oxford: Clarendon P, 1993), 111n. Using a device common in eighteenth-century literature, Fielding claims that the manuscript of *A Journey from This World to the Next* came "accidentally" into his hands, part of a large folio that "had been left in [a] Garret" (Introduction, p. 4). This fictional frame accounts for the fact that Book XIX, Chapter VII, "Wherein Anna Boleyn relates the History of her Life," follows Chapter XXV of Book I. For more on the question of Sarah's authorship see J.F. Burrows and A.J. Hassall, "*Anna Boleyn* and the Authenticity of [Henry] Fielding's Feminine Narratives," *Eighteenth-Century Studies* 21 (1988): 427–53.

development of the novel. Both Leonora's and Anna Boleyn's histories, for example, emphasize the importance of regulating the passions and exercising discernment, practices crucial for women who sought to live virtuous lives. Both Leonora and Anna Boleyn are cautionary figures, women led astray by vanity (a fault many of Fielding's female characters possess). Tellingly, this moral failing is traced to faulty education. Leonora's behavior—she rejects an honorable suitor in favor of a rake who ultimately jilts her—is one "to which young women are often rendered too liable by that blameable levity in the education of [their] sex."[1] Similarly, Anna Boleyn, despite her happy childhood and her parents' indulgence, has no real moral foundation from which to resist the temptations of worldly advancement. Flattered by Henry VIII's desire for her and pleased by the prospect of becoming a queen, she breaks her engagement with the honorable Sir Pearcy, and ultimately loses not only a chance at domestic happiness but her head as well.

Fielding's first full-length publication and most popular novel, *The Adventures of David Simple* (1744), also centers on the tensions between virtue and worldliness. One of the first novels to feature the "Man of Feeling," who would become a staple character in sentimental fiction, *David Simple* depicts the effects emotions have on characters and their behaviors: individuals like David Simple are driven by their "sensibility," that is, by their capacity to feel and to be moved by sympathy and compassion for others.[2] Ironically, given the association between Samuel Richardson and sentimental fiction, when *David Simple* first appeared many readers attributed it to his rival, Henry Fielding. Henry cleared up any such confusion with an extensive preface to the novel's second edition, in which he identifies its author as "a young Woman; one ... nearly and dearly allied to me, in the highest Friendship as well as Relation."[3]

---

[1] Henry Fielding, *Joseph Andrews*. Ed. Paul A. Scanlon (Peterborough: Broadview, 2001), 177.

[2] According to Gerrard A. Barker, David Simple, along with Mary Collyer's Lucius Manly in *Felicia to Charlotte* (1744), "shares the distinction of being one of the two earliest examples of the Man of Feeling in English fiction" ("*David Simple:* The Novel of Sensibility in Embryo," *Modern Language Studies* 12 [1982]: 69). As Barker points out, Fielding's novel "anticipates the novel of feeling decades before such [male] writers as [Henry] Mackenzie, [Oliver] Goldsmith, and Henry Brooke worked in this genre" (69).

[3] *The Adventures of David Simple.* 2nd ed., ed. Malcolm Kelsall (London: Oxford UP, 1969), 5.

In addition to writing the preface, Henry edited and "corrected" the second edition.[1] Janine Barchas argues that Henry's corrections to Sarah's novel indicate an attempt to diminish the role of emotion in the text. In particular, Barchas says, by omitting or replacing Sarah Fielding's numerous dashes—one of her preferred marks of punctuation—Henry lessens the emotional impact of many of the novel's most dramatic scenes. Barchas further suggests that the revisions are a sign of Henry's tendency to identify emotional, sentimental writing as feminine, and thus inferior.[2] Henry's simultaneous attempts to distinguish *David Simple* from his own work in the preface while shaping it into a novel "reflecting his own concept of fiction"[3] can be seen in Henry's discussion of the "Grammatical and other Errors in Style" that appear in the unedited first edition. The "Imperfections of this little Book," Henry writes, which result

> not from want of Genius, but of Learning, lie open to the Eyes
> of every Fool, who has had a little *Latin* inoculated into his
> Tail; but had the same great Quantity of Birch been better
> employ'd, in scourging away his Ill-nature, he would not have
> exposed it in endeavouring to cavil at the first Performance of
> one, whose Sex and Age entitle her to the gentlest Criticism,
> while her Merit, of an infinitely higher kind, may defy the
> severest. But I believe the Warmth of my Friendship hath led
> me to engage a Critic of my own Imagination only....[4]

In many ways, Henry's defense of Sarah's novel reflects his, and the eighteenth century's, differential treatment of men's and women's writing. Because women writers did not have the benefit of a classical education they were to be dealt with gently, especially when their works demonstrated such "a deep and profound Discernment of all the Mazes, Windings and Labyrinths, which perplex the Heart of Man" as Henry found in *David Simple*. Such

[1] From 1969 until 1998, when the University Press of Kentucky reprinted the first
    edition, only the second edition with Henry's revisions was readily available (i.e., the
    1969 Oxford World's Classics edition edited by Malcolm Kelsall).
[2] Janine Barchas, "Sarah Fielding's Dashing Style and Eighteenth-Century Print
    Culture," *ELH* 63 (1996): 633–56.
[3] Sabor xxx.
[4] *David Simple*, ed. Malcolm Kelsall, 6.

discernment in a woman's writing, Henry implies, makes up for any deficiencies in grammar.

That Sarah appreciated her brother's encouragement seems certain judging from their continued collaboration. He contributed a preface to *Familiar Letters Between the Characters in David Simple and Others* (1747), her next publication, as well as five of the 45 letters in the two-volume collection. Unlike *The Adventures of David Simple, Familiar Letters* is not a novel in that it has no sustained plot line. Instead it contains a variety of prose styles, including moral essays, verse, and, of course, letters. And although many of the characters from the novel appear in *Familiar Letters*, it introduces new characters and events unrelated to the earlier work. Like *David Simple*, however, *Familiar Letters* is concerned with moral instruction and the depiction of human virtues and vices. In other words it, too, demonstrates what Henry called Sarah's "vast Penetration into human Nature." Although one of Henry's biographers described *Familiar Letters* as "a dull book, overflowing with moral platitudes, and injudiciously padded with irrelevant matter,"[1] it clearly found an audience among Fielding's contemporaries: according to Sabor, a Dublin edition of *Familiar Letters* was published later in 1747, a second London edition appeared in 1752, and a German translation became available in 1759.[2]

In January 1749, Fielding published *The Governess*, which has been described as the first novel in English written for children (see below). Like Fielding's other works, the book's primary purpose is didactic and, though it is addressed specifically to young women for their "Entertainment and Instruction," it also reflects her engagement with the wider critical conversation about eighteenth-century fiction. For example, in the book's preface, Fielding asks her "young Readers" to consider seriously the "true Use of Reading." It is, she points out, "to make you

---

[1]   F. Homes Dudden, *Henry Fielding; his life, works and times*. 2 vols. (Oxford: Clarendon P, 1952). Qtd. in Jill E. Grey, ed. *The Governess: or, Little Female Academy* (London: Oxford UP, 1968), 17.

[2]   *Familiar Letters* was published by subscription, meaning that readers signed up to receive copies of the book once printed, paying half the price in advance. According to Sabor, Fielding "was among the first women novelists to use this form of publication" (xi). That she was able to gather an impressive list of 507 subscribers, some requesting multiple copies, testifies to her growing reputation as a writer.

wiser and better." To that end Fielding incorporates a variety of texts into the novel, from fairy tales and animal fables to the personal histories of each girl enrolled in the "little female academy." Regardless of genre, Fielding warns, without critical engagement reading is a useless activity.

Fielding's engagement with critical reading practices assumed another form in *Remarks on Clarissa*, a critical essay that appeared the same week as *The Governess*. (See Appendix C for excerpts from *Remarks*.) This work, a valuable contribution to early novel criticism, clearly situates Fielding as a champion of the sentimental novel. Framed as a drawing-room conversation among readers of Richardson's *Clarissa*, *Remarks* raises various criticisms of *Clarissa* and its eponymous heroine in order to override them. One such criticism concerns the novel's conclusion, in which Richardson's heroine dies. Belario, one of Fielding's fictitious readers, confesses that he had been upset by rumors of the book's tragic ending until he read it himself:

> Rightly I think in the Author's [Richardson's] Postscript is it observed, that what is called poetical Justice is chimerical, or rather anti-providential Justice; for God makes his Sun to shine alike on the Just and the Unjust. Why then should Man invent a kind of imaginary Justice, making the common Accidents of Life turn out favourable to the Virtuous only? Vain would be the Comforts spoken to the Virtuous in Affliction, in the sacred Writings, if Affliction could not be their Lot.[1]

Affliction and suffering were certainly primary ingredients in the sentimental novel. Indeed, protagonists were often measured by how patiently they could endure life's misfortunes. Defenders of the genre, like Fielding, based their disregard for poetic justice on Christian values, which emphasized rewards in the afterlife. Clarissa's beautiful death, in other words, was the highest acknowledgement of her virtue and suffering, for only in heaven could she meet with adequate compensation for her earthly trials.

---

[1]   Sarah Fielding, *Remarks on Clarissa, Addressed to the Author. Occasioned by some critical Conversations on the Characters and Conduct of the Work* (London, 1749), 49.

Fielding's next book, *The Adventures of David Simple; Volume the Last, in Which His History Is Concluded*, demonstrates the same disdain for poetic justice that she exhibited in *Remarks on Clarissa*. Published in 1753, nine years after *The Adventures of David Simple* and not long after the deaths of Fielding's three sisters in 1750–51, *Volume the Last* depicts one scene of suffering after another. Whereas David Simple's earlier adventures close with the attainment of his dreams, a double wedding and the establishment of a familial community grounded on the principles of generosity and compassion, *Volume the Last* traces the dissolution of this happy family. Reduced to distress and poverty, David is forced to confront the worst kind of torment, to watch helplessly as his loved ones suffer and die. At the end of the novel, he lays on his deathbed attended by his sister-in-law Cynthia and his one surviving child. With his last words, he sums up the inevitable pain every man (or woman) of feeling suffers in life: "my Eyes were forced wide open, to discover the Fallacy of fancying any real or lasting Happiness can arise from an Attachment to Objects subject to Infirmities, Diseases, and to certain Death."[1] Although we're told that David retains a "strong and lively Hope" in heavenly justice, and despite the fact that Cynthia's last hour with him is described as "a Scene of real Pleasure" given his "Hopes and Resignation," the final words of David's story are dark. Readers are left to take comfort only in the thought that David has at last "escaped from the Possibility of falling into any future Afflictions, and that neither the Malice of his pretended Friends, nor the sufferings of his real ones, can ever again rend and torment his honest Heart."[2]

The year following the publication of *Volume the Last*, Fielding produced a work unlike any she had previously written. *The Cry: A New Dramatic Fable* (1754) was perceived as highly experimental not only by its author but by her readers. Considered with her other works, however, *The Cry* seems a logical step in Fielding's progression as a writer.[3] The thematic concerns dealt with in

---

[1] Sabor 342.

[2] Ibid.

[3] Most critics believe that Jane Collier contributed to *The Cry*, though there's no consensus about how much of the work is hers. Evidence of co-authorship rests on Fielding's instructions to the book's printer to pay half the copyright payment "to

earlier works—the didactic role of fiction, the function (and slipperiness) of language, questions of virtue and vice, gender politics, educational philosophy—all appear here, but they are staged in new ways: *The Cry* is part novel, part moral essay, part drama, part allegory, part philosophy. Fielding was well aware of the risk she was taking by striking "out of a road already so much beaten," and warned her readers that if they were expecting the kind of "stories and novels" that had flooded the market, many of which she considered "trifling performances," *The Cry* would be a disappointment. Those readers interested in tracing with the author "the labyrinths of the human mind" and the "intricate and unopen'd recesses" of the human heart, however, would appreciate the necessity of her assuming "a certain freedom in writing, not strictly ... within the limits prescribed by rules."[1]

Judging from its preface, Fielding obviously felt that her dramatic fable challenged accepted conventions of fiction. Rather than unfolding a novelistic plot, she depicts two protagonists (Portia and Cylinda) placed on trial and compelled to defend their behavior before "The Cry," the name Fielding gives to the worldly assembly who sits in judgment on them, and whose outcries and condemnations are the product of hypocrisy and malice. Although *The Cry*'s biting critique of moral hypocrisy found favor with some readers (Lady Mary Wortley Montagu felt its "Sentiments [were] generally just," and Lady Braidshagh, one of Richardson's correspondents, admired it and hoped "to profit by it"), its experimental form confused and/or frustrated them as well.[2] Many readers, suggest Battestin and Probyn, "mistook its innovation for eccentricity, and were unable to discern its thematic concern for female self-definition in a world that demanded their self-effacement."[3] Whatever the reason, *The Cry* did not go into a second edition and remained out of print until 1974.

---

whomsoever I appoint" (*Correspondence* xx) and the assumption that that "whomsoever" was Collier. Bree points out that "The concept of multiple authorship was congenial among the Fielding-Collier circle," but for the purpose of analysis she assumes Fielding's sole authorship (91).

[1] *The Cry: A New Dramatic Fable.* Introduction (Blackmask Online, 2002). <http://www.blackmask.com/books64c/sarfielcrydex.htm>.

[2] Qtd. in Bree 106, 107.

[3] *Correspondence* xxxiv.

Fielding's next publication, *The Lives of Cleopatra and Octavia* (1757), represents her return to a form she was familiar with, the fictional autobiography. Like the "History of Anna Boleyn," the first-person accounts of Cleopatra and Octavia are presented to the reader from beyond the grave; and again, Fielding chooses historical rather than fictional characters to convey her novel's moral message. Allowing two such (in)famous women to "tell" their stories certainly provided an opportunity for Fielding to exercise her imaginative powers. But *Lives* enabled her to display her extensive and formidable scholarship as well. Indeed, as Christopher D. Johnson suggests, Fielding's narrative is "perhaps the most imaginative work of classical scholarship produced during the Augustan age."[1] Unawed by Fielding's command of classical history, however, one of her contemporaries gently teased that her status as a "virtuous maiden" would skew the text in favor of Octavia (the wife Marc Anthony abandoned for Cleopatra).[2] More recently, Linda Bree argues that, for the first time in Western art, Fielding gives Cleopatra a voice. Before the appearance of Fielding's text, Bree writes, "Cleopatra had always been described by men and regarded primarily as an object of male desire. Now, for the first time, Cleopatra speaks for herself as a woman through the creative intelligence of a woman writer alert to the strategies of sexual politics."[3] In addition to the feminist implications of such a text, Fielding's *Lives* may also be seen as part of the Augustan age's appropriation of classical subjects to critique British culture. As Sara Gadeken points out,

> Classic Rome represents a constant reminder of the evils of luxury and overconsumption, and, as England's commercial enterprise and empire begin to develop, comparisons with the Roman Empire become increasingly uneasy. Against this backdrop, *Cleopatra and Octavia* exploits cultural fears of effeminacy,

---

[1] *Lives of Cleopatra and Octavia*, ed. Christopher D. Johnson (Lewisburg, PA: Bucknell UP, 1994), 16.
[2] Letter from Lady Barbara Montagu to Sarah Scott, qtd. in Bree 24.
[3] Bree 112.

luxury, and moral corruption in an effort to claim a place for strong and active women in the republic of virtue.[1]

For Gadeken, Fielding's classicism carries with it a (proto)feminist condemnation of eighteenth-century patriarchal imperialism. Fielding's next two works followed in fairly quick succession: *The History of the Countess of Dellwyn*, published in 1759, and *The History of Ophelia*, published a year later in 1760. Some critics suggest that these novels were written primarily for the much-needed money they would bring Fielding. This suggestion appears to be borne out in a letter written by Fielding in which she refers to *The Countess of Dellwyn* as "some Stuff I am now about."[2] Fielding's "Stuff" contains a sharp and witty satire of aristocratic life as well as an astute portrayal of an unhappy marriage. Most importantly, Fielding's narrative conforms to her beliefs about the didactic role of fiction. The fate of her heroine, as Fielding claims in the preface, is calculated to show that "Misery is the unavoidable Consequence of vicious Life." Like most of the cautionary figures in Fielding's fiction, Charlotte Lucum (later the Countess of Dellwyn), is unable to regulate her passions, in particular her vanity. Driven by increasing social ambition and the envy she feels whenever a rival threatens to supplant her in the public's admiration, Lady Dellwyn eventually commits adultery—not because she falls in love, but because her lover turns his attentions to another woman.

Embedded within the *Countess of Dellwyn* is the history of Mrs. Bilson, Lady Dellwyn's foil. Whereas Fielding's satire of upper-class manners sometimes echoes Eliza Haywood's scandal novels of the 1720s, the history of Mrs. Bilson reads like a sentimental novel: Mrs. Bilson suffers great trials (her husband is a spendthrift and adulterer), but she remains loyal to him, even when he is thrown into prison for debt. She reforms her husband through patience and forgiveness, and rescues her family by her hard work and ingenuity (though timely intervention by a rich relative secures their fortunes). For Fielding and her readers, Mrs.

---

[1] "Gender, Empire, and Nation in Sarah Fielding's *Lives of Cleopatra and Octavia*," *SEL: Studies in English Literature* 39.3 (1999): 523.

[2] *Correspondence* 139.

Bilson's story serves to show "the natural Tendency of Virtue towards the Attainment of Happiness."[1]

The History of Ophelia, one of Fielding's most popular works and her last novel, delivers a similar message, but does so by sharpening the contrast between nature and art. Ophelia, like Charlotte Lucum, has grown up in seclusion and retirement. Unlike Charlotte, however, Ophelia possesses deeply rooted principles that allow her to withstand the temptations of polite society. In her condemnation of social hypocrisy and artifice, Ophelia resembles Portia in *The Cry*. When, for example, she is expected to dissemble her feelings for Dorchester, the man she loves, she refuses to deny them in the name of modesty. Rather than allow her feelings to lead her astray, however, Ophelia rejects Dorchester when she feels he has betrayed her love—much as Portia rejects Ferdinand when she feels he is unworthy of her.

At first glance, Fielding's last work, *Xenophon's Memoirs of Socrates and the Defence of Socrates before His Judges*, appears quite distinct from Fielding's other writings, particularly her fiction. Certainly this project, a translation of Xenophon's Greek text, is an impressive feat, particularly for a largely self-taught classicist. The *Monthly Review* summed up Fielding's accomplishment, noting the difficulty of translating Xenophon's "elegant simplicity"; Fielding, however, "executed her task in a manner that does her honor."[2] Fielding must have been aware of her achievement before the reviewers, for *Xenophon's Memoirs of Socrates* is the only one of her works that bears her name on the title page.[3] Clearly her pride was well founded, as her translation, which Fielding had worked on for at least four years, went through four more editions in the eighteenth century.[4]

As impressive as Fielding's scholarship is, her choice of subject is also important, particularly as it places her final work within

---

[1] *Countess of Dellwyn.* The Preface (Blackmask Online, 2002). <http://www.black-mask.com/books64c/countdelldex.htm>.

[2] *Monthly Review* 27 (Sept. 1762): 171–76. Qtd. in *Correspondence* xxxix.

[3] Most often Fielding signed her works "By the Author of David Simple."

[4] Fielding's translation was used in nineteenth-century anthologies as well, and in the twentieth century it appeared in the Everyman edition of *Socratic Discourses by Plato and Xenophon*, which remained in print at least until 1933.

the context of the development of eighteenth-century prose. Particularly in *The Defence of Socrates*, Fielding's "hero" exhibits two of the qualities that Fielding conferred on her fictional heroines: moral virtue and strength of character in the face of social condemnation. Fielding, in other words, believed that virtue and strength were asexual. In this sense, her work reflects a departure, not from the concerns and aims of her previous works, but from the wider world of eighteenth-century letters as embodied in the writings of Samuel Richardson and Henry Fielding. Unlike Richardson, Fielding drew heroines who were virtuous *and* active, prepared to fly in the face of social convention in order to uphold their principles; unlike Henry Fielding, she was unafraid to endow her heroines with an intelligence that mirrored her own. In the case of *Xenophon's Memoirs of Socrates*, she unashamedly displayed that intelligence.

Sarah Fielding, *The Governess*, and Female Education

Although *The Governess* is often described as the first English *novel* written for children, it was by no means the first children's book. In fact, by the time Fielding published *The Governess* in 1749, children's literature was a recognized (and lucrative) component of the eighteenth-century book trade. Throughout the 1740s, for example, the publications of John Newbery's press, including the landmark *A Little Pretty Pocket-book* (1744), proved highly popular and set a clear standard for subsequent children's books: they were attractively produced, entertaining for young readers, and, of course, instructive.[1] Most children's books of this

---

[1] In her extensive introduction to the facsimile reprint of the first edition of *The Governess* (1749; London: Oxford UP, 1968), Jill E. Grey lists other children's books on the market at the time, including Mrs. Cooper's *The Child's New Play-thing* (1742) and *Tommy Thumb's Song-Book* (1744), and Thomas Boreman's 10-volume *Gigantick Histories* (1740–43). In addition to these works, Fielding would probably have been familiar with the English translations of French fairy tales like the Comtesse d'Aulnoy's *The History of the Tales of the Fairies* (1721) and R. Samber's translation of Perrault called *Histories, or Tales of Past Times* (1729; 3rd ed. 1741). Other books that would appeal to children were Aesop's *Fables* and a translation of the Abbe Banier's *Mythology and Fables of the Ancients, explained from History*. Henry admired the latter, which was printed by Andrew Millar—Henry's and Sarah's publisher—in 1739–40.

time—including *The Governess*—were influenced by the educational theories of Enlightenment philosopher John Locke. His treatise *Some Thoughts Concerning Education*, first published in 1693 and popular throughout the eighteenth century, encouraged educators and parents to reconceptualize learning as a source of pleasure for children. Learning, he argued, "must never be imposed as a task, nor made a Trouble to them."[1] By piquing their curiosity and adopting gentle tactics, Locke observed, "children may be cozened into a knowledge of their letters ... and play themselves into what others are whipped for."[2] (See Appendix D for excerpts from Locke's treatise.)

In many ways, Fielding's governess, Mrs. Teachum, embodies these Lockean principles. Though Mrs. Teachum strikes awe in her students by her "lively and commanding Eye," she is also "perfectly kind and tender in her Manner." Moreover, she allows her nine students—when they have proved themselves worthy of the privilege—time to pursue their own "amusements," which include reading entertaining stories and fairy tales to each other. Although many educators, including Locke, disapproved of fairy tales for children, Fielding's governess does not mind them so long as they are read with discernment. The story of the two giants Barbarico and Benefico, for example, contain "a very good Moral." So long as the girls remember that "Giants, Magic, Fairies, and all Sorts of supernatural Assistances in a Story, are introduced only to amuse and divert," Mrs. Teachum allows them to read any amusing stories—"provided you read them with the Disposition of a Mind not to be hurt by them" (p. 84).

In addition to its tolerance of fairy tales, *The Governess* marks other new directions in children's literature. Grey observes that Fielding was "the first author for children to establish a distinct contemporary social environment"—the boarding school—"with a definite set of characters taken from ordinary life and using ordinary everyday speech." Moreover, Fielding creates "characters who were supposed to be real children" like her readers.[3] Bree also remarks the originality of *The Governess*'s structure, noting that its

---

[1]   John Locke, *Some Thoughts Concerning Education*. 12th ed. (London: S. Birt, 1752), 224.
[2]   Locke 224. See Appendix D.1 for additional excerpts from Locke's treatise.
[3]   Grey 78–79.

narrative coherence and extended plot distinguish it from the children's books that preceded it. More importantly, Fielding's text is directed at young women, and thus "has no direct precedents in English literature."[1] Indeed, continues Bree, "one of the most striking aspects of *The Governess* is the way in which Locke's ideas, intended by him largely to apply to the education of boys, become principles of female education."[2]

Perhaps Fielding's most provocative appropriation of Lockean educational philosophy is the underlying assumption in *The Governess* that girls as well as boys are capable of exercising reason. According to Locke, all children "love to be treated as rational Creatures."[3] In the eighteenth century, however, females were often depicted as irrational and incapable of learning anything other than domestic employments. Fielding routinely counters this misogynistic assumption by depicting in her fiction intelligent women frustrated by the educational limitations they faced. Cynthia, one of the heroines in *The Adventures of David Simple*, articulates this frustration as she describes her unhappy childhood:

> I loved reading, and had a great Desire of attaining Knowledge; but whenever I asked any Questions ..., I was always told, such Things were not proper for *Girls of my Age* to know. If I got any Book that gave me pleasure, and it was any thing beyond the most silly Story, it was taken from me. For *Miss must not enquire too far into things—it would turn her Brain—she had better mind her Needle-work—and such Things as were useful for Women— Reading and poring on Books, would never get me a Husband....*[4]

Although Fielding was respected and admired by many for her learning, she was aware of the potential pitfalls of being seen as too intelligent. In Henry Fielding's last novel *Amelia* (1751), Sarah's brother satirized learned women in his depiction of Mrs. Bennet (later Mrs. Atkinson), who argues against "the great absurdity, (for so she termed it,) of excluding women from learning; for which

---

[1]   Bree 59.
[2]   Ibid.
[3]   Locke 102.
[4]   Sabor 80.

they were equally qualified with the men."[1] Amelia, the virtuous heroine and moral touchstone of the novel, is too polite to disagree out loud but, the narrator assures us, she does not conform to Mrs. Bennet's notions of female learning.

Biographers have noted that Henry Fielding's bias against women intellectuals was not confined to fiction. In her diary *Thraliana*, Hester Thrale repeats a story told to her by Arthur Collier, Sarah Fielding's Salisbury friend and Latin tutor: "while She only read English Books, and made English Verses it seems, [Henry] fondled her Fancy, & encourag'd her Genius, but as soon [as] he perceived She once read Virgil, Farewell to Fondness, the Author's Jealousy was become stronger than the Brother's Affection, and he saw her future progress in literature not without pleasure only—but with Pain."[2] Bree notes that Collier's account may have been colored by an antipathy between the two men.[3] Yet the fact that Thrale credits the rumor at all demonstrates the believability of a response like the one attributed to Henry, and gives credence to the possibility that a woman who pursued "masculine" knowledge faced resistance, even within her own family.

In light of such resistance, it is not surprising that Fielding's ideas about female education are couched in the relatively unthreatening terms of *The Governess*: There is certainly no mention made of Mrs. Teachum's pupils learning Latin or Greek. Instead, Mrs. Teachum instructs her students in "Reading, Writing, Working, and in all proper Forms of Behaviour" (p. 49). There are passing references to a writing instructor and a dancing master but, as Grey points out, other than these vague suggestions, "The curriculum at Sarah's *Little Female Academy* remains something of a mystery."[4] Though Fielding's curricular details are unclear, she is very explicit about her design in writing *The Governess*, as evidenced by her remarks in the book's dedication:

---

[1] Henry Fielding, *Amelia*. 2 vols. (London: J.M. Dent, 1930), 1.289. See also John Gregory's comments on female learning in Appendix D.2.

[2] *Thraliana* 1.79.

[3] Bree 20.

[4] Grey 55. Mika Suzuki points out that the silence surrounding classroom curriculum was part of a tradition of earlier advice books written by parents, which left such details to parents or tutors ("The Little Female Academy and The Governess," *Women's Writing* 1.3 [1994], 331).

The Design of the following Sheets is to endeavour to cultivate an early Inclination to Benevolence, and a Love of Virtue,
in the Minds of young Women, by trying to shew them, that
their True Interest is concerned in cherishing and improving
those amiable Dispositions into Habits; and in keeping down
all rough and boistrous Passions; and that from this alone they
can propose to themselves to arrive at true Happiness, in any
of the Stations of Life allotted to the Female Character. (p. 45)

At first glance, particularly from a twenty-first-century perspective,
Fielding's position seems to be one of accommodation rather than
resistance to the patriarchal society that imposed strictures on
women's education in the eighteenth century. Certainly *The
Governess* does not contain explicit demands for educational
reform like those found in Mary Astell's *Serious Proposal to the
Ladies* and Mary Wollstonecraft's *Vindication of the Rights of Woman*.
(See Appendix D for extracts from Wollstonecraft's *Vindication*.)
Read another way, however, Fielding's design is highly pragmatic:
given the realities of eighteenth-century British culture, women
were compelled to pursue their "true interests" by proving themselves capable of exercising reason and of subduing the "rough
and boistrous Passions."[1]

The push and pull between reason and passion constituted a
widespread tension in eighteenth-century culture. In *The
Governess*, as in Fielding's other work, this tension is dramatized
in a series of character portraits in which individuals wrestle with
their passions. If characters can regulate their feelings—subordinate them to reason—they attain peace of mind. If not, they
become slaves to their passions and, in consequence, lose all
prospect of happiness. The most obvious illustration of this moral
can be found in the transformation that occurs among Mrs.
Teachum's nine pupils. The book opens, for example, with "an
Account of a Fray, begun and carried on for the sake of an
Apple," during which "they fell to pulling of Caps, tearing of
Hair, and dragging the Cloaths off one another's Backs." By the

---

[1] Another method of pursuing their own interests, and one which Fielding condemns,
is to artfully manipulate gender stereotypes of women as weak and utterly dependent on men.

end of the novel, each individual has overcome her particular character flaw—her reigning passion—and become a happy member of a loving society.

This communal *bildungsroman* provides a frame for the novel, but it also serves to demonstrate Fielding's strong belief in the power of education to reform behavior. The process of reformation is described within the self-narrated histories provided by each of Mrs. Teachum's pupils. Each day during their free time, the girls meet in "a little Arbour" in the school garden. Here the girls exchange life stories, highlighting the various faults that marked their behavior prior to coming to Mrs. Teachum's school: Miss Sukey Jennett was spoiled, Miss Lucy Sly told falsehoods, Nanny Spruce was too fond of fine clothes, and so on. Once the girls see the folly of such behavior and openly confess it to their peers they are free to live in harmony, motivated by an inclination to please each other rather than themselves.

In Fielding's work, as in the educational writings of other "rational moralists," children are led by reason to see the rewards of virtuous living.[1] The emphasis on rationality, suggests M.F. Thwaite, reflects a growing tendency in eighteenth-century culture toward secularization. Children's writings of the period, unlike earlier Puritan writings directed toward children, were more "concerned with character and conduct in the life of this world than with preparation for the life hereafter."[2] This is certainly the case in *The Governess*, but Fielding's rationalism also reflects certain elements of dissenting religious practice, particularly in its emphasis on self-examination, public confession, repentance, and reformation.

---

[1] The rational moralists include Locke, Rousseau, Fielding, Thomas Day, Mary Wollstonecraft, and Maria Edgeworth, among others. Their writings cultivate rational thought and moral judgment and feature "carefully designed narratives, and ... positive as well as negative examples to shape children's understanding. All emphasized tutelage: most of their stories featured a hired tutor, but sometimes a parent is the principal dispenser of information. The purpose remains the same whoever the instructor: to make learning an active, engaging pursuit" (Patricia Demers and Gordon Moyles, eds. *From Instruction to Delight: An Anthology of Children's Literature to 1850* [Toronto: Oxford UP, 1982], 121).

[2] *From Primer to Pleasure: An Introduction to the History of Children's Books in England, from the Invention of Printing to 1900* (London: The Library Association, 1963), 31.

One of the more striking instances of this overlap appears in the "conversion" of Miss Sukey Jennett early in the novel. After the quarrel over the apple, Miss Jenny Peace engages Miss Sukey in a dialogue hoping to lead her to see the folly of her participation in the fray. Their exchange ends with Miss Sukey convinced of Miss Jenny's logic, though she remains unwilling to admit her fault. Left alone Miss Sukey spends a restless night, crying and weeping with frustration. Finally, she confesses to herself that she really is "unhappy; for I hate all my Schoolfellows.... In short, the more I reflect, the more I am afraid Miss Jenny is in the Right; and yet it breaks my Heart to think so." The next morning, Miss Sukey dreads to meet Miss Jenny, for "she knew it would not be possible to resist her Arguments; and yet Shame for having been in Fault overcame her" (p. 57). Fielding's detailed depiction of Miss Sukey's agony—which reveals "a psychological acuteness quite unique in children's stories of the mid-eighteenth century"[1]—recalls the spiritual wrestlings described in writings by dissenters like John Bunyan (*The Pilgrim's Progress*) and Daniel Defoe (*Robinson Crusoe*).[2] And, though Fielding's aims aren't religious conversion, she, like the dissenters, believed in the possibility of redemption.[3]

In the case of *The Governess*, Miss Jenny Peace brings about redemption and reconciliation by gentle persuasion, as she instills "Sincerity and Love" in the hearts of each girl. The girls, in other words, are rescued from their early tendencies—instilled in them by negligent or overindulgent parents, guardians, or servants—and refashioned as members of a harmonious society. As in many

---

1 Demers and Moyles 123.

2 Bunyan describes his conversion in his autobiography *Grace Abounding to the Chief of Sinners*. Many of Defoe's characters (e.g., Robinson Crusoe, Moll Flanders, H.F. in *Journal of the Plague Year*) describe the inner turmoil that leads to their conversion as well. As Linda Bree points out, Bunyan's *The Pilgrim's Progress* and Defoe's *Robinson Crusoe*, though written for adults, were colonized as children's books.

3 Fielding herself was no dissenter; however, her ideas about educational reform were undoubtedly influenced by mainstream elements of dissenting thought. Later in the century, the English Jacobins, including educational writers like Mary Wollstonecraft and William Blake, would demand a variety of social reforms based on their belief in the "doctrine of necessity"—the belief that individuals' circumstances rather than social class determined behavior—that grew out of the dissenting tradition. (See Gary Kelly, *The English Jacobin Novel, 1780–1805* [London: Clarendon P, 1985].)

of Fielding's works, in *The Governess* family ties are replaced by affective social bonds.[1] However, as Terri Nickel observes, even the ties of friendship might, in Fielding's words, "lead you into all manner of Errors" if unrestrained by reason. "One might argue," suggests Nickel, "that in this narrative about the formation of an ideal female society Fielding represents the children in a state of nature. If any sort of social contract is to emerge from such a state, Fielding suggests, discipline of one's natural emotions—a discipline exemplified and stimulated by the exemplary tales which follow—must accompany and regulate natural affection."[2] Although the girls' behaviors have been transformed by Miss Jenny's example and Mrs. Teachum's "wise and kind Instructions," even at the end of the novel the harmony and stability of the group is threatened by unrestrained passion.

This particular threat arises from the impending break-up of the girls' society, necessitated by Miss Jenny Peace's departure. When Mrs. Teachum informs Miss Jenny that her aunt has written requesting her presence at home, the girls burst into tears, unable to restrain their grief. Miss Jenny, always desirous of providing a model for their behavior, tries to soothe them, but they can answer only "by Sobs and Tears; only little Polly Suckling, running to her, clung about her Neck, and cry'd, 'Indeed, indeed, Miss Jenny, you must not go; I shall break my Heart, if I lose you: I'm sure we shan't, nor we can't, be half so happy, when you are gone, tho' our Governess was Ten times better to us than she is" (p. 173). The girls soon get the better of their emotions, persuaded by Miss Jenny that "it is our Duty to do so," and by Mrs. Teachum's assurances that though she "could wish ... never to part with [Miss Jenny] as long as I live ... I consider, that it is for her Advantage; and I would have you all remember, in her Absence, to let her Example and Friendship fill your Hearts with Joy, instead of Grief" (p. 174).

---

[1]   In the writings of the rational moralists, the job of educating children is often assumed by characters outside the family circle, that is, by tutors and governesses. See, e.g., *The History of Sandford and Merton's* Mr. Barclay and *Original Stories's* Mrs. Mason in Appendix D.

[2]   "'Ingenious Torment': Incest, Family, and the Structure of Community in the Work of Sarah Fielding," *The Eighteenth-Century: Theory and Interpretation* 36 (1995): 245.

Miss Jenny's role as exemplum demonstrates one of the most sophisticated textual elements in *The Governess*. For Miss Jenny, even though she physically leaves the group, continues to operate as a regulator of the girls' behavior. If, for example, the harmony of the little female academy threatens to lapse into discord,

> The Story of Miss *Jenny Peace*'s reconciling all her little Companions was told to them; so that Miss *Jenny*, tho' absent, still seemed (by the bright Example which she left behind her) to be the Cement of Union and Harmony in this well-regulated Society. And if any Girl was found to harbour in her Breast a rising Passion, which it was difficult to conquer, the Name and Story of Miss *Jenny Peace* soon gained her Attention, and left her without any other Desire than to emulate Miss *Jenny*'s Virtues. (p. 175–76)

In other words, Miss Jenny has been transfigured, she has become a "Name and Story," a text to be circulated and read, like *The Governess* itself. Indeed, Fielding's entire novel moves on this process of textual transfiguration: stories and life histories are exchanged and discussed; the discussions themselves become part of the texts; the girls who listen and learn from them provide examples for readers; and finally the readers, through active engagement with the text, become examples, too. This metatextual layering of stories within stories, all of which depend on discerning readers for their circulation, in effect confirms and validates fiction as an instructional tool. In this way, Fielding's educational novel becomes part of a larger project to legitimize the social role of the eighteenth-century novel.

Although no critical reviews of *The Governess* were published on its initial appearance, the book's popularity can be seen in its printing history. In August 1749, eight months after the first edition was published, a second edition came out; a third edition was printed in 1751, and a fourth in 1758. Versions of Fielding's text continued to appear throughout the eighteenth and nineteenth centuries, and as late as 1928, extracts from *The Governess* were reprinted in anthologies of children's stories. Numerous imitations of *The Governess* appeared throughout the eighteenth century as well, with titles like *Anecdotes of Mary; or, The Good Governess* (1795) and *Three Days Chat … between Young Ladies and their Governess* (c. 1798). The most famous appropriation of Fielding's text is *The Governess: or, The Little Female Academy. By Mrs. Sherwood*, first published in 1820. As Grey points out, Sherwood's version offers only a vague reference to Fielding's authorship in its introduction. Sherwood's text, moreover, reflects nineteenth-century trends in children's literature that emphasized religious content and deemphasized imaginative play. In rewriting Fielding's novel, Grey tells us, Sherwood "substituted dull, moral tales for Sarah's fairy-stories and … inserted the gloomiest quotations from the Bible on practically every page."[1] For much of the twentieth century, Fielding's *The Governess* remained unavailable until Grey's facsimile reprint appeared in 1968. Pandora Press also reprinted *The Governess* in 1987, but neither of these editions has been available for a number of years. The Broadview edition of *The Governess*, then, represents a recovery of Fielding's innovative educational novel. Along with recent editions of her other works, this text should help readers more fully appreciate Sarah Fielding's position as one of the most popular and talented writers in the eighteenth century.

---

[1] Grey 74.

Sarah Fielding: A Brief Chronology

1706   Colonel Edmund Fielding (b. 1680) marries Sarah Gould (b. 1682; daughter of Sir Henry and Lady Sarah Davidge Gould).

1710   Sir Henry initiates purchase of East Stour farm for the support of his daughter and grandchildren; dies March 1710. Sarah Fielding born 8 November 1710 at East Stour, Dorset, fourth of seven children.

1718/19   Sarah Gould Fielding dies 14 April 1718; Edmund Fielding departs for London leaving his children in the care of Lady Gould's sister, Katherine Cottington.

1719   Edmund remarries Anne Rapha (d. 1727) in January.

1720   Sarah Fielding and sisters Catherine and Ursula enrolled in Mrs. Mary Rookes's school in Salisbury; Henry Fielding enrolled at Eton.

1721   Lady Gould initiates lawsuit against Edmund Fielding on the grounds of misappropriation of East Stour income and neglect of his children.

1722   Lady Gould awarded custody of Sarah and her sisters.

1729   Edmund Fielding marries a third time, to Eleanor Hill (d. 1739).

1733   Lady Gould dies 7 June.

1739   East Stour farm sold 14 May. Sarah's oldest sister Catharine inherits her Aunt Cottington's estate, moves to Westminster, possibly with Sarah and her sisters.

1740/41   Edmund Fielding committed to debtor's prison; marries a fourth time to Elizabeth Sparrye (d. 1770) in March 1741; dies 18 June 1741.

1742   Henry Fielding publishes *Joseph Andrews*, which contains Sarah Fielding's "Letter from Leonora to Horatio."

1743   Henry Fielding publishes *Miscellanies*, containing *A*

Journey from This World to the Next, the last chapter of which is Sarah Fielding's "History of Anna Boleyn."

1744   Henry Fielding's wife Charlotte (*née* Craddock) dies in November; Sarah Fielding possibly moves in to his house in London. Sarah Fielding publishes *The Adventures of David Simple* in May; a second edition follows in July, which contains a preface and editorial changes by Henry.

1747   Sarah Fielding publishes *Familiar Letters Between the Characters in David Simple and Others* in April. Henry remarries in November; Sarah rejoins her sisters in Westminster.

1749   Sarah Fielding publishes *The Governess; or, The Little Female Academy* and *Remarks on Clarissa* in January. A second edition of *The Governess* appears in August.

1750   Sarah Fielding's sister Catharine dies 5 July; Henry Fielding's son Henry (b. 1742?) dies and is buried 3 August; Fielding's sister Ursula dies in December.

1751   Sarah Fielding's last remaining sister, Beatrice, dies in January. Sarah moves in with close friend Jane Collier.

1753   In February, Sarah Fielding publishes *Volume the Last*, the conclusion to *The Adventures of David Simple*, with a preface by Jane Collier.

1754   Sarah Fielding publishes *The Cry* in March; Henry Fielding dies in October, in Portugal. Sarah Fielding moves to Bath for health reasons. She remains in Bath or its environs until her death. There she becomes part of the bluestocking circle whose members include Elizabeth Carter, Sarah Scott, and Lady Barbara Montagu.

1755   Jane Collier dies in the summer.

1757   In May, Sarah Fielding publishes *The Lives of Cleopatra and Octavia*.

1759   In March, Sarah Fielding publishes *The History of the Countess of Dellwyn*.

1760   In March, Sarah Fielding publishes *The History of Ophelia*.

1762   In January, Sarah Fielding publishes her last work, *Xenophon's Memoirs of Socrates, with the Defence of Socrates Before His Judges*.

1766   Sarah Fielding moves in with Sarah Scott.

1768   Sarah Fielding dies on 9 April in Bath; buried 14 April at St. Mary's, Charlcombe, Bath.

A Note on the Text

The text used for this edition is the second revised and corrected edition of *The Governess; or, The Little Female Academy*, published by Andrew Millar in London, 1749, courtesy of the Rare Books and Special Collections Library at the University of Illinois at Urbana-Champaign. Obvious printer's errors have been corrected silently; running quotation marks have been removed and the use of double and single quotation marks in dialogue has been made consistent; the long "s" has been modernized. Fielding's eighteenth-century capitalization, punctuation, and spelling irregularities have been retained.

THE
GOVERNESS;
Or, The LITTLE
-FEMALE ACADEMY.

Calculated for the

ENTERTAINMENT *and* INSTRUCTION

OF
YOUNG LADIES

IN THEIR
EDUCATION.

By the AUTHOR *of* DAVID SIMPLE.

The SECOND EDITION.
Revised and Corrected.

Shall we forget *the Counsel we have shar'd,*
The Sisters Vows, the Hours that we have spent,
When we have chid the hasty-footed Time
For parting Us? O! and is all forgot?
All School-Days Friendship, Childhood Innocence?

SHAKESPEARE's Midsummer Night's Dream.

LONDON:

Printed for A. MILLAR, over against *Catherine*
Street in the *Strand.* M.DCC.XLIX.

[Price bound, 1 *s.* 6 *d.*

To the Honourable *Mrs.* Poyntz.[1]

Madam,

The Design of the following Sheets is to endeavour to cultivate an early Inclination to Benevolence, and a Love of Virtue, in the Minds of young Women, by trying to shew them, that their True Interest is concerned in cherishing and improving those amiable Dispositions into Habits; and in keeping down all rough and boistrous Passions; and that from this alone they can propose to themselves to arrive at true Happiness, in any of the Stations of Life allotted to the Female Character.

This I have endeavoured to inculcate, by those Methods of Fable and Moral, which have been recommended by the wisest Writers, as the most effectual means of conveying useful Instruction.

One Thing only seems to remain; which is, to set before their Eyes one great living Pattern of every Lesson I would teach them; and none who know Mrs. Poyntz, *will wonder that I fix on her as this prevalent Example.*

For what can more strongly enforce the strictest Observance of all those Social Duties, which become the Female Character, *or more plainly tend to take from young Minds all those Desires and Passions, which Vanity or Ambition might inspire, than the Example of a Lady, who, tho' bred in a Court, where she was the Object of Universal Admiration, no sooner became a Wife, than she turned her Thoughts to all the Domestic Duties that Situation requires, and made the maternal Care of her Family her first and chief Study?*

These Considerations, Madame, made me first hope, that a Design of this Nature would not be unacceptable to you; and, particularly, as this Scheme was, in a manner, directed by Mr. Poyntz. *And here I beg Pardon, for indulging my Vanity so far, as not to conceal, that the Execution of it has, in some measure, met with his and your Approbation. I am,*

Madame,

With great Respect,

Your most Obedient,

Humble Servant,

The Author.

---

[1] Anna Maria Mordaunt Poyntz. Prior to her marriage to Stephen Poyntz, she was one of Queen Caroline's Maids of Honor. Mr. Poyntz was Governor (the male equivalent of a governess) of King George II's third son William.

My young Readers,

Before you begin the following Sheets, I beg you will stop a Moment at this Preface, to consider with me, what is the true Use of Reading; and if you can once fix this Truth in your Minds, namely, that the true Use of Books is to make you wiser and better, you will then have both Profit and Pleasure from what you read.

One Thing quite necessary to make any Instructions that come either from your Governors, or your Books, of any Use to you, is to attend with a Desire of Learning, and not to be apt to fansy yourselves too wise to be taught. For this Spirit will keep you ignorant as long as you live, and you will be like the Birds in the following Fable:

The *Magpye* alone, of all the Birds, had the Art of building a Nest, the Form of which was with a Covering over Head, and only a small Hole to creep out at.—The rest of the Birds, being without Houses, desired the *Pye* to teach them how to build one.—A Day is appointed, and they all meet.—The *Pye* then says, "You must lay Two Sticks across, thus."—"Aye, says the *Crow*, I thought that was the way to begin."—"Then lay a little Straw and Moss."—"Certainly, says the *Jack-Daw*, I knew that must follow."—"Then place more Straw, Moss, and Feathers, in such a manner as this."—"Aye, without doubt, cries the *Starling*, that must necessarily follow; any one could tell how to do that."—When the *Pye* had gone on teaching them till the Nest was built half way, and every Bird in his Turn had known either one thing or another, he left off, and said, "Gentlemen, I find you all understand building Nests as well, if not better, than I do; therefore you cannot want any more of my Instructions."—— So saying, he flew away, and left them to upbraid each other with their Folly; which is visible to this Day, as no Bird but the *Magpye* knows how to build more than half a Nest.

The Reason these foolish Birds never knew how to build more than half a Nest, was, that instead of trying to learn what the *Pye* told them, they would boast of knowing more already than he could teach them: And this same Fate will certainly attend all those, who had rather please themselves with the Vanity of fansying they are already wise, than take Pains to become so.

But take care, that, instead of being really humble in your own Hearts, you do not, by a fansied Humility, run into an Error of the other Extreme, and say that you are incapable of understanding it at all; and therefore, from Laziness, and sooner than take any Pains, sit yourselves down contented to be ignorant, and think, by confessing your Ignorance, to make full Amends for your Folly. This is, being as contemptible as the *Owl*, who hates the Light of the Sun; and therefore often makes Use of the Power he has, of drawing a Film over his Eyes, to keep himself in his beloved Darkness.

When you run thro' Numbers of Books, only for the sake of saying, you have read them, without making any Advantage of the Knowlege got thereby, remember this Saying, "That a Head, like a House, when crammed too full, and no regular Order observed in the placing what is there, is only littered instead of being furnished." And that you may the better understand the Force of this Observation, I will tell you a Story.

Mr. *Thomas Watkins* had Two Daughters, Miss *Hannah* and Miss *Fanny*. Their Father and Mother assigned them a very pretty Apartment for their own Use, allowed them all Things in great Plenty, and only desired them to keep their Cloaths, Linen, and all their Things, in such a proper Order, that they might have the Use of them. But these Two foolish Girls, fansying themselves wiser than their Parents, disobeyed their Commands, and threw all their Things about in such irregular Heaps, that whenever they were to be dressed, they found themselves more at a Loss, than any poor Girl would have been, who had not had half their Plenty allowed her. Whenever their Mamma sent them Word she would take them abroad, they were in the greatest Confusion that can be imagined: "Oh! Sister *Hannah* (cries Miss *Fanny*) can you tell where I put my Cap?" "No, indeed (answers Miss *Hannah*) nor can I find my own, nor my Gloves, nor my Hood. Well, what shall I do? My Mamma is in such a Hurry, she will not stay for us."—— Then would these Two Girls tumble all the Things in their Drawers; but in that Confusion could find nothing, till their Mamma was drove from the Door, leaving them at home as they deserved: Whilst, looking ashamed at each other, they were laughed at by the rest of the Family.

Thus will those foolish Children be served, who heap into their Heads a great deal, and yet never observe what they put there, either to mend their Practice, or increase their Knowlege. Their Heads will be in as much Confusion, as were Miss *Watkins's* Chests *of* Drawers. And when in Company they endeavour to find out something to say to the Purpose, they will be hunting in the midst of a Heap of Rubbish, whilst they expose themselves, and become a Laughing-stock to their Companions.

The Design of the following Sheets is to prove to you, that Pride, Stubbornness, Malice, Envy, and, in short, all manner of Wickedness, is the greatest Folly we can be possessed of; and constantly turns on the Head of that foolish Person who does not conquer and get the better of all Inclinations to such Wickedness. Certainly, Love and Affection for each other make the Happiness of all Societies; and therefore Love and Affection (if we would be happy) are what we should chiefly encourage and cherish in our Minds.

I depend on the Goodness of all my little Readers, to acknowlege this to be true. But there is one Caution to be used, namely, That you are not led into many Inconveniencies, and even Faults, by this Love and Affection: For this Disposition will naturally lead you to delight in Friendship; and this Delight in Friendship may lead you into all manner of Errors, unless you take Care not to be partial to any of your Companions, only because they are agreeable, without first considering whether they are good enough to deserve your Love: And there is one Mark in which you can never be deceived; namely That whoever tempts you to fail in your Duty, or justifies you in so doing, is not your real Friend. And if you cannot have Resolution enough to break from such pretended Friends, you will nourish in your Bosoms Serpents, that in the End will sting you to Death.

THE GOVERNESS; OR,
THE LITTLE FEMALE ACADEMY

There lived in the Northern Parts of *England*, a Gentlewoman who undertook the Education of young Ladies; and this Trust she endeavour'd faithfully to discharge, by instructing those committed to her Care in Reading, Writing, Working,[1] and in all proper Forms of Behaviour. And tho' her principal Aim was to improve their Minds in all useful Knowlege; to render them obedient to their Superiors, and gentle, kind, and affectionate to each other; yet did she not omit teaching them an exact Neatness in their Persons and Dress, and a perfect Gentility in their whole Carriage.

This Gentlewoman, whose Name was *Teachum*, was the Widow of a Clergyman, with whom she had lived nine Years in all the Harmony and Concord which form the only satisfactory Happiness in the married state. Two little Girls (the youngest of which was born before the second Year of their Marriage was expired) took up a great Part of their Thoughts; and it was their mutual Design to spare no Pains or Trouble in their Education.

Mr. *Teachum* was a very sensible Man, and took great Delight in improving his Wife; as she also placed her chief Pleasure in receiving his Instructions. One of his constant Subjects of Discourse to her was concerning the Education of Children: So that, when in his last Illness his Physicians pronounced him beyond the Power of their Art to relieve him, he expressed great Satisfaction in the Thought of leaving his Children to the Care of so prudent a Mother.

Mrs. *Teachum*, tho' exceedingly afflicted by such a Loss, yet thought it her Duty to call forth all her Resolution to conquer her Grief, in order to apply herself to the Care of these her dear Husband's Children. But her Misfortunes were not here to end: For within a Twelvemonth after the Death of her Husband, she was deprived of both her Children by a violent Fever that then raged in the Country; and about the same time, by the unforeseen Breaking of a Banker, in whose Hands almost all her Fortune was just then placed, she was bereft of the Means of her future Support.

---

[1] Needlework, embroidery, or the like.

The Christian Fortitude with which (thro' her Husband's Instructions) she had armed her Mind, had not left it in the Power of any outward Accident to bereave her of her Understanding, or to make her incapable of doing what was proper on all Occasions. Therefore, by the Advice of all her Friends, she undertook what she was so well qualified for; namely, the Education of Children. But as she was moderate in her Desires, and did not seek to raise a great Fortune, she was resolved to take no more Scholars than she could have an Eye to herself, without the Help of other Teachers; and, instead of making Interest to fill her School, it was looked upon as a great Favour when she would take any Girl: And as her Number was fixed to Nine, which she on no Account would be prevailed on to increase, great Application was made, when any Scholar went away, to have her Place supplied; and happy were they who could get a Promise for the next Vacancy.

Mrs. *Teachum* was about Forty Years old, tall and genteel in her Person, tho' somewhat inclined to Fat. She had a lively and commanding Eye, insomuch that she naturally created an Awe in all her little Scholars; except when she condescended to smile, and talk familiarly to them; and then she had something perfectly kind and tender in her Manner. Her Temper was so extremely calm and good, that tho' she never omitted reprehending, and that pretty severely, any Girl that was guilty of the smallest Fault proceeding from an evil Disposition; yet for no Cause whatsoever was she provoked to be in a Passion: But she kept up such a Dignity and Authority, by her steady Behaviour, that the Girls greatly feared to incur her Displeasure by disobeying her Commands; and were equally pleased with her approbation, when they had done any-thing worthy her Commendation.

At the Time of the ensuing History, the School (being full) consisted of the Nine following young Ladies:

Miss *Jenny Peace*,

Miss *Sukey Jennett*,	Miss *Nanny Spruce*,
Miss *Dolly Friendly*,	Miss *Betty Ford*,
Miss *Lucy Sly*,	Miss *Henny Fret*,
Miss *Patty Lockit*,	Miss *Polly Suckling*.

The eldest of these was but fourteen Years old, and none of the rest had yet attained their twelfth Year.

An Account of a Fray, begun and carried on for the sake of an Apple: In which are shewn the sad Effects of Rage and Anger

It was on a fine Summer's Evening, when the School-hours were at an End, and the young Ladies were admitted to divert themselves for some time, as they thought proper, in a pleasant Garden adjoining to the House, that their Governess, who delighted in pleasing them, brought out a little Basket of Apples, which were intended to be divided equally amongst them: But Mrs. *Teachum* being hastily called away (one of her poor Neighbours having had an Accident which wanted her Assistance), she left the Fruit in the Hands of Miss *Jenny Peace*, the eldest of her Scholars, with a strict Charge to see that everyone had an equal Share of her Gift.

But here a perverse Accident turned good Mrs. Teachum's Design of giving them Pleasure into their Sorrow, and raised in their little Hearts nothing but Strife and Anger: For, alas! there happened to be one Apple something larger than the rest, on which the whole Company immediately placed their desiring Eyes, and all at once cried out, "Pray, Miss *Jenny*, give me that Apple." Each gave her Reasons why she had the best Title to it: The youngest pleaded her Youth, and the eldest her Age; one insisted on her Goodness, another from her Meekness claimed a Title to Preference; and one, in Confidence of her Strength, said positively, she would have it; but all speaking together, it was difficult to distinguish who said this, or who said that.

Miss *Jenny* begg'd them all to be quiet: But in vain; for she could not be heard: They had all set their Hearts on that fine Apple, looking upon those she had given them as nothing. She told them, they had better be contented with what they had, than be thus seeking what it was impossible for her to give to them all. She offered to divide it into Eight Parts, or to do anything to satisfy them: But she might as well have been silent; for they were all talking, and had no time to hear. At last, as a Means to quiet the Disturbance, she threw this Apple, the Cause of their

Contention, with her utmost Force, over a Hedge, into another Garden, where they could not come at it.

At first they were all silent, as if they were struck dumb with Astonishment with the Loss of this one poor Apple, tho' at the same time they had Plenty before them.

But this did not bring to pass Miss *Jenny's* Design: For now they all began again to quarrel which had the most Right to it, and which *ought* to have had it, with as much Vehemence as they had before contended for the Possession of it: And their Anger by degrees became so high, that Words could not vent half their Rage; and they fell to pulling of Caps, tearing of Hair, and dragging the Cloaths off one another's Backs. Though they did not so much strike, as endeavour to scratch and pinch their Enemies.

Miss *Dolly Friendly* as yet was not engaged in the Battle: But on hearing her Friend Miss *Nanny Spruce* scream out, that she was hurt by a sly Pinch from one of the Girls, she flew on this sly Pincher, as she called her, like an enraged Lion on its Prey: and not content only to return the Harm her Friend had received, she struck with such Force, as felled her Enemy to the Ground. And now they could not distinguish between Friend and Enemy; but fought, scratch'd, and tore, like so many Cats, when they extend their Claws to fix them in their Rival's Heart.

Miss *Jenny* was employed in endeavouring to part them.

In the Midst of this Confusion, appeared Mrs. *Teachum*, who was returning in Hopes to see them happy with the Fruit she had given them: But she was some time there before either her Voice or Presence could awaken them from their Attention to the Fight; when on a sudden they all faced her, and Fear of Punishment began now a little to abate their Rage. Each of the Misses held in her Right-hand, fast clenched, some Marks of Victory; for they beat and were beaten by Turns. One of them held a little Lock of Hair, torn from the Head of her Enemy: Another grasped a Piece of a Cap, which, in aiming at her Rival's Hair, had deceived her Hand, and was all the Spoils she could gain: A third clenched a Piece of an Apron; a fourth, of a Frock. In short, everyone unfortunately held in her Hand a Proof of having been engaged in the Battle. And the Ground was spread with Rags and Tatters, torn from the Backs of the little inveterate Combatants.

Mrs. *Teachum* stood for some time astonished at the Sight: But at last she required Miss *Jenny Peace*, who was the only Person disengaged, to tell her the whole Truth, and to inform her of the Cause of all this Confusion.

Miss *Jenny* was obliged to obey the Commands of her Governess; tho' she was so good-natured, that she did it in the mildest Terms; and endeavoured all she could to lessen, rather than increase, Mrs. Teachum's Anger. The guilty Persons now began all to excuse themselves as fast as Tears and Sobs would permit them.

One said, "Indeed, Madam, it was none of my Fault; for I did not begin; for Miss *Sukey Jennett*, without any Cause in the World (for I did nothing to provoke her), hit me a great Slap in the Face, and made my Tooth ach: The Pain *did* make me angry; and then, indeed, I hit her a little Tap; but it was on her Back; and I am sure it was the smallest Tap in the World; and could not possibly hurt her half so much as her great Blow did me."

"Law, Miss! replied Miss *Jennett*, How can you say so? when you know that you struck me first, and that yours was the great Blow, and mine the little Tap; for I only went to defend myself from your monstrous Blows."

Such-like Defences they would all have made for themselves, each insisting on not being in Fault, and throwing the Blame on her Companion: But Mrs. *Teachum* silenced them by a positive Command; and told them, that she saw they were all equally guilty, and as such she would treat them.

Mrs. *Teachum's* Method of punishing I never could find out. But this is certain, the most severe Punishment she had ever inflicted on any Misses, since she had kept a School, was now laid on these wicked Girls, who had been thus fighting, and pulling one another to Pieces, for a sorry Apple.

The first thing she did, was to take away all the Apples; telling them, that before they had any more Instances of such Kindness from her, they should give her Proofs of their deserving them better. And when she had punished them as much as she thought proper, she made them all embrace one another, and promise to be Friends for the future; which, in Obedience to her Commands, they were forced to comply with, tho' there remained a Grudge and Ill-will in their Bosoms; every one thinking she was punished most, altho' she would have it, that she deserved to be Punished least; and they contrived all the sly Tricks they could think on to vex and teaze each other.

A Dialogue between Miss Jenny Peace, *and Miss* Sukey Jennett; *wherein the latter is at last convinced of her own Folly in being so quarrelsome; and, by her Example, all her Companions are brought to see and confess their Fault*

The next Morning Miss *Jenny Peace* used her utmost Endeavours to bring her School-fellows to be heartily reconciled; but in vain: For each insisted on it, that she was not to blame; but that the whole Quarrel arose from the Faults of others. At last ensued the following Dialogue between Miss *Jenny Peace* and Miss *Sukey Jennett,* which brought about Miss *Jenny's* Designs; and which we recommend to the Consideration of all our young Readers.

Miss *Jenny.* Now pray, Miss *Sukey*, tell me, What did you get by your Contention and Quarrel about that foolish Apple?

Miss *Sukey.* Indeed, Ma'am, I shall not answer you. I know that you only want to prove, that you are wiser than I, because you are older. But I don't know but some People may understand as much at Eleven Years old, as others at Thirteen: But, because you are the oldest in the School, you always want to be tutoring and governing. I don't like to have more than one Governess; and if I obey my Mistress, I think that is enough.

Miss *Jenny.* Indeed, my Dear, I don't want to govern you, nor to prove myself wiser than you: I only want, that, instead of quarrelling and making yourself miserable, you should live at Peace, and be happy. Therefore, pray do, answer my Question, Whether you got any-thing by your Quarrel?

Miss *Sukey.* No! I cannot say I got any-thing by it: For my Mistress was angry, and punished me; and my Hair was pulled off, and my Cloaths torn, in the Scuffle: Neither did I value the Apple: But yet I have too much Spirit to be imposed on. I am sure I had as good a Right to it as any of the others: And I would not give up my Right to any one.

Miss *Jenny.* But don't you know, Miss *Sukey*, it would have shewn much more Spirit to have yielded the Apple to another, than to have fought about it? Then, indeed, you would have proved your Sense; for you would have shewn, that you had too much Understanding to fight about a Trifle. Then your Cloaths had been whole, your Hair not torn from your Head, your Mistress had not been angry, nor had your Fruit been taken away from you.

Miss *Sukey*. And so, Miss, you would fain prove, that it is wisest to submit to every-body that would impose upon one? But I will not believe it, say what you will.

Miss *Jenny*. But is not what I say true? If you had not been in the Battle, would not your Cloaths have been whole, your Hair not torn, your Mistress pleased with you, and the Apples your own?

Here Miss *Sukey* paused for some time: For as Miss *Jenny* was in the Right, and had Truth on her Side, it was difficult for Miss *Sukey* to know what to answer. For it is impossible, without being very silly, to contradict Truth: And yet Miss *Sukey* was so foolish, that she did not care to own herself in the Wrong; tho' nothing could have been so great a Sign of her Understanding.

When Miss *Jenny* saw her thus at a Loss for an Answer, she was in Hopes of making her Companion happy; for, as she had as much Good-nature as Understanding, that was her Design. She therefore pursued her Discourse in the following Manner:

Miss *Jenny*. Pray, Miss *Sukey*, do answer me one question more. Don't you lie awake at Nights, and fret and vex yourself, because you are angry with your School-fellows? Are not you restless and uneasy, because you cannot find a safe Method to be revenged on them, without being punished yourself? Do tell me truly, Is not this your Case?

Miss *Sukey*. Yes, it is. For if I could but hurt my Enemies, without being hurt myself, it would be the greatest Pleasure I could have in the World.

Miss *Jenny*. Oh fy, Miss *Sukey*! What you have now said is wicked. Don't you consider what you say every Day in your Prayers? And this Way of Thinking will make you lead a very uneasy Life. If you would hearken to me, I could put you into a Method of being very happy, and making all those Misses you call your Enemies, become your Friends.

Miss *Sukey*. You could tell me a Method, Miss! Do you think I don't know as well as you what is fit to be done? I believe I am as capable of finding the Way to be happy, as you are of teaching me.

Here Miss *Sukey* burst into Tears, that any-body should presume to tell her the Way to be happy.

Miss *Jenny*. Upon my Word, my Dear, I don't mean to vex you; but only, instead of tormenting yourself all Night in laying Plots to revenge yourself, I would have you employ this one Night in thinking of what I have said. Nothing will shew your Sense so much, as to own that you have been in the Wrong: Nor will any-thing prove a right Spirit so much, as to confess your Fault. All the Misses will be your Friends, and perhaps follow your Example. Then you will have the Pleasure of having caused the Quiet of the whole School; your Governess will love you; and you will be at Peace in your Mind, and never have any more foolish Quarrels, in which you all get nothing but Blows and Uneasiness.

Miss *Sukey* began now to find, that Miss *Jenny* was in the Right, and she herself in the Wrong; but yet she was so proud she would not own it. Nothing could be so foolish as this Pride; because it would have been both good and wise in her to confess the Truth the Moment she saw it. However, Miss *Jenny* was so discreet as not to press her any farther that Night; but begged her to consider seriously on what she had said, and to let her know her Thoughts the next Morning. And then she left her.

When Miss *Sukey* was alone, she stood some time in great Confusion. She could not help seeing how much hitherto she had been in the Wrong; and that Thought stung her to the Heart, She cried, stamped, and was in as great an Agony as if some sad Misfortune had befallen her. At last, when she had somewhat vented her Passion by Tears, she burst forth into the following Speech:

"It is very true what Miss *Jenny Peace* says; for I am always uneasy. I don't sleep in Quiet; because I am always thinking, either that I have not my Share of what is given us, or that I cannot be revenged on any of the Girls that offend me. And when I quarrel with them, I am scratched and bruised, or reproached. And what do I get by all this? Why, I scratch, bruise, and reproach them in my Turn. Is not that Gain enough? I warrant I hurt them as much as they hurt me. But then, indeed, as Miss *Jenny* says, if I could make these Girls my Friends, and did not wish to hurt them, I certainly might live a quieter, and perhaps a happier Life.—But what, then, have I been always in the Wrong all my Life-time? for I always quarrelled and hated every one who had offended me.— Oh! I cannot bear that Thought! It is enough to make me mad! when I imagined myself so wise and so sensible, to find out that I have been always a Fool. If I think a Moment longer about it, I shall die with Grief and Shame. I must think myself in the Right; and I will too.—But, as Miss *Jenny* says, I really am unhappy; for I hate all my School-fellows: And yet, I dare not do them any Mischief; for my Mistress will punish me severely if I do. I should not so much mind that neither: But then those I intend to hurt will triumph over me, to see me punished for their sakes. In short, the more I reflect, the more I am afraid Miss *Jenny* is in the Right; and yet it breaks my Heart to think so."

Here the poor Girl wept so bitterly, and was so heartily grieved, that she could not utter one Word more; but sat herself down, reclining her Head upon her Hand, in the most melancholy Posture that could be: Nor could she close her Eyes all Night; but lay tossing and raving with the Thought how she should act, and what she should say to Miss *Jenny* the next Day.

When the Morning came, Miss *Sukey* dreaded every Moment, as the Time drew nearer when she must meet Miss *Jenny*. She knew it would not be possible to resist her Arguments; and yet Shame for having been in Fault overcame her.

As soon as Miss *Jenny* saw Miss *Sukey* with her Eyes cast down, and confessing, by a Look of Sorrow, that she would take her Advice, she embraced her kindly; and, without giving her the Trouble to speak, took it for granted, that she would leave off quarrelling, be reconciled to her School-fellows, and make herself happy.

Miss *Sukey* did indeed stammer out some Words, which implied a Confession of her Fault; but they were spoke so low they could hardly be heard: Only Miss *Jenny*, who always chose to look at the fairest Side of her Companions Actions, by Miss *Sukey's* Look and Manner, guessed her Meaning.

In the same manner did this good Girl, *Jenny*, persuade, one by one, all her School-fellows to be reconciled to each with Sincerity and Love.

Miss *Dolly Friendly*, who had too much Sense to engage in the Battle for the sake of an Apple, and who was provoked to strike a Blow only for Friendship's Sake, easily saw the Truth of what Miss *Jenny* said; and was therefore presently convinced, that the best Part she could have acted for her Friend, would have been withdrawing her from the Scuffle.

A Scene of Love and Friendship, quite the Reverse of the Battle: Wherein is shewn the different Effects of Love and Goodness from those attending Anger, Strife, and Wickedness: With the Life of Miss Jenny Peace

After Miss *Jenny* had completed the good Work of making all her Companions Friends, she drew them round her in a little Arbour, in that very Garden which had been the Scene of their Strife, and consequently of their Misery; and then spoke to them the following Speech; which she delivered in so mild a Voice, that it was sufficient to charm her Hearers into Attention, and to persuade them to be led by her Advice, and to follow her Example, in the Paths of Goodness.

"My dear Friends and School-fellows, you cannot imagine the Happiness it gives me to see you thus all so heartily reconciled. You will find the joyful Fruits of it. Nothing can shew so much Sense, as thus to own yourselves in Fault: For could anything have been so foolish, as to spend all your Time in Misery, rather than at once to make use of the Power you have of making yourselves happy? Now if you will use as many Endeavours to love, as you have hitherto done to hate each other, you will find, that everyone amongst you, whenever you have any-thing given you, will have double, nay, I may say Eight times (as there are Eight of you) the Pleasure, in considering that your Companions are happy. What is the End of Quarrels, but that every-one is fretted and vexed, and no one gains any thing by it? Whereas by endeavouring to please and love each other, the End is Happiness to ourselves, and Joy to every one around us. I am sure, if you will speak the Truth, none of you have been so easy since you quarreled, as you are now you are reconciled. Answer me honestly, if this is not Truth."

Here Miss *Jenny* was silent, and waited for an Answer. But the poor Girls, who had in them the Seeds of Good-will to each other, altho' those Seeds were choaked and over-run with the Weeds of Envy and Pride; as in a Garden the finest Strawberries will be spoiled by rank Weeds, if Care is not taken to root them out: These poor Girls, I say, now struck with the Force of Truth, and sorry for what they had done, let drop some Tears, which trickled down their Cheeks, and were Signs of Meekness, and Sorrow for their Fault. Not like those Tears which burst from their swoln Eyes, when Anger and Hatred choaked their Words, and their proud Hearts laboured with Stubbornness and Folly; when their Skins reddened, and all their Features were changed and distorted by the Violence of Passion, which made them frightful to the Beholders, and miserable to themselves:—No! Far other Cause had they now for Tears, and far different were the Tears they shed: Their Eyes, melting with Sorrow for their Faults, let fall some Drops, as Tokens of their Repentance: But, as soon as they could recover themselves to speak, they all with one Voice cried out, Indeed, Miss *Jenny*, we are sorry for our Fault, and will follow your Advice; which we now see is owing to your Goodness.

Miss *Jenny* now produced a Basket of Apples, which she had purchased out of the little Pocket-money she was allowed, in order to prove, that the same Things may be a Pleasure, or a Pain, according as the Persons to whom they are given, are good or bad.

These she placed in the Midst of her Companions, and desired them to eat, and enjoy themselves; and now they were so changed, that each helped her next Neighbour before she would touch any for herself: And the Moment they were grown thus good-natured and friendly, they were as well-bred, and as polite, as it is possible to describe.

Miss *Jenny*'s Joy was inexpressible, that she had caused this happy Change: Nor less was the Joy of her Companions, who now began to taste Pleasures, from which their Animosity to each other had hitherto debarred them. They all sat looking pleased on their Companions: Their Faces borrowed Beauty from the Calmness and Goodness of their Minds: And all those ugly Frowns, and all that ill-natured Sourness, which, when they were angry and cross, were but too plain in their Faces, were now intirely fled: Jessamine[1] and Honeysuckles surrounded their Seats, and played round their Heads, of which they gathered Nosegays to present each other with. They now enjoyed all the Pleasure and Happiness that attend those who are innocent and good.

Miss *Jenny*, with her Heart overflowing with Joy at this happy Change, said, "Now, my dear Companions, that you may be convinced what I have said and done was not occasioned by any Desire of proving myself wiser than you, as Miss *Sukey* hinted while she was yet in her Anger, I will, if you please, relate to you the History of my past Life; by which you will see in what manner I came by this Way of thinking; and as you will perceive it was chiefly owing to the Instructions of a kind Mamma, you may all likewise reap the same Advantage under good Mrs. *Teachum*, if you will obey her Commands, and attend to her Precepts: And after I have given you the Particulars of my Life, I must beg that every one of you will, some Day or other, when you have reflected upon it, declare all that you can remember of your own; for, should you not be able to relate any-thing worth remembering as an Example, yet there is nothing more likely to amend the future Part of any one's Life, than the recollecting and confessing the Faults of the past."

All our little Company highly approved of Miss *Jenny*'s Proposal, and promised, in their Turns, to relate their own Lives; and Miss *Polly Suckling* cried out, "Yes indeed, Miss *Jenny*, I'll tell all, when it comes to my Turn: So pray begin; for I long to hear what you did, when you was no bigger than I am now." Miss *Jenny* then kissed little *Polly*, and said, she would instantly begin.

But as, in the reading any one's Story, it is an additional Pleasure to have some Acquaintance with their Persons; and as I delight in giving my little Readers every Pleasure that is in my Power; I shall endeavour, as justly as I can, by Description, to set before their Eyes the Picture of this good young Creature: And the same of every one of our young Company, as they begin their Lives.

---

[1] Jasmine.

The Description *of Miss* Jenny Peace

Miss Jenny Peace was just turned of Fourteen, and could be called neither tall nor short of her Age: But her whole Person was the most agreeable that can be imagined. She had an exceeding fine Complexion, with as much Colour in her Cheeks as is the natural Effect of perfect Health. Her Hair was light-brown, and curled in so regular and yet easy a manner, as never to want any Assistance from Art. Her Eye-brows (which were not of that correct Turn, as to look as if they were drawn with a Pencil), and her Eye-lashes, were both darker than her Hair; and the latter being very long, gave such a Shade to her Eyes, as made them often mistaken for black, tho' they were only a dark Hazle. To give any Description of her Eyes beyond the Colour and Size, which was perfectly the Medium, would be impossible; except by saying they were expressive of every-thing that is amiable and good: For thro' them might be read every single Thought of the Mind; from whence they had such a Brightness and Chearfulness, as seemed to cast a Lustre over her whole Face. She had fine Teeth, and a Mouth answering to the most correct Rules of Beauty; and when she spoke (tho' you were at too great a Distance to hear what she said) there appeared so much Sweetness, Mildness, Modesty, and Good-nature, that you found yourself filled more with Pleasure than Admiration in beholding her. The Delight which every one took in looking on Miss *Jenny* was evident in this; That tho' Miss *Sukey Jennett*, and Miss *Patty Lockit*, were both what might be called handsomer Girls; and if you asked any Persons in Company their Opinion, they would tell you so; yet their Eyes were a direct Contradiction to their Tongues, by being continually fixed on Miss *Jenny*: For, while *She* was in the Room, it was impossible to fix them any-where else. She had a natural Ease and Gentility in her Shape; and all her Motions were more pleasing, tho' less striking, than what is commonly acquired by the Instruction of Dancing-Masters.

Such was the agreeable Person of Miss *Jenny Peace*; who, in her usual obliging Manner, and with an Air pleasing beyond my Power to express, at the Request of her Companions, began to relate the History of her Life, as follows:

The Life *of Miss* Jenny Peace

My Father dying when I was but half a Year old, I was left to the Care of my Mamma; who was the best Woman in the World, and to whose Memory I shall ever pay the most grateful Honour. From the Time she had any Children, she made it the whole Study of her Life to promote their Welfare, and form their Minds in the manner she thought would best answer her Purpose of making them both good and happy: For it was her constant Maxim, that Goodness and Happiness dwelt in the same Bosoms, and were generally found to live so much together, that they could not easily be separated.

My Mother had Six Children born alive; but could preserve none beyond the first Year, except my Brother *Harry Peace* and myself. She made it one of her chief Cares to cultivate and preserve the most perfect Love and Harmony between us. My Brother is but a Twelve-month older than I: So that, till I was Six Years old (for Seven was the Age in which he was sent to School) he remained at home with me; in which time we often had little childish Quarrels: But my Mother always took care to convince us of our Error in wrangling and fighting about nothing, and to teach us how much more Pleasure we enjoyed whilst we agreed. She shewed no Partiality to either, but endeavoured to make us equal in all Things, any otherwise than that she taught me I owed a Respect to my Brother, as the eldest.

Before my Brother went to School, we had set Hours appointed us, in which we regularly attended to learn whatever was thought necessary for our Improvement; my Mamma herself daily watching the opening of our Minds, and taking great Care to instruct us in what manner to make the best Use of the Knowlege we attained. Whatever we read she explained to us, and made us understand, that we might be the better for our Lessons. When we were capable of thinking, we made it so much a Rule to obey our Parent, the Moment she signified her Pleasure, that by that means we avoided many Accidents and Misfortunes: For Example; My Brother was running one Day giddily round the Brink of a Well; and if he had made the least false Step, he must have fallen to the Bottom, and been drowned; my Mamma, by a

Sign with her Finger that called him to her, preserved him from the imminent Danger he was in of losing his Life; and then she took care that we should both be the better for this little Incident, by laying before us, how much our Safety and Happiness, as well as our Duty, were concerned in being obedient.

My Brother and I once had a quarrel about something as trifling as your Apple of Contention; and, tho' we both heartily wished to be reconciled to each other, yet did our little Hearts swell so much with Stubbornness and Pride, that neither of us would speak first: By which means we were so silly as to be both uneasy, and yet would not use the Remedy that was in our own Power to remove that Uneasiness. My Mamma found it out, and sent for me into her Closet,[1] and said, "She was sorry to see her Instructions had no better Effect on me: For, continued she, indeed, *Jenny*, I am ashamed of your Folly, as well as Wickedness, in thus contending with your Brother." A Tear which I believe flowed from Shame, started from my Eyes at this Reproof; and I fixed them on the Ground, being too much overwhelmed with Confusion to dare to lift them up on my Mamma. On which she kindly said, "She hoped my Confusion was a Sign of my Amendment: That she might indeed have used another Method, by commanding me to seek a Reconciliation with my Brother; for she did not imagine I was already so far gone in Perverseness, as not to hold her Commands as inviolable; but she was willing, for my Good, first to convince me of my Folly." As soon as my Confusion would give me leave to speak, on my Knees I gave her a thousand Thanks for her Goodness, and went immediately to seek my Brother. He joyfully embraced the first Opportunity of being reconciled to me: And this was one of the pleasantest Hours of my Life. This Quarrel happened when my Brother came home at a Breaking-up, and I was Nine Years old.

My Mamma's principal Care was to keep up a perfect Amity between me and my Brother. I remember once, when *Harry* and I were playing in the Fields, there was a small Rivulet stopped me in my way. My Brother being nimbler and better able to jump than myself, with one Spring leaped over, and left me on the

---

[1] A small room for privacy or retirement, sometimes used for reading or devotions (*OED*).

other Side of it; but seeing me uneasy that I could not get over to him, his Good-nature prompted him to come back, and to assist me, and, by the Help of his Hand, I easily passed over. On this my good Mamma bid me remember how much my Brother's superior Strength might assist me in his being my Protector; and that I ought in return to use my utmost Endeavours to oblige him; and that then we should be mutual Assistants to each other throughout Life. Thus every-thing that passed was made use of to improve my Understanding, and amend my Heart.

I believe no Child ever spent her Time more agreeably than I did; for I not only enjoyed my own Pleasures, but also those of others. And when my Brother was carried abroad, and I was left at home, that *he* was pleased, made me full Amends for the Loss of any Diversion. The Contentions between us (where our Parent's Commands did not interfere) were always exerted in Endeavours each to prefer the other's Pleasures to Our own. My Mind was easy, and free from Anxiety: For as I always took care to speak Truth, I had nothing to conceal from my Mamma, and consequently had never any Fears of being found in a Lye: For one Lye obliges us to tell a thousand to conceal it; and I have no Notion of any Condition's being so miserable, as to live in a continual Fear of Detection. Most particularly, my Mamma instructed me to beware of all Sorts of Deceit: So that I was accustomed, not only in Words to speak Truth, but also not to endeavour by any means to deceive.

But tho' the Friendship between my Brother and me was so strongly cultivated, yet we were taught, that lying for each other, or praising each other when it was not deserved, was not only a Fault, but a very great Crime: For this, my Mamma used to tell us, was not Love, but Hatred; as it was encouraging one another in Folly and Wickedness: And tho' my natural Disposition inclined me to be very tender of every-thing in my Power, yet was I not suffered to give way even to *this* in an unreasonable Degree: One Instance of which I remember;

When I was about Eleven Years old, I had a Cat that I had bred up from a little Kitten, that used to play round me, till I had indulged for the poor Animal a Fondness that made me delight to have it continually with me where-ever I went; and, in return for my Indulgence, the Cat seemed to have changed its Nature, and assumed the Manner that more properly belongs to Dogs than Cats; for it would follow me about the House and Gardens, mourn for my Absence, and rejoice at my Presence: And, what was very remarkable, the poor Animal would, when fed by my Hand, lose that Caution which Cats are known to be possessed of, and eat whatever I gave it, as if it could reflect, that I meant only its Good, and no Harm could come from me.

I was at last so accustomed to see this little Frisk (for so I called it) playing round me, that I seemed to miss Part of myself in its Absence. But one Day the poor little Creature followed me to the Door; when a Parcel of School-boys coming by, one of them catched her up in his Arms, and ran away with her. All my Cries were to no Purpose; for he was out of Sight with her in a Moment, and there was no Method to trace his Steps. The cruel Wretches, for Sport, as they called it, hunted it the next Day from one to the other, in the most barbarous manner; till at last it took Shelter in that House that used to be its Protection, and came and expired at my Feet.

I was so struck with the Sight of the little Animal dying in that manner, that the great Grief of my Heart overflowed at my Eyes, and I was for some time inconsolable.

My indulgent Mamma comforted me without blaming me, till she thought I had had sufficient time to vent my Grief; and then sending for me into her Chamber, spoke as follows:

"*Jenny*, I have watched you ever since the Death of your little favourite Cat; and have been in Hopes daily, that your Lamenting and Melancholy on that Account would be at an End: But I find you still persist in grieving, as if such a Loss was irreparable. Now tho' I have always encouraged you in all Sentiments of Good-nature and Compassion, and am sensible, that where those Sentiments are strongly implanted, they will extend their Influence even to the least Animal; yet you are to consider, my Child, that you are not to give way to any Passions that interfere with your Duty: For whenever there is any Contention between your Duty and your Inclinations, you must conquer the latter, or become wicked and contemptible. If, therefore, you give way to this Melancholy, how will you be able to perform your Duty towards me, in chearfully obeying my Commands, and endeavouring, by your lively Prattle, and innocent Gaiety of Heart, to be my Companion and Delight? Nor will you be fit to converse with your Brother, whom (as you lost your good Papa when you was too young to know that Loss) I have endeavoured to educate in such a manner, that I hope he will be a Father to you, if you deserve his Love and Protection. In short, if you do not keep Command enough of yourself to prevent being ruffled by every Accident, you will be unfit for all the social Offices of Life, and be despised by all those whose Regard and Love is worth your seeking. I treat you, my Girl, as capable of considering what is for your own Good: For tho' you are but Eleven Years of Age, yet I hope the Pains I have taken in explaining all you read, and in answering all your Questions in Search of Knowlege, has not been so much thrown away, but that you are more capable of judging, than those unhappy Children are, whose Parents have neglected to instruct them: And therefore, farther to enforce what I say, remember, that repining at any Accident that happens to you, is an Offence to that God, to whom I have taught you daily to pray for all the Blessings you can receive, and to whom you are to return humble Thanks for every Blessing.

I expect therefore, *Jenny*, that you now dry up your Tears, and resume your usual Chearfulness. I do not doubt but your Obedience to me will make you at least put on the Appearance of Chearfulness in my Sight: But you will deceive yourself, if you think that is performing your Duty; for if you would obey me as you ought, you must try heartily to root from your Mind all Sorrow and Gloominess. You may depend upon it, this Command is in your Power to obey; for you know I never require any-thing of you that is impossible."

After my Mamma had made this Speech, she went out to take a Walk in the Garden, and left me to consider of what she had said.

The Moment I came to reflect seriously, I found it was indeed in my Power to root all Melancholy from my Heart, when I considered it was necessary, in order to perform my Duty to God, to obey the best of Mothers, and to make myself a Blessing and a chearful Companion to her, rather than a Burden, and the Cause of her Uneasiness, by my foolish Melancholy.

This little Accident, as managed by my Mamma, has been a Lesson to me in governing my Passions ever since.

It would be endless to repeat all the Methods this good Mother invented for my Instruction, Amendment, and Improvement. It is sufficient to acquaint you, that she contrived that every new Day should open to me some new Scene of Knowlege; and no Girl could be happier than I was during her Life. But, alas! when I was Thirteen Years of Age, the Scene changed. My dear Mamma was taken ill of a Scarlet-Fever. I attended her Day and Night whilst she lay ill, my Eyes starting with Tears to see her in that Condition; and yet I did not dare to give my Sorrows vent, for fear of increasing her Pain.

Here a trickling Tear stole from Miss *Jenny's* Eyes. She suppressed some rising Sobs that interrupted her Speech; and was about to proceed in her Story; when, casting her Eyes on her Companions, she saw her Sorrow had such an Effect upon them all, that there was not one of her Hearers who could refrain from shedding a sympathizing Tear. She therefore thought it was more strictly following her Mamma's Precepts to pass this Part of her Story in Silence, rather than to grieve her Friends; and having wiped away her Tears, she hastened to conclude her Story: Which she did as follows:

After my Mamma's Death, my Aunt *Newman*, my Father's Sister, took the Care of me: But being obliged to go to *Jamaica* to settle some Affairs relating to an Estate she is possessed of there, she took with her my Cousin *Harriot* her only Daughter, and left me under the Care of good Mrs. *Teachum* till her Return: And since I have been here, you all know as much of my History as I do myself.

As Miss *Jenny* spoke these Words, the Bell summoned them to Supper, and to the Presence of their Governess, who having narrowly watched their Looks ever since the Fray, had hitherto plainly perceived, that tho' they did not dare to break out again into an open quarrel, yet their Hearts had still harboured unkind Thoughts of one another. She was surprised *now*, as she stood at a Window in the Hall that overlooked the Garden, to see all her Scholars walk towards her Hand in Hand, with such chearful Countenances, as plainly shewed their inward good Humour: And as she thought proper to mention to them her Pleasure in seeing them thus altered, Miss *Jenny Peace* related to her Governess all that had passed in the Arbour, with their general Reconciliation. Mrs. *Teachum* gave Miss *Jenny* all the Applause due to her Goodness, saying, "She herself had only waited a little while to see if their Anger would subside, and Love take its place in their Bosoms, without her interfering again; for *that* she certainly should otherwise have done, to have brought about what Miss *Jenny* had so happily effected."

Miss *Jenny* thanked her Governess for her kind Approbation, and said, "That if she would give them Leave, they would spend what Time she was pleased to allow them from School in this little Arbour, in reading Stories, and such Things as she should think a proper and innocent Amusement."

Mrs. *Teachum* not only gave Leave, but very much approved of this Proposal; and desired Miss *Jenny*, as a Reward for what she had already done, to preside over these Diversions, and to give her an Account in what manner they proceeded. Miss *Jenny* promised in all Things to be guided by good Mrs. *Teachum*. And now, soon after Supper, they retired to Rest, free from those uneasy Passions which used to prevent their Quiet; and as they had passed the Day in Pleasure, at Night they sunk in soft and sweet Repose.

MONDAY

The First Day after their Repentance: And, consequently, the First Day of the Happiness of Miss Jenny Peace *and her Companions*

Early in the Morning, as soon as Miss *Jenny* arose, all her Companions flocked round her; for they now looked on her as the best Friend they had in the World; and they agreed, when they came out of School to adjourn into their Arbour, and divert themselves till Dinner-time; which they accordingly did. When Miss *Jenny* proposed, if it was agreeable to them to hear it, to read them a Story, which she had put in her Pocket for that Purpose; and as they now began to look upon her as the most proper Person to direct them in their Amusements, they all replied, "What was most agreeable to her would please them best." She then began to read the following Story, with which we shall open their First Day's Amusement.

The Story of the cruel Giant Barbarico, *the good Giant* Benefico, *and the little pretty dwarf* Mignon

A Great many hundred Years ago, the Mountains of *Wales* were inhabited by Two Giants; one of whom was the Terror of all his Neighbours, and the Plague of the whole Country. He greatly exceeded the Size of any Giant recorded in History; and his Eyes looked so fierce and terrible, that they frightened all who were so unhappy as to behold them.

The Name of this *enormous Wretch* was *Barbarico*. A Name, which filled all who heard it, with Fear and Astonishment. The whole Delight of this Monster's Life was in Acts of Inhumanity and Mischief; and he was the most miserable as well as the most wicked Creature that ever yet was born. He had no sooner committed one Outrage, but he was in Agonies till he could commit another; never satisfied, unless he could find an Opportunity of either torturing or devouring some innocent Creature. And whenever he happened to be disappointed in any of his malicious Purposes, he would stretch his immense Bulk on the Top of some high Mountain, and groan, and beat the Earth, and bellow with such a hollow Voice, that the whole Country heard and trembled at the Sound.

The other Giant, whose Name was *Benefico*, was not so tall and bulky as the *hideous Barbarico*: He was handsome, and well-proportioned, and of a very good-natured Turn of Mind. His Delight was no less in Acts of Goodness and Benevolence than the other's was in Cruelty and Mischief. His constant Care was to endeavour if possible to repair the Injuries committed by this horrid Tyrant: Which he had sometimes an Opportunity of doing; for tho' *Barbarico* was much larger and stronger than *Benefico*, yet his coward Mind was afraid to engage with him, and always shunned a Meeting; leaving the Pursuit of any Prey, if he himself was pursued by *Benefico*: Nor could the good *Benefico* trust farther to this coward Spirit of his bare Adversary, than only to make the horrid Creature fly; for he well knew, that a close

Engagement might make him desperate; and fatal to himself might be the Consequence of such a brutal Desperation: Therefore he prudently declined any Attempt to destroy this cruel Monster, till he should gain *Some* sure Advantage over him.

It happened on a certain Day, that as the *inhuman Barbarico* was prowling along the Side of a craggy Mountain, o'ergrown with Brambles and briery Thickets, taking most horrid Strides, rolling his ghastly Eyes around in quest of human Blood, and having his Breast tortured with inward Rage and Grief, that he had been so unhappy as to live One whole Day without some Act of Violence, he beheld, in a pleasant Valley at a Distance, a little Rivulet winding its gentle Course thro' Rows of Willows mixt with flowery Shrubs. Hither the *Giant* hasted: And being arrived, he gazed about, to see if in this sweet Retirement any were so unhappy as to fall within his Power: But finding none, the Disappointment set him in a Flame of Rage, which, burning like an inward Furnace, parched his Throat. And now he laid him down upon the Bank, to try if in the cool Stream, that murmured as it flowed, he could asswage or slack the fiery Thirst that burnt within him.

He bent him down to drink: And at the same time casting his baleful Eyes towards the opposite Side, he discovered, within a little natural Arbour formed by the Branches of a spreading Tree within the Meadow's flowery Lawn, the Shepherd *Fidus* and his lov'd *Amata*.

The *gloomy Tyrant* no sooner perceived this happy Pair, than his Heart exulted with Joy; and suddenly leaping up on the Ground, he forgot his Thirst, and left the Stream untasted. He stood for a short Space to view them in their sweet Retirement; and was soon convinced, that in the innocent Enjoyment of reciprocal Affection their Happiness was complete. His Eye, inflamed with Envy to behold such Bliss, darted a fearful Glare; and his Breast swelling with Malice and invenom'd Rage, he with gigantic Pace approached their peaceful Seat.

The happy *Fidus* was at that time busy in entertaining his lov'd *Amata* with a Song which he had that very Morning composed in Praise of Constancy; and the *Giant* was now within one Stride of them, when *Amata*, perceiving him, cried out in a trembling Voice, "Fly, *Fidus*, fly, or we are lost for ever: We are pursued by the *hateful Barbarico*!" She had scarce uttered these Words, when the *Savage Tyrant* seized them by the Waste in either Hand, and holding them up to his nearer View, thus said: "Speak, Miscreants; and, if you would avoid immediate Death, tell me who you are, and whence arises that Tranquillity of Mind, which even at a Distance was visible in your Behaviour."

Poor *Fidus*, with Looks that would have melted the hardest Heart, innocently replied, "That they were wandering that way, without designing Offence to any Creature on Earth: That they were faithful Lovers; and, with the Consent of all their Friends and Relations, were soon to be married; therefore intreated him not to part them."

The *Giant* now no sooner perceived, from the last Words of the affrighted Youth, what was most likely to give them the greatest Torment, than with a spiteful Grin, which made his horrible face yet more horrible, and in a hollow Voice, as loud as Thunder, he tauntingly cried out, "Ho-hoh! You'd not be parted? Would you? For once I'll gratify thy Will, and thou shalt follow this thy whimpering Fondling down my capacious Maw." So saying, he turned his ghastly Visage on the trembling *Amata*, who being now no longer able to support herself under his cruel Threats, fainted away, and remained in his Hand but as a lifeless Corpse. When lifting up his Eyes towards the Hill on the opposite Side, he beheld *Benefico* coming hastily towards him. This good Giant, having been that Morning informed that *Barbarico* was roaming in the Mountains after Prey, left his peaceful Castle, in hopes of giving Protection to whatever unfortunate Creature should fall into the Clutches of this so cruel a Monster.

Barbarico, at the Sight of the friendly *Benefico*, started with Fear: For altho' in Bulk and Stature he was, as we have said, the Superior; yet that Cowardice which ever accompanies Wickedness now wrought in him in such a manner, that he could not bear to confront him, well knowing the Courage and Fortitude that always attend the Good and Virtuous; and therefore instantly putting *Fidus* into the Wallet that hung over his Shoulder, he flung the fainting *Amata*, whom he took to be quite expired, into the Stream that ran hard by, and fled to his Cave, not daring once to cast his Eyes behind him.

The good *Benefico* perceiving the *Monster's Flight*, and not doubting but he had been doing some horrid Mischief, immediately hasted to the Brook; where he found the half-expiring *Amata* floating down the Stream; for her Cloaths had yet borne her up on the Surface of the Water. He speedily stepped in, and drew her out; and taking her in his Arms, pressed her to his warm Bosom; and in a short Space perceiving in her Face the visible Marks of returning Life, his Heart swelled with kind Compassion, and he thus bespoke the tender Maid: "Unhappy Damsel, lift up thy gentle Eyes, and tell me by what hard Fate thou wast fallen into the Power of *that barbarous Monster*, whose savage Nature delights in nothing but Ruin and Desolation. Tremble not thus, but without Fear or Terror behold one who joys in the Thought of having saved thee from Destruction, and will bring thee every Comfort his utmost Power can procure."

The gentle *Amata* was now just enough recovered to open her Eyes: But finding herself in a Giant's Arms, and still retaining in her Mind the frightful Image of the *horrid Barbarico*, she fetched a deep Sigh, crying out in broken Accents, "Fly, *Fidus*, fly;" and again sunk down upon the friendly Giant's Breast. On hearing these Words, and plainly seeing by the Anguish of her Mind that some settled Grief was deeply rooted at her Heart, and therefore despairing to bring her to herself immediately, the kind *Benefico* hastened with her to his hospitable Castle; where every imaginable Assistance was administered to her Relief, in order to recover her lost Senses, and reconcile her to her wretched Fate.

The *cruel Barbarico* was no sooner arrived at his gloomy Cave, than he called to him his little Page; who, trembling to hear the *Tyrant* now again returned, quickly drew near to attend his stern Commands: When drawing out of the Wallet the poor *Fidus*, more dead than alive, the *Monster* cried out, "Here, Caitiff, take in Charge this smooth-faced Miscreant; and, d'ye hear me? see that his Allowance be no more than one small Ounce of mouldy Bread, and half a Pint of standing Water, for each Day's Support, till his now blooming Skin be withered, his Flesh be wasted from his Bones, and he dwindle to a meagre Skeleton." So saying, he left them, as he hoped, to bewail each other's sad condition. But the unhappy *Fidus*, bereft of his *Amata*, was not to be appalled by any of the most horrid Threats; for now his only Comfort was, the Hopes of a speedy End to his miserable Life, and to find a Refuge from his Misfortunes in the peaceful Grave. With this Reflection the faithful *Fidus* was endeavouring to calm the inward Troubles of his Mind, when the little Page, with Looks of the most tender Compassion, and in gentle Words, bid him be comforted, and with Patience endure his present Affliction; adding, that he himself had long suffered the most rigorous Fate, yet despaired not but that one Day would give them an Opportunity to free themselves from the *wicked Wretch*, whose sole Delight was in others Torments. "As to his inhuman Commands, continued he, I will sooner die than obey them; and in a mutual Friendship perhaps we may find some Consolation, even in this dismal Cave."

This little Page the *cruel Barbarico* had stolen from his Parents at Five Years old; ever since which time, he had tortured and abused him, till he had now attained the Age of One-and-twenty. His Mother had given him the Name of *Mignon*; by which Name the *Monster* always called him, as it gratified his Insolence to make use of that fond Appellation whilst he was abusing him: Only when he said *Mignon*, he would in Derision add the Word *Dwarf*; for, to say the Truth, *Mignon* was one of the least Men that was ever seen, tho' at the same time one of the prettiest: His Limbs, tho' small, were exactly proportioned: His Countenance was at once sprightly and soft; and whatever his Head thought, or his Heart felt, his Eyes by their Looks expressed; and his Temper was as sweet as his Person was amiable. Such was the gentle Creature *Barbarico* chose to torment: For wicked Giants, no *less* than wicked Men and Women, are constantly tormented at the Appearance of those Perfections in another, to which they themselves have no Pretensions.

The Friendship and Affection of *Fidus* and *Mignon* now every Day increased; and the longer they were acquainted, the more Delight they took in each other's Company. The faithful *Fidus* related to his Companion the Story of his loved *Amata*, whilst the tender *Mignon* consoled his Friend's inward Sorrows, and supplied him with Necessaries, notwithstanding the Venture he run of the *cruel Tyrant's* heavy Displeasure. The *Giant* ceased not every Day to view the hapless *Fidus*, to see if the Cruelty of his Intentions had in any Degree wrought its desired Effect: But perceiving in him no Alteration, he now began to be suspicious that the little *Mignon* had not punctually obeyed his savage Command. In order therefore to satisfy his wicked Curiosity, he resolved within himself narrowly to watch every Occasion these poor unhappy Captives had of conversing with each other. *Mignon*, well knowing the implacable and revengeful Disposition of this *barbarous Tyrant*, had taken all the Precautions imaginable to avoid Discovery, and therefore generally sought every Opportunity of being alone with *Fidus*, and carrying him his daily Provisions at those Hours he knew the *Giant* was most likely to be asleep.

It so befel, that on a certain Day the *wicked Giant* had, as was his usual Custom, been abroad for many Hours, in Search of some unhappy Creature on whom to glut his hateful Inhumanity; when tired with fruitless Roaming, he returned back to his gloomy Cave, beguiled of all his horrid Purposes; for he had not once that Day espied so much as the Track of Man, or other harmless Animal, to give him even Hopes to gratify his Rage or Cruelty: But now raving with inward Perturbation and Despair, he laid him down upon his Iron Couch, to try if he could close his Eyes, and quiet the tumultuous Passions of his Breast. He tossed, and tumbled, and could get no Rest; starting with fearful Dreams, and horrid Visions of tormenting Furies.

Meanwhile, the gentle *Mignon* had prepared a little delicate Repast, and having seen the *Monster* lay himself at Length, and thinking now that fit Occasion offered in which to comfort and refresh his long-expecting Friend, was hasting with it to the Cell where the faithful *Fidus* was confined. At this fatal Moment the *Giant*, rearing himself up on his Couch, perceived the little *Mignon* just at the Entrance of the Cell: When calling to him in a hollow Voice, that dismally resounded thro' the Cave, he so startled the poor unhappy Page, that he dropped the Cover from his trembling Hand, and stood fixed and motionless as a Statue.

"Come hither, *Mignon*, Caitiff, Dwarf," said then the *taunting Homicide*: But the poor little Creature was so thunderstruck, he was quite unable to stir one Foot. Whereat the *Giant* rousing himself from off his Couch, with one huge Stride, reached out his brawny Arm, and seized him by the Waste; and, pointing to the scattered

Delicates, cried out, "Vile Miscreant! is it thus thou hast obeyed my Orders? Is this the mouldy Bread and muddy Water, with which alone it was my Command thou shouldst sustain that puny Mortal? But I'll——" Here raising him aloft, he was about to dash him to the Ground: When suddenly revolving in his wicked Thoughts, that if at once he should destroy his patient Slave, his Cruelty to him must also have an End, he paused——and then recovering his stretched-out Arm, and bringing the little Trembler near his glaring Eyes, he thus subjoins: "No; I'll not destroy thy wretched Life: But thou shalt waste thy weary Days in a dark Dungeon, as far remote from the least Dawn of Light, as from thy beloved Companion: And I myself will carefully supply you both, so equally, with mouldy Bread and Water, that each by his own Sufferings shall daily know what his dear Friend endures." So saying, he hastened with him to his deepest Dungeon; and having thrust him in, he doubly barred the Iron Door. And now again retiring to his Couch, this new-wrought Mischief, which greatly gratified his raging Mind, soon sunk him down into a sound and heavy Sleep. The Reason this *horrid Monster* had not long ago devoured his little Captive (for he thought him a delicious Morsel) was, that he might never want an Object at hand to gratify his Cruelty: For tho' extremely great was his voracious Hunger, yet greater still was his Desire of Tormenting; and oftentimes when he had teazed, beat, and tortured the poor gentle *Mignon*, so as to force from him Tears, and sometimes a soft Complaint, he would, with a malicious Sneer, scornfully reproach him in the following Words: "Little does it avail to whine, to blubber, or complain; for, remember, abject Wretch,

I am a Giant, and I can eat thee:
Thou art a Dwarf, and thou canst not eat me."

When *Mignon* was thus alone he threw himself on the cold Ground, bemoaning his unhappy Fate. However, he soon recollected, that Patience and Resignation were his only Succour in this distressful Condition; not doubting, but that as Goodness cannot always suffer, he should in time meet with some unforeseen Deliverance from the savage Power of the *inhuman Barbarico.*

Whilst the gentle *Mignon* was endeavouring to comfort himself in his Dungeon with these good Reflections, he suddenly perceived at a little Distance from him, a small glimmering Light. Immediately he rose from the Ground, and going towards it, found that it shone thro' a little Door that had been left a-jar, which led him to a spacious Hall, wherein the *Giant* hoarded his immense Treasures. *Mignon* was at first dazled with the Lustre of so much Gold, and Silver, and sparkling Jewels, as were there heaped together. But casting his Eyes on a Statue that was placed in the Middle of the Room, he read on the Pedestal, written in very small Letters, the following Verses:

Wouldst thou from the Rage be free
Of the Tyrant's Tyranny,
Loose the Fillet[1] which is bound
Thrice three times my Brows around;
Bolts and Bars shall open fly,
By a magic Sympathy.
Take him in his sleeping Hour;
Bind his Neck, and break his Pow'r.
PATIENCE *bids, make no Delay:*
Haste to bind him, haste away.

Mignon's little Heart now leapt for Joy, that he had found the Means of such a speedy Deliverance; and eagerly climbing up the Statue, he quickly unbound the magic Fillet: Which was no sooner done, but suddenly the Bolts and Bars of the great brazen Gates thro' which the Giant used to pass to this his Treasury, were all unloosed, and the Folding-doors of their own accord flew open, grating harsh Thunder on their massy Hinges. At the same Instant, stretched on his Iron Couch in the Room adjoining to the Hall, the Giant gave a deadly Groan. Here again the little *Mignon's* trembling Heart began to fail; for he feared the Monster was awakened by the Noise, and that he should now suffer the cruellest Torments his wicked Malice could invent. Wherefore

---

[1] A ribbon, string, or narrow band of material used for binding the hair, or worn round the head as ornament, or to keep a headdress in place (*OED*).

for a short Space he remained clinging round the Statue, till he perceived that all again was hushed and silent. When getting down, he gently stole into the Giant's chamber; where he found him still in a profound Sleep.

But here, to the great Mortification of Miss *Jenny*'s attentive Hearers, the Hour of entertaining themselves being at an End, they were obliged to leave the poor little *Mignon* in the greatest Distress and Fright lest the Giant should awake before he could fulfil the Commands of the Oracle, and to wait for the Remainder of the Story till another Opportunity.

In the Evening as soon as School was over, the little Company again met in their Arbour; and nothing could be greater than their Impatience to hear the Event of *Mignon*'s hazardous Undertaking. Miss *Dolly Friendly* said, that if the poor little Creature was destroyed, she should not sleep that Night: But they all joined in intreating Miss *Jenny* to proceed: Which she did in the following Manner:

A Continuation of the Story of the Giants

Now, thought *Mignon*, is the lucky Moment to fulfil the Instructions of the Oracle: And then cautiously getting up the Side of the Couch, with trembling Hands he put the Fillet round the Monster's Neck, and tied it firmly in a threefold Knot: And again softly creeping down, he retired into a Corner of the Room, to wait the wished Event. In a few Minutes the Giant waked; and opening his enormous Eyes, he glared their horrid Orbs around (but without the least Motion of his Head or Body) and spy'd the little *Mignon* where he lay, close shrinking, to avoid his baleful Sight.

The Giant no sooner perceived his little Page at Liberty, but his Heart sorely smote him, and he began to suspect the worst that could befal: For, recollecting that he had carelessly left open the little Door leading from the Dungeon to the great Hall wherein was placed the fatal magic Statue, he was now intirely convinced that *Mignon* had discovered the secret Charm on which his Power depended; for he already found the Magic of the Fillet round his Neck fully to operate, his Sinews all relax, his joints all tremble; and when he would by his own Hand have tried to free himself, his shivering Limbs, he found, refused Obedience to their Office. Thus bereft of all his Strength, and well nigh motionless, in this Extremity of Impotence he cast about within himself, by what sly Fraud (for Fraud and Subtilty were now his only Refuge) he best might work upon the gentle *Mignon* to lend his kind Assistance to unloose him. Wherefore with guileful Words, and seeming Courtesy, still striving to conceal his curst Condition, he thus bespake his little Captive:

"Come hither, *Mignon*; my pretty gentle Boy, come near me. This Fillet thou hast bound around my Neck, to keep me from the Cold, gives me some Pain. I know thy gentle Nature would not let thee see thy tender Master in the least Uneasiness, without affording him thy chearful Aid and kind Relief. Come hither, my dear Child, I say, and loose the Knot which in thy kind Concern (I thank thee for thy Care) thou'st tied so hard, it somewhat frets my Neck."

These Words the insidious Wretch uttered in such a low trembling Tone of Voice, and with such an Affectation of Tenderness, that the little Page, who had never before experienced from him any such kind of Dialect, and but too well knew his savage Nature to believe that any-thing but Guile, or Want of Power, could move him to the least friendly Speech, or kind Affection, began now strongly to be persuaded that all was as he wished, and that the Power of the inhuman Tyrant was at an End. He knew full well, that if the Giant had not lost the Ability of rising from the Couch, he should ere now too sensibly have felt the sad Effects of his malicious Resentment; and therefore boldly adventured to approach him; and coming near the Couch, and finding not the least Effort in the Monster to reach him, and from thence quite satisfied of the Giant's total Incapacity of doing farther Mischief, he flew with Raptures to the Cell where *Fidus* lay confined.

Poor *Fidus* all this time was quite disconsolate: Nor could he guess the Cause why his little Friend so long had kept away: One while he thought the Giant's stern Commands had streighten'd him of all Subsistence; another while his Heart misgave him for his gentle Friend, lest unawares his kind Beneficence towards *him* had caused him to fall a Sacrifice to the Tyrant's cruel Resentment.

With these, and many other like Reflections, the unhappy Youth was busied, when *Mignon*, suddenly unbarring the Cell, flew to his Friend, and eagerly embracing him, cried out, "Come, *Fidus*, haste, my dearest Friend; for thou, and all of us, are from this Moment free. Come and behold the cruel Monster, where he lies, bereft of all his Strength. I cannot stay to tell thee now the Cause; but haste, and thou shalt see the dreaded Tyrant stretched on his Iron Couch, deprived of all his wicked Power: But first let us unbar each Cell, wherein is pent some wretched Captive, that we may share a general Transport for this our glad Deliverance."

The faithful *Fidus*, whose Heart had known but little Joy since he had lost his lov'd *Amata,* now felt a dawning Hope that he might once more chance to find her, if she had survived their fatal Separation; and, without one Word of Answer, he followed *Mignon* to the several Cells, and soon released all the astonished Captives.

Mignon first carried them to behold their former Terror, now, to Appearance, almost a lifeless Corpse; who, on seeing them all surround his Couch, gave a most hideous Roar, which made them tremble, all but the gentle *Mignon*, who was convinced of the Impotence of his Rage, and begged them to give him their Attendance in the Hall; where they were no sooner assembled, than he shewed them the Statue, read them the Oracle, and told them every Circumstance before related.

They now began to bethink themselves of what Method was to be taken to procure their intire Liberty; for the Influence of the magic Fillet extended only to the Gates of the Hall; and still they remained imprisoned within the dismal Cave: And though they knew from the Oracle, as well as from what appeared, that the Monster's Power was at an End; yet still were they to seek the Means of their Escape from this his horrid Abode. At length *Mignon* again ascended the Couch to find the massy Key; and, spying one End of it peep out from under the Pillow, he called to *Fidus*, who first stepped up to his Friend's Assistance; the rest by his Example quickly followed: And now, by their united Force, they dragged the ponderous Key from under the Monster's Head; and then descending, they all went to the outer Door of the Cave, where, with some Difficulty, they set wide open the folding Iron Gates.

They now determined to dispatch a Messenger to the good *Benefico*, with the News which they knew would be so welcome to him and all his Guests; and with one Voice agreed, that *Fidus* should bear the joyful Tidings; and then returned to observe the Monster, and to wait the coming of *Benefico*. The nimble *Fidus* soon reached the Giant's dwelling, where, at a little Distance from the Castle, he met the good *Benefico*, with a Train of happy Friends, enjoying the Pleasures of the Evening, and the instructive and chearful Conversation of their kind Protector. *Fidus* briefly told his Errand; and instantly *Benefico*, with all his Train, joyfully hastened to behold the Wonders he had related; for now many Hearts leapt for Joy, in Hopes of meeting some Friend of whom they had been bereft by the Cruelty of the savage *Barbarico*.

They were not long before they arrived at the horrid Cave, where *Benefico*, proceeding directly to the Monster's Chamber, suddenly appeared to him at the Side of his Couch. *Barbarico*, on seeing him, gave a hideous Yell, and rolled his glaring Eyes in such a manner, as expressed the Height of Rage and envious Bitterness.

Benefico, turning to all the Company present, thus spoke: "How shall I enough praise and admire the gentle *Mignon*, for having put it in my Power to do Justice on this execrable Wretch, and freeing you all from an insufferable Slavery, and the whole Country from their Terror?" Then reaching the Monster's own Sword, which hung over his Couch, his Hand yet suspended over the impious Tyrant, he thus said: "Speak, Wretch, if yet the Power of Speech is left thee; and with thy latest Breath declare, what Advantage hast thou found of all thy wicked Life?"

Barbarico well knew, that too bad had been that Life, to leave the least room for Hope of Mercy; and therefore, instead of an Answer, he gave another hideous Yell, gnashing his horrid Teeth, and again rolling his ghastly Eye on all around.

Benefico, seeing him thus impenitent and sullen, lifted on high the mighty Sword, and, with one Blow severed his odious Head from his enormous Body.

The whole Assembly gave a Shout for Joy; and *Benefico* holding in his Hand the Monster's yet grinning Head, thus addressed his half-astonished Companions: "See here, my Friends, the proper Conclusion of a rapacious cruel Life. But let us hasten from this Monster's gloomy Cave; and on the Top of one of our highest Mountains, fixed on a Pole, will I set up this joyful Spectacle, that all the Country round may know themselves at Liberty to pursue their rural Business, or Amusements, without the Dread of any Annoyance from a devouring vile Tormentor: And when his Treasures, which justly all belong to the good patient *Mignon*, are removed, we will shut up the Mouth of this abominable Dwelling; and, casting on the Door a Heap of Earth, we hope, that both the Place and the Remembrance of this cruel Savage may in time, be lost."

The sweet little *Mignon* declared, "That he should never think of accepting more than a Part of that mighty Wealth; for it was his Opinion, that every Captive who had suffered by the Tyrant's Cruelty, had an equal Right to share in all the Advantages of his Death: But if they thought he had any just Title to those Treasures, he begged they might instantly be removed to *Benefico's* Castle: For, continued *Mignon*, He who has already shewn how well he knows the true Use of Power and Riches, by employing them for the Happiness of others; 'tis he alone who has the just and true Claim to them; and I doubt not but you all willingly consent to this Proposal."

Every one readily cried out, "That to *Benefico*, the good *Benefico*, alone belonged the Tyrant's Treasures; that *Benefico* should ever be, as heretofore, their Governor, their Father, and their kind Protector."

The beneficent Heart of the *good Giant* was quite melted with this their kind Confidence and Dependence upon him, and assured them, he should ever regard them as his Children: And now, exulting in the general Joy that must attend the Destruction of this savage Monster, when the whole Country should find themselves freed from the Terror of his Rapine and Desolation, he sent before to his Castle, to give Intelligence to all within that happy Place of the grim Monster's Fall, and little *Mignon's* Triumph; giving in Charge to the Harbinger of these Tidings, that it should be his first and chiefest Care to glad the gentle Bosom of a fair Disconsolate (who kept herself retired and pent up within her own Apartment) with the Knowlege that the inhuman Monster was no more; and that henceforth sweet Peace and rural Innocence might reign in all their Woods and Groves. The Hearts of all within the Castle bounded with Joy, on hearing the Report of the inhuman Monster's Death, and the Deliverance of all his Captives, and with speedy Steps they hastened to meet their kind Protector; nor did the melancholy Fair-one, lest she should seem unthankful for the general Blessing, refuse to join the Train.

It was not long after the Messenger that *Benefico*, and those his joyful Friends, arrived: But the faithful *Fidus* alone, of all this happy Company, was tortured with the inward Pangs of a sad Grief he could not conquer, and his fond Heart remained still captivated to a melting Sorrow: Nor could even the tender Friendship of the gentle *Mignon* quite remove, tho' it alleviated, his Sadness; but the Thoughts of his loved lost *Amata* embitter'd every Joy, and overwhelmed his generous Soul with Sorrow.

When the Company from the Castle joined *Benefico*, he declared to them in what manner their Deliverance was effected; and, as a general Shout of Joy resounded thro' the neighbouring Mountains, *Fidus*, lifting up his Eyes, beheld in the midst of the Multitude, standing in a pensive Posture, the fair Disconsolate. Her tender Heart was at that Instant overflowing in soft Tears, caused by a kind Participation of their present Transport, yet mixed with the deep sad Impression of a Grief her Bosom was full fraught with. Her Face, at first, was almost hid by her white Handkerchief, with which she wiped away the trickling Drops, which falling had bedew'd her beauteous Cheeks: But as she turned her lovely Face to view the joyful Conquerors, and to speak a Welcome to her kind Protector, what Words can speak the Raptures, the Astonishment, that swell'd the Bosom of the faithful Youth, when in this fair Disconsolate he saw his loved, his constant, his long-lost *Amata*! Their delighted Eyes in the same Instant beheld each other; and, breaking on each Side from their astonished Friends, they flew like Lightning into each other's Arms.

After they had given a short Account of what had passed in their Separation, *Fidus* presented to his loved *Amata* the kind, the gentle *Mignon*, with lavish Praises of his generous Friendship, and steady Resolution, in hazarding his Life by disobeying the Injunctions of the cruel Tyrant. No sooner had *Amata* heard the

Name of *Mignon*, but she cried out, "Surely my Happiness is now complete, and all my Sorrows, by this joyful Moment, are more than fully recompensed; for, in the kind Preserver of my *Fidus*, I have found my Brother. My Mother lost her little *Mignon* when he was Five Years old; and pining Grief, after some Years vain Search, ended her wretched Life."

The generous Hearts of all who were present shared the Raptures of the faithful *Fidus,* the lovely *Amata,* and gentle *Mignon,* on this happy Discovery; and in the warmest Congratulations they expressed their Joy. *Benefico* now led all the delighted Company into his Castle, where Freedom was publicly proclaimed; and everyone was left at Liberty either to remain there with *Benefico,* or, loaded with Wealth sufficient for their Use, to go where their Attachments or Inclinations might invite them.

Fidus, Amata, and the little *Mignon,* hesitated not one Moment to declare their Choice of staying with the generous *Benefico.*

The Nuptials of the faithful *Fidus,* and his loved *Amata,* were solemnized in the Presence of all their Friends.

Benefico pass'd the Remainder of his Days in pleasing Reflections on his well-spent Life.

The Treasures of the dead Tyrant were turned into Blessings, by the Use they were now made of: Little *Mignon* was loved and cherished by all his Companions. Peace, Harmony, and Love reigned in every Bosom; Dissension, Discord, and Hatred were banished from this friendly Dwelling; and that Happiness, which is the natural Consequence of Goodness, appeared in every chearful Countenance throughout the Castle of the good *Benefico*; and as heretofore Affright and Terror spread itself from the Monster's hateful Cave, so now from this peaceful Castle was diffused tranquillity and Joy thro' all the happy Country round.

Thus ended the Story of the Two Giants: And Miss *Jenny* being tired with reading, her little Company left the Arbour for that Night, and agreed to meet there again the next Day.

As soon as they had supp'd, Mrs. *Teachum* sent for Miss *Jenny Peace* into her Closet, and desired an exact Account from her of this their First Day's Amusement, that she might judge from thence how far they might be trusted with the Liberty she had given them.

Miss *Jenny* shewed her Governess the Story she had read; and said, "I hope, Madam, you will not think it an improper one; for it was given me by my Mamma; and she told me, that she thought it contained a very excellent Moral."

Mrs. *Teachum*, having looked it over, thus spoke: "I have no Objection, Miss *Jenny*, to your reading any Stories to amuse you, provided you read them with the Disposition of a Mind not to be hurt by them. A very good Moral may indeed be drawn from the Whole, and likewise from almost every Part of it; and as you had this Story from your Mamma, I doubt not but you are very well qualified to make the proper Remarks yourself upon the Moral of it to your Companions. But here let me observe to you (which I would have you communicate to your little Friends) that Giants, Magic, Fairies, and all Sorts of supernatural Assistances in a Story, are introduced only to amuse and divert: For a Giant is called so only to express a Man of great Power; and the magic Fillet round the Statue was intended only to shew you, that by Patience you will overcome all Difficulties. Therefore by no means let the Notion of Giants or Magic dwell upon your Minds. And you may farther observe, that there is a different Stile adapted to every Sort of Writing; and the various sounding Epithets given to *Barbarico* are proper to express the raging Cruelty of his wicked Mind. But neither this high-sounding Language, nor the supernatural Contrivances in this Story, do I so thoroughly approve, as to recommend them much to your reading; except as I said before, great Care is taken to prevent your being carried away, by these high-flown Things, from that Simplicity of Taste and Manners which it is my chief Study to inculcate."

Here Miss *Jenny* looked a little confounded; and, by her down-cast Eye, shewed a Fear that she had incurred the Disapprobation, if not the Displeasure, of her Governess: Upon which Mrs. *Teachum* thus proceeded:

"I do not intend by this, my Dear, to blame you for what you have done; but only to instruct you how to make the best Use of even the most trifling Things: And if you have any more Stories of this kind, with a equally good Moral, when you are not better employed, I shall not be against your reading them; always remembring the Cautions I have this Evening been giving you."

Miss *Jenny* thanked her Governess for her Instructions, and kind Indulgence to her, and promised to give her an exact Account of their daily Amusements; and, taking Leave, retired to her Rest.

TUESDAY

The Second Day

At Miss *Jenny's* Meeting with her Companions in the Morning, after School, she asked them how they liked the History of the Giants. They all declared they thought it a very pretty diverting Story. Miss *Jenny* replied, "Tho' she was glad they were pleased, yet she would have them look farther than the present Amusement: For, continued she, my Mamma always taught me to understand what I read; otherwise, she said, it was to no manner of Purpose to read ever so many Books, which would only stuff my Brain, without being any Improvement to my Mind."

The Misses all agreed, that certainly it was of no Use to read, without understanding what they read; and began to talk of the Story of the Giants, to prove they could make just Remarks on it.

Miss *Sukey Jennett* said, "I am most pleased with that Part of the Story where the good *Benefico* cuts off the Monster's Head, and puts an End to his Cruelty, especially as he was so sullen he would not confess his Wickedness; because, you know, Miss *Jenny*, if he had had Sense enough to have owned his Error, and have followed the Example of the good Giant, he might have been happy."

Miss *Lucy Sly* delivered the following Opinion: "My greatest Joy was whilst *Mignon* was tying the magic Fillet round the Monster's Neck, and conquering him"

"Now I (said Miss *Dolly Friendly*) am most pleased with that Part of the Story, where *Fidus* and *Amata* meet the Reward of their Constancy and Love, when they find each other after all their Sufferings."

Miss Polly Suckling said, with some Eagerness, "My greatest Joy was in the Description of *Mignon;* and to think that it should be in the Power of that little Creature to conquer such a great Monster."

Miss *Patty Lockit,* Miss *Nanny Spruce,* Miss *Betty Ford,* and Miss *Henny Fret,* advanced no new Opinions; but agreed some to one, and some to another, of those that were already advanced. And as everyone was eager to maintain her own Opinion, an Argument followed, the Particulars of which I could never learn: Only thus much I know, that it was concluded by Miss *Lucy Sly,* saying, with an Air and Tone of Voice that implied more Anger than had been heard since the Reconciliation, "That she was sure Miss *Polly Suckling* liked that Part about *Mignon,* only because she was the least in the School; and *Mignon* being such a little Creature, put her in Mind of herself."

Miss *Jenny Peace* now began to be frighted, lest this Contention should raise another Quarrel; and therefore begged to be heard before they went any farther. They were not yet angry enough to refuse hearing what she had to say: And then Miss *Jenny* desired them to consider the Moral of the Story, and what Use they might make of it, instead of contending which was the prettiest Part: "For otherwise, continued she, I have lost my Breath in reading to you; and you will be worse rather than better, for what you have heard. Pray observe, that *Benefico's* Happiness arose intirely from his Goodness: He had less Strength, and less Riches, than the cruel Monster; and yet, by the good Use he made of what he possessed, you see how he turned all Things to his Advantage. But particularly remember, that the *Mignon,* in the Moment that he was patiently submitting to his Sufferings, found a Method of relieving himself from them, and of overcoming a barbarous Monster, who had so cruelly abused him.

Our good Governess last Night not only instructed me in this Moral I am now communicating to you, but likewise bid me warn you by no means to let the Notion of Giants or Magic dwell upon your Minds; for by a Giant is meant no more than a Man of great Power; and the magic Fillet round the Head of the Statue was only intended to teach you, that by the Assistance of Patience you may overcome all Difficulties.

In order therefore to make what you read of any Use to you,

you must not only think of it thus in general, but make the Application to yourselves. For when (as now) instead of improving yourselves by Reading, you make what you read a Subject to quarrel about, what is this less than being like the Monster *Barbarico*, who turned his very Riches to a Curse? I am sure it is not following the Example of *Benefico*, who made every-thing a Blessing to him. Remember, if you pinch and abuse a Dog or Cat, because it is in your Power, you are like the cruel Monster, when he abused the little *Mignon*, and said,

'*I am a Giant, and I can eat thee;*
Thou art a Dwarf, and thou canst not eat me.'

In short, if you will reap any Benefit from this Story towards rendering you happy, whenever you have any Power, you must follow the Example of the Giant *Benefico*, and do Good with it; And when you are under any Sufferings, like *Mignon*, you must patiently endure them till you can find a Remedy: Then, in one Case, like *Benefico*, you will enjoy what you possess; and, in the other, you will in time, like *Mignon*, overcome your Sufferings: For the natural Consequence of indulging Cruelty and Revenge in the Mind, even where there is the highest Power to gratify it, is Misery."—

Here Miss *Sukey Jennett* interrupted Miss *Jenny*, saying, "That she herself had experienced the Truth of that Observation in the former Part of her Life: For she never had known either Peace or Pleasure, till she had conquered in her Mind the Desire of hurting and being revenged on those who she thought did not, by their Behaviour, shew the same Regard for her, that her own good Opinion of herself made her think she deserved." Miss *Jenny* then asked her, "If she was willing to lead the Way to the rest of her Companions, by telling her past Life?" She answered, "She would do it with all her Heart; and, by having so many and great Faults to confess, she hoped she should, by her true Confessions, set them an Example of Honesty and Ingenuousness."

The Description *of Miss* Sukey Jennett

Miss *Sukey Jennett*, who was next in Years to Miss *Jenny Peace*, was not quite Twelve Years old; but so very tall of her Age, that she was within a Trifle as tall as Miss *Jenny Peace*; and, by growing so fast, was much thinner: And tho' she was not really so well made, yet, from an assured Air in her manner of carrying herself, she was called much the genteelest Girl. There was, on the first View, a great Resemblance in their Persons. Her Face was very handsome, and her Complexion extremely good; but a little more inclined to pale than Miss *Jenny*'s. Her Eyes were a Degree darker, and had a Life and Fire in them which was very beautiful: But yet her Impatience on the least Contradiction often brought a Fierceness into her Eyes, and gave such a Discomposure to her whole Countenance, as immediately took off your Admiration. But her Eyes had now, since her hearty Reconciliation with her Companions, lost a great Part of their Fierceness; and with great Mildness, and an obliging Manner, she told her Story as follows:

The Life *of Miss* Sukey Jennett

My Mamma died when I was so young that I cannot remember her; and my Papa marrying again within half a Year after her Death, I was chiefly left to the Care of an old Servant, that had lived many Years in the Family. I was a great Favourite of hers, and in every-thing had my own Way. When I was but Four Years old, if ever any-thing crossed me, I was taught to beat it, and be revenged of it, even tho' it could not feel. If I fell down and hurt myself, the very Ground was to be beat for hurting the sweet Child: So that, instead of fearing to fall, I did not dislike it; for I was pleased to find, that I was of such Consequence, that every-thing was to take care that I came by no Harm.

I had a little Play-fellow, in a Child of one of my Papa's Servants, who was to be intirely under my Command. This Girl I used to abuse and beat, whenever I was out of Humour; and when I had abused her, if she dared to grumble, or make the least Complaint, I thought it the greatest Impudence in the World;

and, instead of mending my Behaviour to her, I grew very angry that she should dare to dispute my Power: For my Governess always told her, that she was but a Servant's Girl, and I was a Gentleman's Daughter; and that therefore she ought to give way to me; for that I did her great Honour in playing with her. Thus I thought the Distance between us was so great, that I never considered that she could feel: But whilst I myself suffered nothing, I fansied every-thing was very right; and it never once came into my Head, that I could be in the Wrong.

This Life I led till I came to School, when I was Eleven Years old. Here I had no-body in my Power; for all my School-fellows thought themselves my Equals: So that I could only quarrel, fight, and contend for every-thing: But being liable to be punished, when I was trying to be revenged on any of my Enemies, as I thought them, I never had a Moment's Ease or Pleasure, till Miss *Jenny* was so good to take the Pains to convince me of my Folly, and to make me be reconciled to you, my dear Companions.

Here Miss *Sukey* ceased; and Miss *Jenny* smiled with Pleasure, at the Thoughts that she had been the Cause of her Happiness.

Mrs. *Teachum* being now come into the Arbour, to see in what manner her little Scholars passed their Time, they all rose up to do her Reverence. Miss *Jenny* gave her an Account how they had been employed; and she was much pleased with their innocent and useful Entertainment; but especially with the Method they had found out of relating their past Lives. She took little *Polly Suckling* by the Hand, and bidding the rest follow, it being now Dinner-time, she walked towards the House, attended by the whole Company.

Mrs. *Teachum* had a great Inclination to hear the History of the Lives of all her little Scholars: But she thought, that her presence at those Relations might be a Balk to the Narration, as perhaps they might be ashamed freely to confess their past Faults before her; and therefore, that she might not be any Bar in this Case to the Freedom of their Speech, and yet might be acquainted with their Stories (tho' this was not merely a vain Curiosity, but a Desire, by this means, to know their different Dispositions), she called Miss *Jenny Peace* in to her Parlour after Dinner, and told her, "She would have her get the Lives of her Companions in Writing, and bring them to her;" and Miss *Jenny* readily promised to obey her Commands.

In the Evening our little Company again met in their charming Arbour; where they were no sooner seated, with that Calmness and Content which now always attended them, than the Cries and Sobs of a Child, at a little Distance from their Garden, disturbed their Tranquillity.

Miss *Jenny*, ever ready to relieve the Distressed, ran immediately to the Place whence the Sound seemed to come, and was followed by all her Companions: When, at a small Distance from Mrs. *Teachum's* Garden-Wall, over which from the Terrass our young Company looked, they saw, under a large spreading Tree, Part of the Branches of which shaded a Seat at the End of that Terrass, a middle-aged Woman beating a Girl, who looked to be about Eight Years old, so severely, that it was no Wonder her Cries had reached their Arbour.

Miss *Jenny* could not forbear calling out to the Woman, and begging her to forbear: And little *Polly Suckling* cried as much as the Girl, and desired she might not be beat any more. The Woman, in respect to them, let the Child go; but said, "Indeed, young Ladies, you don't know what a naughty Girl she is: For tho' you now see me correct her in this manner, yet I am in all respects very kind to her, and never strike her but for Lying. I have tried all Means, good and bad, to break her of this vile Fault; but hitherto all I have done has been in vain: Nor can I ever get one Word of Truth out of her Mouth. But I am resolved to break her of this horrid Custom, or I cannot live with her: For tho' I am but poor, yet I will breed up my Child to be honest, both in Word and Deed."

Miss *Jenny* could not but approve of what the poor Woman said. However, they all joined in begging Forgiveness for the Girl this time, provided she promised Amendment for the future: And then our little Society returned to their Arbour.

Miss *Jenny* could not help expressing her great Detestation of all Lying whatsoever; when Miss *Dolly Friendly*, colouring, confessed she had often been guilty of this Fault, tho' she never scarcely did it but for her Friend.

Here Miss *Jenny*, interrupting her, said, "That even That was no sort of Excuse for Lying; besides that the Habit of it on any

Occasion, even with the Appearance of a good Intention, would but too likely lead to the Use of it on many others: And as she did not doubt, by Miss *Dolly's* blushing, that she was now very sensible of the Truth of what she had just been saying, she hoped she would take this Opportunity of obliging them with the History of her past Life": Which Request she made no Hesitation to grant, saying, "The Shame of her past Faults should by no means induce her to conceal them."

The Description *of Miss* Dolly Friendly

Miss *Dolly Friendly* was just turned of Eleven Years of Age. Her Person was neither plain nor handsome: And though she had not what is properly called one fine Feature in her Face, yet the Disposition of her Features was so regular, that her Countenance was rather agreeable than otherwise. She had generally something very quiet, or rather indolent, in her Look, except when she was moved by Anger; which seldom happened, but in Defence of some Favourite or Friend; and she had then a Fierceness and Eagerness which altered her whole Countenance: For she could not bear the least Reflection or Insult on those she loved. This Disposition made her always eager to comply with her Friends Requests; and she immediately began, as follows:

The Life *of Miss* Dolly Friendly

I was bred up, till I was Nine Years of Age, with a Sister, who was One Year younger than myself. The chief Care of our Parents was to make us love each other; and, as I was naturally inclined to have very strong Affections, I became so fond of my Sister *Molly*, which was her Name, that all my Delight was to please her; and this I carried to such a Height, that I scrupled no Lyes to excuse her Faults: And whatever she did, I justified, and thought right, only because she did it.

I was ready to fight her Quarrels, whether right or wrong; and hated every-body that offended her. My Parents winked at whatever I did in Defence of my Sister; and I had no Notion that any thing done for her could be unreasonable. In short, I made it my Study to oblige and please her, till I found at last it was out of my Power: For she grew so very humoursome, that she could not find out what she had most Mind to have; and I found her always miserable; for she would cry only because she did not know her own Mind.

She never minded what Faults she committed, because she knew I would excuse her; and she was forgiven in Consideration of our Friendship, which gave our Parents great Pleasure.

My poor little Sister grew very sickly, and she died just before I came to School: But the same Disposition still continued; and it was my Friend's Outcries of being hurt, that drew me into that odious Quarrel, that we have all now repented of.

Here Miss *Dolly Friendly* ceased; and Miss *Jenny* said, "She hoped Miss *Dolly* would remember, for the rest of her Life, what *her* good Mamma had always taught her; namely, that it was not the Office of Friendship, to justify or excuse our Friends when in the Wrong; for that was the Way to prevent their ever being in the Right: That it was rather Hatred, or Contempt, than Love, when the Fear of other Peoples Anger made us forego their Good, for the sake of our own present Pleasure; and that the Friends who expected such Flattery, were not worth keeping."

The Bell again summoned our little Company to Supper: But, before they went in, Miss *Dolly Friendly* said, "If Miss *Jenny* approved of it, she would the next Morning read them a Story given her by an Uncle of hers, that, she said, she was sure would please her, as its Subject was Friendship." Miss *Jenny* replied, "That she was certain it would be a great Pleasure to them all, to hear any Story Miss *Dolly* thought proper to read them."

WEDNESDAY

The Third Day

As soon as School was over in the Morning, our little Company were impatient to go into the Arbour, to hear Miss *Dolly's* Story:

But Mrs. *Teachum* told them they must be otherwise employed; for their Writing-Master, who lived some Miles off, and who was expected in the Afternoon, was just then come in, and begged that they would give him their Attendance, tho' out of School-time; because he was obliged to be at home again before the Afternoon, to meet a Person who would confer some Favour on him, and would be highly disobliged should he not keep his Appointment: "And I know (said Mrs. *Teachum*) my little Dears, you would rather lose your own Amusement, than let anyone suffer a real Inconvenience on your Accounts." They all readily complied, and chearfully set to their Writing; and in the Afternoon Mrs. *Teachum* permitted them to leave off Work an Hour sooner than usual, as a Reward for their Readiness to lose their Amusement in the Morning: And being met in their Arbour, Miss *Dolly* read to them as follows:

The Story of Cælia and Chloe

Cælia and *Chloe* were both Orphans, at the tender Age of Six Years. *Amanda* their Aunt, who was very rich, and a Maiden, took them directly under her Care, and bred them up as her own Children. *Cælia's* Mother was *Amanda's* Sister; and *Chloe's* Father was her Brother; so that she was equally related to both.

They were left intirely unprovided for; were both born on the same Day; and both lost their Mothers on the Day of their Birth: Their Fathers were Soldiers of Fortune; and were both killed in one Day, in the same Engagement. But the Fortunes of the Girls were not more similar than their Persons and Dispositions. They were both extremely handsome; and in their Childhoood were so remarkable for Liveliness of Parts, and Sweetness of Temper, that they were the Admiration of the whole Country where they lived.

Their Aunt loved them with a sincere and equal Affection; and took the greatest Pleasure imaginable in their Education, and particularly in encouraging that Love and Friendship which she perceived between them. *Amanda* being (as was said) very rich, and having no other Relations, it was supposed that these her Nieces would be very great Fortunes; and as soon as they became Women, they were addressed by all the Men of Fortune and no Fortune round the Neighbourhood. But as the Love of Admiration, and a Desire of a large Train of Admirers, had no Place in their Minds, they soon dismissed, in the most civil and obliging manner, one after another, all these Lovers.

The refusing such Numbers of Men, and some such as by the World were called good Offers, soon got them the Name of Jilts; and by that means they were freed from any farther Importunity, and for some Years enjoyed that Peace and Quiet they had long wished. Their Aunt, from being their Mother and their Guardian, was now become their Friend. For, as she endeavoured not in the least to force their Inclinations, they never kept any-thing concealed from her; and every Action of their Lives was still guided by her Advice and Approbation.

They lived on in this way, perfectly happy in their own little Community, till they were about Two-and-twenty Years old; when there happened to be a Regiment quartered in the neighbouring Town, to which their House was nearly situated; and the Lieutenant-Colonel, a Man about Four-and-thirty Years old, hearing their Names, had a great Desire to see them. For when he was a Boy of Sixteen, he was put into the Army under the Care of *Chloe's* Father, who treated him with the greatest Tenderness; and in a certain famous Engagement received his Death's Wound by endeavouring to save him from being taken by the Enemy. And Gratitude to the Memory of so good a Friend was as great an Inducement to make him desire to see his Daughter, as the Report he had heard both of hers and her Cousin's great Beauty.

Sempronius (for so this Colonel was called) was a very sensible, well-bred, agreeable Man; and from the Circumstances of his former Acquaintance, and his present proper and polite Behaviour, he soon became very intimate in the Family. The old Lady was particularly pleased with him; and secretly wished, that, before she died, she might be so happy as to see one of her Nieces married to *Sempronius*. She could not from his Behaviour see the least particular Liking to either, for he shewed equally a very great Esteem and Regard for both.

He in reality liked them both extremely; and the Reason of making no Declaration of Love was, his being so undetermined in any Preference that was due to either. He saw plainly that he was very agreeable to both; and with Pleasure he observed, that they made use of none of those Arts which Women generally do to get away a disputed Lover: And this sincere Friendship which subsisted between them raised in him the highest Degree of Love and Admiration. However he at last determined to make the following Trial:

He went first to *Chloe*, and (finding her alone) told her, that he had the greatest Liking in the World to her Cousin, and had really a mind to propose himself to her: But as he saw a very great Friendship between them, he was willing to ask her Advice in the Matter; and conjured her to tell him sincerely, whether there was any-thing in *Cælia's* Temper (not discoverable by him) which as a Wife would make him unhappy. He told her, "That if she knew any such thing, it would be no Treachery, but rather kind in her to declare it, as it would prevent her Friend's being unhappy; which must be the Consequence, in Marriage, of her making him so."

Chloe could not help seeing very plainly, that if *Cælia* was removed she stood the very next in *Sempronius's* Favour. Her Lover was present—her Friend was absent—and the Temptation was too strong and agreeable to be resisted. She then answered, "That since he insisted upon the Truth, and had convinced her that it was in reality acting justly and kindly by her Friend, she must confess, that *Cælia* was possessed (tho' in a very small Degree) of what she had often heard him declare most against of any-thing in the World; and that was, an Artfulness of Temper, and some few Sparks of Envy."

Chloe's confused Manner of speaking, and frequent Hesitation, as unwilling to pronounce her Friend's Condemnation (which, as she was unused to Falsehood, was really unaffected) *Sempronius* imputed to Tenderness and Concern for *Cælia*; but he did not in the least doubt, but on his Application to her, he should soon be convinced of the Truth of what *Chloe* had said.

He then went directly to the Arbour at the End of the Garden, and there to his Wish he found *Cælia* quite alone; and he addressed her exactly in the same manner concerning her Cousin, as he had before spoken to *Chloe* concerning her. *Cælia* suddenly blushed (from Motives I leave those to find out who can put themselves in her Circumstances) and then fetched a soft Sigh, from the Thought that she was hearing a Man she loved declare a Passion of which she was not the Object. But after some little Pause, she told him, "That if *Chloe* had any Faults, they were to her yet undiscovered; and she really and sincerely believed her Cousin would make him extremely happy." *Sempronius* then said, "That of all other Things, *Treachery* and *Envy* were what he had the greatest Dislike to:" And he asked her, "If she did not think her Cousin was a little tainted with these?"——

Here *Cælia* could not help interrupting, and assuring him, "That she believed her totally free from both." And, from his casting on her Friend an Aspersion which her very Soul abhorred, forgetting all Rivalship, she could not refrain from growing quite lavish in her Praise. "Suppose then (said *Sempronius*) I was to say the same to your Cousin concerning my Intentions towards you as I have to you concerning her; do you think she would say as many fine things in your Praise as you have done in hers?"

Cælia answered, "That she verily believed her Cousin would say as much for her as she really deserved; but whether that would be equal to what with Justice she could say of *Chloe*, her Modesty left her in some doubt of."

Sempronius had too much Penetration not to see the real and true Difference in the Behaviour of these Two Women; and could not help crying out, "O *Cælia!* your honest Truth and Goodness in every Word and Look are too visible to leave me one Doubt of their Reality. But could you believe it? This Friend of yours is false. I have already put her to the Trial, by declaring to her my sincere and unalterable Passion for you: When, on my insisting, as I did to you, upon her speaking the Truth, she accused you of what nothing should now convince me you are guilty of. I own, that hitherto my Regard, Esteem, and Love, have been equal to both; but now I offer to the sincere, artless, and charming *Cælia*, my whole Heart, Love, and Affection, and the Service of every Minute of my future Life; and from this Moment I banish from my Mind the false and ungrateful *Chloe*."

Cælia's Friendship for *Chloe* was so deeply rooted in her Breast, that even a Declaration of Love from *Sempronius* could not blot it one Moment from her Heart; and on his speaking the Words *false*

Chloe, she burst into Tears, and said, "Is it possible that *Chloe* should act such a Part towards her *Cælia*? You must forgive her, *Sempronius*: It was her violent Passion for you, and Fear of losing you, which made her do what hitherto her Nature has ever appeared averse to."

Sempronius answered, "That he could not enough admire her Goodness to her Friend *Chloe*: But such Proofs of Passion, he said, were to him at the same time Proofs of its being such a Passion as he had no Regard for; since it was impossible for anyone to gain or increase his Love, by an Action, which at the same time lessened his Esteem." This was so exactly *Cælia's* own way of thinking, that she could not but assent to what he said.

But just as they were coming out of the Arbour, *Chloe*, unseen by them, passed by; and from seeing him kiss her Hand, and the Complacency of *Cælia's* Look, it was easy for her to guess what had been the Result of their private Conference. She could not however help indulging her Curiosity, so far as to walk on the other Side of a thick Yew Hedge, to listen to their Discourse: And as they walked on, she heard *Sempronius* intreat *Cælia* to be chearful, and think no more of her treacherous Friend, whose Wickedness he doubted not would sufficiently punish itself. She then heard *Cælia* say, "I cannot bear, *Sempronius*, to hear you speak so hardly of my *Chloe*. Say that you forgive her, and I will indeed be chearful."

Nothing upon Earth can be conceived so wretched as poor *Chloe*: For on the first Moment that she suffered herself to reflect on what she had done, she thoroughly repented, and heartily detested herself for such Baseness. She went directly into the Garden in hopes of meeting *Sempronius*, in order to throw herself at his Feet, confess her Treachery, and to beg him never to mention it to *Cælia*: But now she was conscious her Repentance would come too late; and he would despise her, if possible, still more for such a Recantation, after her Knowlege of what had passed between him and *Cælia*.

She could indeed have gone to him, and not have owned what she had seen [or] heard: But now her Abhorrence of even the Appearance of Treachery or Cunning was so great, that she could not bear to add the smallest Grain of Falsehood or Deceit to the Weight of her Guilt, which was already almost insupportable: And should she tell him of her Repentance, with a Confession of her

Knowlege of his Engagement with *Cælia*, it would (as has been before observed) appear both servile and insincere.

Nothing could now appear so altered as the whole Face of this once happy Family. *Sempronius* as much as possible shunned the Sight of *Chloe*; for as she was the Cause of all the Confusion amongst them, he had almost an Aversion to her. Though he was not of an implacable Temper; yet, as the Injury was intended to one he sincerely loved, he found it much harder to forgive it, than if it had even succeeded against himself: And as he still looked upon *Chloe* as the Cause of Melancholy in his dear *Cælia*, he could hardly have any Patience with her.

No Words can describe the various Passions which were expressed in the sad Countenance of *Chloe*, when first she met her Friend. They were both afraid of speaking. Shame, and the Fear of being (and with too good Reason) suspected of Insincerity, with-held *Chloe*; and an Unwillingness to accuse or hurt her Friend with-held the gentle *Cælia*. She sometimes indeed thought she saw Repentance in *Chloe*'s Face, and wished for nothing more than to seal her Pardon: But till it was asked, she was in doubt (from what had passed) whether such Pardon and proffer'd Reconciliation might not be rejected. She knew that her Friend's Passions were naturally stronger than hers; and she therefore trembled at the Consequences of coming to an Explanation.

But there was hardly a greater Sufferer in this Scene of Confusion than the poor old Lady *Amanda*. She saw a sort of Horror and Wildness in the Face of *Chloe*; and in *Cælia*'s a settled Melancholy, and such an unusual Reserve in both towards each other, as well as to herself, as quite astonished her.

Sempronius came indeed to the House as often as usual; but in his Countenance she could perceive a sort of Anger and Concern, which perfectly frightened her. But as they did not speak to her, she could not bring herself to ask the Cause of this woful Change, for fear of hearing something too bad to bear.

Cælia had absolutely refused granting to *Sempronius* Leave to ask her Aunt's Consent, till she should come to some Explanation with *Chloe*; which seemed every Day farther off than ever.

The great Perturbation of *Chloe's* Mind threw her into a Disorder not many Degrees short of Madness; and at last she was seized with a violent Fever, so as to keep her Bed. She said she could not bear to look on *Amanda*; but begged *Cælia* to be with her as much as possible: Which she did, in hopes of bringing herself to ease her Mind, by speaking to her of what had given them all this Torment.

Cælia watched with her Night and Day for Three Days; when the Physician who attended her pronounced, that there was no Hope of her Life. *Cælia* could not any longer bear to stay in the Room; and went down-stairs, expecting every Moment to hear she was expired.

Chloe soon perceived by *Cælia*'s abrupt leaving the Room, and by the Looks of those who were left in it, that her Fate was pronounced; which, instead of sinking her Spirits, and making her dejected, gave a Tranquillity to her Mind: For she thought within herself, "I shall now make my dear Cousin happy, by removing out of her Way an Object that must imbitter all her Joy: And now likewise, as she is convinced I am on my Death-bed, she will once more believe me capable of speaking Truth; and will in the manner I could wish receive my sincere Repentance." Then sending for *Cælia* up to her Bed-side, she in a weak Voice, with hardly Strength for Utterance, spoke in this manner: "My dear *Cælia*, tho' you know me to be a worthless base Wretch, yet do not think so hardly of me, as to imagine I would deceive you with my last Breath. Believe me then when I tell you, that I sincerely repent of my Treachery towards you; and as sincerely rejoice, that it has in reality been the Cause of your Happiness with *Sempronius*. Tell him this; and then, perhaps, he will not hate my Memory." Here she fainted away; and they forced *Cælia* out of the Room, as thinking *Chloe*'s Breath was forever flown. But in some time she came again to herself, and cried out, "What! would not my dear *Cælia* say that she forgave me? Methinks I would not die, till I had obtained her Pardon. She is too good to refuse her Friend this last Request." Her Attendants then told her, that seeing her faint away, they had forced *Cælia* out of the Room: And they begged her to try to compose herself; for they were sure that seeing her Friend again, at this time, would only disturb her Mind, and do her an Injury.

Chloe, from the Vent she had given her Grief in speaking to *Cælia*, found herself something more easy and composed; and desiring the Room to be made perfectly quiet, she fell into a gentle Sleep, which lasted Two Hours: And when she awaked, she found herself so much better, that those about her were convinced, from her composed manner of Speaking, that she was now able to bear another Interview.

They again called for *Cælia*, and told her of her Cousin's Amendment. She flew with all Speed to her Chamber; and the Moment she entered, *Chloe* cried out, "Can you forgive me, *Cælia?*" "Yes, with the greatest Joy and Sincerity imaginable, my dearest *Chloe*," answered *Cælia*: "And never let it be again mentioned or remembered."

The sudden Recovery of *Chloe* was almost incredible; for in less than a Week she was able to quit both her Bed and Room, and go into her Aunt's Chamber. The good old Lady shed tears of Joy, to see such a Return of *Chloe's* Health, and of Chearfulness in the Family; and was perfectly contented, now she saw their Melancholy removed, not to inquire into the late Cause of it, for fear of renewing their Trouble even one Moment by the Remembrance of it.

Sempronius, in the mean time, upon some Affairs of his Duty in the Army, had been called away, and was absent the whole time of *Chloe's* Illness; and was not yet returned. *Cælia* spent almost her whole Time with *Chloe*: But Three Weeks passed on, and they were often alone; yet they had never once mentioned the Name of *Sempronius*: Which laid *Cælia* still under the greatest Difficulty how to act, so as to avoid giving her Friend any Uneasiness, and yet not disoblige *Sempronius*: For she had promised him at his Departure, that she would give him Leave to ask her Aunt's Consent immediately upon his Return. But the very Day he was expected, she was made quite easy by what passed between her and her Friend.

Chloe, in this time, by proper Reflections, and a due Sense of *Cælia's* great Goodness and Affection to her, had so intirely got the better of herself in this Affair, that she found she could now without any Uneasiness see them married: And calling *Cælia* to her, she raid with a Smile, "I have, my dear Friend, been so long accustomed to read in that intelligible Index, your Countenance, all your most inmost Thoughts; that I have not been unobserving of those kind

Fears you have had on my Account: And the reason I have so long delayed speaking, was, my Resolution, if possible, never again to deceive you. I can with Pleasure now assure you, that nothing can give me so much Joy as to see your Wedding with *Sempronius*. I make no doubt, but if you ask it, you will have my Aunt's Consent: And, if any Intercession should be wanting towards obtaining it, I will (if you can trust me) use all my Influence in your Behalf. Be assured, my dear *Cælia*, I have now no farther Regard left for *Sempronius*, than as your Husband: And that Regard will increase in proportion as he is the Cause of your Happiness."

They were interrupted in their Discourse by News being brought of the Arrival of *Sempronius*: And *Chloe* received him with such Chearfulness as convinced *Cælia* her Professions were unfeigned.

Cælia related to *Sempronius* all that had passed between her and *Chloe*: And by her continued Chearfulness of Behaviour, the Peace and Tranquillity of the Family were perfectly restored, and their Joy greatly increased by *Amanda's* ready Consent to the Marriage of *Sempronius* and *Cælia*, having first settled all her Fortune to be divided at her Death equally between her Nieces; and in her Life-time there was no Occasion of Settlements, or Deeds of Gift; for they lived all together, and separate Property was not so much as mentioned or thought of in this Family of Harmony and Peace.

Here Miss *Dolly* ceased reading; and all her Hearers sat some little time silent, and then expressed their great Joy that *Cælia* and *Chloe* were at last happy; for none of them had been able to refrain from Tears whilst they were otherwise. On which Miss *Jenny Peace* begged them to observe from this Story, the miser-able Effects that attend Deceit and Treachery: "For, continued she, you see you could not refrain from Tears, only by imagin-ing what *Chloe* must feel after her Wickedness (by which indeed she lost the very Happiness she intended treacherously to gain): Nor could she enjoy one Moment's Peace, till by confessing her Fault, and heartily repenting of it, her Mind was restored to its former Calm and Tranquility." Miss *Dolly* thanked Miss *Jenny* for her Remarks: But Miss *Lucy Sly* was most sensibly touched with this Story, as Cunning had formerly intirely possessed *her* Mind; and said, that if her Companions were not weary at present of their Arbour, she would now recount to them the History of her Life, as this Story was a proper Introduction to it.

The Description of Miss Lucy Sly

Miss *Lucy Sly* was of the same Age as Miss *Dolly Friendly*; but shorter, at least, by half the Head. She was generally called a pretty Girl, from having a Pair of exceeding fine black Eyes, only with the Allay of something cunning in their Look. She had a high Forehead, and very good curling black Hair. She had a sharp high Nose, and a very small Mouth. Her Complexion was but indifferent; and the lower Part of her Face ill turned; for her Chin was too long for due Proportion.

The Life of Miss Lucy Sly

From the time I was Two Years old (said Miss *Lucy*) my Mamma was so sickly, that she was unable to take any great Care of me herself: And I was left to the Care of a Governess, who made it her Study to bring me to do what she had a mind to have done, without troubling her Head what induced me so to do. And whenever I did any-thing wrong, she used to say it was the *Foot-boy*, and not *Miss*, that was naughty. Nay, she would say, it was the Dog, or the Cat, or any-thing she could lay the Blame upon, sooner than own it was I. I thought this pure, that I was never in Fault; and soon got into a way of telling any Lyes, and of laying my own Faults on others, since I found I should be believed. I remember once, when I had broken a fine *China* Cup, that I artfully got out of the Scrape, and hid the broken Cup in the Foot-boy's Room. He was whipt for breaking it; and the next Day whilst I was at Play about the Room, I heard my Governess say to a Friend who was with her, "Yesterday Miss *Lucy* broke a *China* Cup; but the artful little Hussy went and hid it in the Foot-boy's Room, and the poor Boy was whipt for it. I don't believe there was ever a Girl of her Age that had half her Cunning and Contrivance." I knew by her Tone of Voice, and her Manner of speaking, that she did not blame me in her Heart, but rather commended my Ingenuity. And I thought myself so wise, that I could thus get off the Blame from myself, that I every Day improved in new Inventions to save myself, and have others punished in my Place.

This Life of endeavouring to deceive I led till I came to School. But here I found that I could not so well carry on my little Schemes; for I was found out and punished for my own Faults: And this created in me a Hatred to my Companions. For whatever Miss I had a mind to serve as I used to serve our Foot-boy, in laying the Blame falsly upon her, if she could justify herself, and prove me in the wrong, I was very angry with her, for daring to contradict me, and not submitting as quietly to be punished wrongfully, as the Foot-boy was forced to do.

This is all I know of my Life hitherto.

Thus ended Miss *Lucy Sly*: And Miss *Jenny Peace* commended Miss *Lucy* for her free Confession of her Faults, and said, "She doubted not but she would find the Advantage of amending, and endeavouring to change a Disposition so very pernicious to her own Peace and Quiet, as well as to that of all her Friends." But they now obeyed the Summons of the Supper-bell; and soon after retired to Rest.

THURSDAY

The Fourth Day

Our little Company, as soon as the Morning School-Hours were over, hastened to their Arbour, and were attentive to what Miss *Jenny Peace* should propose to them for their Amusement till Dinner-time: When Miss *Jenny*, looking round upon them, said, "That she had not at present any Story to read; but that she hoped, from Miss *Dolly Friendly*'s Example Yesterday, some of the rest might endeavour sometimes to furnish out the Entertainment of the Day:" Upon which Miss *Sukey Jennett* said, "That tho' she could not promise them such an agreeable Story as Miss *Dolly*'s;

yet she would read them a Letter she had received the Evening before from her Cousin *Peggy Smith*, who lived at *York*; in which there was a Story that she thought very strange and remarkable." They were all very desirous of it, when Miss *Sukey* read as follows:

Dear Cousin,

I Promised, you know, to write to you, when I had any-thing to tell you: And as I think the following Story very extraordinary, I was willing to keep my Word.

Some time ago there came to settle in this City a Lady, whose Name was *Dison*. We all visited her: But she had so deep a Melancholy, arising, as it appeared, from a settled State of ill Health, that nothing we could do could afford her the least Relief, or make her chearful. In this Condition she languished amongst us Five Years, still continuing to grow worse and worse.

We all grieved at her Fate. Her Flesh was withered away; her Appetite decayed by degrees, till all Food became nauseous to her Sight; her Strength failed her; her Feet could not support her tottering Body, lean and worn away as it was; and we hourly expected her Death. When, at last, she one Day called her most intimate Friends to her Bed-side, and, as well as she could, spoke to the following Purpose: "I know you all pity me: But, alas! I am not so much the Object of your Pity, as your Contempt; for all my Misery is of my own seeking, and owing to the Wickedness of my own Mind. I had Two Sisters, with whom I was bred up; and I have all my Life-time been unhappy, for no other Cause but for their Success in the World. When we were young, I could neither eat nor sleep in Peace, when they had either Praise or Pleasure. When we grew up to be Women, they were both soon married much to their Advantage and Satisfaction. This galled me to the Heart; and, though I had several good Offers, yet as I did not think them in all respects equal to my Sisters, I would not accept them; and yet, was inwardly vexed to refuse them, for fear I should get no better. I generally deliberated so long that I lost my Lovers, and then I pined for that Loss. I never wanted for any-thing; and was in a Situation in which I might have been happy, if I pleased. My Sisters loved me very well; for I concealed as much as possible from them my odious Envy; and yet never did any poor Wretch lead so miserable a Life as I have done; for every Blessing they enjoyed was a Dagger to my Heart. 'Tis this Envy that has caused all my ill Health, has preyed upon my very Vitals, and will now bring me to my Grave."

In a few Days after this Confession she died; and her Words and Death made such a strong Impression on my Mind, that I could not help sending you this Relation; and begging you, my dear *Sukey*, to remember how careful we ought to be to curb in our Minds the very first Risings of a Passion so detestable, and so fatal, as this proved to poor Mrs. *Dison*. I know I have no particular Reason for giving you this Caution; for I never saw any-thing in you, but what deserved the Love and Esteem of

Your very affectionate Cousin,

M. SMITH.

As soon as Miss *Sukey* had finished her Letter, Miss *Patty Lockit* rose up, and, flying to Miss *Jenny Peace*, embraced her, and said, "What Thanks can I give you, my dear Friend, for having put me into a Way of examining my Heart, and reflecting on my own Actions; by which you have saved me, perhaps, from a Life as miserable as that of the poor Woman in Miss *Sukey's* Letter!" Miss *Jenny* did not thoroughly understand her Meaning; but imagining it might be something relating to her past Life, desired her to explain herself; which she said she would do, telling now, in her Turn, all that had hitherto happened to her.

The Description of Miss Patty Lockit

Miss *Patty Lockit* was but Ten Years old; tall, and inclined to Fat. Her Neck was short; and she was not in the least genteel. Her Face was very handsome; for all her Features were extremely good. She had large blue Eyes; was exceeding fair; and had a great Bloom in her Cheeks. Her Hair was the very first Degree of light brown; was bright and shining; and hung in Ringlets half-way down her Back. Her Mouth was rather too large; but she had such fine Teeth, and looked so agreeably when she smiled, that you was not sensible of any Fault in it.

This was the Person of Miss *Patty Lockit*, who was now to relate her past Life: Which she did, in the following manner:

The Life *of Miss* Patty Lockit

I lived, till I was Six Years old, in a very large family; for I had Four Sisters, all older than myself, and Three Brothers. We played together, and passed our Time much in the common Way: Sometimes we quarrelled, and sometimes agreed, just as Accident would have it. Our Parents had no Partiality to any of us: So we had no Cause to envy one another on that Account; and we lived tolerably well together.

When I was Six Years old, my Grandmother by my Father's Side (and who was also my Godmother) offering to take me to live with her, and promising to look upon me as her own Child, and intirely to provide for me; my Father and Mother, as they had a large Family, very readily accepted her Offer, and sent me directly to her House.

About Half a Year before this, she had taken another God-daughter, the only Child of my Aunt *Bradly*, who was lately dead, and whose Husband was gone to the *West Indies*. My Cousin *Molly Bradly*, was Four Years older than I; and her Mother had taken such Pains in her Education, that she understood more than most Girls of her Age; and had so much Liveliness, Good-humour, and Ingenuity, that every-body was fond of her; and where-ever we went together, all the Notice was taken of my Cousin, and I was very little regarded.

Though I had all my Life before lived in a Family where everyone in it was older, and knew more than myself, yet I was very easy; for we were generally together, in the Nursery; and no-body took much Notice of us, whether we knew any-thing, or whether we did not. But now, as I lived in the House with only one Companion, who was so much more admired than myself, the Comparison began to vex me, and I found a strong Hatred and Aversion for my Cousin arising in my Mind: And yet, I verily believe I should have got the better of it, and been willing to have learnt of my Cousin, and should have loved her for teaching me, if any one had told me it was right; and if it had not been that *Betty*, the Maid who took care of us, used to be for ever teazing me about the Preference that was shewn to my Cousin, and the Neglect I always met with. She used to tell me, that she wondered how I could bear to see Miss *Molly* so caressed; and that it was Want of Spirit not to think myself as good as she was; and, if she was in my Place, she would not submit to be taught by a Child; for my Cousin *Molly* frequently offered to instruct me in any-thing she knew: But I used to say (as *Betty* had taught me) that I would not learn of her; for she was but a Child, tho' she was a little older; and that I was not put under her Care, but that of my Grandmamma. But she, poor Woman, was so old and unhealthy, that she never troubled her Head much about us, but only to take care that we wanted for nothing. I lived in this manner three Years, fretting and vexing myself that I did not know so much, nor was so much liked, as my Cousin *Molly*, and yet resolving not to learn any-thing she could teach me; when my Grandmamma was advised to send me to School: But, as soon as I came here, the Case was much worse; for, instead of one Person to envy, I found many; for all my School-fellows had learned more than I; and, instead of endeavouring to get Knowlege, I began to hate all those who knew more than myself: And this, I am now convinced, was owing to that odious Envy, which, if not cured, would always have made me as miserable as Mrs. *Dison* was; and which constantly tormented me, til we came to live in that general Peace and Good-humour we have lately enjoyed: And as I hope this wicked Spirit was not natural to me, but only blown up by that vile *Betty*'s Instigations, I don't doubt but I shall now grow very happy, and learn something every Day, and be pleased with being instructed; and that I shall always love those who are so good as to instruct me.

Here Miss *Patty Lockit* ceased; and the Dinner-Bell called them from their Arbour.

Mrs. *Teachum*, as soon as they had dined, told them, "That she thought it proper they should use some bodily Exercise, that they might not, by sitting constantly still, impair their Health." Not but that she was greatly pleased with their innocent and instructive Manner of employing their leisure Hours: But this wise

Woman knew, that the Faculties of the Mind grow languid and useless, when the Health of the Body is lost.

As soon as they understood their Governess's Pleasure, they readily resolved to obey her Commands, and desired, that, after School, they might take a Walk as far as the *Dairy-House*, to eat some Curds and Cream. Mrs. *Teachum* not only granted their Request, but said she would dispense with their School-attendance that Afternoon, in order to give them more time for their Walk, which was between two and three Miles; and she likewise added, that she herself would go with them. They all flew like Lightning to get their Hats, and to equip themselves for their Walk; and, with chearful Countenances, attended Mrs. *Teachum* in the School-room. This good Gentlewoman, so far from laying them under a Restraint by her Presence, encouraged them to run in the Fields, and to gather Flowers; which they did, each Miss trying to get the best to present to her Governess. In this agreeable manner, with Laughing, Talking, and Singing, they arrived at the *Dairy-House*, before they imagined they had walked a Mile.

There lived at this *Dairy-House* an old Woman, near Seventy Years of Age. She had a fresh Colour in her Face; but was troubled with the Palsy, that made her Head shake a little. She was bent forward with Age, and her Hair was quite grey: But she retained much Good-humour, and received this little Party with a hearty Welcome.

Our little Gentry flocked about this good Woman, asking her a thousand questions. Miss *Polly Suckling* asked her, "Why she shook her Head so?" and Miss *Patty Lockit* said, "She hoped her Hair would never be of such a Colour."

Miss *Jenny Peace* was afraid they would say something that would offend the old Woman, and advised them to turn their Discourse. "Oh! let the dear Rogues alone," says the old Woman; "I like their Prattle;" and, taking Miss *Polly* by the Hand, said, "Come, my Dear, we will go into the Dairy, and skim the Milk-pans." At which Words they all run into the Dairy, and some of them dipped their Fingers in the Cream; which when Mrs. *Nelly* perceived (who was the eldest Daughter of the old Woman, and managed all the Affairs) she desired they would walk out of the Dairy, and she would bring them what was fit for them: Upon which Miss *Dolly Friendly* said,

"She had rather be as old and good-natured as the Mother, than as young and ill-natured as the Daughter."

The old Woman desired her Company to sit down at a long Table, which she soon supplied with Plenty of Cream, Strawberries, Brown-bread, and Sugar. Mrs. *Teachum* took her Place at the upper End, and the rest sat down in their usual Order, and eat plentifully of these good Things. After which, Mrs. *Teachum* told them they might walk out and see the Garden and Orchard, and by that time it would be proper to return home.

The good old Woman shewed them the Way into the Garden; and gathered the finest Roses and Pinks she could pick, and gave them to Miss *Polly*, to whom she had taken a great Fancy.

At their taking Leave, Mrs. *Teachum* rewarded the good old Woman for her Trouble; who, on her part, expressed much Pleasure in seeing so many well-behaved young Ladies; and said, "She hoped they would come often."

These little Friends had not walked far in their Way home, before they met a miserable ragged Fellow, who begged their Charity. Our young Folks immediately gathered about this poor Creature, and were hearkening very earnestly to his Story, which he set forth in a terrible manner, of having been burnt out of his House, and, from one Distress to another, reduced to that miserable State they saw him in, when Mrs. *Teachum* came up to them. She was not a little pleased to see all the Misses Hands in their Pockets, pulling out Half-pence, and some Sixpences. She told them, she approved of their Readiness to assist the poor Fellow, as he appeared to them: But oftentimes those Fellows made up dismal Stories without much Foundation, and because they were lazy, and would not work. Miss *Dolly* said, "Indeed she believed the poor Man spoke Truth; for he looked honest; and, besides, he seemed almost starved."

Mrs. *Teachum* told them it would be too late before they could get home: So, after each of them had given what they thought proper, they pursued their Walk, prattling all the Way.

They got home about Nine o' Clock; and, as they did not choose any Supper, the Bell rang for Prayers; after which our young Travellers retired to their Rest, where we doubt not but they had a good Repose.

FRIDAY

The Fifth Day

Mrs. *Teachum*, in the Morning, inquired how her Scholars did after their Walk, and was pleased to hear they were all very well. They then performed their several Tasks with much Chearfulness; and, after the School-hours, they were hastening, as usual, to their Arbour, when Miss *Jenny* desired them all to go thither without her, and she would soon follow them; which they readily consented to; but begged her not to deprive them long of the Pleasure of her sweet Company.

Miss *Jenny* then went directly into her Governess's Parlour, and told her, that she had some Thoughts of reading to her Companions a Fairy-Tale, which was also given her by her Mamma: And tho' it was not in such a pompous Stile, nor so full of wonderful Images, as the Giant-Story; yet she would not venture to read any-thing of that Kind without her Permission: But, as she had not absolutely condemned all that Sort of Writing, she hoped she was not guilty of a Fault in asking that Permission. Mrs. *Teachum*, with a gracious Smile, told her, that she seemed so thoroughly well to understand the whole Force of her *Monday* Night's Discourse to her, that she might be trusted almost in any-thing; and desired her to go and follow her own Judgment and Inclinations in the Amusement of her happy Friends. Miss *Jenny*, overjoyed with this kind Condescension in her Governess, thanked her, with a low Courtesy, and said, "She hoped she should never do any-thing unworthy of the Confidence reposed in her;" and, hastening to the Arbour, she there found all her little Companions quite impatient of this short Absence.

Miss *Jenny* told them, that she had by her a Fairy-Tale, which, if they liked it, she would read; and, as it had pleased her, she did not doubt but it would give them equal Pleasure.

It was the Custom now so much amongst them to assent to any Proposal that came from Miss *Jenny*, that they all with one Voice desired her to read it; till Miss *Polly Suckling* said, "That altho' she was very unwilling to contradict any-thing Miss *Jenny* liked, yet she could not help saying, she thought it would be better if they were to read some true History, from which they might learn something; for she thought Fairy-Tales were fit only for little Children."

Miss *Jenny* could not help smiling at such an Objections coming from the little Dumpling, who was not much above Seven Years of Age; and then said, "I will tell you a Story, my little *Polly*, of what happened to me whilst I was at home."

"There came into our Village, when I was Six Years old, a Man who carried about a Raree-Show;[1] which all the Children of the Parish were fond of seeing: But I had taken it into my Head, that it was beneath my *Wisdom* to see Raree-Shows; and therefore would not be persuaded to join my Companions to see this Sight: And altho' I had as great an Inclination as any of them to see it; yet I avoided it, in order to boast of my own great Sense, in that I was above such Trifles.

When my Mamma asked me, 'Why I would not see the Show, when she had given me Leave?' I drew up my Head, and said, 'Indeed I did not like Raree-Shows: That I had been reading; and I thought That much more worth my while, than to lose my Time at such foolish Entertainments.' My Mamma, who saw the Cause of my refusing this Amusement was only a Pretence of being wise, laughed, and said, 'She herself had seen it, and it was really very comical and diverting.' On hearing this, I was heartily vexed to think I had denied myself a Pleasure, which I fansied was beneath me, when I found even my Mamma was not above seeing it. This in a great measure cured me of the Folly of thinking myself above any innocent Amusement. And when I grew older, and more capable of hearing Reason, my Mamma told me, 'She had taken this Method of laughing at me, as Laughing is the proper Manner of treating Affectation; which, of all Things, she said, she would have me carefully avoid; otherwise, whenever I was found out, I should become contemptible.'"

Here Miss *Jenny* ceased speaking; and Miss *Polly Suckling*, blushing that she had made any Objection to what Miss *Jenny* had

---

[1]   A show contained or carried about in a box; a peep show (*OED*). In his *Dictionary*, Samuel Johnson suggests the term is formed in imitation of the foreign way of pronouncing "rare show." According to the *Oxford English Dictionary*, the early exhibitors of peep shows appear to have been Savoyards, from whom the form was likely adopted.

proposed, begged her to begin the Fairy Tale; when just at this Instant, Mrs. *Teachum*, who had been taking a Walk in the Garden, turned into the Arbour to delight herself with the View of her little School united in Harmony and Love. Miss *Jenny*, with great Good-humour, told her Mistress the small Contest she had just had with Miss *Polly*, about reading a Fairy-Tale, and the Occasion of it. Mrs. *Teachum* kindly chucking the little Dumpling under the Chin, said, "She had so good an Opinion of Miss *Jenny*, as to answer for her, that she would read nothing to them but what was proper; and added, that she herself would stay and hear this Fairy-Tale," which Miss *Jenny*, on her Commands, immediately began.

The *Princess* Hebe: *A* Fairy Tale

Above Two thousand Years ago, there reigned over the Kingdom of Tonga, a King whose Name was *Abdallah.* He was married to a young Princess, the Daughter of a King of a neighbouring Country, whose Name was *Rousignon.* Her Beauty and Prudence engaged him so far in Affection to her, that every Hour he could possibly spare from attending the Affairs of his Kingdom, he spent in her Apartment. They had a little Daughter, to whom they gave the Name of Hebe, who was the Darling and mutual Care of both.

The King was quiet in his Dominions, beloved by his Subjects, happy in his Family, and all his Days rolled on in calm Content and Joy. The King's Brother *Abdulham* was also married to a young Princess, named *Tropo*, who in Seven Years had brought him no Children: And she conceived so mortal a Hatred against the Queen (for she envied her Happiness in the little Princess *Hebe*) that she resolved to do her some Mischief. It was impossible for her, during the King's Life-time, to vent her Malice without being discovered; and therefore she pretended the greatest Respect and Friendship imaginable for the unsuspecting Queen.

Whilst Things were in this Situation, the King fell into a violent Fever, of which he died: And during the Time that the Queen was in the Height of her Affliction for him, and could think of nothing but his Loss, the Princess *Tropo* took the Opportunity of putting in Execution her malicious Intentions. She inflamed her Husband's

Passions, by setting forth the Meanness of his Spirit, in letting a Crown be ravished from his Head by a Female Infant, till Ambition seized his Mind, and he resolved to wield the *Tongian* Sceptre himself. It was very easy to bring this about; for, by his Brother's Appointment, he was Protector of the Realm, and Guardian to the young Princess his Niece: And the Queen taking him and the Princess his Wife for her best Friends, suspected nothing of their Designs, but in a manner gave herself up to their Power.

The Protector *Abdulham*, having the whole Treasure of the Kingdom at his Command, was in Possession of the Means to make all his Schemes successful: And the Princess *Tropo*, by lavishly rewarding the Instruments of her Treachery, contrived to make it generally believed, that the Queen had poisoned her Husband; who was so much beloved by his Subjects, that the very Horror of the Action, without any Proof of her Guilt, raised against the poor unhappy Queen an universal Clamour, and a general Aversion throughout the whole Kingdom. The Princess had so well laid her Scheme, that the Guards were to seize the Queen, and convey her to a Place of Confinement, till she could prove her Innocence; which that she might never be able to do, proper Care was taken by procuring sufficient Evidences to accuse her on Oath; and the Princess *Hebe*, her Daughter, was to be taken from her, and educated under the Care of her Uncle. But the Night before this cruel Design was to have been put in Execution, a faithful Attendant of the Queen's, named *Loretta*, by the Assistance of one of the Princess *Tropo*'s Confidants (who had long professed himself her Lover) discovered the whole Secret, of which she immediately informed her Royal Mistress.

The Horrors which filled the Queen's Mind at the Relation of the Princess *Tropo*'s malicious Intentions, were inexpressible, and her Perturbation so great, that she could not form any Scheme that appeared probable to execute for her own Preservation. *Loretta* told her, that the Person who had given her this timely Notice, had also provided a Peasant who knew the Country, and would meet her at the Western Gate of the City, and, carrying the young Princess *Hebe* in his Arms, would conduct her to some Place of Safety; but she must consent to put on a Disguise and escape that very Night from the Palace, or she would be lost forever. Horses or Mules, she said, it would be impossible to come at without Suspicion; therefore she must endeavour (tho' unused to such Fatigue) to travel a-foot till she got herself concealed in some Cottage from her Pursuers, if her Enemies should think of endeavouring to find her out. *Loretta* offered to attend her Mistress, but she absolutely forbad her going any farther than to the Western Gate; where delivering the little Princess *Hebe* into the Arms of the Peasant, who was there waiting for them, she reluctantly withdrew.

The good Queen, who saw no Remedy to this her terrible Disgrace, could have borne this barbarous Usage without much repining, had she herself been the only Sufferer by it: For the Loss of the good King her Husband so far exceeded all her other Misfortunes, that every thing else was trifling in Comparison of so dreadful an Affliction. But the young Princess *Hebe*, whom she was accustomed to look on as her greatest Blessing, now became to her an Object of Pity and Concern; for, from being Heiress to a Throne, the poor Infant, not yet Five Years old, was with her wretched Mother become a Vagabond, and knew not whither to fly for Protection.

Loretta had prevailed on her Royal Mistress to take with her a few little Necessaries, besides a small Picture of the King, and some of her Jewels, which the Queen contrived to conceal under her Night-cloaths, in the midst of that Hair they were used to adorn, when her beloved Husband delighted to see it displayed in flowing Ringlets round her snowy Neck. This Lady, during the Life of her fond Husband, was by his tender Care kept from every Inclemency of the Air, and preserved from every Inconvenience that it was possible for human Nature to suffer. What then must be her Condition now! when thro' By-Paths and thorny Ways, she was obliged to fly with all possible Speed, to escape the Fury of her cruel Pursuers: For she too well knew the merciless Temper of her Enemies, to hope that they would not pursue her with the utmost Diligence, especially as she was accompanied by the young Princess *Hebe*; whose Life was the principal Cause of their Disquiet, and whose Destruction they chiefly aimed at.

The honest Peasant, who carried the Princess *Hebe* in his Arms, followed the Queen's painful Steps; and seeing the Day begin to break, he begged her, if possible, to hasten on to a Wood which was not far off; where it was likely she might find a Place of Safety. But the afflicted Queen at the Sight of the opening Morn (which once used to fill her Mind with rising Joy) burst into a Flood of Tears, and, quite overcome with Grief and Fatigue) cast herself on the Ground, crying out in the most affecting Manner, "The End of my Misfortunes is at hand. My weary Limbs will no longer support me. My Spirits fail me——In the Grave alone must I seek for Shelter." The poor Princess, seeing her Mother in Tears, cast her little Arms about her Neck, and wept also, though she knew not why.

Whilst she was in this deplorable Condition, turning round her Head, she saw behind her a little Girl, no older in Appearance than the Princess *Hebe*; who with an amiable and tranquil countenance begged her to rise and follow her, and she would lead her where she might refresh and repose herself.

The Queen was surprised at the Manner of speaking of this little Child, as she took her to be; but soon thought it was some kind Fairy sent to protect her; and was very ready to submit herself to her Guidance and Protection.

The little Fairy (for such indeed was the seeming Child, who had thus accosted them) ordered the Peasant to return back, and said that she would take care of the Queen, and her young Daughter; and he, knowing her to be the good Fairy *Sybella* very readily obeyed.

Sybella then striking the Ground three times with a little Wand, there suddenly rose up before them a neat plain Car,[1] and a Pair of Milk-white Horses; and placing the Queen with the Princess *Hebe* in her Lap by her Side, she drove with excessive Swiftness full West-ward for Eight Hours; when (just as the Sun began to have Power enough to make the Queen almost faint with the Heat, and her former Fatigue) they arrived at the Side of a shady Wood; upon entering of which, the Fairy made her Horses slacken their Speed; and, having travelled about a Mile and a half, thro' Rows of Elms and Beech Trees, they came to a thick Grove of Firs, into which there seemed to be no Entrance. For

---

[1]   A wheeled vehicle or conveyance, e.g., a carriage or chariot (*OED*).

there was not any Opening to a Path, and the Under-wood, consisting chiefly of Rose-bushes, White-thorn, Eglantine, and other flowering Shrubs, was so thick, that it appeared impossible to force her way through them. But alighting out of the Car (which immediately disappeared) the Fairy (bidding the Queen follow her) pushed her Way thro' a large Bush of jessamine, whose tender Branches gave Way for their Passage, and then closed again, so as to leave no Traces of an Entrance into this charming Grove.

Having gone a little Way thro' an extreme narrow Path, they came into an Opening (quite surrounded by these Firs, and sweet Underwood) not very large, but in which was contained everything that is necessary towards making Life comfortable. At the End of a green Meadow was a plain neat House, built more for Convenience than Beauty, fronting the rising Sun; and behind it was a small Garden, stored only with Fruits and useful Herbs. *Sybella* conducted her Guests into this her simple Lodging; and as Repose was the chief Thing necessary for the poor fatigued Queen, she prevailed with her to lie down on a Couch. Some Hours sound Sleep, which her Weariness induced, gave her a fresh Supply of Spirits: The Ease and Safety from her Pursuers, in which she then found herself, made her for a short time tolerably composed; and she begged the Favour of knowing to whom she was so greatly obliged for this her happy Deliverance: But the Fairy, seeing her Mind too unsettled to give any due Attention to what she should say, told her that she would defer the Relation of her own Life (which was worth her Observation) till she had obtained a Respite from her Sorrows; and in the mean time, by all manner of obliging Ways, she endeavoured to divert and amuse her. The Queen, after a short Interval of Calmness of Mind, occasioned only by her so sudden Escape from the Terrors of Pursuit, returned to her former Dejection, and for some time incessantly wept at the dismal Thought, that the Princess seemed now, by this Reverse of Fate, to be for ever excluded all Hopes of being seated on her Father's Throne; and, by a strange perverse Way of adding to her own Grief, she afflicted herself the more, because the little Princess was ignorant of her Misfortune; and whenever she saw her diverting herself with little childish Plays, instead of being pleased with such her innocent Amusement, it added to her

Sorrow, and made her Tears gush forth in a larger Stream than usual. She could not divert her Thoughts from the Palace from which she had been driven, to fix them on any other Object; nor would her Grief suffer her to reflect, that it was possible for the Princess to be happy without a Crown.

At length, Time, the great Cure of all Ills, in some measure abated her Sorrows; her Grief began to subside; and, spite of herself, the Reflection that her Misery was only in her own Fancy, would sometimes force itself on her Mind. She could not avoid seeing, that her little Hostess enjoyed as perfect a State of Happiness, as is possible to attain in this World: That she was free from anxious Cares, undisturbed by restless Passions, and Mistress of all Things that could be of any Use to make Life easy or agreeable. The oftener this Reflection presented itself to her Thoughts, the more Strength it gained; and at last, she could even bear to think, that her beloved Child might be as happy in such a Situation, as was her amiable Hostess. Her Countenance now grew more chearful: She could take the Princess *Hebe* in her Arms, and, thinking the Jewels she had preserved would secure her from any Fear of Want, look on her with Delight; and began even to [be] convinced, that her future Life might be spent in calm Content and Pleasure.

As soon as the Voice of Reason had gained this Power over the Queen, *Sybella* told her, that now her Bosom was so free from Passion, she would relate the History of her Life. The Queen, overjoyed that her Curiosity might now be gratified, begged her not to delay giving her that Pleasure one Moment; on which our little Fairy began in the following Manner:

But there Mrs. *Teachum* told Miss *Jenny* that the Bell rung for Dinner; on which she was obliged to break off. But meeting again in the same Arbour, in the Evening, when their good Mistress continued to them the Favour of her Presence, Miss *Jenny* pursued her Story.

Fairy Tale *continued*

My Father, said the Fairy, was a Magician: He married a Lady for Love, whose Beauty far outshone that of all her Neighbours; and by means of that Beauty, she had so great an Influence over her Husband, that she could command the utmost Power of his Art. But better had it been for her, had that Beauty been wanting; for her Power only served to make her wish for more, and the Gratification of every Desire begot a new one, which often it was impossible for her to gratify. My Father, tho' he saw his Error in thus indulging her, could not attain Steadiness of Mind enough to mend it, nor acquire Resolution enough to suffer his beloved Wife once to grieve or shed a Tear to no Purpose tho' in order to cure her of that Folly which made her miserable.

My Grandfather so plainly saw the Temper and Disposition of his Son towards Women, that he did not leave him at Liberty to dispose of his Magic Art to any but his Posterity, that it might not be in the Power of a Wife to teaze him out of it. But his Caution was to very little Purpose; for although my Mother could not from herself exert any Magic Power, yet such was her unbounded Influence over her Husband, that she was sure of Success in every Attempt to persuade him to gratify her Desires. For if every Argument she could invent happened to fail, yet the shedding but one Tear was a certain Method to prevail with him to give up his Reason, whatever might be the Consequence.

When my Father and Mother had been married about a Year, She was brought to bed of a Daughter, to whom she gave the Name of *Brunetta*; Her first Request to my Father was, That he would endow this Infant with as much Beauty as she herself was possessed of, and bestow on her as much of his Art as should enable her to succeed in all her Designs. My Father foresaw the dreadful Tendency of granting this Request, but said he would give it with this Restriction, that she should succeed in all her Designs that were not wicked; for, said he, the Success of wicked Designs always turns out as a Punishment to the Person so succeeding. In this Resolution he held for Three Days, till my Mother (being weak in Body after her Lying-in) worked herself with her violent Passions to such a Degree, that the Physicians told my Father, they despaired of her Life, unless some Method could be found to make her Mind more calm and easy. His Fondness for his Wife would not suffer him to bear the Thoughts of losing her, and the Horror with which that Apprehension had but for a Moment possessed his Mind, prevailed with him to bestow on the little *Brunetta*, (tho' foreseeing it would make her miserable) the fatal Gift in its full Extent. But one Restriction it was out of his Power to take off, namely, that all wicked Designs ever could and should be rendered ineffectual by the Virtue and Perseverance of those against whom they were intended, if they in a proper manner exerted that Virtue.

I was born about Two Years after *Brunetta*, and was called *Sybella*: But my Mother was so taken up with her Darling *Brunetta*, that she gave herself not the least Concern about me; and I was left wholly to the Care of my Father.

In order to make the Gift she had extorted from her fond Husband, as fatal as possible to her favourite Child, she took Care in her Education (by endeavouring to cultivate in her the Spirit of Revenge and Malice against those who had in the least Degree offended her) to turn her Mind to all manner of Mischief; by which means she lived in a continual Passion.

My Father, as soon as I was old enough to hearken to Reason, told me of the Gift he had conferred on my Sister; said he could not retract it; and therefore, if she had any mischievous Designs against me, they must in some measure succeed; but he would endow me with a Power superior to this Gift of my Sister's, and likewise superior to any thing else that he was able to bestow, which was Strength and Constancy of Mind enough to bear patiently any Injuries I might receive; and this was a Strength, he said, which would not decay, but rather increase, by every new Exercise of it: And, to secure me in the Possession of this Gift, he also gave me a perfect Knowlege of the true Value of every-thing around me, by which means I might learn, whatever outward Accidents befel me, not to lose the greatest Blessing in this World, namely, a calm and contented Mind. He taught me so well my Duty, that I chearfully obeyed my Mother in all things, tho' she seldom gave me a kind Word, or even a kind Look; for my spiteful Sister was always telling some Lyes to make her angry with me. But my Heart overflowed with Gratitude to my Father, that he should give me Leave to love him, whist he instructed me that it was my Duty to pay him the most strict Obedience.

Brunetta was daily encouraged by her Mother to use me ill, and chiefly because my Father loved me; and altho' she succeeded in all her Designs of Revenge on me; yet was she very uneasy, because she could not take away the Chearfulness of my Mind; for I bore with Patience whatever happened to me: And she would often say, Must I with all my Beauty, Power, and Wisdom (for so she called her low Cunning) be suffering perpetual Uneasiness? And shall you, who have neither Beauty, Power, nor Wisdom, pretend to be happy and chearful? Then would she cry and stamp, and rave like a mad Creature, and set her Invention at Work, to make my Mother beat me, or lock me up, or take from me some of my best Cloaths to give to her; yet still could not her Power extend to vex my Mind: And this used to throw her again into such Passions, as weakened her Health, and greatly impair'd her so much boasted Beauty.

In this Manner we lived, till on a certain Day, after *Brunetta* had been in one of her Rages with me for nothing, my Father came in and chid her for it; which when my Mother heard, she threw herself into such a violent Passion, that her Husband could not pacify her. And, being big with Child, the Convulsions, caused by her Passions, brought her to her Grave. Thus my Father lost her, by the same uncontroulable Excesses, the fatal Effects of which he had before ruined his Daughter to preserve her from. He did not long survive her; but, before he died, gave me a little Wand, which, by striking three times on the Ground, he said, would at any time produce me any Necessary or Convenience of Life, which I really wanted, either for myself, or the Assistance of others: And this he gave me, because he was very sensible, he said, that as soon as he was dead, my Sister would never rest till she had got from me both his Castle, and every thing that I had belonging to me, in it. But, continued he, whenever you are driven from thence, bend your Course directly into the pleasant Wood *Ardella*; there strike with your Wand, and every Thing you want, will be provided for you. But keep this Wand a profound Secret, or *Brunetta* will get it from you; and then (tho' you can never, while you preserve your Patience, be unhappy) you will not have it in your Power to be of so much Use as you would wish to be, to those who shall stand in Need of your Assistance. Saying these Words, he expired, as I kneeled by his Bed-side, attending his last Commands, and bewailing the Loss of so good a Father.

In the midst of this our Distress, we sent to my Uncle *Sochus*, my Father's Brother, to come to us, and to assist us in an equal Division of my deceased Father's Effects: But my Sister soon contrived to make him believe, that I was the wickedest Girl alive, and had always set my Father against her by my Art, which she said I pretended to call Wisdom; and by several handsome Presents she soon persuaded him (for he did not care a Farthing for either of us) to join with her in saying, "That as she was the eldest Sister, she had a full Right to the Castle, and every Thing in it;" but she told me I was very welcome to stay there, and live with her, if I pleased: and while I behaved myself well, she should be very glad of my Company.

As it was natural for me to love all People that would give me Leave to love them, I was quite overjoyed at this kind Offer of my Sister's, and never once thought on the Treachery she had so lately been guilty of: And I have since reflected, that happy was it for me, that Passion was so much uppermost with her, that she could not execute any Plot that required a Dissimulation of any long Continuance: For, had her Good-humour lasted but one Four-and-twenty Hours, 'tis very probable that I should have opened my whole Heart to her; should have endeavoured to have begun a Friendship with her, and perhaps have betrayed the Secret of my Wand: But just as it was Sun-set, she came into the Room where I was, in the most violent Passion in the World, accusing me to my Uncle of Ingratitude to her great generosity, in suffering me to live in *her* Castle. She said, "That she had found me out, and that my Crimes were of the blackest Dye," altho' she would not tell me either what they were, or who were my Accusers. She would not give me Leave to speak, either to ask what my Offence was, or to justify my Innocence: And I plainly perceived, that her pretended Kindness was designed only to make my Disappointment the greater; and that she was now determined to find me guilty, whether I pleaded, or not. And after she had raved on for some time, she said to me with a Sneer, "Since you have always boasted of your calm and contented Mind, you may now try to be contented this Night with the Softness of the Grass for your Bed; for here in *my* Castle you shall not stay one Moment longer." And so saying, she and my Uncle led me to the outer Court, and thrusting me with all their Force from them, they shut up the Gates, bolting and barring them as close as if to keep out a Giant; and left me at that Time of Night, friendless, and, as they thought, destitute of any Kind of Support.

I then remembred my dear Father's last Words, and made what Haste I could to this Wood, which is not above a Mile distant from the Castle; and being, as I thought, about the middle of it, I struck three times with my Wand, and immediately up rose this Grove of Trees, which you see, this House, and all the other Conveniencies, which I now enjoy; and getting that very Night into this my plain and easy Bed, I enjoyed as sweet a Repose as ever I did in my Life, only delayed, indeed, a short time, by a few Sighs, for the Loss of so good a Parent, and the unhappy State of a self-tormented Sister, whose Slumbers (I fear) on a Bed of Down, were more restless and interrupted that Night than mine would have been, even had not my Father's Present of the Wand prevented me from the Necessity of using the Bed of Grass, which she, in her Wrath, allotted me. In this Grove, which I call *Placid Grove*, is contained all that I want; and 'tis so well secured from any Invaders, by the thick Briars and Thorns, which surround it, having no Entrance but thro' that tender Jessamine, that I live in no Apprehensions of any Disturbance, tho' so near my Sister's Castle. But once, indeed, she came with a large Train, and, whilst I was asleep, set Fire to the Trees all around me; and waking, I found myself almost suffocated with Smoke, and the Flames had reached one Part of my House. I started from my Bed, and striking on the Ground three times with my Wand, there came such a Quantity of Water from the Heavens, as soon extinguished the Fire; and the next Morning, by again having recourse to my Wand, all Things grew up into their convenient and proper Order. When my Sister *Brunetta* found that I had such a supernatural Power at my Command, tho' she knew not what it was, she desisted from ever attempting any more by Force to disturb me; and now only uses all sorts of Arts and Contrivances to deceive me, or any Persons whom I would wish to secure. One of my Father's daily Lessons to me was, that I should never omit any one Day of my Life endeavouring to be as serviceable as I possibly could to any Person in Distress. And I daily wander, as far as my Feet will carry me, in Search of any such, and hither I invite them to Peace and calm Contentment. But my Father added also this Command, that I should never endeavour doing any farther Good to those whom Adversity had not taught to hearken to the Voice of Reason, enough to enable them so to conquer their Passions, as not to think themselves miserable in a safe Retreat from Noise and Confusion. This was the Reason I could not gratify you in relating the History of my Life, whilst you gave Way to raging Passions, which only serve to blind your Eyes, and shut your Ears from Truth. But now, great Queen (for I know your State, from what you vented in your Grief) I am ready to endow this little Princess with any Gift in my Power, that I know will tend really to her Good: And I hope your Experience of the World has made you too reasonable to require any other.

The Queen consider'd a little while, and then desired *Sybella* to endow the Princess with that only Wisdom, which would enable her to see and follow what was her own true Good, to know the Value of every Thing around her, and to be sensible, that following the Paths of Goodness, and performing her Duty, was the only Road to Content and Happiness.

Sybella was overjoyed at the Queen's Request, and immediately granted it, only telling the Princess *Hebe*, that it was absolutely necessary towards the Attainment of this great Blessing, that she should intirely obey the Queen her Mother, without ever pretending to examine her Commands; for "True Obedience (said she) consists in Submission; and when we pretend to choose what Commands are proper and fit for us, we don't obey, but set up our own Wisdom in Opposition to our Governors: This, my dear *Hebe*, you must be very careful of avoiding, if you would be happy." She then cautioned her against giving Way to the Persuasions of any of the young Shepherdesses thereabouts, who would endeavour to allure her to Disobedience, by striving to raise in her Mind a Desire of thinking herself wise, whilst they were tearing from her what was indeed true Wisdom. "For (said *Sybella*) my Sister *Brunetta*, who lives in the Castle she drove me from (about a Mile from this Wood), endows young Shepherdesses with great Beauty, and every Thing that is in Appearance amiable, and likely to persuade, in order to allure away, and make wretched, those Persons I would preserve: And all the Wisdom with which I have endow'd the Princess *Hebe*, will not prevent her falling into my Sister's Snares, if she gives the least Way to Temptation: For my Father's Gift to *Brunetta*, in her Infancy, enables her (as I told you) to succeed in all her Designs, except they are resisted by the Virtue of the Person she is practising against. Many poor Wretches has my Sister already decoy'd away from me, whom she now keeps in her Castle; where they live in Splendor and seeming Joy, but in real Misery, from perpetual Jars and Tumults, raised by Envy, Malice, and all the Train of tumultuous and tormenting Passions."

The Princess *Hebe* said, "She doubted not but she should be able to withstand any of *Brunetta's* Temptations." Her Mother interrupting her, cry'd out, "Oh, my dear Child, tho' you are endow'd with Wisdom enough to direct you in the Way to Virtue; yet if you grow conceited and proud of that Wisdom, and fansy yourself above Temptation, it will lead you into the worst of all Evils." Here the Fairy interposed, and told the Princess *Hebe*, "That if she would always carefully observe and obey her Mother, who had learn'd Wisdom in that best School Adversity, she would then, indeed, be able to withstand and overcome every Temptation; and would likewise be happy herself, and able to dispense Happiness to all around her." Nothing was omitted by the Fairy to make this Retirement agreeable to her Royal Guests: And they had now passed near Seven Years in this delightful Grove, in perfect Peace and Tranquillity; when one Evening, as they were walking in the pleasant Wood which surrounded their Habitation, they espy'd, under the Shade, and leaning against the Bark of a large Oak, a poor old Man, whose Limbs were wither'd and decay'd, and whose Eyes were hollow, and sunk with Age and Misery. They stopped as soon as they saw him, and heard him in the Anguish of his Heart, with a loud Groan, utter these Words: "When will my Sorrow end? Where shall I find the good Fairy *Sybella*?" The Fairy immediately begg'd to know his Business with her; and said, if his Sorrows would end on finding *Sybella*, he might set his Heart at Ease; for she stood now before him, and ready to serve him, if his Distresses were such as would admit of Relief, and he could prove himself worthy of her Friendship. The old Man appeared greatly overjoy'd at having found the Fairy, and began the following Story:

"I live from hence a Thousand Leagues. All this tiresome Way have I come in Search of you. My whole Life has been spent in amassing Wealth, to enrich one only Son whom I doated on to Distraction. It is now five Years since I have given to him all the Riches I had labour'd to get, only to make him happy. But, alas! how am I disappointed! His Wealth enables him to command whatever this World produces; and yet the poorest Wretch that begs his Bread cannot be more miserable. He spends his Days in Riot and Luxury; has more Slaves and Attendants than wait in the Palace of a Prince; and still he sighs from Morning till Night, because, he says, there is nothing in this World worth living for. All his Dainties only sate his Palate, and grow irksome to his Sight. He daily changes his Opinion of what is Pleasure, and on the Trial finds none that he can call such; and then falls to sighing again, for the Emptiness of all that he has enjoy'd. So that, instead of being my Delight, and the Comfort of my old Age, sleepless Nights, and anxious Days, are all the Rewards of my past Labours for him. But I have had many Visions and Dreams to admonish me, that if I would venture with my old Frame to travel hither a-foot, in Search of the Fairy *Sybella*, she had a Glass, which if she shew'd him, he would be cur'd of this dreadful Melancholy; and I have borne the Labour and Fatigue of coming this long tiresome Way, that I may not breathe my last with the agonizing Reflection, that all the Labours of my Life have been thrown away. But what shall I say to engage you to go with me? Can Riches tempt, or Praise allure you?"

"No (answer'd the Fairy), neither of them has Power to move me: But I compassionate your Age; and if I thought I could succeed, would not refuse you. The Glass which I shall bid him look in, will shew him his inward Self; but if he will not open both his Eyes and Heart enough to Truth, to let him understand, that the Pleasures he pursues not only are not, but cannot be satisfactory, I can be of no sort of Service to him. And know, old Man, that the Punishment you now feel, is the natural Result of your not having taught him this from his Infancy: For, instead of heaping up Wealth, to allure him to seek for Happiness from such deceitful Means, you should have taught him, that the only Path to it was to be virtuous and good."

The old Man said, "He heartily repented of his Conduct;" and then on his Knees so fervently implor'd *Sybella's* Assistance, that at last she consented to go with him. Then striking on the Ground three times with her Wand, the Car and Horses rose up; and placing the old Man by her, after taking Leave of the Queen, and begging the Princess *Hebe* to be careful to guard against all Temptations to Disobedience, she set out on her Journey.

It being now come to the latest Hour, that Mrs. *Teachum* thought proper for her little Scholars to stay out in the Air, she told Miss *Jenny*, that she must defer reading the remaining Part of her Story till the next Day. Miss *Jenny* always, with great Chearfulness, obeyed her Governess, and immediately left off reading; and said she was ready to attend her: And the whole Company rose up to follow her.

Mrs. *Teachum* had so much Judgment, that, perceiving such a ready Obedience to all her Commands, she now endeavour'd, by all means she could think of to make her Scholars throw off that Reserve before her, which must ever make it uneasy to them for her to be present whilst they were following their innocent Diversions: For such was the Understanding of this good Woman, that she could keep up the Authority of the Governess in her School, yet at times become the Companion of her Scholars. And as she now saw, by their good Behaviour, they deserv'd that Indulgence, she took the little Dumpling by the Hand, and, follow'd by the rest, walked towards the House, and discoursed familiarly with them the rest of the Evening, concerning all their past Amusements.

SATURDAY

The Sixth Day

It was the Custom on *Saturdays* to have no School in the Afternoon; and it being also their Writing-Day from Morning-School till Dinner; Mrs. *Teachum*, knowing how eager Miss

Jenny's Hearers were for the rest of the Story, accompanied them into the Arbour, early in the Afternoon, when Miss *Jenny* went on as follows.

The Fairy Tale *continued*

The Queen, and the Princess *Hebe*, remain'd, by the good Fairy's Desire, in her Habitation, during her Absence. They spent their Time in Serenity and Content; the Princess daily improving herself in Wisdom and Goodness, by hearkening to her Mother's Instructions, and obeying all her Commands, and the Queen in studying what would be of most Use to her Child. She had now forgot her Throne and Palace, and desir'd nothing farther than her present peaceful Retreat. One Morning, as they were sitting in a little Arbour at the Corner of a pleasant Meadow, on a sudden they heard a Voice, much sweeter than they had ever heard, warble thro' the following Song.

A Song.

I.

Virtue, *soft Balm of ev'ry Woe,*
Of ev'ry Grief the Cure,
'Tis thou alone that canst bestow
　　Pleasures unmix'd and pure.

II.

The shady Wood, the verdant Mead,
Are Virtue's flow'ry Road;
Nor painful are the Steps which lead
　　To her Divine Abode.

III.

'Tis not in Palaces or Halls,
　　She or her Train appear:
Far off she flies from pompous Walls;
　　Virtue and Peace dwell here.

The Queen was all Attention, and, at the End of the Song, she gazed around her, in Hopes of seeing the Person, whose inchanting Voice she had been so eagerly listening to; when she espied a young Shepherdess, not much older than the Princess *Hebe*; but possessed of such uncommon and dazling Beauty, that it was some time before she could disengage her Eyes from so agreeable an Object. As soon as the young Shepherdess found herself observed, she seemed modestly to offer to withdraw; but the Queen begged her not to go till she had informed them who she was, that, with such a commanding Aspect, had so much engaged them in her Favour.

The Shepherdess coming forward, with a bashful Blush, and profound Obeisance, answered, that her Name was *Rozella*, and she was the Daughter of a neighbouring Shepherd and Shepherdess, who lived about a Quarter of a Mile from thence; and, to confess the Truth, she had wandered thither, in hopes of seeing the young Stranger, whose Fame for Beauty and Wisdom had filled all that Country round.

The Princess *Hebe*, well knowing of whom she spoke, conceived from that Moment such an Inclination for her Acquaintance, that she begged her to stay and spend that whole Day with them in *Placid Grove*. Here the Queen frown'd upon her; for she had, by the Fairy's Desire, charged her never to bring any one, without her Permission, into that peaceful Grove.

The young *Rozella* answered, that nothing could be more agreeable to her Inclinations; but she must be at home by Noon; for so in the Morning had her Father commanded her, and never yet in her Life had she either disputed or disobey'd her Parents Commands. Here the young Princess look'd on her Mother with Eyes expressive of her Joy, at finding a Companion, which she, and even the Fairy herself, could not disapprove.

When *Rozella* took her Leave, she begg'd the Favour, that the little *Hebe* (for so she call'd her, not knowing her to be a Princess) might come to her Father's small Cottage, and there partake such homely Fare as it afforded: A Welcome, she said, she could insure her; and tho' poor, yet, from the Honesty of her Parents, who would be proud to entertain so rare a Beauty, she was certain no sort of Harm could happen to the pretty *Hebe*, from such a friendly Visit:

And she would be in the same Place again To-morrow, to meet her, in hopes, as she said, to conduct her to her humble Habitation. When *Rozella* was gone, the Queen, tho' highly possessed in her Favour, both by her Beauty and modest Behaviour, yet ponder'd some time on the Thought, whether or no she was a fit Companion for her Daughter. She remember'd what *Sybella* had told her concerning *Brunetta*'s adorning young Shepherdesses with Beauty, and other Excellences, only to enable them the better to allure and intice others into Wickedness. *Rozella*'s beginning her Acquaintance too with the Princess, by Flattery, had no good Aspect; and the sudden Effect it had upon her, so as to make her forget, or wilfully disobey, her Commands, by inviting *Rozella* to *Placid Grove*, were Circumstances which greatly alarmed her. But, by the repeated Intreaties of the Princess, she gave her Consent, that she should meet *Rozella* the next Day, and walk with her in that Meadow, and in the Wood; but upon no Account should she go home with her, or bring *Rozella* back with her. The Queen then, in gentle Terms, chid the Princess for her Invitation to the young Shepherdess, which was contrary to an absolute Command; and said, "You must, my dear *Hebe*, be very careful to guard yourself extremely well against those Temptations which wear the Face of Virtue. I know, that your sudden Affection to this apparent good Girl, and your Desire of her Company, to partake with you the innocent Pleasures of this happy Place, arise from a good Disposition: But where the Indulgence of the most laudable Passion, even Benevolence and Compassion itself, interferes with, or runs counter to, your Duty, you must endeavour to suppress it, or it will fare with you, as it did with that Hen, who, thinking that she heard the Voice of a little Duckling in Distress, flew from her Young ones, to go and give it Assistance, and, following the Cry, came at last to an Hedge, out of which jump'd a subtle and wicked Fox, who had made that Noise to deceive her, and devoured her in an Instant. A Kite[1] at the same time, taking Advantage of her Absence, carried away, one by one, all her little innocent Brood, robbed of that Parent, who should have been their Protector." The Princess promised her Mother, that

---

[1] A bird of prey of the falcon family (*OED*).

she would punctually obey all her Commands, and be very watchful and observant of every thing *Rozella* said and did, till she had approved herself worthy of her Confidence and Friendship.

The Queen the next Morning renew'd her Injunctions to her Daughter, that she should by no means go farther out of the Wood than into the Meadow, where she was to meet *Rozella*; and that she should give her a faithful Account of all that should pass between them.

They met according to Appointment, and the Princess brought home so good an Account of their Conversation, which the Queen imagined would help to improve, rather than seduce her Child, that she indulg'd her in the same Pleasure as often as she asked it. They passed some Hours every Day in walking round that delightful Wood, in which were many small green Meadows, with little Rivulets running thro' them, on the Banks of which, covered with Primroses and Violets, *Rozella*, by the Side of her sweet Companion, used to sing the most inchanting Songs in the World: The Words were chiefly in Praise of Innocence, and a Country-Life.

The Princess came home every Day more and more charm'd with her young Shepherdess, and recounted, as near as she could remember, every Word that passed between them. The Queen highly approved of their manner of amusing themselves; but again injoin'd her to omit nothing that passed in Conversation, especially if it had the least Tendency towards alluring her from her Duty.

One Day, as the Princess *Hebe* and *Rozella* were walking alone, and talking, as usual, of their own happy State, and the Princess was declaring how much her own Happiness was owing to her thorough Obedience to her Mother, *Rozella*, with a Tone of Voice as half in Jest, said, "But don't you think, my little *Hebe*, that, if I take a very great Pleasure in any thing that will do me no Hurt, tho' it is forbidden, I may disobey my Parents by enjoying it, provided I don't tell them of it to vex them with the Thoughts that I have disobey'd them? And then, my Dear, what Harm is done?"

"Great Harm (answer'd the Princess, looking grave, and half angry): I am asham'd to hear you talk so, *Rozella*. Are you not guilty of Treachery, as well Disobedience? Neither ought you to determine, that no Harm is done, because you do not feel the immediate Effects of your Transgression; for the Consequence may be out of our narrow unexperienced View: And I have been taught, whenever my Mother lays any Commands on me, to take it for granted, she has some Reason for so doing; and I obey her, without examining what those Reasons are; otherwise, it would not be obeying her, but setting up my own Wisdom, and doing what she bid me only when I thought proper."

They held a long Argument on this Head, in which *Rozella* made use of many a Fallacy to prove her Point; but the Princess, as she had not yet departed from Truth, nor fail'd in her Duty, could not be imposed upon. *Rozella*, seeing every Attempt to persuade her was in vain, turn'd all her past Discourse into a Jest; said she had only a Mind to try her; and was overjoy'd to find her so steady in the Cause of Truth and Virtue. The Princess resumed her usual Chearfulness and good Humour. *Rozella* sung her a Song in Praise of Constancy of Mind; and they passed the rest of the Time they stay'd together, as they used to do.

But, just before they parted, *Rozella* begg'd she would not tell her Mother of the first Part of the Conversation that had passed between them. The Princess reply'd, "That it would be breaking thro' one of her Mother's Commands; and therefore she dared not grant her Request." Then said *Rozella*, "Here I must for ever part with my dear little *Hebe*. Your Mother, not knowing the manner in which I spoke, will have an ill Opinion of me, and will never trust you again in my Company. Thus will you be torn from me; and my Loss will be irreparable." These Words she accompanied with a Flood of Tears, and such little Tendernesses, as quite melted the Princess into Tears also. But she still said, that she could not dare to conceal from her Mother any thing that had happen'd, tho' she could not but own, she believ'd their Separation would be the Consequence. "Well then (cry'd *Rozella*) I will endeavour to be contented, as our Separation will give you less Pain, than what you call this mighty Breach of your Duty: And tho' I would willingly undergo almost any Torments that could be invented, rather than be debarr'd one Moment the Company of my dearest *Hebe*; yet I will not expect that she should suffer the smallest Degree of Pain or Uneasiness, to save me from losing what is the whole Pleasure of my Life."

The Princess could not bear the Thought of appearing ungrateful to such a warm Friendship as *Rozella* expressed; and, without farther Hesitation, promis'd to conceal what she had said, and to undergo any thing, rather than lose so amiable a Friend.

After this they parted. But when the Princess enter'd the Grove, she did not, as usual, run with Haste and Joy into the Presence of her indulgent Mother; for her Mind was disturb'd: She felt a conscious Shame on seeing her, and turned away her face, as wanting to shun the piercing Look of that Eye, which she imagin'd would see the Secret lurking in her Bosom. Her Mother observed with Concern her downcast Look, and Want of Chearfulness: And being asked what was the Matter, she answered, Her Walk had fatigued her, and she begged early to retire to Rest. Her kind Mother consented: But little Rest had the poor Princess that whole Night; for the Pain of having her Mind touched with Guilt, and the Fear she was under of losing her dear Companion, kept her Thoughts in one continued Tumult and Confusion. The Fairy's Gift now became her Curse; for the Power of seeing what was right, as she had acted contrary to her Knowlege, only tormented her.

She hastened the next Morning to meet *Rozella*, and told her all that had passed in her own Mind the preceding Night; declaring that she would not pass such another for the whole World; but yet would not dispense with her Promise to her without her Consent; and therefore came to ask her Leave to acquaint her good Mother with all that had passed: "For (said she), my dear *Rozella*, we must, if we would be happy, do always what is right, and trust for the Consequences." Here *Rozella* drew her Features into the most contemptuous Sneer imaginable, and said, "Pray what are all these mighty Pains you have suffered? Are they not owing only to your Want of Sense enough to know, that you can do your Mother no Harm by concealing from her this, or any thing else that will vex her? And, my dear Girl (continued she) when you have once enter'd into this Way of thinking, and have put this blind Duty out of your Head, you will spend no more such restless Nights, which you must see was intirely owing to your own Imaginations."

This startled the Princess to such a Degree, that she was breaking from her; but, putting on a more tender Air *Rozella* cry'd, "And can you then, my dear *Hebe*, determine to give me up for such a trifling Consideration?" Then raising her Voice again, in a haughty manner, she said, "I ought to despise and laugh at you for your Folly, or at best pity your Ignorance, rather than offer a sincere Friendship to one so undeserving."

The Princess, having once swerved from her Duty, was now in the Power of every Passion that should attack her. Pride and Indignation, at the Thought of being despised, bore more Sway with her, than either her Duty or Affection to her fond Mother; and she was now determined, she said, to think for herself, and make use of her own Understanding, which, she was convinced, would always teach her what was right. Upon this *Rozella* took her by the Hand, and, with Tears of Joy, said, "Now, my dearest Girl, you are really wise, and cannot therefore (according to your own Rule) fail of being happy. But, to shew that you are in Earnest in this Resolution, you shall this Morning go home with me to my Father's Cott: It is not so far off, but you will be back by the Time your Mother expects you; and as that will be obeying the chief Command, it is but concealing from her the Thing that would vex her, and there will be no Harm done."

Here a Ray of Truth broke in upon our young Princess; but as a false Shame, and Fear of being laughed at, had now got Possession of her, she, with a soft Sigh, consented to the Proposal.

Rozella led the Way. But just as they were turning round the Walk, which leads out of the Wood, a large Serpent darted from one Side out of a Thicket, directly between them; and, turning its hissing Mouth towards the Princess, as seeming to make after her, she fled hastily back, and ran with all her Speed towards the Grove, and panting for Breath, flew into the Arms of her ever kind Protectress.

Her Mother was vastly terrified to see her tremble, and look so pale; and as soon as she was a little recovered, asked her the Occasion of her *Fright*; and added (with Tears running down her Cheeks) "I am afraid, my dear *Hebe*, some sad Disaster has befallen you; for, indeed, my Child, I but too plainly saw last Night—"

Here the Princess was so struck with true Shame and Confusion for her past Behaviour, that she fell down upon her Knees, confessed the whole Truth, and implored Forgiveness for her Fault.

The Queen kindly raised her up, kissed and forgave her. "I am overjoyed, my dear Child (said she) at this your sweet Repentence, though the Effect of mere Accident, as it appears; but sent, without doubt, by some good Fairy, to save you from Destruction: And I hope you are thoroughly convinced, that the Serpent which drove you home, was not half so dangerous as the false *Rozella*."

The Princess answered, "That she was thoroughly sensible of the Dangers she had avoided; and hoped she never should again, by her own Folly and Wickedness, deserve to be exposed to the Danger from which she had so lately escaped."

Some Days passed, without the Princess's offering to stir out of the Grove; and in that time she gave a willing and patient Ear to all her Mother's Instructions, and seemed thoroughly sensible of the great Deliverance she had lately experienced. But yet there appeared in her Countenance an Uneasiness, which the Queen wishing to remove, asked her the Cause of it.

"It is, dear Madam," answered the Princess, "because I have not yet had it in my Power to convince you of my Repentance, which (tho' I know it to be sincere) you have had no Proof of, but in Words only; and, indeed, my Heart longs for an Occasion to shew you, that I am now able to resist any Allurement which would tempt me from my Duty; and I cannot be easy till you have given me an Opportunity of shewing you the Firmness of my Resolution; and if you will give me Leave to take a Walk in the Wood alone, this Evening, I shall return to you with Pleasure, and will promise not to exceed any Bounds that you shall prescribe."

The Queen was not much pleased with this Request; but the Princess was so earnest with her to grant it, that she could not well refuse, without seeming to suspect her Sincerity; which she did not, but only feared for her Safety; and, giving her a strict Charge, not to stir a Step out of the Wood, or to speak to the false *Rozella*, if she came in her Way, she reluctantly gave her Consent.

The Princess walked thro' all the flowery Labyrinths, in which the had so often strayed with *Rozella*; but she was so shocked with the Thoughts of her Wickedness, that she hardly gave a Sigh for the Loss of a Companion once so dear to her: And as a Proof, that her Repentance was sincere, tho' she heard *Rozella* singing in an Arbour (purposely perhaps to decoy her) she turned away without the least Emotion, and went quite to the other Side of the Wood; where looking into the Meadow, in which she first beheld that false Friend, she saw a Girl about her own Age, leaning against a Tree, and crying most bitterly. But the Moment she came in Sight, the young Shepherdess (for such by her Dress she appeared to be) cry'd out, "O help, dear young lady, help me; for I am tied here to this Tree, by the spiteful Contrivance of a wicked young Shepherdess, called *Rozella*: My Hands, too, you see, are bound behind me, so that I cannot myself unloose the Knot; and if I am not released, here must I lie all Night: And my wretched Parents will break their Hearts, for fear some sad Accident should have befallen their only Child, their poor unhappy *Florimel!*"

The Princess, hearing her speak of *Rozella* in that manner, had no Suspicion of her being one of that false Girl's deluding Companions; but rather thought that she was a Fellow-sufferer with herself; and therefore, without any Consideration of the Bounds prescribed, she hastened to relieve her, and even thought that she should have great Pleasure in telling her Mother, that she had saved a poor young Shepherdess from *Rozella's* Malice, and restored her to her fond Parents. But as soon as she had unloosed the Girl from the Tree, and unbound her Hands, instead of receiving Thanks for what she had done, the wicked *Florimel* burst into a Laugh, and suddenly snatching from the Princess *Hebe's* Side her Father's Picture, which she always wore hanging in a Ribband, [1] she ran away with it, as fast as she could, over the Meadow.

The Princess was so astonished at this strange Piece of Ingratitude and Treachery, and was so alarmed for fear of losing what she knew her Mother so highly valued, that, hardly knowing what she was about, she pursued *Florimel* with all her Speed; begging and intreating her not to bereave her so basely and ungratefully of that Picture, which she would not part with for the World: But it was all to no Purpose; for *Florimel* continued her Flight, and the Princess her Pursuit, till they arrived at *Brunetta's* Castle-Gate; where the Fairy herself appeared dressed and adorned in the most becoming Manner, and, with the most bewitching Smile that can come from dazling Beauty, invited the Princess to enter her Castle (into which *Florimel* was run to hide herself) and promised her, on that Condition, to make the idle Girl restore the Picture.

---

[1]   Riband, or ribbon (*OED*).

It was now so late, that it was impossible for the Princess to think of returning home that Night; and the pleasing Address of *Brunetta*, together with the hopes of having her Picture restored, soon prevailed with her to accept of the Fairy's Invitation. The Castle glittered with gaudy Furniture; sweet Music was heard in every Room; the whole Company, who were all of the most beautiful Forms that could be conceived, strove who should be most obliging to this their new Guest. They omitted nothing that could amuse and delight the Senses. And the Princess *Hebe* was so entranced with Joy and Rapture, that she had not time for Thought, or for the least serious Reflection: And she now began to think, that she had attained the highest Happiness upon Earth.

After they had kept her Three Days in this Round of Pleasure and Delight, they began to pull off the Mask: Nothing was heard but Quarrels, Jars, and galling Speeches: Instead of sweet Music, the Apartments were filled with Screams and Howling; for every one giving way to the most outrageous Passions, they were always doing each other some malicious Turn, and one universal Horror and Confusion reigned.

The Princess was hated by all, and was often asked, with insulting Sneers, Why she did not return to her peaceful Grove, and condescending Mother? But her Mind having been thus turned aside from what was right, could not bear the Thoughts of returning; and tho' by her daily Tears, she shewed her Repentance, Shame prevented her Return: But this again was not the right sort of Shame; for then she would humbly have taken the Punishment due to her Crime; and it was rather a stubborn Pride; which, as she knew herself so highly to blame, would not give her Leave to suffer the Confusion of again confessing her Fault; and till she could bring herself to such a State of Mind, there was no Remedy for her Misery.

Just as Miss *Jenny* had read these Words, Mrs. *Teachum* remembring some Orders necessary to be given in her Family, left them; but bid them go on, saying she would return again in a Quarter of an Hour. But she was no sooner gone from them, than our little Company, hearing the Sound of Trumpets and Kettle-drums, which seemed to be playing at some little Distance from Mrs. *Teachum's* House, suddenly started from their Seats, running directly to the Terrace; and, looking over the Garden Wall, they saw a Troop of Soldiers riding by, with these Instruments of Music playing before them.

They were highly delighted with the gallant and splendid Appearance of these Soldiers, and watched them out of Sight; and were then returning to the Arbour, where Miss *Jenny* had been reading; but Miss *Nanny Spruce* espied another Troop coming out of the Lane from whence the first had issued, and cry'd out, "O! here is another fine Sight; let us stay and see these go by too." "Indeed (said Miss *Dolly Friendly*) I am in such Pain for the poor Princess *Hebe*, while she is in that sad Castle, that I had rather hear how she escaped (for that I hope she will) than see all the Soldiers in the World; and besides, it is but seeing the same thing we have just looked at before." Here some were for staying, and others for going back; but as Miss *Dolly's* Party was the strongest, the few were ashamed to avow their Inclinations; and they were returning to their Arbour, when they met Mrs. *Teachum*, who informed them their Dancing-Master was just arrived, and they must attend him; but in the Evening they might finish their Story.

They were so curious (and especially Miss *Dolly Friendly*) to know what was to become of the Princess, that they could have wished not to have been interrupted; but yet, without one Word of Answer, they complied with what their Governess thought most proper; and in the Evening, hastening to their Arbour, Mrs. *Teachum* herself being present, Miss *Jenny* went on in the following Manner.

Fairy Tale *continued*

The Queen, in the mean time, suffered for the Loss of her Child more than Words can express, till the good Fairy *Sybella* returned. The Queen burst into Tears at the Sight of her; but the Fairy immediately cry'd out, "You may spare yourself, my Royal Guest, the Pain of relating what has happened. I know it all; for that old Man, whom I took such Pity on, was a Phantom, raised by *Brunetta*, to allure me hence, in order to have an Opportunity, in my Absence, of *seducing* the Princess from her Duty. She knew nothing but a probable Story could impose on me; and therefore raised that Story of the Misery of the old Man's Son (*from Motives which too often, indeed, cause the Misery of Mortals*); as knowing I should think it my Duty to do what I could to relieve such a Wretch. I will not tell you all my Journey, nor what I have gone thro'. I know your Mind is at present too much fixed on the Princess, to attend to such a Relation: I'll only tell you what concerns yourself. When the Phantom found, that by no Distress he could disturb my Mind, he said he was obliged to tell the Truth; what was the Intention of my being deluded from home, and what had happened since; and then vanished away." Here the Fairy related to the Queen every thing that had happened to the Princess, as has already been written; and concluded with saying, that she would wander about the Castle-Walls (for *Brunetta* had no Power over her); and if she could get a Sight of the Princess, she would endeavour to bring her to a true Sense of her Fault, and then she might again be restored to Happiness.

The Queen blessed the Fairy for her Goodness; and it was not long before *Sybella's* continual Assiduity got her a Sight of the Princess; for she often wandered a little way towards that Wood she had once so much delighted in, but never could bring herself to enter into it; the Thought of seeing her injured Mother made her start back, and run half wild into the fatal Castle. *Rozella* used frequently to throw herself in her Way; and on hearing her Sighs, and seeing her Tears, would burst into a sneering Laugh at her Folly; to avoid which Laugh, the poor Princess first suffered herself to throw off all her Principles of Goodness and Obedience, and was now fallen into the very Contempt she so much dreaded.

The first time the Fairy got a Sight of her, she called to her with the most friendly Voice; but the Princess, stung to the Soul with the Sight of her, fled away, and did not venture out again in several Days. The kind *Sybella* began almost to despair of regaining her lost Child; but never failed walking round the Castle many Hours every Day. And one Evening, just before the Sun set, she heard within the Gates a loud tumultuous Noise, but more like riotous Mirth, than the Voice either of Rage or Anger; and immediately she saw the Princess rush out at the Gate, and about a Dozen Girls laughing and shouting, running after her. The poor Princess flew with all her Speed, till she came to a little Arbour, just by the Side of the Wood; and her Pursuers, as they intended only to teaze her, did not follow her very close; but as soon as they lost Sight of her, returned all back again to the Castle.

Sybella went directly into the Arbour, where she found the little Trembler prostrate on the Ground, crying and sobbing as if her Heart was breaking. The Fairy seized her Hand, and would not let her go, till she had prevailed with her to return to the *Placid Grove*, to throw herself once more at her Mother's Feet, assuring her, that nothing but this humble State of Mind would cure her Misery, and restore her wonted Peace.

The Queen was filled with the highest Joy to see her Child; but restrained herself so much, that she shewed not the least Sign of it, till she had seen her some time prostrate at her Feet, and had heard her with Tears properly confess, and ask Pardon for, all her Faults. She then raised, and once more forgave her; but told her, that she must learn more Humility, and Distrust of herself, before she should again expect to be trusted.

The Princess made no Answer; but by a modest downcast Look expressed great Concern, and true Repentance; and in a short time recover'd her former Peace of Mind; and as she never afterwards disobeyed her indulgent Mother, she daily increased in Wisdom and Goodness.

After having lived on in the most innocent and peaceful Manner for Three Years (the Princess being just turned of Eighteen Years old) the Fairy told the Queen, that she would now tell her some News of her Kingdom, which she had heard in her Journey: Namely, That her Sister-in-law was dead, and her Brother-in-law had made Proclamation throughout the Kingdom, of great Rewards to any one, who should produce the Queen and the Princess *Hebe*, whom he would immediately reinstate in the Throne.

The Princess *Hebe* was by, when she related this; and said she begged to lead a private Life, and never more be exposed to the Temptation of entering into Vice, for which she already had so severely smarted.

The Fairy told her, that, since she doubted herself, she was now fit to be trusted; for, said she, "I did not like your being so sure of resisting Temptation, when first I conferred on you the

Gift of Wisdom. But you will, my Princess, if you take the Crown, have an Opportunity of doing so much Good, that, if you continue virtuous, you will have perpetual Pleasures; for Power, if made a right Use of, is indeed a very great Blessing."

The Princess answered, that if the Queen, her Mother, thought it her Duty to take the Crown, she would chearfully submit, tho' a private Life would be otherwise her Choice.

The Queen reply'd, that she did not blame her for chusing a private Life; but she thought she could not innocently refuse the Power that would give her such Opportunities of doing Good, and making Others happy; since, by that Refusal, the Power might fall into Hands that would make an ill Use of it.

After this Conversation, they got into the same Car in which they travelled to the Wood of *Ardella*; arrived safely at the City of *Algorada*, and the Princess *Hebe* was seated, with universal Consent, on her Father's Throne; where she and her People were reciprocally happy, by her great Wisdom and Prudence: And the Queen-Mother spent the Remainder of her Days in Peace and Joy, to see her beloved Daughter prove a Blessing to such Numbers of human Creatures; whilst she herself enjoyed that only true Content and Happiness this World can produce; namely, *A peaceful Conscience, and a quiet Mind.*

When Miss *Jenny* had finished her Story, Mrs. *Teachum* left them for the present, that they might, with the utmost Freedom, make their own Observations; for she knew she should be acquainted with all their Sentiments from Miss *Jenny* afterwards.

The little Hearts of all the Company were swelled with Joy, in that the Princess *Hebe* was at last made happy; for Hope and Fear had each by Turns possessed their Bosoms for the Fate of the little Princess; and Miss *Dolly Friendly* said, that *Rozella's* artful manner was enough to have drawn in the wisest Girl into her Snares; and she did not see how it was possible for the Princess *Hebe* to withstand it, especially when she cry'd for fear of parting with her.

Miss *Sukey Jennet* said, that *Rozella's* laughing at her, and using her with Contempt, she thought was insupportable; for who could bear the Contempt of a Friend?

Many and various were the Remarks made by Miss *Jenny's* Hearers, on the Story she had read to them. But now they were so confirmed in Goodness, and every one was so settled in her Affection for her Companions, that, instead of being angry at any Opposition that was made to their Judgments, every one spoke her Opinion with the utmost Mildness.

Miss *Jenny* sat some time silent to hear their Conversation on her Fairy Tale. But her seeing them so much altered in their Manner of talking to each other, since the time they made their little Remarks on her Story of the Giants, filled her whole Mind with the most sincere Pleasure: And with a Smile peculiar to herself, and which diffused a Chearfulness to all around her, she told her Companions the Joy their present Behaviour had inspired her with; but saying, that it was as late as their Governess chose they should stay out, she rose, and walked towards the House, whither she was chearfully followed by the whole Company.

Mrs. *Teachum* after Supper, again, in a familiar manner, talked to them on the Subject of the Fairy Tale, and encouraged them, as much as possible, to answer her freely in whatever she asked them; and at last said, "My good Children, I am very much pleased when you are innocently amused; and yet I would have you consider seriously enough of what you read, to draw such Morals from your Books, as may influence your future Practice: And as to Fairy Tales in general, remember, that the Fairies, as I told Miss *Jenny* before of Giants and Magic, are introduced, by the Writers of those Tales, only by way of Amusement to the Reader. For if the Story is well written, the common Course of Things would produce the same Incidents, without the Help of Fairies.

As for Example, In this of the Princess *Hebe* you see the Queen her Mother was not admitted to know the Fairy's History, till she could calm her Mind enough to hearken to Reason: Which only means, that whilst we give way to the Raging of our Passions, nothing useful can ever sink into our Minds. For by the Fairy *Sybella's* Story you find, that by our own Faults we may turn the greatest Advantages into our own Misery, as *Sybella's* Mother did her Beauty, by making use of the Influence it gave her over her Husband, to teaze him into the Ruin of his Child; and as also *Brunetta* did, by depending on her Father's Gift, to enable her to complete her Desires, and therefore never endeavouring to conquer them.

You may observe also on the other Side, that no Accident had any Power to hurt *Sybella*; because she followed the Paths of Virtue, and kept her Mind free from restless Passions.

You see Happiness in the good *Sybella*'s peaceful Grove, and Misery in the wicked *Brunetta*'s gaudy Castle. The Queen desiring the Fairy to endow her Child with true Wisdom, was the Cause that the Princess *Hebe* had it in her Power to be happy. But take notice, that when she swerved from her Duty, all her Knowlege was of no Use; but only rendered her more miserable, by letting her see her own Folly in the stronger Light. *Rozella* first tempted the Princess to Disobedience, by moving her Tenderness, and alarming her Friendship, in fearing to part with her; and then by persuading her to set up her own Wisdom, in Opposition to her Mother's Commands, rather than be laughed at, and despised, by her Friends. You are therefore to observe, that if you would steadily persevere in Virtue, you must have Resolution enough to stand the Sneers of those who would allure you to Vice; for it is the constant Practice of the Vicious, to endeavour to allure others to follow their Example, by an affected Contempt and Ridicule of Virtue.

By the Princess *Hebe*'s being drawn at last beyond the prescribed Bounds, by the Cries and Intreaties of that insidious Girl, you are to learn, that whatever Appearance of Virtue any Action may be attended with; yet, if it makes you go contrary to the Commands of those who know better what is for your Good, than you do yourselves, and who can see farther into the Consequences of Actions than can your tender Years, it will certainly lead you into Error and Misfortune; and you find, as soon as the Princess had once o'erleaped the Bounds, another plausible Excuse arose to carry her on; and by a false Fear of incurring her Mother's Displeasure, she really deserved that Displeasure, and was soon seduced into the Power of her Enemy.

The Princess, you see, could have no Happiness till she returned again to her Obedience, and had confessed her Fault. And tho' in this Story all this is brought about by Fairies; yet the Moral of it is, that whenever we give way to our Passions, and act contrary to our Duty, we must be miserable.

But let me once more observe to you, that these Fairies are intended only to amuse you; for remember that the Misery which attended the Princess *Hebe*, on her Disobedience, was the natural Consequence of that Disobedience; as well as the natural Consequence of her Amendment, and Return to her Duty, was Content and Happiness for the rest of her Life."

Here good Mrs. *Teachum* ceased; and Miss *Jenny*, in the Name of the Company, thanked her for her kind Instructions, and promised that they would endeavour, to the utmost of their Power, to imprint them on their Memory for the rest of their Lives.

SUNDAY

The Seventh Day

This Morning our little Society rose very early, and were all dressed with Neatness and Elegance, in order to go to Church. Mrs. *Teachum* put Miss *Polly Suckling* before her, and the rest followed, Two and Two, with perfect Regularity.

Mrs. *Teachum* expressed great Approbation, that her Scholars, at this solemn Place, shewed no sort of Childishness, notwithstanding their tender Age; but behaved with Decency and Devotion, suitable to the Occasion.

They went again in the same Order, and behaved again in the same Manner, in the Afternoon; and when they returned from Church, Two young Ladies, Lady *Caroline* and Lady *Fanny Delun*, who had formerly known Miss *Jenny Peace*, and who were at present in that Neighbourhood, with their Uncle, came to make her a Visit.

Lady *Caroline* was Fourteen Years of Age, tall and genteel in her Person, of a fair Complexion, and a regular Set of Features; so that, upon the Whole, she was generally complimented with being very handsome.

Lady *Fanny*, who was one Year younger than her Sister, was rather little of her Age, of a brown Complexion, her Features irregular; and, in short, she had not the least real Pretensions to Beauty.

It was but lately that their Father was, by the Death of his eldest Brother, become Earl of *Delun*; so that their Titles were new, and they had not been long used to *Your Ladyship*.

Miss *Jenny Peace* received them as her old Acquaintance: However, she paid them the Deference due to their Quality, and, at the same time, took care not to behave as if she imagined they thought of nothing else.

As it was her chief Delight to communicate her Pleasures to others, she introduced her new-made Friends to her old Acquaintance, and expected to have spent a very agreeable Afternoon. But to describe the Behaviour of these Two young Ladies, is very difficult. Lady *Caroline*, who was dressed in a Pink Robe, embroidered thick with Gold, and adorned with very fine Jewels, and the finest *Mechlin* Lace,[1] addressed most of her Discourse to her Sister, that she might have the Pleasure every Minute of uttering *Your Ladyship*, in order to shew what she herself expected. And as she spoke, her Fingers were in perpetual Motion, either adjusting her Tucker,[2] placing the Plaits of her Robe, or fiddling with a Diamond Cross, that hung down on her Bosom, her Eyes accompanying her Fingers as they moved, and then again suddenly snatched off, that she might not be observed to think of her own Dress; yet was it plain, that her Thoughts were employed only on that and her Titles. Miss *Jenny Peace*, altho' she would have made it her Choice always to be in such Company as did not deserve Ridicule; yet had she Humour enough to treat Affectation as it deserved. And she addressed herself to Lady *Caroline*, with so many Ladyships, and such Praises of her fine Cloaths, as she hoped would have made her ashamed; but Lady *Caroline* was too full of her own Vanity, to see her Design, and only exposed herself Ten times the more, till she really got the better of Miss *Jenny*, who blushed for her, since she was incapable of blushing for herself.

Lady *Fanny's* Dress was plain and neat only, nor did she mention any-thing about it; and it was very visible her Thoughts were otherwise employed; neither did she seem to take any Delight in the Words *Your Ladyship*; but she tossed and threw her Person about into so many ridiculous Postures, and, as there

---

[1] Lace originally produced at Mechelen (Mechlin), a town in Belgium (OED).

[2] A piece of lace or the like, worn by women within or around the top of the bodice in the seventeenth and eighteenth centuries; a frill of lace worn around the neck (OED).

happened unfortunately to be no Looking-glass in the Room where they sat, she turned and rolled her Eyes so many different Ways, in endeavouring to view as much of herself as possible, that it was very plain to the whole Company she thought herself a Beauty, and admired herself for being so.

Our little Society, whose Hearts were so open to each other, that they had not a Thought they endeavoured to conceal, were so filled with Contempt at Lady *Caroline* and Lady *Fanny's* Behaviour, and yet so strictly obliged, by good Manners, not to shew that Contempt, that the Reserve they were forced to put on, laid them under so great a Restraint, that they knew not which Way to turn themselves, or how to utter one Word; and great was their Joy when Lady *Caroline*, as the eldest, led the Way, and with a swimming Courtesy, her Head turned half round on one Shoulder, and a disdainful Eye, took her Leave, repeating Two or Three times the Word Misses, to put them in mind, that she was a Lady. She was followed by her Sister Lady *Fanny*, who made a slow distinct Courtesy to everyone in the Room, that she might be the longer under Observation. And then taking Miss *Jenny* by the Hand, said, "Indeed, Miss, you are very pretty," in order to put them in mind of her own Beauty.

Our little Society, as soon as they were released, retired to their Arbour, where, for some time, they could talk of nothing but this Visit. Miss *Jenny Peace* remarked how many Shapes Vanity would turn itself into, and desired them to observe, how ridiculously Lady *Caroline Delun* turned her whole Thoughts on her Dress, and Condition of Life; and how absurd it was in Lady *Fanny*, who was a very plain Girl, to set up for a Beauty, and to behave in a manner which would render her contemptible, even tho' she had that Beauty her own Vanity made her imagine herself possessed of.

Miss *Nanny Spruce* said, "She was greatly rejoiced that she had seen her Folly; for she could very well remember when she had the same Vanity of Dress and Superiority of Station with Lady *Caroline*, tho' she had not, indeed, a Title to support it; and in what manner (she said) she would tell them in the Story of her Life."

The Description *of Miss* Nanny Spruce

Miss *Nanny Spruce* was just Nine Years old, and was the very
Reverse of *Patty Lockit*, in all Things; for she had little Limbs, little
Features, and such a Compactness in her Form, that she was often
called the *Little Fairy.* She had the Misfortune to be lame in one
of her Hips; but by good Management, and a Briskness and
Alacrity in carrying herself, it was a very small Blemish to her,
and looked more like an idle childish Gait, than any real Defect.

The Life *of Miss* Nanny Spruce

My Delight, said Miss *Nanny Spruce*, ever since I can remember,
has been in Dress and Finery; for whenever I did as I was bid, I
was promised fine Coats, Ribbands, and laced Caps; and when I
was stubborn and naughty, then my fine Things were all to be
locked up, and I was to wear only an old Stuff Coat; so that I
thought the only Reward I could have, was, to be dressed fine;
and the only Punishment was, to be plainly dressed. By this means
I delighted so much in fine Cloaths, that I never thought of any-
thing but when I should have something new to adorn myself in;
and I have sat whole Days considering what should be my next
new Coat; for I had always my Choice given me of the Colour.

We lived in a Country Parish, my Papa being the only
Gentleman, so that all the little Girls in the Parish used to take
it as a great Honour to play with me. And I used to delight to
shew them my fine Things, and to see that they could not come
at any but very plain Coats. However, as they did not pretend to
have any-thing equal with me, I was kind enough to them. As
to those Girls whose Parents were so very poor, that they went
in Rags, I did not suffer them to come near me.

Whilst I was at Home, I spent my time very pleasantly, as no
one pretended to be my Equal: But as soon as I came to School,
where other Misses were as fine as myself, and some finer, I grew
very miserable. Every new Coat, every Silver Ribband, that any
of my Schoolfellows wore, made me unhappy. Your Scarlet
Damask, Miss *Betty Ford*, cost me a Week's Pain; and I lay awake,

and sighed and wept all Night, because I did not dare to spoil it. I had several Plots in my Head, to have dirted it, or cut it, so as to have made it unfit to wear; but by some Accident my Plots were prevented; and then I was so uneasy, I could not tell what to do with myself; and so afraid, lest any-body should suspect me of such a Thing, that I could not sleep in Peace, for fear I should dream of it, and in my Sleep discover it to my Bedfellow. I would not go through the same Dreads and Terrors again for the World. But I am very happy now, in having no Thoughts but what my Companions may know; for since that Quarrel, and Miss *Jenny Peace* was so good as to shew me what I'm sure I never thought of before, that is, that the Road to Happiness is by conquering such foolish Vanities, and the only Way to be pleased is to endeavour to please others, I have never known what it was to be uneasy.

As soon as Miss *Nanny* had finished speaking, Miss *Betty Ford* said, that she heartily forgave her all her former Designs upon her Scarlet Coat: But, added she, Lady *Fanny Delun* put me no less in mind of my former Life, than Lady *Caroline* did you of yours; and if Miss *Jenny* pleases, I will now relate it.

The Description *of Miss* Betty Ford

Miss Betty Ford was of the same Age with Miss *Nanny Spruce*, and much of the same Height, and might be called the plainest Girl in the School; for she had nothing pleasing either in her Person or Face, except an exceeding fair Skin, and tolerable good black Eyes; but her Face was ill-shaped and broad, her Hair very red, and all the Summer she was generally very full of Freckles; and she had also a small Hesitation in her Speech. But without Preamble, she began her Life as follows:

The Life *of Miss* Betty Ford

My Life, said Miss *Betty Ford*, has hitherto passed very like that
of Miss *Nanny Spruce*, only with this Difference, that as all her
Thoughts were fixed on Finery, my Head ran on nothing but
Beauty. I had an elder Sister, who was, I must own, a great deal
handsomer than I; and yet, in my own Mind, at that time, I did
not think so, though I was always told it was not for me to
pretend to the same Things with pretty *Miss Kitty* (which was
the Name of my Sister): And in all respects she was taken so
much more Notice of than I was, that I perfectly hated her, and
could not help wishing, that, by some Accident, her Beauty
might be spoiled: Whenever any Visitors came to the House,
their Praises of her gave me the greatest Vexation; and as I had
made myself believe I was a very great Beauty, I thought that it
was Prejudice and Ill-nature in all around me, not to view me in
that Light. My Sister *Kitty* was very good-natured; and tho' she
was thus cry'd up for her Beauty, and more indulged on that
account; yet she never insulted me, but did all in her Power to
oblige me. But I could not love her, and sometimes would raise
Lyes against her; which did not signify, for she could always
justify herself. I could not give any Reason for hating her, but
her Beauty; for she was very good; but the better she was, I
thought the worse I appeared. I could not bear her Praises, without teazing and vexing myself. At last, little *Kitty* died of a Fever,
to my great Joy; though, as every-body cry'd for her, I cry'd too
for Company, and because I would not be thought ill-natured.

After *Kitty*'s Death, I lived tolerably easy, till I came to School.
Then the same Desire of Beauty returned, and I hated all the
Misses who were handsomer than myself, as much as I had before
hated my Sister; and always took every Opportunity of quarrelling
with them, till I found my own Peace was concerned in getting
the better of this Disposition; and that if I would have any
Content, I must not repine at my not being so handsome as others.

When Miss *Betty Ford* ceased, Miss *Jenny* said, "Indeed, my Dear,
it is well you had not at that time the Power of the Eagle in the

Fable; for your poor Sister might then, like the Peacock, have said in a soft Voice, 'You are, indeed, a great Beauty; but it lies in your Beak and your Talons, which make it Death to me to dispute it.' "

Miss *Betty Ford* rejoiced, that her Power did not extend to enable her to do Mischief, before she had seen her Folly. And now this little Society, in good Humour and Chearfulness, attended their kind Governess's Summons to Supper; and then, after the Evening Prayers, they retired to their peaceful Slumbers.

MONDAY

The Eighth Day

Early in the Morning, after the public Prayers, which Mrs. *Teachum* read every Day, our little Company took a Walk in the Garden, whilst the Breakfast was preparing.

The fine Weather, the Prospects round them, all conspired to increase their Pleasure. They looked at one another with Delight; their Minds were innocent and satisfied; and therefore every outward Object was pleasing in their Sight.

Miss *Jenny Peace* said, "She was sure they were happier than any other Society of Children whatever, except where the same Harmony and Love were preserved, as were kept up in their Minds; For (continued she) I think now, my dear Companions, I can answer for you all, that no mischievous, no malicious Plots, disturb the Tranquillity of your Thoughts; Plots, which in the End constantly fall on the Heads of those who invent them, after all the Pains they cost them in forming, and endeavouring to execute."

Whilst Miss *Jenny Peace* was talking, Miss *Dolly Friendly* looked at her very earnestly. She would not interrupt her; but the Moment she was silent, Miss *Dolly* said, "My dear Miss *Jenny*, what is the Matter with you? Your Eyes are swelled, and you look as if you had been crying. If you have any Grief that you keep to yourself, you rob us of the Share we have a Right to demand in all that belongs to you."

"No, indeed (answered Miss *Jenny*), I have nothing that grieves me; tho', if I had, I should think it increased, rather than lessened, by your being grieved too: But last Night, after I went up Stairs, I found amongst my Books the Play of the *Funeral*, or, *Grief A-la-mode*;[1] where the faithful and tender Behaviour of a good old Servant, who had long lived in his Lord's Family, with many other Passages in the Play (which I cannot explain, unless you knew the whole Story) made me cry, so that I could hardly stop my Tears."

"Pray, Miss *Jenny*, let us hear this Play, that had such an Effect on you," was the general Request; and Miss *Jenny* readily promised, when they met in their Arbour, to read it to them.

They eagerly ran to their Arbour as soon as School was over; and Miss *Jenny* performed her Promise, and was greatly pleased to find such a Sympathy between her Companions and herself; for they were most of them affected just in the same manner, and with the same Parts of the Play as had before affected her.

By the time they had wiped their Eyes, and were rejoicing at the Turn at the End of the Play, in favour of the Characters with which they were most pleased, Mrs. *Teachum* entered the Arbour, and inquired what they had been reading. Miss *Jenny* immediately told her; adding, "I hope, Madam, you will not think reading a Play, an improper Amusement for us; for I should be very sorry to be guilty myself, or cause my Companions to be guilty, of any thing that would meet with your Disapprobation." Mrs. *Teachum* answered, that she was not at all displeased with her having read a Play, as she saw by her Fear of offending, that her Discretion was to be trusted to. "Nay (continued this good Woman) I like that you should know something of all kinds of Writings, where neither Morals nor Manners are offended; for if you read Plays, and consider them as you ought, you will neglect and despise what is light and useless, whilst you'll imprint on your Minds every useful Lesson that is to be drawn from them. I am very well acquainted with the Play you have been reading; but that I may see whether you give the proper Attention to what you have heard, I desire, my little Girls, that one of you will give me an Account of the chief Incidents in the Play, and tell me the Story, just as you would do to one of your Companions, that had happened to have been absent."

---

[1] A comedy by Sir Richard Steele (1672-1729), first printed in 1701 and reprinted throughout the eighteenth century. Steele was one of Fielding's favorite authors.

Here they all looked upon Miss *Jenny Peace*, as thinking her the most capable of doing what their Governess required. But Mrs. *Teachum*, reading their Thoughts in their Looks, said, "I exclude Miss *Jenny* in this Case; for, as the Play was of her own chusing, I doubt not but she is thoroughly enough acquainted with every Part of it; and my Design was, to try the Memory and Attention of some of the others."

They all remained silent, and seemed to wait for a more particular Command, before any one would offer at the Undertaking; not through any Backwardness to comply with Mrs. *Teachum's* Request, but each from a Diffidence of herself to perform it.

Miss *Jenny Peace* then said, that she had observed a great Attention in them all; and she did not doubt but every one was able to give a very good Account of what they had heard. "But as Miss *Sukey Jennet* is the eldest, I believe, Madam (continued she) if you approve it, they will all be very ready to depute her as their Speaker."

Each smiled at being so relieved by Miss *Jenny*; and Mrs. *Teachum*, taking Miss *Sukey Jennett* by the Hand, said, "Come, my Dear, throw off all Fear and Reserve; imagine me one of your Companions, and tell me the Story of the Play you have been reading."

Miss *Sukey*, thus encouraged by her kind Governess, without any Hesitation spoke in the following manner:

"If I understand your Commands, Madam, by telling the Story of the Play, you would not have me tell you the Acts and Scenes as they followed one another; for that I am afraid I can hardly remember, as I have heard it only once; but I must describe the chief People in the Play, and the Plots and Contrivances that are carried on amongst them."

Mrs. *Teachum* nodded her Head, and Miss *Sukey* thus proceeded:

"There is an old Lord *Brumpton*, who had married a young Wife that had lived with him some Years, and by her deceitful and cunning Ways had prevailed with him to disinherit his only Son Lord *Hardy* (who was a very sensible good young Man) and to leave him but a Shilling. And this Lord *Brumpton* was taken in a Fit, so that all the House thought he was dead; and his Lady sent for an Undertaker, one Mr. *Sable*, to bury him. But coming out of his Fit, when no-body but this Mr. *Sable*, and an old Servant, called

Trusty, were by, he was prevailed upon by the good old *Trusty* to feign himself still dead (and the Undertaker promises Secrecy) in order to detect the Wickedness of his Wife, which old *Trusty* assures him is very great; and then he carries his Lord where he overhears a Discourse between the Widow (as she thinks herself) and her Maid *Tattleaid*: And he hears his once beloved Wife rejoicing in his supposed Death, and in the Success of her own Arts to deceive him. Then there are Two young Ladies, Lady *Charlotte* and Lady *Harriot Lovely*, to whom this Lord *Brumpton* was Guardian; and he had left them also in the Care of this wicked Woman. And this young Lord *Hardy* was in Love with Lady *Charlotte*; and Mr. *Camply*, a very lively young Gentleman, his Friend, was in Love with Lady *Harriot*; and Lady *Brumpton* locked the Two young Ladies up, and would not let them be seen by their Lovers. But there at last they contrived, by the Help of old *Trusty*, who had their real Guardian's Consent for it, both to get away; and Lady *Harriot* married Mr. *Camply* directly; but Lady *Charlotte* did not get away so soon, and so was not married till the End of the Play. This Mr. *Camply* was a very generous Man, and was newly come to a large Fortune; and in the Beginning of the Play he contrives, in a very genteel manner, to give his Friend Lord *Hardy*, who very much wanted it, Three Hundred Pounds; but he takes care to let us know, that my Lord had formerly, when he wanted his Assistance, been very kind to him. And there at last, when Lady *Brumpton* finds out that the Two young Ladies are gone, she goes away in a Rage to Lord *Hardy*'s Lodgings; and in an insulting manner she pays all due Legacies, as she calls it; that is, she gives Lord *Hardy* the Shilling, which, by her wicked Arts, was all his Father had left him; and she was insulting the young Ladies, and glorying in her Wickedness, when honest old *Trusty* came in, and brought in old Lord *Brumpton*, whom they imagined to be dead; and all but Lady *Brumpton* were greatly overjoyed to see him alive; but when he taxed her with her Falshood, she defied him, and said that she had got a Deed of Gift under his Hand, which he could not revoke, and she *would* enjoy his Fortune in spite of him: Upon which they all looked sadly vexed, till the good old *Trusty* went out and came in again, and brought in a Man called *Cabinet*, who confessed himself the Husband to the pretended Lady *Brumpton*, and that he was married to her half a Year before she was married to my Lord *Brumpton*; but as my Lord happened to fall in Love with her, they agreed to keep their Marriage concealed, in order that she should marry my Lord, and cheat him in the manner she had done; and the Reason that *Cabinet* came to confess all this was, that he looked into a Closet, and saw my Lord writing, after he thought he was dead; and, taking it for his Ghost, was by that means frightened into this Confession, which he first made in Writing to *Old Trusty*, and therefore could not now deny it. They were all rejoiced at this Discovery, except the late pretended Lady *Brumpton*, who sneaked away with *Cabinet* her Husband; and my Lord *Brumpton* embraced his Son, and gave his Consent that he should marry Lady *Charlotte*; and they were all pleased and happy."

Here Miss *Sukey* ceased, and Mrs. *Teachum* told her, "She was a very good Girl, and had remembred a great deal of the Play, But (said she) in time, with using yourself to this Way of repeating what you have read, you will come to a better Manner, and a more regular Method, of telling your Story, which you was now so intent upon finishing, that you forgot to describe what sort of Women these two young Ladies were; tho', as to all the rest, you have been particular enough."

"Indeed, Madam (said Miss *Sukey*) I had forgot that; but Lady *Charlotte* was a very sensible, grave young Lady, and Lady *Harriot* was extremely gay and coquettish; but Mr. *Camply* tells her how much it misbecomes her to be so; and she having good Sense, as well as good Nature, is convinced of her Folly, and likes him so well for his Reproof, that she consents to marry him."

Mrs. *Teachum*, addressing herself to them all, told them, that this was a Method she wished they would take with whatever they read; for nothing so strongly imprinted any-thing on the Memory as such a Repetition: And then turning to Miss *Jenny Peace*, she said, "And now, Miss *Jenny*, I desire you will speak freely what you think is the chief Moral to be drawn from the Play you have just read."

Miss *Jenny* being thus suddenly asked a Question of this Nature, considered some time before she gave an Answer; for she was naturally very diffident of her own Opinion in any thing where she had not been before instructed by some one she thought wiser than herself. At last, with a modest Look, and an humble Voice, she said, "Since, Madam, you have commanded me to speak my Sentiments freely, I think by what happened to each Character in this Play, the Author intended to prove what my good Mamma first taught me, and what you, Madam, since have so strongly confirmed me in; namely, that Folly, Wickedness, and Misery, all Three, as constantly dwell together, as Wisdom, Virtue, and Happiness do."

"'Tis very true (answered Mrs. *Teachum*); but this Moral does not arise only from the happy Turn in the Conclusion of the Play, in favour of the virtuous Characters, but is strongly inculcated, as you see all along, in the Peace of Mind that attends the Virtuous, even in the midst of Oppression and Distress, while the Event is yet doubtful, and seemingly against them; and, on the contrary, in the Confusion of Mind which the Vicious are tormented with, even whilst they falsly imagine themselves triumphant."

Mrs. *Teachum* then taking the Book out of Miss *Jenny's* Hands, and turning to the Passage, said, "How does Lady *Brumpton* shew us the wretched Condition of her own Mind, when she says,

—'How miserable 'tis to have One one hates always about one! And when one can't endure one's own Reflections upon some Actions, who can bear the Thoughts of another upon them?'

Then with what Perturbation of Mind does she proceed, to wish it was in her Power to increase her Wickedness, without making use enough of her Understanding, to see that by that means she would but increase her own Misery!

On the other hand, what a noble Figure does Lord *Hardy* make, when, by this wicked Woman's Contrivances, he thinks himself disinherited of his whole Fortune, ill-treated and neglected by a Father he never had in Thought offended! He could give an Opportunity to a sincere Friend, who would not flatter him, to say,

'No; you are, my Lord, the extraordinary Man, who, on the Loss of an almost princely Fortune, can be Master of a Temper that makes you the Envy, rather than Pity, of your more fortunate, not more happy Friends.'

This is a fine Distinction between *Fortunate* and *Happy*; and intimates that Happiness must dwell in the Mind, and depends upon no outward Accidents.

Fortune, indeed, is a Blessing, if properly used; which *Camply* shews, when by that means he can assist and relieve his worthy Friend.

With what Advantage does Lady *Charlotte* appear over her Sister, when the latter is trifling and dancing before the Glass, and the former says,

'—If I am at first so silly as to be a little taken with myself, I know it is a Fault, and take Pains to correct it!'

And on Lady *Harriot's* saying, very giddily, that it was too soon for her to think at that rate, Lady *Charlotte* properly adds,

'They that think it too soon to understand themselves, will very soon find it too late.'

In how ridiculous a Light does Lady *Harriot* appear, while she is displaying all that foolish Coquetry! And how different a Figure does she make, when she has got the better of it!

My Lady *Brumpton*, when alarmed with the least Noise, breaks out into all the convulsive Starts natural to conscious Guilt.

'Ha! what Noise is that—that Noise of Fighting?—Run, I say—Whither are you going?—What, are you mad?—Will you leave me alone?—Can't you stir?—What, you can't take your Message with you!—Whatever 'tis, I suppose you are not in the Plot, not you—Nor that now they're breaking open my House for *Charlotte*, not you—Go see what's the Matter, I say; I have no-body I can trust—One Minute I think this Wench honest, and the next false—Whither shall I turn me?'

This is a Picture of the confused, the miserable Mind of a close, malicious, cruel, designing Woman, as Lady *Brumpton* was, and as Lady *Harriott* very properly calls her.

Honesty and Faithfulness shine forth in all their Lustre, in the good old *Trusty*. We follow him throughout with anxious Wishes for his Success, and Tears of Joy for his Tenderness. And when he finds that he is likely to come at the whole Truth, and to save his Lord from being deceived and betrayed into unjustly ruining his noble Son, you may remember that he makes this pious Reflection:

'*All that is ours, is to be justly bent;*
And Heav'n in its own time will bless th' Event.'

This is the natural Thought that proceeds from Innocence and Goodness; and surely this State of Mind is Happiness.

I have only pointed out a few Passages, to shew you, that though it is the Nature of Comedy to end happily, and therefore the good Characters must be successful in the last Act; yet the Moral lies deeper, and is to be deduced from a Proof throughout this Play, that the natural Consequence of Vice is Misery within, even in the midst of a seeming Triumph; and the natural Consequence of Goodness is a calm Peace of Mind, even in the midst of Oppression and Distress.

I have endeavoured, my little Dears, to shew you, as clearly as I can, not only what Moral is to be drawn from this Play, but what is to be sought for in all others; and where that Moral is not to be found, the Writer will have this to answer for, that he has been guilty of one of the worst of Evils; namely, That he has cloathed Vice in so beautiful a Dress, that, instead of deterring, it will allure and draw into its Snares the young and tender Mind. And I am sorry to say, that too many of our dramatic Performances are of this latter Cast; which is the Reason that wise and prudent Parents and Governors in general discourage in very young People the Reading of Plays. And tho' by what I have said (if it makes a proper Impression) I doubt not but you will all have a just Abhorrence of such immoral Plays, instead of being pleased with them, should they fall in your Way; yet I would advise you rather to avoid them, and never to read any but such as are approved of, and recommended to you, by those who have the Care of your Education."

Here good Mrs. *Teachum* ceased, and left her little Scholars to reflect on what she had been saying; when Miss *Jenny Peace* declared, for her Part, that she could feel the Truth of her Governess's Observations; for she had rather be the innocent Lord *Hardy*, though she was to have but that One Shilling in the World, which was so insolently offered him as his Father's Last Legacy, than be the Lady *Brumpton*, even tho' she had possessed the Fortune she so treacherously endeavoured to obtain.

"Nay (said Miss *Dolly Friendly*) I had rather have been old *Trusty*, with all the Infirmities of Age, following my Lord *Hardy* thro' the World, had his Poverty and Distress been ever so great, than have been the malicious Lady *Brumpton*, in the Height of her Beauty, surrounded by a Croud of Lovers and Flatterers."

Miss *Henny Frett* then declared, how glad she was, that she had now no Malice in her Mind; though she could not always have said so, as she would inform them in the History of her past Life.

The Description *of Miss* Henny Frett

Miss *Henny Frett* was turned of Nine Years old. She was very prettily made, and remarkably genteel. All her Features were regular. She was not very fair, and looked pale. Her upper Lip seemed rather shorter than it should be; for it was drawn up in such a manner, as to shew her upper Teeth; and tho' this was in some Degree natural; yet it had been very much increased by her being continually disturbed at every trifling Accident that offended her, or at every Contradiction that was offered to her. When you came to examine her Face, she had not one Feature but what was pretty; yet from that constant Uneasiness which appeared in her Countenance, it gave you so little Pleasure to look at her, that she seldom had common Justice done her, but had generally hitherto passed for a little insignificant plain Girl, tho' her very Face was so altered since she was grown good-natured, and had got the better of that foolish Fretfulness she used to be possessed of, that she appeared from her good-humoured Smiles quite a different Person; and, with a mild Aspect, she thus began her Story:

The Life *of Miss* Henny Frett

I had one Brother, said Miss *Henny*, as well as Miss *Jenny Peace*; but my Manner of living with him was quite the Reverse to that in which she lived with her Brother. All my Praise or Blame was to arise from my being better or worse than my Brother. If I was guilty of any Fault, it was immediately said, Oh! Fye, Miss! Master *George* (that was my Brother's Name) would not be guilty of such a thing for the World. If he was carried abroad, and I staid at home, then I was bemoaned over, that poor Miss *Henny* was left at home, and her Brother carried abroad. And then I was told, that I should go abroad one of these Days, and my Brother be left at home; so that whenever I went abroad, my greatest Joy was, that he was left at home; and I was pleased to see him come out to the Coach-door with a melancholy Air, that he could not go too. If my Brother happened to have any Fruit given him, and was in a peevish Humour, and would not give me as much as I desired, the Servant that attended me was sure to bid me take care, when I had any thing he wanted, not to give him any. So that I thought, if I did not endeavour to be revenged of him, I should shew a Want of Spirit, which was of all things what I dreaded most. I had a better Memory than my Brother, and whenever I learnt any-thing, my Comfort was to laugh at him, because he could not learn so fast; by which means I got a good deal of Learning, but never minded what I learnt, nor took any Pains to keep it; so that what I was eager to learn one Day, to shew *George* how much I knew more than he, I forgot the next. And so I went on learning, and forgetting as fast as I learnt; and all the Pains I took, served only to shew that I *could* learn.

I was so great a Favourite, that I was never denied any-thing I asked for; but I was very unhappy for the same Reason that Miss *Dolly Friendly's* Sister was so; and I have often sat down, and cry'd, because I did not know what I would have, till at last I own I grew so peevish and humoursome, that I was always on the Fret, and harboured in my Mind a kind of Malice, that made me fansy whatever my Brother got, I lost: And in this unhappy Condition I lived, till I came to School, and here I found that other Misses wanted to have their Humours as well as myself. This I could not bear; because I had been used to have my own Will, and never to trouble myself about what others felt. For whenever I beat or abused my Brother, his Pain did not make me cry: But I believe it was thinking wrong, made me guilty of these Faults; for I don't find I am ill-natured; for now I have been taught to consider that my Companions can feel as well as myself, I am sorry for their Pain, and glad when they are pleased, and would be glad to do any-thing to oblige them.

Here Miss *Henny* ceased, and Miss *Jenny Peace* then told her how glad she was to hear that she had subdued all Malice in her Mind; adding, "These Weeds, my Dear, unless early plucked up, are (as I have heard our good Governess observe upon a like Occasion) very apt to take such deep Root, as to choak every good Seed around them; and then who can tell whether, with the same Opportunities, they might not become Lady *Brumptons* before the End of their Lives?"

Little *Polly Suckling* remembered, that all the Company had told the History of their past Lives, except herself: and she was determined not to be left out; but yet the had a mind to be asked to tell it, hoping that her Companions thought her of Consequence enough not to leave her out of any Scheme: Therefore, addressing herself to Miss *Jenny*, she said, "She thought it was very pleasant to hear People tell the History of their own Lives." Miss *Jenny* saw her Meaning; and answer'd, "So it is, my little Dear; and now, if you please, you shall oblige us with relating the History of yours." *Polly* smiled at this Request, and said the was ready to comply.

The Description *of Miss* Polly Suckling

Miss *Polly Suckling* was just turned of Eight Years old, but so short of her Age, that few People took her to be above Five. It was not a dwarfish Shortness; for she had the most exact-proportioned Limbs in the World, very small Bones, and was as fat as a little Cherub. She was extremely fair, and her Hair quite flaxen. Her Eyes a perfect Blue, her Mouth small, and her Lips quite plump and red. She had the Freshness of a Milk-maid; and when she smiled and laughed, she seemed to shew an hundred agreeable Dimples. She was, in short, the very Picture of Health and Good-humour, and was the Play-thing and general Favourite of the whole School.

The Life *of Miss* Polly Suckling

Now, said little *Polly*, I will tell you my whole History. I hardly remember any-thing before I came to School; for I was but Five Years old when I was brought hither.

All I know is, that I don't love quarrelling; for I like better to live in Peace and Quietness. But I have been always less than any of my Companions, ever since I have been here; and so I only followed the Example of the rest; and as I found they contended about every thing, I did so too. Besides, I have been always in fear, that my Schoolfellows wanted to impose on me, because I was little; and so I used to engage in every Quarrel, rather than be left out, as if I was too little to give any Assistance; but, indeed, I am very glad now we all agree, because I always came by the worst of it. And besides, it is a great Pleasure to me to be loved, and every Miss is kind and good to me, and ready to assist me whenever I ask her. And this is all know of my whole Life.

When little *Polly* ceased, she was kissed and applauded by the whole Company, for the agreeable Simplicity of her little History.

And thus ended the Eighth Day's Amusement.

TUESDAY

The Ninth Day

Miss *Jenny* rose early in the Morning, and, having collected the Lives of her Companions (which she had wrote down each Day, as they related them), she carried them, after Morning School, according to her Promise, to her Governess.

Mrs. *Teachum*, when she had perused them, was much pleased; and said, that she perceived, by the manner in which her Scholars had related their Lives; how much they were in Earnest in their Design of Amendment. "For (continued she) they have all confessed their Faults without Reserve; and the untowardly Bent of their Minds, which so strongly appeared before the Quarrel, has not broke out in these their little Histories; but, on the contrary, they all seem, according to their Capacities, to have endeavoured to imitate your Stile, in the Account you gave of your own Life. I would have you continue to employ your leisure Hours in the manner you have lately done, only setting apart a proper Time for Exercise; and To-day I will dispense with your Attendance in the School-Room and indulge you this Afternoon in another Walk, either to the Dairy-House, or to the Cherry-Garden, which-ever you all agree on. But as I shall not go with you myself, and shall only send a Servant to take care of you, I hope to hear from you, Miss *Jenny*, so good an Account of the Behaviour of your little Friends and Companions, that I shall have no Cause to repent my Indulgence."

Miss *Jenny Peace* respectfully took Leave of her Governess, and hastened to the Arbour, where her little Friends were met, in Expectation of her Coming. She told them how well pleased their Governess was with them all, for the ingenuous Confession of their Faults in their past Lives; and she then declared Mrs. *Teachum's* kind Permission to them to take another Walk that Afternoon.

As no one had at present any Story to read or relate, they employed their Time till Dinner, some in walking and running about the Garden; others, in looking after, and tending some Plant or Flower, that they had taken particularly under their Care, which Mrs. *Teachum* both permitted and encouraged them in; whilst Miss *Jenny Peace*, Miss *Sukey Jennett* and Miss *Dolly Friendly*, remained in the Arbour, the two latter asking a thousand Questions of the former, both concerning all the Instructions the had ever learned from her Mamma, and by what means they should best be able to preserve that Friendship and Happiness, which had of late subsisted amongst them; saying, how pleased their Friends and Relations would be, to see such a Change in their Temper and Behaviour, and how much they should be beloved by every one.

When they met at Dinner, Mrs. *Teachum* asked them, whether they had determined upon the Choice she had given them in their Afternoon's Walk; and they were all desirous of going to the Dairy-House; for little *Polly* said, "She longed to see the good-humoured old Woman again: And indeed, she would not now say any thing to her of her shaking Head, or her grey Hair." Mrs. *Teachum* was pleased, that little *Polly* so gratefully remembered the old Woman, who had been so kind to her; and readily consented to their Choice, and approved of their Determination.

Being soon equipped for their Walk, they set out, attended by Two Maid Servants; and as soon as they arrived, the good old Woman expressed the highest Joy on seeing them, and told little *Polly*, that she should have Plenty of Cream and Strawberries; for her Daughter had been that Day in the Wood, and had brought home Three Baskets of very fine ones. Mrs. *Nelly*, her Daughter, said very crossly, that she supposed there would be fine Work amongst them, now their Governess was not with them; but 'twas her Mother's Way, to let all Children be as rude as they pleased. Miss *Sukey Jennett*, with some Indignation in her Look, was going to answer her; but Miss *Jenny Peace*, fearing she would say something less mild than she wished, gave her a Nod; and, turning to the young Woman, with great Modesty and Temper, thus said: "You shall see, Mrs. *Nelly*, that our good Governess's Instructions are of more Force with us, than to lose all their Effect when we are out of her Presence; and I hope you will have no Cause, when we go away, to complain of the ill Behaviour of any of us."

The good old Woman declared, "She never saw such sweet-tempered Children in all her Life;" and after they had eat their Strawberries and Cream, and were loaded with Pinks and Roses by the good Woman's Bounty (for they did not gather one without her Permission), they took their Leave with the utmost Civility, and Miss *Jenny* handsomely rewarded the old Woman for her good Chear. Mrs. *Nelly* herself was so pleased with their regular and inoffensive Behaviour, that she could not help telling Miss *Jenny*, that she, and all her Companions, had, indeed, behaved as well as if their Governess had been with them: On which Miss *Jenny* (as they were walking home) observed to Miss *Sukey Jennett* (whom she had prevented from making any Reply to Mrs. *Nelly's* Speech) how much better it was to gain another's good Will by our own Endeavours to be obliging, than to provoke them to be more cross, by our angry Answers and Reproaches.

When this little Company, employed in pleasing Talk, and lively Observations, were come within about a Mile of Mrs. *Teachum's* House, and within View of a Nobleman's fine Seat, Miss *Jenny* said, that the next time their Governess permitted them to walk out, she would ask her Leave, that they might go and see that fine House; for some time ago she had told them, that they should go thither when the Family were absent. Mrs. *Wilson*, the Housekeeper, who by chance was walking that way, and heard what Miss *Jenny* said, came up to them, and told Miss *Jenny*, that her Lord and Lady were now both absent, having set out, one for *London*, and the other for another fine Seat, Forty Miles off, that very Morning; and as she knew them to be Mrs. *Teachum's* well-regulated Family, they should be welcome to see the House and Gardens now, if they liked it. Miss *Jenny* thanked her, and said, As it was near Two Hours sooner than their Governess expected them home, she would accept of her kind Offer. The Housekeeper led them through an Avenue of tall Elm-trees, into this magnificent House, in which were many spacious Apartments, furnished with the utmost Grandeur and Elegance. Some of the Rooms were adorned with fine Pictures, others were hung with Tapestry almost as lovely as those Paintings, and most of the Apartments above Stairs were furnished with the finest Sorts of Needlework. Our little Company were struck into a sort of silent Wonder and Admiration at the splendid Appearance of every thing around them; nor could they find Words to express the various Reflections that passed in their Minds, on seeing such a Variety of dazling gaudy Things: But when they came to the Needle-work, Miss *Jenny* could not help smiling, to see how every one seemed most fixed in Attention upon that sort of Work, which she herself was employed in; and she saw in the Faces of all a secret Wish, that their own Piece of Work might be finished with equal Neatness and Perfection. The Housekeeper was greatly pleased to see them so much delighted, and answered all their Questions concerning the Stories that were represented in the Pictures and Tapestry, as fully as the Time would permit: But Miss *Jenny*, being fearful of exceeding the Hour in which they would be expected home, told them they must not now stay any longer; but if their Governess would give them Leave, and it would not be trouble-some to Mrs. *Wilson* they would come another time. She answered, that it was so far from being troublesome, that she never had more Pleasure in her Life, than to see so many well-behaved young Ladies, who all seemed not only pleased with what they saw, but doubly delighted, and happy, in seeing each other so; and for her

Part, she could wish they were to stay with her all their Lives: And, in short, they should not go till they had been in her Room, and eat some Sweetmeats of her own making. The good Woman seemed to take so much Delight in giving them any Pleasure, that Miss *Jenny* could not refuse accepting her Offer; and when they were all in her Room, *Polly Suckling* said, "Well, this is a most charming House: I wish we could all live here for ever. How happy must the Lord and Lady of this fine Place be!"

"Indeed, my little *Polly*, said Miss *Jenny*, you may be very much mistaken; for you know our good Governess has taught us, that there is no Happiness but in the Content of our own Minds; and perhaps we may have more Pleasure in viewing these fine Things, than the Owners have in the Possession of them."

"It is very true (said the Housekeeper); for my Lord and Lady have no Delight in all this Magnificence; for, by being so accustomed to it, they walk through all these Apartments, and never so much as observe, or amuse themselves with the Work, the Pictures, or any thing else; or if they observe them at all, it is rather with a Look that denotes a sort of Weariness, at seeing the same Things continually before them, than with any kind of Pleasure." And then, with a deep Sigh, she added, "You are indeed, young Lady, perfectly in the right, when you say, Grandeur and Happiness do not always go together." But turning off the Discourse, Mrs. *Wilson* forced them to take as many dried Sweetmeats as they could carry away with them, and insisted upon their Promise (with Mrs. *Teachum's* Consent) that they should come another time to see the Gardens. They then took their Leave with many Thanks, and the greatest Civility; and discoursed, all the way home, on the fine Things they had seen. Miss *Betty Ford* said, that the fine Gilding, and so many glittering Looking-glasses, made her think herself in *Barbarico's* great Hall, where he kept all his Treasure.

"No (says Miss *Nancy Spruce*) it was not half so much like that, as it was little *Brunetta's* fine Castle; and I could not help thinking myself the Princess *Hebe*, and how much I should have been pleased with such a fine Place at first, just as she was."

"Indeed, says Miss *Betty Ford*, you are in the right of it, Miss *Nanny*; for 'twas much more like the Description of *Brunetta's* Castle, than what I said myself."

Miss *Jenny* was pleased to hear Miss *Betty* so ready to own herself mistaken; and said to Miss *Nanny Spruce*, "I am glad, my Dear, to find that you so well remember what you read; for it is by recalling frequently into our Memories the Things we have read, that they are likely to be of any Service to us."

Being now come home, they entered into the Presence of their Governess with that Pleasure, and proper Confidence, which ever attends Innocence and Goodness; and Mrs. *Teachum* received them with a pleasing Smile.

Miss *Jenny* gave her Governess a faithful Account of all that had passed, with the agreeable Entertainment they had accidentally met with, of seeing Lord *X*—'s fine House, and the great Civility of Mrs. *Wilson*; "which I hope, Madam (said Miss *Jenny*), I did not do wrong in accepting." "You did very properly, my Dear (said Mrs. *Teachum*); for when People are willing to oblige you, without any Inconvenience to themselves, it is always right to accept their Offer, as you thereby gratify them, by putting it in their Power to give you Pleasure."

Miss *Jenny* then, with great Chearfulness and Freedom, told her Governess all that had passed in Conversation, both in their Walk to the Dairy-House, and at Lord *X*—'s, what little *Polly* had said in the Housekeeper's Room, as also Mrs. *Wilson*'s Answer; and said, by Mrs. *Wilson*'s downcast Look, she was afraid that poor Lord *X*— and his Lady were not so happy as might be wished. "But (continued she) I did not ask Mrs. *Wilson* any Questions; because you have taught me, Madam, carefully to avoid the least Appearance of impertinent Curiosity."

"You was very right, my Dear (said Mrs. *Teachum*), in asking no farther Questions; nor would she, I dare say, as she is a prudent Woman, have gratified you, if you had; for tho' the unhappy Story is too well known all over the Country; yet it would have been very unbecoming in one of the Family to have published it." Mrs. *Teachum* saw in her little Scholars Eyes, a secret Wish of knowing what this Story was; and, after a short Pause, she said, "Since I find you disposed, my good Girls, to make the proper Use of what you hear, I will indulge your Curiosity.

Lord *X*— and his Lady have been married Seven Years: Lord *X*— is the wretchedest Creature breathing, because he has no

Children, and therefore no Heir to his Title, and large Estate. He was naturally of a haughty impetuous Temper, and impatient of any the least Disappointment; and this Disposition not being subdued in his Youth, has led him into all sort of Excesses. His Lady is not much better tempered than himself, and valuing herself highly upon her Beauty, and the large Fortune she brought him, greatly resents his sometimes insolent, and always neglectful Usage of her. They have hitherto lived on in the most jarring disputing manner, never minding to conceal their Quarrels from the World; but at last they have agreed to part by Consent, and the different Journeys they this Morning took, were taken, I suppose, with an Intent of a final Separation.

That Grandeur and Happiness do not always go together (as Mrs. *Wilson* observed to you) is seen by this Story; which I was the more willing to tell you, as it was a proper Introduction to a Fable I have been collecting together from others, for your Use. You know that all my Endeavours to make you good, are only intended to make you happy; and if you thoroughly reflect upon the Truth of this Maxim, which I so often endeavour to inculcate, you will doubtless reap no small Advantage from it."

Here Mrs. *Teachum* ceased speaking, and, giving Miss *Jenny Peace* a Paper, she bid her read it aloud; which she did; and it contained the following Fable.

The Assembly *of the* Birds
A Fable

In antient Days there was a great Contention amongst the Birds, which, from his own Perfections, and peculiar Advantages, had the strongest Title to Happiness; and at last they agreed to refer the Decision of the Debate to the Eagle.

A Day was appointed for their Meeting; the *Eagle* took his Seat, and the Birds all attended to give in their several Pleas.

First spoke the *Parrot*. Her Voice so nearly resembling human Speech, which enabled her to converse with such a superior Race, she doubted not (she said) would have its just Weight with the *Eagle*, and engage him to grant a Decree in her Favour; and to this Plea she also added, that she dwelt in a fine Cage adorned with Gold, and was fed every Day by the Hands of a fair Lady. And pray, Mrs. *Poll*, said the *Eagle*, how comes it, since you fare so sumptuously, that you are so lean and meagre, and seem scarcely able to exert that Voice, you thus make your Boast of? "Alas! (replied the *Parrot*) poor *Poll's* Lady has kept her Bed almost this Week; the Servants have all forgot to feed me; and I am almost starved." "Pray observe (said the *Eagle*) the Folly of such Pride! Had you been able to have conversed only with your own Kind, you would have fared in common with them; but it is to this vaunted Imitation of the human Voice, that you owe your Confinement, and consequently (though living in a Golden Cage) your Dependence upon the Will and Memory of others, even for common necessary Food." Thus reproved, the *Parrot*, with Shame, hastily retired from the Assembly.

Next stood forth the *Daw*, and, having tricked himself in all the gay Feathers he could muster together, on the Credit of these borrowed Ornaments, pleaded his Beauty, as a Title to the Preference in Dispute. Immediately the Birds agreed to divest the silly Counterfeit of all his borrowed Plumes; and, more abashed than the *Parrot*, he secretly slunk away.

The *Peacock*, proud of native Beauty, now flew into the midst of the Assembly. He displayed before the Sun his gorgeous Tail. "Observe (said he) how the vivid Blue of the Sapphire glitters in my Neck; and when thus I spread my Tail, a gemmy Brightness strikes the Eye from a Plumage varied with a thousand glowing Colours." At this Moment, a *Nightingale* began to chant forth his melodious Lay; at which the *Peacock*, dropping his expanded Tail, cried out, "Ah! what avails my silent unmeaning Beauty, when I am so far excelled in Voice by such a little Russet-feathered Wretch as that!" And, by retiring, he gave up all Claim to the contended-for Preference.

The *Nightingale* was so delighted with having got the better of the *Peacock*, that he exerted his little Voice; and was so lost in the Conceit of his own Melody, that he did not observe a *Hawk*, who flew upon him, and carried him off in his Claws.

The *Eagle* then declared, "That as the *Peacock's* Envy had taken away all his Claim, so no less had the *Nightingale's* Self-conceit frustrated all his Pretensions; for those who are so wrapped up in their own Perfections, as to mind nothing but themselves, are for ever liable to all sorts of Accidents." And, besides, it was plain, by the Exultation the *Nightingale* expressed on his imagined Victory over the *Peacock*, that he would have been equally dejected on any Preference given to another.

And now the *Owl*, with an affected Gravity, and whooting Voice, pleaded his well-known Wisdom; and said, "He doubted not but the Preference would be granted to him without Contest, by all the whole Assembly; for what was so likely to produce Happiness as Wisdom?" The *Eagle* declared, "That, if his Title to Wisdom could be proved, the Justice of his Claim should be allowed; and then asked him, how he could convince them of the Truth of what he had advanced?" The *Owl* answered, "That he would willingly appeal to the whole Assembly for their Decision in this Point; for he was positive no-body could deny his great Superiority as to Wisdom." Being separately asked, they most of them declared, that they knew no one Reason, either from his Words or Actions, to pronounce him a wise Bird; though it was true, that by an affected Solemnity in his Looks, and by frequent Declarations of his own, that he was very wise, he had made some very silly Birds give him that Character; but, since they were called upon to declare their Opinions, they must say, that he was ever the Object of Contempt to all those Birds who had any Title to common Understanding. The *Eagle* then said, "He could by no means admit a Plea, which as plainly appeared to be counterfeit, as were the *Jay's* borrowed Feathers." The *Owl*, thus disappointed, flew away, and has ever since shunned the Light of the Sun, and has never appeared in the Day-time, but to be scorned and wondered at.

It would be endless to repeat all the several Pleas brought by the Birds, each desiring to prove, that Happiness ought to be his own peculiar Lot. But the *Eagle*, observing that the Arguments made use of to prove their Point, were chiefly drawn from the Disadvantages of others, rather than from any Advantage of their own, told them, "There was too much Envy and Malice amongst them, for him to pronounce any of them deserving or capable of being happy; but I wonder, says he, Why the *Dove* alone is absent from this Meeting?" "I know of one in her Nest, hard by (answered the *Red-breast*): Shall I go and call her?" "No (says the *Eagle*); Since she did not obey our general Summons, 'tis plain she had no Ambition for a public Preference; but I will take Two or Three chosen Friends, and we will go softly to her Nest, and see in what manner she is employing herself; for from our own Observations upon the Actions of any one, we are more likely to form a Judgment of them, than by any Boasts they can make."

The *Eagle* was obeyed; and, accompanied only by the *Linnet*, the *Lark*, the *Lapwing*, and the *Red-breast* for his Guide, he stole gently to the Place where the *Dove* was found hovering over her Nest, waiting the Return of her absent Mate; and, thinking herself quite unobserved,

"[1] *While o'er her callow Brood she hung,*
She fondly thus address'd her Young:
Ye tender Objects of my Care,
Peace! Peace! ye little helpless Pair.
Anon! he comes, your gentle Sire,
And brings you all your Hearts require;
For Us, his Infants and his Bride,
For us with only Love to guide,
Our Lord assumes an Eagle's Speed;
And, like a Lion, dares to bleed:
Nor yet by wintry Skies confin'd,
He mounts upon the rudest Wind,
From Danger tears the vital Spoil,
And with Affection sweetens Toil.
Ah! Cease, too vent'rous, cease to dare;
In thine, our dearer Safety spare.
From him, ye cruel Falcons, stray;
And turn, ye Fowlers, far away.
—All-giving Pow'r, great Source of Life,
Oh! hear the Parent, hear the Wife:
That Life thou lendest from above,

---

[1] Author's footnote: These Verses are a Quotation from that tender Fable of the Sparrow and the Dove in the Fables for the *Female Sex*. [Ed.: *Fables for the Female Sex* (1744) was written by Edward Moore and Henry Brooke. A third edition of this popular work appeared in 1749, the year *The Governess* was published.]

Tho' little, make it large in Love.
Oh! bid my feeling Heart expand,
To ev'ry Claim on ev'ry Hand,
To those, from whom my Days I drew,
To these, in whom those Days renew,
To all my Kin, however wide,
In cordial Warmth as Blood ally'd,
To Friends in steely Fetters twin'd,
And to the cruel not unkind;
But chief the Lord of my Desire,
My Life, myself, my Soul, my Sire,
Friends, Children, all that Wish can claim,
Chaste Passion clasp, and Rapture name.
Oh! spare him, spare him, gracious Pow'r:
Oh! give him to my latest Hour.
Let me my Length of Life employ,
To give my sole Enjoyment Joy.
His Love let mutual Love excite;
Turn all my Cares to his Delight,
And ev'ry needless Blessing spare,
Wherein my Darling wants a Share,
—Let one unruffled calm Delight,
The Loving and Belov'd unite;
One pure Desire our Bosoms warm;
One Will direct, one Wish inform:
Thro' Life one mutual Aid sustain;
In Death one peaceful Grave contain.
While, swelling with the darling Theme,
Her Accents pour'd an endless Stream,
The well-known Wings a Sound impart,
That reach'd her Ear, and touch'd her Heart.
Quick dropp'd the Music of her Tongue,
And forth, with eager Joy she sprung.
As swift her ent'ring Consort flew,
And plum'd, and kindled, at the View.
Their Wings, their Souls embracing meet;
Their Hearts with answ'ring Measure beat;
Half lost in sacred Sweets, and bless'd

With Raptures felt, but ne'er express'd,
    Strait to her humble Roof she led
The Partner of her spotless Bed;
Her Young, a flutt'ring Pair, arise,
Their Welcome sparkling in their Eyes,
Transported, to their Sire they bound,
And hang, with speechless Action, round.
In Pleasure wrapt, the Parents stand,
And see their little Wings expand;
The Sire his Life-sustaining Prize,
To each expecting Bill applies;
There fondly pours the Wheaten Spoil,
With Transport giv'n, tho' won with T'oil;
While all, collected at the Sight,
And silent, thro' supreme Delight,
The Fair high Heav'n of Bliss beguiles,
And on her Lord and Infants smiles."

The *Eagle* now, without any Hesitation, pronounced the *Dove* to be deservedly the happiest of the feathered kind; and however unwilling the rest of the Birds were to assent to the Judgment given, yet could they not dispute the Justice of the Decree.

Here Miss *Jenny* ceased reading, and all the little Company expressed by their Looks, that they were overjoyed at the *Eagle's* Determination; for they had all in their own Minds forestalled the *Eagle's* Judgment, of giving the Preference to the *Dove*. "Now, my good Children (said Mrs. *Teachum*), if you will pass thro' this Life with real Pleasure, imitate the *Dove*; and remember, that Innocence of Mind, and Integrity of Heart, adorn the Female Character; and can alone produce your own Happiness, and diffuse it to all around you."

Our little Company thanked their Governess for her Fable; and, just at that Instant, they heard a Chariot drive into the Court, and Mrs. *Teachum* went out to see what Visitor could be arrived so late in the Evening; for it was near Eight o'Clock.

They all remained in the Room where their Governess left

them; for they had been taught never to run out to the Door, or to the Windows, to look at any Strangers that came, till they knew whether it was proper for them to see them or not.

Mrs. *Teachum* soon returned with a Letter open in her Hand, and remained some little time silent; but cast on every one round such a tender and affectionate Look, a Tear almost starting from her Eye, that the sympathizing Sorrow seemed to spread through the whole Company, and they were all silent, and ready to cry, tho' they knew not for what Reason. "I am sorry, my little Dears (said Mrs. *Teachum*), to give your tender Bosoms the Uneasiness I fear the Contents of this Letter will do, as it will deprive you of that your Hearts so justly hold most dear." And, so saying, she delivered to Miss *Jenny Peace* the following Letter:

To Miss Jenny Peace.

My dear Niece,   *Monday Night, June* 24.
I Arrived safe at my own House, with your Cousin Harriot, *last* Saturday *Night, after a very tedious Voyage by Sea, and fatiguing Journey by Land. I long to see my dear* Jenny *as soon as possible, and* Harriot *is quite impatient for that Pleasure.*

I have ordered my Chariot to be with you To-morrow *Night; and I desire you would set out on* Wednesday *Morning, as early as your Inclination shall prompt you to come to*
Your truly affectionate Aunt,
M. Newman.
I have writ a Letter of thanks to your kind Governess, for her Care of you.

It is impossible to describe the various Sensations of Miss *Jenny's* Mind, on the reading this Letter. Her rising Joy at the Thoughts of seeing her kind Aunt safely returned from a long and tedious Voyage, was suppressed by a Sorrow which could not be resisted, on parting with such dear Friends, and so good a Governess; and the Lustre which such a Joy would have given to her Eye, was damped by rising Tears. Her Heart for some time was too full for Utterance. At last, turning to her Governess, she said; "And is the Chariot really come, to carry me to my dear Aunt?" Then, after a Pause, the Tears trickling down her Cheeks, "And must I so soon leave you, Madam, and all my kind Companions?" Mrs. *Teachum*, on seeing Miss *Jenny's* tender Struggles of Mind, and all her Companions at once bursting into Tears, stood up, and left the Room, saying, "She would come to them again after Supper." For this prudent Woman well knew, that it was in vain to contend with the very first Emotions of Grief on such an Occasion; but intended, at her Return, to shew them how much it was their Duty and Interest to conquer all sorts of extravagant Sorrow.

They remained some time silent, as quite struck dumb with Concern, till at last Miss *Dolly Friendly*, in broken Accents, cry'd out, "And must we lose you, my dear Miss *Jenny*, now we are just settled in that Love and Esteem for you, which your Goodness so well deserves?"

Miss *Jenny* endeavoured to dry up her Tears, and then said, "Altho' I cannot but be pleased, my dear Companions, at every Mark of your Affection for me; yet I beg that you would not give me the Pain to see that I make so many dear Friends unhappy. Let us submit chearfully to this Separation (which, believe me, is as deeply felt by me as any of you), because it is our Duty so to do: And let me intreat you to be comforted, by reflecting, how much my good Aunt's safe Return must be conducive to my future Welfare; nor can you be unhappy, while you continue with so good a Governess, and persist in that Readiness to obey her, which you have lately shewn. She will direct who shall preside over your innocent Amusements in my Place. I will certainly write to you, and shall always take the greatest Delight in hearing from each of you, both while you continue here, and when your Duty and different Connexions shall call you elsewhere. We may some, and perhaps all, of us, happen often to meet again; and I hope a Friendship, founded on so innocent and so good a Foundation as ours is, will always subsist, as far as shall be consistent with our future Situations in Life."

Miss *Jenny's* Friends could not answer her but by Sobs and Tears; only little *Polly Suckling*, running to her, clung about her Neck, and cry'd, "Indeed, indeed, Miss *Jenny*, you must not go; I shall break my Heart, if I lose you: I'm sure we shan't, nor we can't, be half so happy, when you are gone, tho' our Governess was Ten times better to us than she is."

Miss *Jenny* again intreated them to dry up their Tears, and to be more contented with the present Necessity; and, begged, that they would not let their Governess see them at her Return so overwhelmed in Sorrow; for she might take it unkindly, that they should be so afflicted at the Loss of one Person, while they still remained under her indulgent Care and Protection.

It was with the utmost Difficulty, that Miss *Jenny* refrained from shedding Tear for Tear with her kind Companions; but as it was her constant Maxim to partake with her Friends all her Pleasure, and to confine her Sorrows as much as possible within her own Bosom, she chose rather to endeavour, by her own Chearfulness, and innocent Talk, to steal insensibly from the Bosoms of her little Companions half their Sorrow; and they began to appear tolerably easy.

After Supper, Mrs. *Teachum* returned; and, seeing them all striving who should most conceal their Grief, for fear of giving Uneasiness to the rest: yet with a deep Dejection fixed in every Countenance, and little *Polly* still sobbing behind Miss *Jenny's* Chair, she was so moved herself with the affecting Scene, that the Tears stole from her Eyes; and the sympathizing Company once more eased their almost bursting Hearts, by another general Flow of melting Sorrow.

"My dear Children (said Mrs. *Teachum*), I am not at all surprised at your being so much concerned to part with Miss *Jenny*. I love her myself with a motherly Affection (as I do all of you, and shall ever continue to do so while you so well deserve it); and I could wish, for my own sake, never to part with her as long as I live; but I consider, that it is for her Advantage; and I would have you all remember, in her Absence, to let her Example and Friendship fill your Hearts with Joy, instead of Grief. It is now pretty late in the Evening, and as Miss *Jenny* is to set out very early in the Morning, I must insist upon shortening your Pain (for such is your present Situation); and desire you would take your Leave of this your engaging Friend."

They none of them attempted to speak another Word; for their Hearts were still too full for Utterance: And Miss *Jenny* took everyone by the Hand as they went out of the Room, saluted them with the tenderest Affection, mingling Tears with those which flowed from every streaming Eye; and, wishing them all Happiness and Joy till their next Meeting, they all, with heavy Hearts, retired to Rest.

Miss *Jenny* returned the warmest and most grateful Acknowlegements to her good Governess, for all her Care of her; and said, "I shall attribute every happy Hour, Madam, that I may hereafter be blessed with, to your wise and kind Instructions, which I shall always remember with the highest Veneration, and shall ever consider you as having been to me no less than a fond and indulgent Mother."

Mrs. *Teachum* kept Miss *Jenny* in the Room with her no longer than to assure her how sincerely she should regret her Absence; and confessed how much of the Regularity and Harmony of her School she owed to her good Example, her Sweetness of Temper, and Conformity to Rules.

The End of the Ninth Day.

The Conclusion

Altho' Miss *Jenny Peace* did not return any more to School; yet she ever gratefully remembred the Kindness of her Governess, and frequently corresponded with all her Companions. And as they continued their innocent Amusements and Meetings in the Arbour, whenever the Weather would permit, there was no Day thought to be better employed, than that in which they received a Letter from their absent instructive Friend, whose Name was always mentioned with Gratitude and Honour.

Mrs. *Teachum* continued the same watchful Care over any young Persons who were intrusted to her Management; and she never increased the Number of her Scholars, tho' often intreated so to do. All Quarrels and Contentions were banished her House; and if ever any such Thing was likely to arise, the Story of Miss *Jenny Peace's* reconciling all her little Companions was told to them; so that Miss *Jenny*, tho' absent, still seemed (by the bright Example which she left behind her) to be the Cement of Union and Harmony in this well-regulated Society. And if any Girl was found to harbour in her Breast a rising Passion, which it was difficult to conquer, the Name and Story of Miss *Jenny Peace* soon gained her Attention, and left her without any other Desire than to emulate Miss *Jenny's* Virtues. In short, Mrs. *Teachum's* School was always mentioned throughout the Country, as an Example of Peace and Harmony: And also by the daily Improvement of all her Girls, it plainly appeared, how early young People might attain great Knowlege, if their Minds were free from foolish Anxieties about Trifles, and properly employed on their own Improvement; for never did any young Lady leave Mrs. *Teachum,* but that her Parents and Friends were greatly delighted with her Behaviour, as she had made it her chief Study to learn always to pay to her Governors the most exact Obedience, and to exert towards her Companions all the good Effects of a Mind filled with Benevolence and Love.

FINIS.

Appendix A: Sarah Trimmer's Review of The Governess in The Guardian of Education (June 1802)

[Sarah Trimmer (1741–1810) was an educational writer and reviewer whose teaching philosophy grew out of her own experiences educating her children (she had twelve children, nine of whom survived her). Trimmer was active in the Sunday School movement of the late eighteenth and early nineteenth centuries, and her book *The Economy of Charity* was influential in promoting the establishment of Sunday Schools for poor children. Her most famous children's work was *Fabulous Histories* (1786), an excerpt of which can be found in Appendix D. *The Guardian of Education* was a periodical that Trimmer produced from 1802 to 1806, which was specifically addressed to governesses and parents. It has been read as the earliest attempt to survey the history of children's literature and to systematically review contemporary children's books.]

ART.VII.—*The Governess; or, the Little Female Academy. Calculated for the Entertainment and Instruction of Young Ladies in their Education.* By the Author of David Simple

Whether this agreeable and instructive little volume is still among the favourite Books of young Ladies at school, we are not able to say; but from the date of a copy lately purchased, viz. 1765, we fear it has lain for years upon the shelf, or in the warehouse, with the works of other neglected Authors. Yet we are much mistaken if there has not been a later edition than that which our bookseller supplied us. But be that as it may, the desire is irresistible of speaking a word or two in praise of an old acquaintance which certainly deserves a better fate, than to be shoved aside to make way for Books of inferior merit now standing in proud array, blazing in scarlet, purple, and gold, to tempt the curiosity of childhood and youth—too frequently to the injury of their principles and morals!—Nothing of this sort is to be apprehended, from the engaging history of *Mrs. Teachum's* nine young ladies; on the contrary, much good is to be learned; and we cannot but wish that this little volume, which had for its author one of the best female scholars England has produced,[1] may be estimated according to its real merit, as long as the world lasts; for when such Works as this cease to be admired and approved, we may regard it as a certain sign, that good morals and simplicity of manners, are banished from the system of English Education, to make room for *false Philosophy* and *artificial refinement*.

[*The Guardian of Education* 1.2 (June 1802): 137–38]

---

1   Mrs. Fielding, the learned translator of Xenophon. [Trimmer's note.]

Appendix B: Selected Correspondence of Sarah Fielding

[According to Martin C. Battestin and Clive T. Probyn, until recently only five letters written by Sarah Fielding "were even known to exist" (*Correspondence* xv). The discovery of a collection of letters—49 in all, 21 by Sarah Fielding and 26 by Henry—among the family papers of the Earl of Malmesbury, then, proved an exciting addition to Fielding scholarship. These and other surviving letters, edited by Battestin and Probyn, and published in 1993, primarily revolve around practical matters: requests to borrow books, thanks for gifts, and updates on the status of works in progress. But they also provide a glimpse into Sarah Fielding's everyday life, and reveal the extent of her friendships with such writers as Samuel Richardson and Jane Collier. The following letters are reprinted from *The Correspondence of Henry and Sarah Fielding*, ed. Martin C. Battestin and Clive T. Probyn (Oxford: Oxford UP, 1993), by permission of Oxford University Press.]

To Samuel Richardson[1] [Duke Street], 8 Jan. 1748/49[2]

Sir,

You cannot imagine the pleasure Miss Collier[3] and I enjoyed at the receipt of your kind epistles. We were at dinner with a *hic, haec, hoc* man,[4] who said, well, I do wonder Mr. Richardson will be troubled

---

1 Samuel Richardson (1689–1761), one of the most popular novelists of the eighteenth century, author of *Pamela, or, Virtue Rewarded* (1740–41), *Clarissa, or the History of a Young Lady* (1747–48), and *The History of Sir Charles Grandison* (1753–54). See the introduction for more on Fielding's relationship with Richardson.

2 The slash indicates Fielding's reference to both the Julian calendar (which did not begin the New Year until March 25) and the Gregorian calendar (which we use today, and which begins the new year on January 1). England officially switched to the Gregorian calendar on December 31, 1751.

3 Jane Collier, Fielding's childhood friend from Salisbury with whom she resided in London for a period in the early 1750s.

4 "Hic, haec, hoc" are Latin declensions of "this" in the masculine, feminine, and neuter forms; the satiric reference here is to the intellectual pretensions of Fielding's dining companion and his contempt of women who presume to bother Richardson.

with such *silly women*; on which we thought to ourselves (though we did not care to say it) if Mr Richardson will bear us, and not think us impertinent in pursuing the pleasure of his correspondence, we don't care in how many languages you fancy you despise us; not but we know you do love and like us too, say what you will to the contrary.

'Tis but a sham quarrel between you and your pen; for had it been real, I flatter myself, that, knowing how delighted, how overjoyed, I should have been, with making your pen my master, you would have solicited him to have admitted me as his servant. Humble and faithful would I have been; I would have obeyed his call; his hours, though six, or even five, in the morning, should have been mine. Indeed, what is there I would not have done? Pleasantly surprised should I have been, suddenly to have found all my thoughts strengthened, and my words flow into an easy and nervous style: never did I so much wish for it as in this daring attempt of mentioning Clarissa:[1] but when I read of her, I am all sensation; my heart glows; I am overwhelmed; my only vent is tears; and unless tears could mark my thoughts as legibly as ink, I cannot speak half I feel. I become like the Harlowes' servant, when he spoke not; he could not speak; he looked, he bowed, and withdrew. In short, Sir, no pen but your's can do justice to Clarissa. Often have I reflected on my own vanity in daring but to touch the hem of her garment; and your excuse for both what I have done, and what I have not done, is all the hopes of,
Sir,
Your ever faithful
humble Servant,
S. Fielding

---

[1] Fielding's *Remarks on Clarissa*. See Appendix C for extracts.

Sarah Fielding and Jane Collier to James Harris[1]

Beauford Buildings, 28 Dec. 1751

Sir,
We return you our sincerest thanks for that most agreable [sic] mark of your favour we received from Mr Vaillant.[2]

We should indeed verify the truth of Mr Popes[3] observation that 'a little Learning is a dang'rous thing' should we vainly attempt to express our approbation of your work; and by such an attempt deservedly should we incur the censure cast on those Women who, having pick'd up a few scraps of Horace, immediately imagine themselves fraught with all knowledge. But altho it would be indecent for Chilldren [sic] in the pride of their hearts to tell their Parents or Tutors that they approve their sentiments, yet would it not be unbecoming for them from the gratitude of their hearts to express their highest acknowledgements for every kind Instruction, and every new field of knowledge, and consequently of pleasure open'd to their minds.

As little Children then Sir give us leave to consider ourselves, and as our kind Instructor accept our thanks for turning our studies from the barren Desarts or arbitrary words, into cultivated Plains where amidst the greatest variety we may in every part trace the footsteps of Reason, and where how much soever we wander, yet with such a guide we may still avoid confusion.

With our best compliments to Mrs Harris and all your Family, we beg leave to subscribe ourselves.
Sir
your most obliged
Obed^t,
Hum^ble Servants
Beauford Buildings Dec: 28th 1751   Sarah Fielding
                                                                          Jane Collier

---

1 James Harris, another of Fielding's Salisbury friends, was a classical scholar who had helped Fielding in her studies. Harris had written a biographical memoir of Henry Fielding (who died in Lisbon in 1754) in May 1758.
2 According to Battestin and Probyn, Harris's publisher, Paul Vaillant, had sent Fielding a copy of Harris's most recent book, *Hermes: or, a Philosophical Inquiry Concerning Language and Universal Grammar* (*Correspondence* 125n).
3 Alexander Pope (1688–1744). The quotation is from *Essay on Criticism*.

Dear Sir, I was in town two days. I sought you out, but you was no where to be found; for you were gone to Parson's Green,[1] from whence, Monday se'ennight, I ran away, being frightened with a pain in my stomach, which put me in mind of an old story of a lady, whose friend said she was very rude and uncivil to go a visiting to her friend, and die whilst she was there.

My love to Mrs. Richardson, and all who have the happiness to be under your roof.

To live in a family where there is but one heart, and as many good strong heads as persons, and to have a place in that enlarged single heart, is such a state of happiness as I cannot hear of without feeling the utmost pleasure. Methinks, in such a house, each word that is uttered must sink into the hearer's mind, as the kindly falling showers in April sink into the teeming earth, and enlarge and ripen every idea, as those friendly drops do the new-sown grain, or the water-wanting plant. There is nothing in all the works of nature or of art too trifling to give pleasure, where there is such a capacity to enjoy it, as must be found in such an union. Give me leave, dear Sir, to return your pleasingly cordial expression, and to say I am, with unabated affection, every your's,

S. Fielding

To James Harris, Bathwick, 25 Dec. [1759]

Bath-wick Dec^br, ye 25th

Sir,

I sometime ago sent you a Translation, or rather a Schoolboy's Exercise wherein I aimed at putting into English Xenophon's Defence of Socrates; your not returning any answer to that Letter, I impute to your Politeness and Good-Nature, that would not suffer you to tell me how very ill it was done. I have since taken a good deal of pains, and hope it is a Proof of my having made some Improvement as it has served to shew me how greatly I often erred in that premature attempt of mine.

I should be obliged to you if you would please to return it the

---

[1] Richardson's country house.

first convenient Opportunity—I dare not ask you to correct what I now find must want so much correcting—for as I have now published proposals for a Subscription it will be necessary for me to be endeavouring to make the whole as free from Faults as is in my Power. I would gladly think that it was owing to your unwillingness to tell me how often I had erred that I had not the Pleasure of hearing from you, as I could not forbear saying to Doctor Hoadly[1] when I last saw him in Bath, for it would grieve me very much if I thought I had done any thing to disoblige a Person for whom I have so true an Esteem. I beg my Compliments to Mrs Harris. My sincere good Wishes attend your little Family, and I am Dear Sir
with true Respect your
Obliged and Obed^t Hum^ble Servt.

S. Fielding

I hope you will give me leave to credit my List with your Name. Be so kind to give the enclosed Letter to Mrs Doi'lys[2]

---

[1] A mutual friend of Henry and Sarah Fielding, John Hoadly wrote the inscription on Sarah's memorial tablet in Bath Abbey.

[2] Mrs. Elizabeth D'Oyly, a friend of Harris's mother Lady Elizabeth Ashley and one of the subscribers to Sarah's *Familiar Letters*.

Appendix C: Excerpts from Sarah Fielding's Remarks on 'Clarissa' (1749)

[Although *Remarks on 'Clarissa'* was published anonymously the same year as *The Governess*, most critics agree that the essay is Fielding's. (Evidence includes Fielding's reference to the work in her letter to Richardson, included in Appendix B.) As a work of literary criticism, *Remarks* is noteworthy for several reasons. First, it is an astute analysis not only of Richardson's novel but also of the reader's relationship to it. Second, Fielding presents her criticism in a highly imaginative way. The essay opens with the anonymous critic's claim to have collected and reported the various criticisms of Richardson's novel, as expressed by a variety of people gathered together over the course of several social evenings. By creating a number of different characters to condemn or praise *Clarissa*, Fielding engages in her own fictional enterprise. Indeed, as a work of fiction, *Remarks* goes beyond establishing a moral and artistic kinship between Fielding and Richardson. The work continues to develop many of the themes central to *The Governess* and to her earlier writings: the nature and significance of reading; the necessity of self-discipline and discernment; and, finally, the need to recognize and negotiate the conflict between male expectations and female behavior.]

Sir,

Perhaps an Address of this Nature may appear very unaccountable, and whimsical; when I assure you, my Design is fairly to lay before you all the Criticisms, as far as I can remember them, that I have heard on your History of *Clarissa*; from the Appearance of the two first Volumes, to the Close of the Work.[1] I have not willingly omitted any

---

[1] Volumes i and ii of *Clarissa; or the History of a Young Lady: Comprehending the Most Important Concerns of Private Life, and Particularly Showing the Distresses That May Attend the Misconduct Both of Parents and Children, in Relation to Marriage*, were published in December of 1747, volumes iii and iv in April 1748, volume v in October, and volumes vi and vii in November 1748. The length of the novel was indeed prodigious: the most readily available unabridged edition currently available is the Penguin Classics paperback, which is about 1,466 pages long, set in 8-point type.

one Objection I have heard made to your favourite Character, from her first Appearance in the World; nor, on the contrary, have I either diminished or added to the favourable Construction put on her Words or Actions. If the Grounds for the Objections are found to be deducible from the Story, I would have them remain in their full Force; but if the Answers her Admirers have given to those Objections are found to result from an impartial and attentive perusal of the Story, I would not have her deny'd the Justice they have done her. …

In the first Conversation I heard on this Subject, the whole Book was unanimously condemned, without the least Glimpse of Favour from any one present who sat in judgment on it. It was tedious stuff!—low!—Letters wrote between Misses about their Sweet-hearts!—There was an Uncle *Anthony*—a Brother *James!*—a Goody *Norton!*—and a Servant *Hannah.*—In short, *one* had no Patience to read it, *another* could not bear it, a *third* did not like it, &c. Such general Censurers, I knew, could be very little worth attending to; and this Judgment I should have formed had I been a Stranger to the Book thus unmercifully treated; but as I had read *Clarissa*, and observed some Beauties in it, yet heard not one of them mentioned, I was determined to say nothing, and to make my Visit as short as possible.

From hence I went to spend the Evening with a Family in whose Conversation I am always agreeably entertained. There happened, that Night, to be a pretty large Assembly of mix'd Company. *Clarissa* immediately became the Subject of our Conversation, when, after a few general Remarks, one of the Gentlemen said, "His chief Objection was to the Length of it, for that he was certain he could tell the whole Story contained in the two first Volumes in a few Minutes; for Example, (continued he) There is a Family who live in the Country, consisting of an old positive,[1] gouty Gentleman, two old Batchelors as positive as their gouty Brother, a meek Wife, an ambitious Son, an envious elder Sister, and a handsome younger Sister; who, having refused many offered Matches, engages the Attention and Liking of one Mr. *Lovelace*, a young Gentleman of a noble Family; her Brother has an absolute Aversion to him; a Rencounter follows between them; the Lady corresponds with *Lovelace* to prevent farther Mischief; a disagreeable Man is proposed to her by all her Family; she will not consent; they all combine to insist on her Compliance; she is lock'd up; forbid all Correspondence

---

[1]   In this context, opinionated or dictatorial.

out of the Family, but still persists in her Refusal; they call it Obstinance; she calls it Resolution; Mr. *Lovelace* takes the Advantage of her Friends Usage of her, and presses her to throw herself on his Protection: at last, for fear of being forced to marry the Man she hates, she appoints to go off with *Lovelace*; but fearing the Consequence of such a rash Step, and thinking it a Breach of her Duty to leave her Father's House till urged by the last Necessity, she would have retracted the Appointment, and waited yet a little longer, in hopes her Friends might be influenced to change their Mind; Mr. *Lovelace* does not take the Letter she puts in the usual Place for that purpose, and we see by her last Letter to her Friend, dated at St. *Albans*, that she is there with *Lovelace*. Now, how is it possible for this Story, without being exceeding tedious, to be spun out to two Volumes, containing each above 300 Pages?"

When the Gentleman ceased, a young Lady, whose Name was *Gibson*, took a little Almanack out of her Pocket, and, turning to the Place where the Births and Deaths of the Kings of *England* were marked, gave it to the Gentleman, and said, "that by his Rule of Writing, that was the best History of *England*, and Almanack-makers were the best Historians."

★   ★   ★

The next Scene of Criticism (if I may so call it) on *Clarissa* that I was present at, was on the Publication of the two succeeding Volumes.

The same Company met, with the Addition only of one Gentleman, whom I shall call *Bellario*; his known Taste and Impartiality made all those who wished Reason instead of Prejudice might judge of the Subject before them, rejoice[d] at his Presence. The Objections now arose so fast, it was impossible to guess where they would end. *Clarissa* herself was a Prude—a Coquet.... She was an undutiful Daughter—too strict in her Principles of Obedience to such Parents— too fond of a Rake[1] and a Libertine—her Heart was as impenitrable and unsusceptible of Affection, as the hardest Marble. In short, the many contradictory faults that she was at once accused of, is almost incredible: So many, that those who had attended enough to her Character, to have an Inclination to justify her, found it difficult to

---

[1]   A womanizer. In eighteenth-century literature the rake is a stock character, though Richardson's Lovelace is a complex study of the type.

know where to begin to answer such a complicated Charge. But after a short Silence, Miss *Gibson*, with her usual Penetration, said; "Whenever any Person is accused of a Variety of Faults, which are plainly impossible to dwell in the same Mind, I am immediately convinced the Person so accused is innocent of them all. A Prude cannot, by an observing Eye, be taken for a Coquet, nor a Coquet for a Prude, but a good Woman may be called either, or both, according to the Dispositions of her resolved Censurers; and hence I believe we may trace the Cause, why the Characters even of those Persons who do not endeavour to wear any Disguise are so very liable to be mistaken; for Partiality or Prejudice generally sit as Judges: If the former mount the Judgment-seat, how many different Terms do we make use of to express that Goodness in another, which our own fluctuating Imaginations only have erected? If the latter, how do we vary Expressions to paint that Wickedness which we are resolve[d] to prove inhabits the Mind we think proper to condemn?" ...

Bellario, who had hitherto been silent, said, "He thought *Clarissa* could not justly be accused of any material Fault, but that of wanting[1] Affection for her Lover; for that he was sure, a Woman whose Mind was incapable of Love, could not be amiable, nor have any of those gentle Qualities which chiefly adorn the female Character. And as to her whining after her Papa and Mamma, who had used her so cruelly, (added he) I think 'tis contemptible in her."

"But, Sir, (said Miss *Gibson*) please only to consider, first, *Clarissa* is accused of want of Love, and then in a Moment she is condemned for not being able suddenly to tear from her Bosom an Affection that had been daily growing and improving from the Time of her Birth, and this built on the greatest paternal Indulgence imaginable. Affections that have taken such deep Root, are little Treasures hoarded up in the good Mind, and cannot be torn from thence without causing the strongest convulsive Pangs in the Heart where they have long been nourished: And when they are so very easily given up as you now, Sir, seem to contend for, I confess I am very apt to suspect they have only been talked of by the Persons who can part with them with so little Pain, either from Hypocrisy, or from another very obvious Cause, namely, the using Words we are accustomed to hear, without so much as thinking of their Meaning. Such

---

[1] In the eighteenth century, "to want" meant "to lack" (as in this case) as well as "to desire."

Hearts I think may be much more properly compared to the Hardness of Marble, than could that of the gentle *Clarissa*.

"There is in her Behaviour, I own, a good deal of apparent Indifference to *Lovelace*; but let her Situation and his manner of treating her be considered, and I fancy the whole will be seen in a different Light from what it may appear on the first View.... That *Clarissa* positively did not intend to go off with *Lovelace* when she met him, to me is very plain; nor could he have prevailed on her, had not the Terrors raised in her Mind, by apprehended Murder, almost robbed her of her Senses, and hurried her away, not knowing what she did....[1]

"She was vexed to her soul afterwards to find she was tricked, as she calls it, out of herself, when *Lovelace*, instead of comforting and assuring her Mind, begins such a Train of shufling artful Tricks, as no one but *Lovelace* could have thought on: And altho' she did not know all his Design, for if she had, she would certainly have left him, yet she sees enough of his *crooked ways*, to be convinced that he acted ungenerously by her, because she was in *his Power* ....

"But if, Sir, you cannot think *Lovelace's* Usage of *Clarissa* a full Justification of her in this Point, I think the Author has a just Right to be heard out before his Heroine is condemned in so heavy a Charge, as that of being void of all Affection. You know enough of my Sentiments, Sir, to be convinced that I do think this the heaviest Charge a Woman can be accused of; for Love is the only Passion I should wish to be harboured in the gentle Bosom of a good Woman. Ambition, with all the Train of turbulent Passions the World is infested with, I would leave to Men: And could I make my whole Sex of my Opinion, they would be resigned without the least Grudge or Envy; for Peace and Harmony dwell not with them, but on the contrary, Discord, Perturbation and Misery are their constant Companions. ...

"[I]f I can guess any Thing of the Author's Intention by what is already published, I fancy, when we have read the Conclusion of this Story, we shall be convinced that Love was the strongest Characteristic of *Clarissa's* Mind."

---

[1] Lovelace convinces Clarissa that her family is going to force her to marry a man she does not love. This fear prompts her to agree to leave her family to stay with his, though she soon changes her mind. When she meets Lovelace to tell him she won't go with him, he tricks her into thinking the Harlowes have discovered their plans and are giving chase, at which point he hurries her into his waiting carriage. This is the first of many elaborate subterfuges Lovelace engages in to keep Clarissa in his power.

Bellario answered, with that Candor, which is known to be one of the most distinguishing Marks of his Character by all who have the Pleasure of his Acquaintance, "That if it proved so, he should have the greatest Esteem and highest Veneration for *Clarissa*, and would suspend his Judgment till he saw the remaining Part of the Story."

★   ★   ★

[The last objection to the novel during this exchange is expressed by Bellario.] *Bellario* said, that the Report that the Catastrophy[1] was to be unhappy had made a deep Impression on him; for that he could not avoid thinking that, if it was true, it must be a great Error, and destroy all the Pleasure a good-natur'd Reader might already have received: However, he said, he would keep his Word in not absolutely giving his Judgment till he saw the Conclusion.

And thus ended the second Scene of Criticism on *Clarissa*; only, as we went down Stairs, a Lady, who had not spoke one Word the whole Evening, mutter'd out a strong Dislike, that the agreeable Mr. *Lovelace* should not become a Husband.

And now, in the Month of *December*, appears the long expected, much wished for Conclusion of *Clarissa*'s Story.

The Company we have already mentioned being again assembled, the Lady who had before grieved that the agreeable Mr. *Lovelace* should not become a Husband, now lamented that Miss *Howe* should be married to so insipid a Man (that was the Epithet she chose for him) as Mr. *Hickman*.[2] This passed some little time without any Answer. Miss *Gibson* was silent; and I saw by her Looks that she thought there was some Weight in her Objection. At last an old Lady, who had three Daughters marriagable, said, she wondered to hear Mr. *Hickman* called insipid; for she thought there could be no Reason for giving him that Appellation, unless young Women would confess what she should be very sorry to hear them confess, namely, that, in their Opinion, Sobriety intitles a Man to the Character of Insipidity. ... I think Miss *Howe* is very censurable

---

1   The change or revolution that produces the conclusion or final event of a dramatic work (*OED*).

2   Miss Anna Howe is Clarissa's closest friend and her primary correspondent. Mr. Hickman is the man Miss Howe's mother would like her to marry. Although Anna admits she will eventually marry him, she, like Clarissa, often voices her desire for "the single life."

for the Liberties she takes with a worthy Man, whom also it is plain she intends to make her Husband.

Miss *Gibson* agreed in censuring Miss *Howe* for the Liberties she takes with him; but at the same time said, she thought even his bearing that Usage did lower his Character. Now you see, replied the Lady, how you are taken in; that you can condemn Miss *Howe* for her Contempt of Mr. *Hickman*, and yet at the same time let the lively Strokes that fall from her Pen have their full force against the abused worthy Man. Yet Miss *Howe* herself owns, as early as the second Volume, that Mr. *Hickman* is humane, benevolent, generous,—No Fox-hunter—No Gamester—That he is sober, modest, and virtuous; and has Qualities that Mothers would be fond of in a Husband for their Daughters; and for which, perhaps, their Daughters would be the happier, could they judge as well for themselves as Experience may teach them to judge for their future Daughters. ... And Miss *Howe* owns he never disobliged her by Word or Look. What then is the Objection to Mr. *Hickman*? Why truly, he has not *Lovelace's* fine Person!—*Lovelace's* fine Address!—*Lovelace's* impetuous Spirit.... But, indeed, I am afraid whoever prefers a *Lovelace* to a *Hickman*, will wish all her life-time she could have sooner found out, that tho' *Lovelace* was the best Partner at a Ball; yet, when a Companion for Life was to be chose, that Mr. *Hickman's* Goodness of Heart rendered him in all respects more essential to Happiness; much more eligible than all the gay, fluttering, and parading Spirit of a *Lovelace* could possibly have done....

Nay, Madam, says Miss *Gibson*, I do not dispute Mr. *Hickman's* being preferable for a Husband to Mr. *Lovelace*; the Heart is certainly the first thing to be considered in a Man to whose Government a Woman resigns herself; but I should not chuse either *Lovelace* or *Hickman*. I must confess I should desire Humour and Spirit in a Man. ...

Ah! Miss *Gibson*, replied the Lady, in every Word you speak, you prove how necessary the Author's Moral is to be strongly inculcated; when even *your* serious and thoughtful Turn of Mind will not suffer you to see through the Glare of what you call Humour and Spirit with that Clearness which would enable you to distinguish how very seldom that Humour and Spirit is bestowed on a Wife. Mr. *Hickman's* whole Mind being at Home, would enliven him into a chearful Companion with his Wife; whilst a *Lovelace's* Mind, engaged on foreign Objects, would often make him fall into Peevishness and Ill-humour, instead of this so much dreaded *Insipidity*.

Indeed, Madam, said Miss *Gibson*, I don't plead for Mr. *Lovelace*; for I detest him of all the Men I ever read of.

That is true, replied the Lady; but that is because you have *read* of him, and know the Villanies he was capable of. But yet, I think, you have plainly proved, if a *Lovelace* and a *Hickman* contend for your Favour, which would have the best Chance of succeeding. ... The Gentlemen, during this Debate, had all sat silent; but they often smiled to see how few Advocates Mr. *Hickman* was likely to have amongst the Ladies.

At last *Bellario* said, If I had not thought so before, I should now be convinced by this Conversation, how judicious the Author of *Clarissa* was in setting forth so very strongly as he does, the Necessity of Sobriety and Goodness in a Husband, in order to render a married State happy. For you have shown clearly, Ladies, how difficult it is for a Man to be esteemed by you who has those Qualities; since I can see no one Objection to Mr. *Hickman*, but that he has not that Gaiety of Disposition which from a vast Flow of animal Spirits, without Restraint or Curb from either Principles of Religion or Good-nature, shines forth in *Lovelace*'s wild Fancies. And this Man you find such a Reluctance to speak well of ... is respected by all the World!—And a *Clarissa* for ever acknowleges his Merit.—And, in one of the last Actions of her Life, praises him as he deserves to be praised. And earnestly recommends it to her best and dear Friend, to give both her Hand and Heart to so worthy a Man. The steady Principles of Mr. *Hickman* was a firm Basis to depend on, for Protection and good Usage.

Miss *Gibson* was so much pleased with seeing *Bellario* enter so heartily into the Design of the Author of *Clarissa*, that she dropp'd the Argument, (tho' she did not seem quite convinc'd that Mr. *Hickman* could be an agreeable Husband) and with some Earnestness desired *Bellario* to tell her, whether he was not now convinced that *Clarissa* was capable of the strongest Affection, could she but have found the least Foundation to have built that Affection on: Yes, replied *Bellario*, I am convinced of it, and am surprised that I did not before see how much *Lovelace*'s base unmanly Behaviour justifies her in this Point....

[Pr]ay, Sir, continued Miss *Gibson*, pardon my asking you one Question more, namely; whether you are not now satisfied with the Conduct of the Author in the Management of his whole Story?

Bellario answered, That he was not only satisfied with it, but highly applauded all the material Parts of it; that the various distressful

Situations in which you had placed your Heroine, were noble beyond Expression; that these three last Volumes contained many Scenes, each singly arising to as high a Tragedy as can possibly be wrote; that the Tears you had drawn from his Eyes were such Tears as flow'd from a Heart at once filled with Admiration and Compassion, and labouring under Sensations too strong for any Utterance in Words; and that for the Sake of *Clarissa*, he would never form any Judgment of a Work again till the whole was lain before him. This was noble! this was candid! this was like *Bellario*! ...

★ ★ ★

Mr. *Barker* said, "that he thought there was one great Fault in the Conduct of your Story; and that was, the Indelicacy of making *Clarissa* seek *Lovelace* after the Outrage."... [1]

As to the Indelicacy of *Clarissa's* seeking *Lovleace*, said *Bellario*, "I confess I do not see it; however, I will leave that matter to be decided by the Ladies," who all agreed, that they thought it no Breach of the strictest Modesty to declare it was their Opinion, that the whole Scene, as it now stands, is what it *should be*, and would have admitted of no Alteration, but for the worse. ... In short, this Scene was allowed to be Virtue's Triumph, and *Clarissa's* Conduct to be a direct Opposition to that of all those whining Women, who blubber out an humble Petition to be joined for Life to the Men who have betrayed them. [2]

Had not *Clarissa* seen *Lovelace*, said Miss *Gibson*, her Triumph could never have been so compleat; and as I think the Impossibility of her Escape at that time, from Mrs. *Sinclair's*, is very apparent, had she not sought him, the true Lovers of *Clarissa* must have mourned the Loss of seeing her Behaviour in such an uncommon Situation.

Bellario gave these Sentiments a Sanction by his Approbation, and the rest of the Company either concurr'd with his Opinion, or at least did not contradict him; and the next Day Miss *Gibson* received the following Letter from *Bellario*.

MADAM,

You seem'd so pleased last Night with my Conversion, if I may

---

[1]   Lovelace, after trying every art to seduce Clarissa, eventually resorts to violence: he drugs her and rapes her while she is unconscious.

[2]   In the eighteenth century, a convicted rapist could be forced to marry his victim as the only restitution in her power. After Clarissa is raped, she confronts Lovelace and cows him with her moral superiority.

be allowed the Expression, to your Favourite *Clarissa*, that I could not seek any Repose till I had thrown together my Thoughts on that Head, in order to address them to you; nor am I ashamed to confess, that the Author's Design is more noble, and his Execution of it much happier, than I even suspected till I had seen the whole....

* * *

I confess I was against the Story's ending unhappily, till I saw the Conclusion; but I now think the different Deaths of the many Persons (for in this Point also the Difference is as essentially preserved, as in the Characters or Scenes) who fall in the winding up the Catastrophy in the seventh Volume, produce as noble a Moral as can be invented by the Wit of Man....

Nothing ever made so strong a Contrast as the Deaths of *Lovelace* and *Clarissa*. Wild was the Life of *Lovelace*, rapid was his Death; gentle was *Clarissa*'s Life, softly flowed her latest Hours; the very Word *Death* seems too harsh to describe her leaving Life, and her last Breath was like the soft playing of a western Breeze, all calm! all Peace! all Quiet!....

Rightly I think in the Author's Postscript is it observed, that what is called poetical Justice is chimerical; or rather anti-providential Justice; for God makes his Sun to shine alike on the Just and the Unjust. Why then should Man invent a kind of imaginary Justice, making the common Accidents of Life turn out favourable to the Virtuous only? Vain would be the Comforts spoken to the Virtuous in Affliction, in the sacred writings, if Affliction could not be their Lot.

But the Author of *Clarissa* has in his Postscript quoted such undoubted Authorities, and given so many Reasons on the Christian System for his Catastrophy, that to say more on that Head would be but repeating his Words. The Variety of Punishments also of more guilty Persons in this Work who do not die, and the Rewards of those who are innocent, I could go through, had not that Postscript, and the Conclusion supposed to be writ by Mr. *Belford*, already done it. ...

If what I have here said can be any Amusement to you, as it concerns your favourite *Clarissa*, my End will be answered. I am, *Madam*,

Your's, &c. BELLARIO.

Miss GIBSON *to* BELLARIO.

SIR,

Your Good-nature in sending me your Thoughts on *Clarissa*, with a Design to give me Pleasure, I assure you is not thrown away; may you have equal Success in every generous Purpose that fills your Heart, and greater Happiness in this World, I am sure I cannot wish you.

Most truly, Sir, do you remark, that a Story told in this Manner can move but slowly, that the Characters can be seen only by such as attend strictly to the Whole; yet this Advantage the Author gains by writing in the present Tense, as he himself calls it, and in the first Person, that his Strokes penetrate immediately to the Heart, and we feel all the Distresses he paints; we not only weep for, but with *Clarissa*, and accompany her, step by step, through all her Distresses....

★ ★ ★

I think [one] could not find a better Close to her Misfortunes than a triumphant Death. Triumphant it may very well be called, when her Soul, fortified by a truly Christian Philosophy, melted and softened in the School of Affliction, had conquered every earthly Desire, baffled every uneasy Passion, lost every disturbing Fear, while nothing remained in her tender Bosom but a lively Hope of future Happiness. When her very Griefs were in a manner forgot, the Impression of them as faint and languid as a feverish Dream to one restored to Health, all calm and serene her Mind, forgiving and praying for her worst Enemies, she retired from all her Afflictions, to meet the Reward of her Christian Piety....

Surely the Tears we shed for *Clarissa* in her last Hours, must be Tears of tender Joy! Whilst we seem to live, and daily converse with her through her last Stage, our Hearts are at once rejoiced and amended, are both soften'd and elevated, till our Sensations grow too strong for any Vent, but that of Tears; nor am I ashamed to confess, that Tears without Number have I shed, whilst Mr. *Belford* by his Relation has kept me (as I may say) with fixed Attention in her Apartment, and made me perfectly present at her noble exalted Behaviour; nor can I hardly refrain from crying out, "Farewell, my dear *Clarissa*! may every Friend I love in this World imitate you in their Lives, and thus joyfully quit all the Cares and Troubles that disturb this mortal Being!"

May *Clarissa's* Memory be as triumphant as was her Death! May all the World, like *Lovelace*, bear Testimony to her Virtues, and acknowledge her Triumph!

I am with many Thanks, Sir, for your obliging Letter,

Your most obedient, &c.

HARRIOTE GIBSON.

These Letters were shewn me by Miss *Gibson*, and thus, Sir, have I collected together all I have heard on your History of *Clarissa*; and if every thing that Miss *Gibson* and *Bellario* has said, is fairly deducible from the Story, then I am certain, by the candid and good-natured Reader, this will be deemed a fair and impartial Examination, tho' I avow myself the sincere Admirer of *Clarissa*, and

Your very humble Servant,

FINIS

Appendix D: Excerpts from Eighteenth-Century Educational Literature

[The following extracts are taken from a variety of educational and children's literature popular during the eighteenth and early nineteenth centuries.]

1. From John Locke, *Some Thoughts Concerning Education*, 1693

[*Some Thoughts Concerning Education* by John Locke (1632–1704) was an extremely popular work, reprinted throughout the eighteenth century. As can be seen from the passages below, Locke's theories clearly informed Fielding's *Governess*. Although Locke believed that instruction should be a pleasant activity for children, he also emphasized children's capacity for reason and the need for them to become self-disciplined in order to be productive members of society.]

From the Dedication[1]

... I myself have been consulted of late by so many, who profess themselves at a loss how to breed their children, and the early corruption of youth is now become so general a complaint, that he cannot be thought wholly impertinent, who brings the consideration of this matter on the stage, and offers something, if it be but to excite others, or afford matter for correction; for errors in education should be less indulged than any. ...

But my business is not to recommend this treatise to you, whose opinion of it I know already; nor it to the world, either by your opinion or patronage. The well educating of their children is so much the duty and concern of parents, and the welfare and prosperity of the nation so much depends on it, that I would have every one lay it seriously to heart; and after having well examined and distinguished what fancy, custom, or reason advises in the case, set

---

[1] Locke dedicated his essay to his friend Edward Clarke. The work was based on a series of letters Locke had written to Clarke containing advice about how to raise his son. Locke himself never married and had no children.

his helping hand to promote that way in the several degrees of men, which is the easiest, shortest, and likeliest to produce virtuous, useful, and able men in their distinct callings. Though that most to be taken care of is the gentleman's calling; for if those of that rank are by their education once set right, they will quickly bring all the rest into order....

From Section 1

A sound mind in a sound body, is a short but full description of a happy state in this world: he that has these two, has little more to wish for; and he that wants either of them, will be but little the better for any thing else. Men's happiness or misery is most part of their own making. He whose mind directs not wisely, will never take the right way; and he whose body is crazy and feeble will never be able to advance in it. I confess there are some men's constitutions of body and mind so vigorous and well framed by nature that they need not much assistance from others but by the strength of their natural genius they are from their cradles carried towards what is excellent and by the privilege of their happy constitutions are able to do wonders. But examples of these are but few; and I think I may say that, of all the men we meet with, nine parts of ten are what they are, good or evil, useful or not, by their education. 'Tis that which makes the great difference in mankind. The little, and almost insensible impressions on our tender infancies, have very important and lasting consequences; and there 'tis, as in the fountains of some rivers where a gentle application of the hand turns the flexible waters into channels, that make them take quite contrary courses, and by this little direction given them at first in the source they receive different tendencies and arrive at last at very remote and distant places.

From Section 6

I have said *He* here, because the principal aim of my discourse is, how a young gentleman should be brought up from his infancy, which in all things will not so perfectly suit the education of daughters; though, where the difference of sex requires different treatment, 'twill be no hard matter to distinguish.

From Section 32

If what I have said in the beginning of this discourse be true, as I do not doubt but it is, viz. that the difference to be found in the manners and abilities of men, is owing more to their education than to any thing else; we have reason to conclude, that great care is to be had of the forming children's minds, and giving them that seasoning early, which shall influence their lives always after. For when they do well or ill, the praise or blame will be laid there: and when any thing is done untowardly, the common saying will pass upon them, that it is suitable to their breeding.

From Section 33

As the strength of the body lies chiefly in being able to endure hardships, so also does that of the mind. And the great principle and foundation of all virtue and worth is placed in this, that a man is able to deny himself his own desires, cross his own inclinations, and purely follow what reason directs as best, though the appetite lean the other way.

From Section 34

The great mistake I have observed in people's breeding their children has been, that this has not been taken care enough of in its due season; that the mind has not been made obedient to rules, and pliant to reason, when at first it was most tender, most easy to be bowed. Parents being wisely ordained by nature to love their children, are very apt, if reason watch not that natural affection very warily; are apt, I say, to let it run into fondness. They love their little ones, and 'tis their duty: but they often with them cherish their faults too. They must not be crossed, forsooth; they must be permitted to have their wills in all things; and they being in their infancies not capable of great vices, their parents think they may safely enough indulge their little irregularities and make themselves sport with that pretty perverseness which they think well enough becomes that innocent age. But to a fond parent that would not have his child corrected for a perverse trick but excused it saying it was a small matter, Solon very well replied, "Ay, but custom is a great one."

From Section 42

... Fear and awe ought to give you the first power over [your children's] minds, and love and friendship in riper years to hold it: for the time must come, when they will be past the rod and correction; and then, if the love of you make them not obedient and dutiful, if the love of virtue and reputation keep them not in laudable courses, I ask, what hold will you have upon them, to turn them to it? Indeed, fear of having a scanty portion, if they displease you, may make them slaves to your estate, but they will be never the less ill and wicked in private; and that restraint will not last always. Every man must some time or other be trusted, to himself, and his own conduct; and he that is a good, a virtuous, and able man, must be made so within. And therefore, what he is to receive from education, what is to sway and influence his life, must be something put into him betimes, habits woven into the very principles of his nature; and not a counterfeit carriage, and dissembled outside, put on by fear, only to avoid the present anger of a father, who perhaps may disinherit him.

From Section 45

That this is so, will be easily allowed, when it is but considered what is to be aimed at in an ingenuous education, and upon what it turns.
1. Self-denial. He that has not a mastery over his inclinations, he that knows not how to resist the importunity of present pleasure or pain, for the sake of what reason tells him is fit to be done, wants the true principle of virtue and industry, and is in danger never to be good for any thing. This temper, therefore, so contrary to unguided nature, is to be got betimes; and this habit, as the true foundation of future ability and happiness, is to be wrought into the mind, as early as may be, even from the first dawnings of any knowledge or apprehension in children; and so to be confirmed in them, by all the care and ways imaginable, by those who have the oversight of their education.

From Section 52

Rewards.—Beating them [children], and all other sorts of slavish and corporal punishments, are not the discipline fit to be used in the education of those we would have wise, good, and ingenuous men; and therefore very rarely to be applied, and that only in great occasions, and cases of extremity. On the other side, to flatter children by rewards of things that are pleasant to them, is as carefully to be avoided. He that will give to his son apples, or sugar-plums, or what else of this kind he is most delighted with, to make him learn his book, does but authorize his love of pleasure, and cocker up that dangerous propensity, which he ought by all means to subdue and stifle in him. You can never hope to teach him to master it whilst you compound for the check you give his inclination in one place, by the satisfaction you propose to it in another. To make a good, a wise, and a virtuous man, it is fit he should learn to cross his appetite, and deny his inclination to riches, finery, or pleasing his palate, etc., whenever his reason advises the contrary, and his duty requires it. But when you draw him to do anything that is fit, by the offer of money; or reward the pains of learning his book, by the pleasure of a luscious morsel; when you promise him a lace-cravat, or a fine new suit, upon performance of some of his little tasks; what do you, by proposing these as rewards, but allow them to be the good things he should aim at, and thereby encourage his longing for them, and accustom him to place his happiness in them? Thus people, to prevail with children to be industrious about their grammar, dancing, or some other such matter of no great moment to the happiness or usefulness of their lives by misapplied rewards and punishments, sacrifice their virtue, invert the order of their education, and teach them luxury, pride, or covetousness, etc. For in this way, flattering those wrong inclinations, which they should restrain and suppress, they lay the foundations of those future vices, which cannot be avoided, but by curbing our desires, and accustoming them early to submit to reason.

From Section 53

I say, not this, that I would have children kept from the conveniences or pleasures of life, that are not injurious to their health or virtue. On the contrary, I would have their lives made as pleasant, and as agreeable to them as may be, in a plentiful enjoyment of whatsoever might innocently delight them: provided it be with this caution, that they have those enjoyments only as the consequences of the state of esteem and acceptation they are in with their parents and governors; but they should never be offered or bestowed on them, as the reward of this or that particular performance, that they show an aversion to, or to which they would not have applied themselves without that temptation.

From Section 54

But if you take away the rod on one hand, and these little encouragements, which they are taken with, on the other, How then (will you say) shall children be governed? Remove hope and fear, and there is an end of all discipline. I grant, that good and evil, reward and punishment, are the only motives to a rational creature; these are the spur and reins whereby all mankind are set on work and guided, and therefore they are to be made use of to children too. For I advise their parents and governors always to carry this in their minds, that they are to be treated as rational creatures.

From Section 73

1. Task. None of the things they are to learn should ever be made a burden to them, or imposed on them as a task. Whatever is so proposed, presently becomes irksome: the mind takes an aversion to it, though before it were a thing of delight or indifferency. Let a child be but ordered to whip his top at a certain time every day, whether he has, or has not a mind to it; let this be but required of him as a duty, wherein he must spend so many hours morning and afternoon, and see whether he will not soon be weary of any play at this rate. Is it not so with grown men? What they do cheerfully of themselves, do they not presently grow sick of, and can no more endure, as soon as they find it is expected of them as a duty? Children have as much a mind to show that they are free, that their own good actions come from themselves, that they are absolute and independent, as any of the proudest of you grown men, think of them as you please.

From Section 74

2. Disposition. As a consequence of this, they should seldom be put upon doing even those things you have got an inclination in them to,

but when they have a mind and disposition to it. He that loves reading, writing, music, etc., finds yet in himself certain seasons wherein those things have no relish to him; and, if at that time he forces himself to it, he only pothers and wearies himself to no purpose. So it is with children. This change of temper should be carefully observed in them, and the favourable seasons of aptitude and inclination be heedfully laid hold of, to set them upon anything. By this means a great deal of time and tiring would be saved: for a child will learn three times as much when he is in tune, as he will with double the time and pains, when he goes awkwardly, or is dragged unwillingly to it. If this were minded as it should, children might be permitted to weary themselves with play, and yet have time enough to learn what is suited to the capacity of each age. And if things were ordered right, learning anything they should be taught, might be made as much a recreation to their play, as their play is to their learning. The pains are equal on both sides: nor is it that which troubles them, for they love to be busy, and the change and variety is that which naturally delights them. The only odds is, in that which we call play they act at liberty, and employ their pains (whereof you may observe them never sparing) freely; but what they are to learn, they are driven to it, called on or compelled. This is that, that at first entrance balks and cools them; they want their liberty: get them but to ask their tutor to teach them, as they do often their playfellows, instead of this calling upon them to learn, and they being satisfied that they act as freely in this, as they do in other things they will go on with as much pleasure in it, and it will not differ from their other sports and play. By these ways, carefully pursued, I guess a child may be brought to desire to be taught any thing you have a mind he should learn. The hardest part, I confess, is with the first or eldest; but when once he is set right, it is easy by him to lead the rest whither one will.

From Section 156

When by these gentle ways he begins to be able to read, some easy, pleasant book, suited to his capacity, should be put into his hands, wherein the entertainment that he finds might draw him on, and reward his pains in reading; and yet not such as should fill his head with perfectly useless trumpery, or lay the principles of vice and folly. To this purpose I think Aesop's *Fables* the best, which being stories apt to delight and entertain a child, may yet afford useful reflections to a grown man; and if his memory retain them all his life after, he will not repent to find them there, amongst his manly thoughts and serious business. If his Aesop has pictures in it, it will entertain him much the better, and encourage him to read when it carries the increase of knowledge with it: for such visible objects children hear talked of in vain, and without any satisfaction, whilst they have no ideas of them; those ideas being not to be had from sounds, but from the things themselves, or their pictures. And therefore, I think, as soon as he begins to spell, as many pictures of animals should be got him as can be found, with the printed names to them, which at the same time will invite him to read, and afford him matter of inquiry and knowledge. *Reynard the Fox* is another book, I think, that may be made use of to the same purpose. And if those about him will talk to him often about the stories he has read, and hear him tell them, it will, besides other advantages, add encouragement and delight to his reading, when he finds there is some use and pleasure in it, which in the ordinary method, I think, learners do not till late; and so take books only for fashionable amusements, or impertinent troubles, good for nothing.

2. From John Gregory, *A Father's Legacy to His Daughters*, 1774

[John Gregory (1724-73), a respected and influential Edinburgh physician, wrote *A Father's Legacy to His Daughters* almost thirty years after Fielding's *Governess*. Reprinted throughout the last decades of the eighteenth century and translated into foreign languages, Gregory's advice to young women reflected popular notions of appropriate female conduct. Like Fielding's *The Governess*, Gregory's text promotes modesty and self-regulation as highly desirable characteristics. However, Fielding encouraged all rational human beings—men as well as women—to develop these traits, whereas Gregory emphasized them as peculiarly feminine.]

From the Introduction

My Dear Girls,
    You had the misfortune to be deprived of your mother, at a time of life when you were insensible of your loss, and could receive little benefit, either from her instruction, or her example.—Before this comes to your hands, you will likewise have lost your father.

I have had many melancholy reflections on the forlorn and help-less situation you must be in, if it should please God to remove me from you, before you arrive at that period of life, when you will be able to think and act for yourselves. I know mankind too well. I know their falsehood, their dissipation, their coldness to all the duties of friendship and humanity. I know the little attention paid to helpless infancy.—You will meet with few friends disinterested enough to do you good offices, when you are incapable of making them any return, by contributing to their interest or their pleasure, or even to the gratification of their vanity.

I have been supported under the gloom naturally arising from these reflections, by a reliance on the goodness of that Providence which has hitherto preserved you, and given me the most pleasing prospect of the goodness of your dispositions; and by the secret hope that your mother's virtues will entail a blessing on her children.

The anxiety I have for your happiness has made me resolve to throw together my sentiments relating to your future conduct in life. If I live for some years, you will receive them with much greater advantage, suited to your different geniuses and dispositions. If I die sooner, you must receive them in this very imperfect manner,—the last proof of my affection.

You will all remember your father's fondness, when perhaps every other circumstance relating to him is forgotten. This remem-brance, I hope, will induce you to give a serious attention to the advices I am now going to leave with you.—I can request this atten-tion with the greater confidence, as my sentiments on the most interesting points that regard life and manners, were entirely corre-spondent to your mother's, whose judgment and taste I trusted much more than my own.

You must expect that the advices which I shall give you will be very imperfect, as there are many nameless delicacies, in female manners, of which none but a woman can judge.—You will have one advantage by attending to what I am going to leave with you; you will hear, at least for once in your lives, the genuine sentiments of a man who has no interest in flattering or deceiving you.—I shall throw my reflections together without any studied order, and shall only, to avoid confusion, range them under a few general heads.

You will see, in a little Treatise of mine just published,[1] in what an

---

[1] I have been unable to identify this treatise.

honourable point of view I have considered your sex; not as domestic drudges, or the slaves of our pleasures, but as our companions and equals; as designed to soften our hearts and polish our manners; and, as Thomson finely says,

> To raise the virtues, animate the bliss,
> And sweeten all the toils of human life.[1]

I shall not repeat what I have there said on this subject, and shall only observe, that from the view I have given of your natural character and place in society, there arises a certain propriety of conduct peculiar to your sex. It is this peculiar propriety of female manners of which I intend to give you my sentiments, without touching on those general rules of conduct by which men and women are equally bound.

While I explain to you that system of conduct which I think will tend most to your honour and happiness, I shall, at the same time, endeavour to point out those virtues and accomplishments which render you most respectable and most amiable in the eyes of my own sex.[2]

Conduct and Behaviour

One of the chief beauties in a female character is that modest reserve, that retiring delicacy, which avoids the public eye, and is disconcerted even at the gaze of admiration.—I do not wish you to be insensible to applause. If you were, you must become, if not worse, at least less amiable women. But you may be dazzled by that admiration, which yet rejoices your hearts.

When a girl ceases to blush, she has lost the most powerful charm of beauty. That extreme sensibility which it indicates, may be a weakness and incumbrance in our sex, as I have too often felt; but in yours it is peculiarly engaging. Pedants, who think themselves philosophers, ask why a woman should blush when she is conscious of no crime. It is a sufficient answer, that Nature has made you to

---

[1] This particular quotation from James Thomson's 1730 poem *Autumn* (in *A Hymn on the Seasons*) was often cited as a concise description of women's purpose in life.

[2] See the extract below from *A Vindication of the Rights of Woman* for Mary Wollstonecraft's response to Gregory's advice to his daughters.

blush when you are guilty of no fault, and has forced us to love you because you do so.—Blushing is so far from being necessarily an attendant on guilt, that it is the usual companion of innocence.

This modesty, which I think so essential in your sex, will naturally dispose you to be rather silent in company, especially in a large one.—People of sense and discernment will never mistake such silence for dulness. One may take a share in conversation without uttering a syllable. The expression in the countenance shews it, and this never escapes an observing eye.

I should be glad that you had an easy dignity in your behaviour at public places, but not that confident ease, that unabashed countenance, which seems to set the company at defiance.—If, while a gentleman is speaking to you, one of superior rank addresses you, do not let your eager attention and visible preference betray the flutter of your heart. Let your pride on this occasion preserve you from that meanness into which your vanity would sink you. Consider that you expose yourselves to the ridicule of the company, and affront one gentleman, only to swell the triumph of another, who perhaps thinks he does you honour in speaking to you.

Converse with men even of the first rank with that dignified modesty, which may prevent the approach of the most distant familiarity, and consequently prevent them from feeling themselves your superiors.

Wit is the most dangerous talent you can possess. It must be guarded with great discretion and good-nature, otherwise it will create you many enemies. Wit is perfectly consistent with softness and delicacy; yet they are seldom found united. Wit is so flattering to vanity, that they who possess it become intoxicated, and lose all self-command.

Humour is a different quality. It will make your company much solicited; but be cautious how you indulge it.—It is often a great enemy to delicacy, and a still greater one to dignity of character. It may sometimes gain you applause, but will never procure you respect.

Be even cautious in displaying your good sense. It will be thought you assume a superiority over the rest of the company.—But if you happen to have any learning, keep it a profound secret, especially from the men, who generally look with a jealous and malignant eye on a woman of great parts, and a cultivated understanding.

A man of real genius and candour is far superior to this meanness. But such a one will seldom fall in your way; and if by accident he should, do not be anxious to shew the full extent of your knowledge. If he has any opportunities of seeing you, he will soon discover it himself; and if you have any advantages of person or manner, and keep your own secret, he will probably give you credit for a great deal more than you possess.—The great art of pleasing in conversation consists in making the company pleased with themselves. You will more readily hear than talk yourselves into their good graces.

Beware of detraction, especially where your own sex are concerned. You are generally accused of being particularly addicted to this vice.—I think unjustly.—Men are fully as guilty of it when their interests interfere.—As your interests more frequently clash, and as your feelings are quicker than ours, your temptations to it are more frequent. For this reason, be particularly tender of the reputation of your own sex, especially when they happen to rival you in our regards. We look on this as the strongest proof of dignity and true greatness of mind.

Shew a compassionate sympathy to unfortunate women, especially to those who are rendered so by the villainy of men. Indulge a secret pleasure, I may say pride, in being the friends and refuge of the unhappy, but without the vanity of shewing it.

Consider every species of indelicacy in conversation, as shameful in itself, and as highly disgusting to us. All double entendre is of this sort.—The dissoluteness of men's education allows them to be diverted with a kind of wit, which yet they have delicacy enough to be shocked at, when it comes from your mouths, or even when you hear it without pain and contempt.—Virgin purity is of that delicate nature, that it cannot hear certain things without contamination. It is always in your power to avoid these. No man, but a brute or a fool, will insult a woman with conversation which he sees gives her pain; nor will he dare to do it, if she resent the injury with a becoming spirit.—There is a dignity in conscious virtue which is able to awe the most shameless and abandoned of men.

You will be reproached perhaps with prudery. By prudery is usually meant an affectation of delicacy. Now I do not wish you to affect delicacy; I wish you to possess it. At any rate, it is better to run the risk of being thought ridiculous than disgusting.

The men will complain of your reserve. They will assure you that a franker behaviour would make you more amiable. But trust me, they are not sincere when they tell you so.—I acknowledge, that on some occasions it might render you more agreeable as companions, but it would make you less amiable as women: An important distinction, which many of your sex are not aware of.—After all, I wish you to have great ease and openness in your conversation. I only point out some considerations which ought to regulate your behaviour in that respect.

Have a sacred regard to truth. Lying is a mean and despicable vice.—I have known some women of excellent parts, who were so much addicted to it, that they could not be trusted in the relation of any story, especially if it contained any thing of the marvellous, or if they themselves were the heroines of the tale. This weakness did not proceed from a bad heart, but was merely the effect of vanity, or an unbridled imagination.—I do not mean to censure that lively embellishment of a humorous story, which is only intended to promote innocent mirth.

There is a certain gentleness of spirit and manners extremely engaging in your sex; not that indiscriminate attention, that unmeaning simper, which smiles on all alike. This arises, either from an affectation of softness, or from perfect insipidity.

There is a species of refinement in luxury, just beginning to prevail among the gentlemen of this country, to which our ladies are yet as great strangers as any women upon earth; I hope, for the honour of the sex, they may ever continue so: I mean, the luxury of eating. It is a despicable selfish vice in men, but in your sex it is beyond expression indelicate and disgusting.

Every one who remembers a few years back, is sensible of a very striking change in the attention and respect formerly paid by the gentlemen to the ladies. Their drawing-rooms are deserted; and after dinner and supper, the gentlemen are impatient till they retire. How they came to lose this respect, which nature and politeness so well intitle them to, I shall not here particularly inquire. The revolutions of manners in any country depend on causes very various and complicated. I shall only observe, that the behaviour of the ladies in the last age was very reserved and stately. It would now be reckoned ridiculously stiff and formal. Whatever it was, it had certainly the effect of making them more respected.

A fine woman, like other fine things in nature, has her proper point of view, from which she may be seen to most advantage. To fix this point requires great judgment, and an intimate knowledge of the human heart. By the present mode of female manners, the ladies seem to expect that they shall regain their ascendancy over us, by the fullest display of their personal charms, by being always in our eye at public places, by conversing with us with the same unreserved freedom as we do with one another; in short, by resembling us as nearly as they possibly can.—But a little time and experience will shew the folly of this expectation and conduct.

The power of a fine woman over the hearts of men, of men of the finest parts, is even beyond what she conceives. They are sensible of the pleasing illusion, but they cannot, nor do they wish to dissolve it. But if she is determined to dispel the charm, it certainly is in her power: she may soon reduce the angel to a very ordinary girl.

There is a native dignity in ingenuous modesty to be expected in your sex, which is your natural protection from the familiarities of the men, and which you should feel previous to the reflection that it is your interest to keep yourselves sacred from all personal freedoms. The many nameless charms and endearments of beauty should be reserved to bless the arms of the happy man to whom you give your heart, but who, if he has the least delicacy, will despise them, if he knows that they have been prostituted to fifty men before him.—The sentiment, that a woman may allow all innocent freedoms, provided her virtue is secure, is both grossly indelicate and dangerous, and has proved fatal to many of your sex.

Let me now recommend to your attention that elegance, which is not so much a quality itself, as the high polish of every other. It is what diffuses an ineffable grace over every look, every motion, every sentence you utter. It gives that charm to beauty without which it generally fails to please. It is partly a personal quality, in which respect it is the gift of nature; but I speak of it principally as a quality of the mind. In a word, it is the perfection of taste in life and manners;—every virtue and every excellence, in their most graceful and amiable forms.

You may perhaps think that I want to throw every spark of nature out of your composition, and to make you entirely artificial. Far from it. I wish you to possess the most perfect simplicity of heart and manners. I think you may possess dignity without pride, affability without meanness, and simple elegance without affectation. Milton had my idea, when he says of Eve,

> Grace was in all her steps, Heaven in her eye,
> In every gesture dignity and love.[1]

---

[1] In *Paradise Lost*, first published in 1667, John Milton (1608–74) describes Eve with these often-quoted lines in Book 8.

From Amusements

Every period of life has amusements which are natural and proper to it. You may indulge the variety of your tastes in these, while you keep within the bounds of that propriety which is suitable to your sex. Some amusements are conducive to health, as various kinds of exercise: some are connected with qualities really useful, as different kinds of women's work, and all the domestic concerns of a family: some are elegant accomplishments, as dress, dancing, music, and drawing. Such books as improve your understanding, enlarge your knowledge, and cultivate your taste, may be considered in a higher point of view than mere amusements. There are a variety of others, which are neither useful nor ornamental, such as play of different kinds....

The intention of your being taught needle-work, knitting, and such like, is not on account of the intrinsic value of all you can do with your hands, which is trifling, but to enable you to judge more perfectly of that kind of work, and to direct the execution of it in others. Another principal end is to enable you to fill up, in a tolerably agreeable way, some of the many solitary hours you must necessarily pass at home.—It is a great article in the happiness of life, to have your pleasures as independent of others as possible. By continually gadding abroad in search of amusement, you lose the respect of all your acquaintances, whom you oppress with those visits, which, by a more discreet management, might have been courted....

I am at the greatest loss what to advise you in regard to books. There is no impropriety in your reading history, or cultivating any art or science to which genius or accident leads you. The whole volume of Nature lies open to your eye, and furnishes an infinite variety of entertainment. If I was sure that Nature had given you such strong principles of taste and sentiment as would remain with you, and influence your future conduct, with the utmost pleasure would I endeavour to direct your reading in such a way as might form that taste to the utmost perfection of truth and elegance. "But when I reflect how easy it is to warm a girl's imagination, and how difficult deeply and permanently to affect her heart; how readily she enters into every refinement of sentiment, and how easily she can sacrifice them to vanity or convenience;" I think I may very probably do you an injury by artificially creating a taste, which, if Nature never gave it you, would only serve to embarrass your future conduct.—I do not want to *make* you any thing: I want to know what Nature has made you, and to perfect you on her plan. I do not wish you to have sentiments that might perplex you: I wish you to have sentiments that may uniformly and steadily guide you, and such as your hearts so thoroughly approve, that you would not forego them for any consideration this world could offer....

3. From Thomas Day, *The History of Sandford and Merton, A Work Intended for the Use of Children*, 1784

[Thomas Day's *Sandford and Merton*, like *The Governess*, was heavily influenced by Locke's educational philosophies. Locke's emphasis on children's rational and moral development became a central tenet for a large group of writers publishing from the mid-eighteenth to mid-nineteenth centuries. Referred to as rational moralists, these writers often placed a wise and benevolent tutor at the center of their works—like Mrs. Teachum in *The Governess*, Mr. Barlow in *Sandford and Merton*, and Mrs. Mason in Mary Wollstonecraft's *Original Stories*. Day and Wollstonecraft were also influenced by the writings of Jean-Jacques Rousseau (1712-78), who celebrated children's innocence and curiosity. Although Rousseau's ideas about male education are still influential, his theories about the education of young women were limited to preparing their minds to be "well-tilled soil ready for the sower," that is, their future husbands. Day took Rousseau's advice to heart, and in his search for a perfect wife, took two twelve-year-old girls from orphanages and educated them according to the system Rousseau outlined in his educational treatise *Émile* (1762). Apparently neither young woman proved suitable, and Day eventually married someone else.]

In the western part of England lived a gentleman of great fortune, whose name was Merton. He had a large estate in the island of Jamaica, where he had past the greater part of his life, and was master of many servants, who cultivated sugar and other valuable things for his advantage.[1] He had only one son, of whom he was excessively

---

[1] As an abolitionist writer Day was concerned about the effects of slavery not only on slaves, but on slaveholders as well. Most abolitionists believed that the institution corrupted the morals of slaveholders, turning them into tyrants. Given Day's abolitionist tendencies, it is ironic that he uses the euphemistic "servant" rather than "slave."

fond; and to educate this child properly was the reason of his determining to stay some years in England. Tommy Merton, who, at the time he came from Jamaica, was only six years old, was naturally a very good-natured boy, but unfortunately had been spoiled by too much indulgence. While he lived in Jamaica, he had several black servants to wait upon him, who were forbidden upon any account to contradict him. If he walked, there always went two negroes with him, one of whom carried a large umbrella to keep the sun from him, and the other was to carry him in his arms, whenever he was tired. Besides this, he was always dressed in silk or laced cloaths, and had a fine gilded carriage, which was borne upon men's shoulders, in which he made visits to his play-fellows. His mother was so excessively fond of him, that she gave him every thing he cried for, and would never let him learn to read, because he complained that it made his head ache.

The consequence of this was, that, though Master Merton had every thing he wanted, he became very fretful and unhappy. Sometimes he ate sweetmeats till he made himself sick, and then he suffered a great deal of pain, because he would not take bitter physic[1] to make him well. Sometimes he cried for things that it was impossible to give him, and then, as he had never been used to be contradicted, it was many hours before he could be pacified. When any company came to dine at the house, he was always to be helped first, and to have the most delicate parts of the meat, otherwise he would make such a noise as disturbed the whole company. When his father and mother were sitting at the tea-table with their friends, instead of waiting till they were at leisure to attend to him, he would scramble upon the table, seize the cake and bread and butter, and frequently over-set the tea-cups. By these pranks he not only made himself disagreeable to every body, but often met with very dangerous accidents. Frequently he cut himself with knives, at other times thrown heavy things upon his head, and once he narrowly escaped being scalded to death, by a kettle of boiling water. He was also so delicately brought up that he was perpetually ill; the least wind or rain gave him a cold, and the least sun was sure to throw him into a fever. Instead of playing about, and jumping, and running like other children, he was taught to sit still for fear of spoiling his cloaths, and to stay in the house for fear of injuring his complection. By this kind of education, when Master Merton came over to England, he could

---

[1] That is, medicine.

neither write, nor read, nor cipher; he could use none of his limbs with ease, nor bear any degree of fatigue; but he was very proud, fretful, and impatient.

Very near to Mr. Merton's seat lived a plain, honest farmer, whose name was Sandford. This man had, like Mr. Merton, an only son, about six years old, whose name was Harry. Harry, as he had been always accustomed to run about in the fields, to follow the labourers while they were ploughing, and to drive the sheep to their pasture, was active, strong, hardy, and fresh coloured.[1] He was neither so fair, nor so delicately shaped as Master Merton; but he had an honest, good-natured countenance, which made every body love him; was never out of humour, and took the greatest pleasure in obliging every body. If little Harry saw a poor wretch who wanted victuals, while he was eating his dinner, he was sure to give him half, and sometimes the whole: nay, so very good-natured was he to every thing, that he would never go into the fields to take the eggs of poor birds, or their young ones, nor practise any other kind of sport which gave pain to poor animals, who are as capable of feeling as we ourselves, though they have no words to express their sufferings. Once, indeed, Harry was caught twirling a cockchafer[2] round, which he had fastened by a crooked pin to a long piece of thread, but then this was through ignorance and want of thought: for as soon as his father told him that the poor, helpless insect felt as much, or more than he would do, were a knife thrust through his hand, he burst into tears, and took the poor animal home, where he fed him during a fortnight upon fresh leaves; and when he was perfectly recovered, turned him out to enjoy liberty and the fresh air. Ever since that time, Harry was so careful and considerate, that he would step out of the way for fear of hurting a worm, and employed himself in doing kind offices to all the animals in the neighbourhood. He used to stroke the horses as they were at work, and fill his pockets with acorns for the pigs: if he walked in the fields, he was sure to gather green boughs for the sheep, who were so fond of him, that they followed him wherever he went. In the winter time, when the ground was covered with frost and snow, and the poor little birds could get at no food, he would often go supperless to bed, that he

---

[1]   That is, rosy-cheeked or suntanned.
[2]   A stout broad insect or beetle of comparatively large size and grayish chestnut color, also called Maybug, which flies with a loud whirring sound. Both the perfect insect and the larva are very destructive to vegetation (*OED*).

might feed the robin redbreasts. Even toads, and frogs, and spiders and such kind of disagreeable animals, which most people destroy where-ever they find them, were perfectly safe with Harry: he used to say they had a right to live as well as we, and that it was cruel and unjust to kill creatures only because we did not like them.

These sentiments made little Harry a great favourite with every body, particularly with the clergyman of the parish, who became so fond of him, that he taught him to read and write, and had him almost always with him. Indeed, it was not surprising that Mr. Barlow shewed so particular an affection for him; for, besides learning every thing that he was taught with the greatest readiness, little Harry was the most honest, obliging creature in the world. He was never discontented, nor did he ever grumble, what-ever he was desired to do. And then you might believe Harry in every thing he said; for though he could have gained a plumb-cake by telling an untruth, and was sure that speaking the truth would expose him to a severe whipping, he never hesitated in declaring it. ...

As [Master Merton] and the maid were once walking in the fields upon a fine summer's morning, diverting themselves with gathering different kinds of wild flowers, and running after butter-flies, a large snake, on a sudden, started up from among some long grass, and coiled itself round little Tommy's leg. You may imagine the fright they were both in at this accident: the maid ran away shrieking for help, while the child, who was in agony of terror, did not dare to stir from the place where he was standing. Harry, who happened to be walking near the place, came running up, and asked what was the matter? Tommy, who was sobbing most piteously, could not find words to tell him, but pointed to his leg, and made Harry sensible of what had happened. Harry, who, though young, was a boy of a most courageous spirit, told him not to be fright-ened, and instantly seizing the snake by the neck with as much dexterity as resolution, tore him from Tommy's leg, and threw him to a great distance off. Just as this happened, Mrs. Merton and all the family, alarmed by the servant's cries, came running breathless to the place, as Tommy was recovering his spirits, and thanking his brave little deliverer. Her first emotions were to catch her darling up in her arms, and, after giving him a thousand kisses, to ask him whether he had received any hurt? No, says Tommy, indeed I have not, mama; but I believe that nasty, ugly beast would have bitten me, if that little boy had not come and pulled him off. And who are you, my dear, says she, to whom we are all so obliged? Harry Sandford, madam. Well, my child, you are a dear, brave little creature, and you shall go home and dine with us. No, thank you, madam; my father will want me. And who is your father, my sweet boy? Farmer Sandford, madam, that lives at the bottom of the hill. Well, my dear, you shall be my child henceforth, will you? If you please, madam, if I may have my own father and mother, too.

Mrs. Merton instantly dispatched a servant to the farmer's, and taking little Harry by the hand, she led him to the mansion-house, where she found Mr. Merton, whom she entertained with a long account of Tommy's danger and Harry's bravery. Harry was now in a new scene of life. He was carried through costly apartments, where every thing that could please the eye, or contribute to convenience, was assembled. He saw large looking-glasses in gilded frames, carved tables and chairs, curtains made of the finest silk, and the very plates and knives and forks were silver. At dinner he was placed close to Mrs. Merton, who took care to supply him with the choicest bits, and engaged him to eat with the most endearing kindness. But, to the astonishment of every body, he neither appeared pleased or surprised at any thing he saw. Mrs. Merton could not conceal her disappointment; for as she had always been used to a great degree of finery herself, she had expected it should make the same impression upon every body else. At last, seeing him eye a small silver cup, with great attention, out of which he had been drinking, she asked him, whether he should not like to have such a fine thing to drink out of; and added, that, though it was Tommy's cup, she was sure he would give it with great pleasure to his little friend. Yes, that I will, says Tommy; for you know, mama, I have a much finer than that, made of gold, besides two large ones made of silver. Thank you with all my heart, says little Harry; but I will not rob you of it, for I have a much better one at home. How! Says Mrs. Merton, what does your father eat and drink out of silver? I don't know, madam, what you call this, but we drink at home out of long things made of horn, just such as the cows wear upon their heads. The child is a simpleton, I think, says Mrs. Merton;—and why is that better than silver ones? Because, says Harry, they never make us uneasy. Make you uneasy, my child, says Mrs. Merton; what do you mean? Why, madam, when the man threw that great thing down, which looks just like this, I saw that you were very sorry about it, and looked as if you had been just ready to drop. Now, ours at home are thrown about by all the family, and nobody minds it.

I protest, says Mrs. Merton to her husband, I do not know what to say to this boy, he makes such strange observations. The fact was, that during dinner one of the servants had thrown down a large piece of plate, which, as it was very valuable, had made Mrs. Merton not only look very uneasy, but give the man a very severe scolding for his carelessness.

After dinner, Mrs. Merton filled a large glass with wine and, giving it to Harry, bade him drink it up; but he thanked her, and said he was not dry. But, my dear, says she, this is very sweet and pleasant, and, as you are a good boy, you may drink it up. Aye! but, madam, Mr. Barlow says, that we must only eat when we are hungry, and drink when we are dry; and that we must only eat and drink such things as are easily met with, otherwise we shall grow peevish and vexed when we can't get them....

... Upon my word, says Mr. Merton, this little man is a great philosopher, and we should be much obliged to Mr. Barlow if he would take our Tommy under his care; for he grows a great boy, and it is time that he should know something. What say you, Tommy, should you like to be a philosopher? Indeed, papa, I don't know what a philosopher is, but I should like to be a king; because he's finer and richer than any body else, and has nothing to do, and every body waits upon him, and is afraid of him. Well said, my dear, says Mrs. Merton, and rose and kissed him; and a king you deserve to be with such a spirit, and here's a glass of wine for you for making such a pretty answer. And should you not like to be a king too, little Harry? Indeed, madam, I don't know what that is; but I hope I shall soon be big enough to go to plough, and get my own living; and then I shall want nobody to wait upon me. What a difference there is between the children of farmers and gentle-men! whispered Mrs. Merton to her husband, looking rather contemptuously upon Harry. I am not sure, said Mr. Merton, that for this time the advantage is on the side of our son. But should you not like to be rich, my dear, says he to Harry? No, indeed, sir. No, simpleton, says Mrs. Merton, and why not? Because the only rich man I ever saw is squire Chace, who lives hard by, and he rides among people's corn,[1] and breaks down their hedges, and lames their cattle, and abuses the

---

[1] As a general term "corn" includes all the cereals: wheat, rye, barley, oats, maize, rice, etc. Locally, the word, when not otherwise qualified, refers to the kind of cereal that is the leading crop of the district; hence in the greater part of England "corn" refers to wheat, in North Britain and Ireland, to oats, and in the US, to Indian corn, or maize (OED).

poor, and they say he does all this because he's rich; but every body hates him, though they dare not tell him so to his face—and I would not be hated for any thing in the world. But should not you like to have a fine laced coat, and a coach to carry you about, and servants to wait upon you? As to that, madam, one coat is as good as another, if it will but keep one warm; and I don't want to ride, because I can walk wherever I chuse; and, as to servants, I should have nothing for them to do, if I had an hundred of them. Mrs. Merton continued to look at him with a sort of contemptuous astonishment, but did not ask him any more questions....

... [A]t the mansion-house, much of the conversation ... was employed in examining the merits of little Harry. Mrs. Merton acknowledged his bravery and openness of temper; she was also struck with the general good-nature and benevolence of his character; but she contended there were a certain grossness and indelicacy in his ideas which distinguish the children of the lower and middling classes of people from those of persons of fashion.[1] Mr. Merton, on the contrary, contended that he had never before seen a child whose sentiments and dispositions would do so much honour even to the most elevated situations. Nothing, he affirmed, was more easily acquired than those external manners, and that superficial address, upon which too many of the higher classes pride themselves as their greatest, or even as their only accomplishment.... Indeed, the real feat of all superiority, even of manners, must be placed in the mind: dignified sentiments, superior courage, accompanied with genuine and universal courtesy, are always necessary to constitute the real gentleman; and where these are wanting, it is the greatest absurdity to think they can be supplied by affected tones of voice, particular grimaces, or extravagant and unnatural modes of dress.... I cannot help, therefore, asserting, said he very seriously, that this little peasant has within his mind the seeds of true gentility and dignity of character; and, though I shall also wish that our son may possess all the common accomplishments of his rank, nothing would give me more pleasure than a certainty hat he would never in any respect fall below the son of farmer Sandford.

Whether Mrs. Merton fully acceded to these observations of her husband I cannot decide; but without waiting to hear her particular

---

[1]   That is, sophisticated, wealthier people; those who know the ways of so-called polite society. For Day, such worldliness is less attractive than simplicity and honesty.

sentiments, he thus went on:—Should I appear more warm than usual upon this subject, you must pardon me, my dear, and attribute it to the interest I feel in the welfare of our little Tommy. I am too sensible, that our mutual fondness has hitherto treated him with rather too much indulgence. While we have been over solicitous to remove from him every painful and disagreeable impression, we have made him too delicate and fretful: our desire of constantly consulting his inclinations has made us gratify even his caprices and humours; and, while we have been too studious to preserve him from restraint and opposition, we have in reality been the cause why he has not acquired even the common acquisitions of his age and situation. All this I have long observed in silence; but have hitherto concealed, both from my fondness for our child, and my fear of offending you. But at length a consideration of his real interests has prevailed over every other notice, and has compelled me to embrace a resolution which I hope will not be disagreeable to you, that of sending him directly to Mr. Barlow....

... The day after Tommy came to Mr. Barlow's, as soon as breakfast was over, he took him and Harry into the garden: when he was there, he took a spade into his own hand, and giving Harry an hoe, they both began to work with great eagerness. Every body that eats, says Mr. Barlow, ought to assist in procuring food, and therefore little Harry and I begin our daily work; this is my bed, and that other is his; we work upon it every day, and he that raises the most out of it, will deserve to fare the best. Now, Tommy, if you chuse to join us, I will mark you out a piece of ground, which you shall have to yourself, and all the produce shall be your own. No, indeed, says Tommy, very sulkily, I am a gentleman, and don't chuse to slave like a ploughboy. Just as you please, Mr. Gentleman, said Mr. Barlow; but Harry and I, who are not above being useful, will mind our work. In about two hours Mr. Barlow said it was time to leave off, and, taking Harry by the hand, he led him into a very pleasant summer-house, where they sat down, and Mr. Barlow, taking out a plate of very fine ripe cherries, divided them between Harry and himself. Tommy, who had followed, and expected his share, when he saw them both eating without taking any notice of him, could no longer restrain his passion, but burst into a violent fit of sobbing and crying. What is the matter, said Mr. Barlow very coolly to him? Tommy looked upon him very sulkily, but returned no answer. Oh! sir, if you don't chuse to give me an answer, you may be silent; nobody is obliged to speak here. Tommy became still more disconcerted at this, and, being unable to conceal his anger, ran out of the summerhouse, and wandered very disconsolately about the garden; equally surprised and vexed that he was now in a place where nobody felt any concern whether he was pleased or the contrary....

4. From Sarah Trimmer, *Fabulous Histories. Designed for the Instruction of Children, Respecting Their Treatment of Animals*, 1786

[As evidenced by her review of *The Governess* (see Appendix A), Sarah Trimmer (1741-1810) appreciated the moral lessons imparted by Fielding's educational novel. Trimmer herself was an influential educationalist, much of her philosophy derived from the practical experience of teaching her own twelve children. Although Trimmer was a prolific writer, her most famous children's book remains her *Fabulous Histories*, an excerpt from which is printed below. As with much of the literature produced by the Sunday School movement, *The History of the Robins* (the more familiar title of *Fabulous Histories*), promotes cheerful obedience to authority and a willingness to perform (and accept) acts of charity.]

Chapter III

It happened one day, that both the Redbreasts, who always went together to Mr. Benson's (because, if one had waited for the other's return, it would have missed the chance of being fed) it happened, I say, that they were both absent longer than usual, for their little benefactors having been fatigued with a very long walk the evening before, lay late in bed that morning; but as soon as Frederick was dressed, his sister, who was waiting for him, took him by the hand, and led him down stairs, where he hastily demanded to the cook the collection of crumbs reserved for him. As soon as he entered the breakfast parlour, he ran eagerly to the window, and attempted to fling it up. What is the cause of this mighty bustle? said his mamma. Do you not perceive that I am in the room, Frederick? Oh, my birds! my birds! cried he. I understand, rejoined Mrs. Benson, that you have neglected to feed your little pensioners; how came this about, Harriet? We were so tired last night, answered Miss Benson, that we overslept ourselves, mamma. This excuse may satisfy you and your brother, added the Lady, but I fear your birds would bring heavy complaints against you, were they able to talk our language. But make haste to supply their present wants; and for the future, whenever you give any living creature cause to depend on you for sustenance, be careful on no account to disappoint it; and if you are prevented feeding it yourself, employ another person to do it for you. But though it is very commendable, and indeed an obligation on your humanity, to be attentive to your dependants, yet you must not let this make you forgetful of your duty to your friends. It is customary for little boys and girls to pay their respects to their papa's and mamma's, every morning, as soon as they see them. This, Frederick, you ought to have done to me, on entering the parlour, instead of tearing across it, crying out, my birds! my birds! It would have taken you but a very little time to have done so: however, I will excuse your neglect now, my dear, as you did not intend to offend me; but I expect that you will so manage the business you have undertaken, that it may not break in on your higher obligations. You depend on your papa and me, for every thing you want, as these little birds do on you: nay, more so, for they could supply their own wants, by seeking food in other places; but children can do nothing towards their support: therefore it is particularly requisite, that they should be dutiful and respectful to those, whose tenderness and care are constantly exerted on their benefit. Miss Harriet promised her mamma, that she would, on all occasions, endeavour to behave as she wished her to do; but I am sorry to say, Frederick was more intent on opening the window, than on imbibing the good instructions that were given him: this he could not effect, and therefore Harriet, by her mamma's permission, went to his assistance, and the store of provisions was dispensed. As many of the birds had nests, they eat their meal with all possible expedition; amongst this number were the Robins, who dispatched the business as soon as they could, for the hen was anxious to return to her little ones, and the cock to procure them a breakfast; and having given his young friends a serenade, before they left their bed-chambers, he did not think it necessary to stay to sing any more, they therefore departed. When the mother-bird arrived at the ivy wall, she stopt at the entrance of the nest, with a palpitating heart; but seeing her brood all safe and well, she hastened to take them under her wings. As soon as she was seated, she observed that they were not so cheerful as usual. What is the matter, said she? How have you agreed during my absence? To these questions all were unwilling to reply, for the truth was, that they had been quarrelling almost the whole time. What, all silent? said she; I fear you have not obeyed my commands, but have been contending. I desire you will tell me the truth. Robin, knowing that he was the greatest offender, began to justify himself, before the others could have time to lay an accusation against him.

I am sure, mother, said he, I only gave Dicky a little peck, because he crowded me so; and all the others joined with him, and fell upon me at once.

Since you have begun, Robin, answered Dicky, I must speak, for you gave me a very hard peck indeed, and I was afraid you had put out my eye. I am sure I made all the room I could for you; but you said you ought to have half the nest, and to be master, when your father and mother were out, because you are the eldest.

I do not love to tell tales, said Flapsy, but what Dicky says is very true, Robin; and you plucked two or three little feathers out of me, only because I begged you not to use us ill.

And you set your foot very hard upon me, cried Pecksy, for telling you that you had forgot our dear mother's injunction.

This is a sad story indeed, said the mother. I am very sorry to find, Robin, that you already discover such a turbulent disposition. If you go on in this manner, we shall have no peace in the nest, nor can I leave it with any degree of satisfaction. As for your being the eldest, though it makes me shew you a preference on all proper occasions, it does not give you a privilege to domineer over your brothers and sisters. You are all equally the objects of our tender care, which we shall exercise equally amongst you, provided you do not forfeit it by bad behaviour. To shew that you are not master of the nest, I desire you to get from under my wing, and sit on the outside, whilst I cherish those who are dutiful and good. Robin, greatly mortified, retired from his mother; on which Dicky, with the utmost kindness, began to intercede for him. Pardon Robin, my dear mother, I entreat you, said he, I heartily forgive his treatment of me, and would not have complained to you, had it not been necessary for my own justification. You are a good bird, Dicky, said his mother, but such an offence as this must be repented of before it is pardoned. At this instant her mate returned with a fine worm, and looked as usual for Robin, who lay skulking by himself. Give it, said the mother, to Dicky, Robin must be served last this morning; nay, I do not know whether I shall permit him to have any victuals all day. Dicky was very unwilling to mortify his brother, but on his mother's commanding him not to detain his father, he opened his mouth and swallowed the delicious mouthful. What can be the matter, said the good father, surely none of the little ones have been naughty? But I cannot stop to enquire at present, for I left another fine worm, which may be gone if I do not make haste back.

As soon as he departed, Dicky renewed his solicitations that Robin might be forgiven; but as he sat swelling with anger and disdain, because he fancied that the eldest should not be shoved to the outside of his mother's wing, whilst the others were fed, she would not hear a word in his behalf. The father soon came and fed Flapsy, and then thinking it best for his mate to continue her instructions, he made another excursion; during which, Pecksy, whose little heart was full of affectionate concern for the punishment of her brother, thus attempted to comfort him.

Dear Robin, do not grieve, I will give you my breakfast, if my mother will let me. O, said Robin, I do not want any breakfast; if I may not be served *first*, I will have *none*. Shall I ask my mother to forgive you? I don't want any of your intercessions, replied he; if you had not been a parcel of ill-natured things, I should not have been pushed about as I am.

Come back, Pecksy, said the mother, who overheard them, I will not have you hold converse with so naughty a bird. I forbid every one of you even to go near him. The father then arrived, and Pecksy was fed. You may rest yourself, my dear, said the mother, your morning's task is ended. Why, what has Robin done? asked he. What I am sorry to relate, she replied: Quarrelled with his brothers and sisters. Quarrelled with his brothers and sisters! you surprize me: I could not have suspected he would have been either so foolish or so unkind.—O, this is not all, said the mother, for he presumes on being the eldest, and claims half the nest to himself when we are absent, and now is sullen because he is disgraced, and not fed first as usual. If that is the case, replied the father, leave me to settle this business, my dear, and pray go into the air a little, for you seem to be sadly agitated. I am disturbed, said she, I confess; for after all my care and solicitude, I did not expect such a sad recompense as this. I am sorry to expose this perverse bird, even to you, but he resists my efforts to reform him. I will do as you desire, go into the air a little; so saying, she repaired to a neighbouring tree, where she waited, with anxious expectation, the event of her mate's interposition.

As soon as the mother departed, the father thus addressed the delinquent. And so, Robin, you want to be master of the nest? A pretty master you will make indeed, who do not know even how to govern your own temper! I will not stand to talk much to you now, because, in your present disposition, you would in all probability turn a deaf ear to my admonitions; but depend upon it, I will not suffer you to use any of the family ill, particularly your good mother; and if you persist in obstinacy, I will certainly turn you out of the nest before you can fly. These threatenings intimidated Robin, and he also began to be very hungry, as well as cold; he therefore promised to behave better for the future, and his brothers and sisters pleaded earnestly that he might be forgiven and restored to his usual place. I can say nothing in respect to the last particular, replied the father, that depends upon his mother; but as it is his first offence, and he seems to be very sorry, I will myself pardon it, and intercede for him with his mother, who I fear is at this time lamenting his obduracy. On this he left the nest to seek for her. Return, my dear, said he, to your beloved family; Robin seems sensible of his offence, and longs to ask your forgiveness. Pleased at this intelligence, the mother raised her drooping head, and closed her wings, which hung mournfully at her sides, expressive of the dejection of her spirits. I fly to give it him, said [s]he, and hastened into the nest. In the mean while Robin wished for, yet dreaded her return. As soon as he saw her, he lifted up a supplicating eye, and with feeble accents (for hunger concurred with sorrow to make him faint) he chirped, "Forgive me, dear mother, I will not again offend you." I accept your submission, Robin, said she, and will once more receive you to my wing; but indeed, your behaviour has made me very unhappy. She then made room for him, he nestled closely to her side, and soon found the benefit of her foster-ing heat; yet he had not confidence to ask his father to fetch him any victuals: but this kind parent waited not for solicitation, for seeing that his mother had received him into favour, he went with all speed to an adjacent field, where he soon met with refreshment for him, which with tender love he presented, and Robin swallowed with gratitude. Thus was peace restored to the nest, and the happy mother once more rejoiced that harmony reigned in the family.

5. From Mary Wollstonecraft, *Original Stories from Real Life*, 1788

[As mentioned in the introductory note to Day's *Sandford and Merton*, Mary Wollstonecraft (1759-97) belonged to that group of educational philosophers known as the rational moralists. Wollstonecraft's second work on education—her first publication was *Thoughts on the Education of Daughters* (1787)—features the governess Mrs. Mason, who assumes the task of educating two young girls, Caroline and Mary. The lessons she imparts are designed to appeal to Caroline and Mary's reason, and by the end of the text, Mrs. Mason is happy to see that their virtue and understanding have been strengthened under her guidance. Unlike Wollstonecraft's later treatise, *A Vindication of the Rights of Woman*, *Original Stories* does not represent a radical departure from conventional educational literature that emphasized self-denial and self-regulation. Even so, it is useful to see how this early work—based on Wollstonecraft's experience running a school for girls and her brief career as a governess—laid the foundation for her more famous argument on women's education.]

From the Preface

These conversations and tales are accommodated to the present state of society; which obliges the author to attempt to cure those faults by reason, which ought never to have taken root in the infant mind. Good habits, imperceptibly fixed, are far preferable to the precepts of reason; but, as this task requires more judgment than generally falls to the lot of parent, substitutes must be sought for, and medicines given, when regimen would have answered the purpose much better. I believe those who examine their own minds, will readily agree with me, that reason, with difficulty, conquers settled habits, even when it is arrived at some degree of maturity: why then do we suffer children to be bound with fetters, which their half-formed faculties cannot break....

The Benefit of Bodily Pain: Fortitude the Basis of Virtue

The children had been playing in the garden for some time, whilst Mrs. Mason was reading alone. But she was suddenly alarmed by the cries of Caroline, who ran in to the room in great distress. Mary quickly followed, and explaining the matter said, that her sister had accidently disturbed some wasps, who were terrified, and of course stung her. Remedies were applied to assuage the pain; yet all the time she uttered the loudest and most silly complaints, regardless of the uneasiness she gave those who were exerting themselves to relieve her. In a short time the smart abated, and then her friend thus addressed her, with more than usual gravity. I am sorry to see a girl of your age weep on account of bodily pain; it is a proof of a weak mind—a proof that you cannot employ yourself about things of consequence. How often must I tell you that the Most High is educating us for eternity?

'The term virtue, comes from a word signifying strength. Fortitude of mind is, therefore, the basis of every virtue, and virtue belongs to a being, that is weak in its nature, and strong only in will and resolution.'

Children early feel bodily pain, to habituate them to bear the conflicts of the soul, when they become reasonable creatures. This, I say, is the first trial, and I like to see that proper pride which strives to conceal its sufferings. Those who, when young, weep if the least trifle annoys them, will never, I fear, have sufficient strength of mind, to encounter all the miseries that can afflict the body, rather than act meanly to avoid them. Indeed, this seems to be the essential difference between a great and a little mind: the former knows how to endure—whilst the latter suffers an immortal soul to be depressed, lost in its abode; suffers the inconveniences which attack the one to overwhelm the other. The soul would always support the body, if its superiority was felt, and invigorated by exercise. The Almighty, who never afflicts but to produce some good end, first sends diseases to children to teach them patience and fortitude; and when by degrees they have learned to bear them, they have acquired some virtue....

Mrs. Mason's Farewell Advice to Her Young Friends

The day before Mrs. Mason was to leave her pupils, she took a hand of each, and pressing them tenderly in her own, tears started into her eyes—I tremble for you, my dear girls, for you must now practise by yourselves some of the virtues which I have been endeavouring to inculcate; and I shall anxiously wait for the summer, to see what progress you have made by yourselves.

We have conversed on several very important subjects; pray do not forget the conclusions I have drawn.

I now, as my last present, give you a book, in which I have written the subjects that we discussed. Recur frequently to it, for the stories illustrating the instruction it contains, you will not feel in such a great degree the want of my personal advice. Some of the reasoning you may not thoroughly comprehend, but, as your understandings ripen, you will feel its full force.

Avoid anger; exercise compassion; and love truth. Recollect, that from religion your chief comfort must spring, and never neglect the duty of prayer. Learn from experience the comfort that arises from making known your wants and sorrows to the wisest and best of Beings, in whose hands are the issues, not only of this life, but of that which is to come.

Your father will allow you a certain stipend; you have already *felt* the pleasure of doing good; ever recollect that the wild pursuits of fancy must be conquered, to enable you to gratify benevolent wishes, and that you must practice œconomy in trifles to have it in your power to be generous on great occasions. And the good you intend to do, do quickly;—for know that a trifling duty neglected, is a great fault, and the present time only is at your command.

You are now candidates for my friendship, and on your advancement in virtue my regard will in future depend. Write often to me, I will punctually answer your letters; but let me have the genuine sentiments of your hearts. In expressions of affection and respect, do not deviate from truth to gain what you wish for, or to turn a period[1] prettily.

Adieu! when you think of your friend, observe her precepts; and let the recollection of my affection, give additional weight to the truths which I have endeavoured to instill; and, to reward my care, let me hear that you love and practice virtue.

6. From Mary Wollstonecraft, *A Vindication of the Rights of Woman*, 1792

[Wollstonecraft's famous polemic on women's rights remains one of the most impassioned statements for equal educational opportunities for women ever published. Although Wollstonecraft was by no means the first female writer to challenge the patriarchal status quo, she wrote during a revolutionary period that lent excitement and urgency to her argument. In developing her ideas about women's

---

[1] A complete sentence; here, the term applies to language that is rhetorically attractive but untrue or unsound.

ability to exercise reason—introduced earlier in *Original Stories*—Wollstonecraft challenges both long-held perceptions of women as inferior to men and those male writers whose educational theories perpetuate those perceptions. One such writer is John Gregory, whose *A Father's Legacy to His Daughters* is excerpted above.]

Chapter II, The Prevailing Opinion of a Sexual Character Discussed

To account for, and excuse the tyranny of man, many ingenious arguments have been brought forward to prove, that the two sexes, in the acquirement of virtue, ought to aim at attaining a very different character: or, to speak explicitly, women are not allowed to have sufficient strength of mind to acquire what really deserves the name of virtue. Yet it should seem, allowing them to have souls, that there is but one way appointed by Providence to lead *mankind* to either virtue or happiness.

If then women are not a swarm of ephemeron triflers, why should they be kept in ignorance under the specious name of innocence? Men complain, and with reason, of the follies and caprices of our sex, when they do not keenly satirize our headstrong passions and grovelling vices. Behold, I should answer, the natural effect of ignorance! The mind will ever be unstable that has only prejudices to rest on, and the current will run with destructive fury when there are no barriers to break its force. Women are told from their infancy, and taught by the example of their mothers, that a little knowledge of human weakness, justly termed cunning, softness of temper, *outward* obedience, and a scrupulous attention to a puerile kind of propriety, will obtain for them the protection of man; and should they be beautiful, every thing else is needless, for, at least, twenty years of their lives.

Thus Milton describes our first frail mother; though when he tells us that women are formed for softness and sweet attractive grace, I cannot comprehend his meaning, unless, in the true Mahometan strain, he meant to deprive us of souls, and insinuate that we were beings only designed by sweet attractive grace, and docile blind obedience, to gratify the senses of man when he can no longer soar on the wing of contemplation.[1]

---

[1]   Wollstonecraft takes great offense at Milton's portrayal of Eve in *Paradise Lost*. The "Mahometan strain" refers to eighteenth-century Western conceptions of Muslim culture, including the common (unfounded) criticism that Islamic teachings denied the existence of women's souls (which meant they could not enter heaven).

How grossly do they insult us who thus advise us only to render ourselves gentle, domestic brutes! For instance, the winning softness so warmly, and frequently, recommended, that governs by obeying. What childish expressions, and how insignificant is the being—can it be an immortal one? who will condescend to govern by such sinister methods! 'Certainly,' says Lord Bacon, 'man is of kin to the beasts by his body; and if he be not of kin to God by his spirit, he is a base and ignoble creature!'[1] Men, indeed, appear to me to act in a very unphilosophical manner when they try to secure the good conduct of women by attempting to keep them always in a state of childhood. Rousseau[2] was more consistent when he wished to stop the progress of reason in both sexes, for if men eat of the tree of knowledge, women will come in for a taste; but, from the imperfect cultivation which their understandings now receive, they only attain a knowledge of evil. Children, I grant, should be innocent; but when the epithet is applied to men, or women, it is but a civil term for weakness. For if it be allowed that women were destined by Providence to acquire human virtues, and by the exercise of their understanding, that stability of character which is the firmest ground to rest our future hopes upon, they must be permitted to turn to the fountain of light, and not forced to shape their course by the twinkling of a mere satellite. Milton, I grant, was of a very different opinion; for he only bends to the indefeasible right of beauty ...

By individual education, I mean, for the sense of the word is not precisely defined, such an attention to a child as will slowly sharpen the senses, form the temper, regulate the passions, as they begin to ferment, and set the understanding to work before the body arrives at maturity; so that the man may only have to proceed, not to begin, the important task of learning to think and reason.

To prevent any misconstruction, I must add, that I do not believe that a private education can work the wonders which some sanguine writers have attributed to it. Men and women must be educated, in a great degree, by the opinions and manners of the society they live in. In every age there has been a stream of popular opinion that has

---

[1]   Francis Bacon (1561–1626). The quotation is from "Of Atheism."

[2]   Jean-Jacques Rousseau (1712–78), the famous Enlightenment educator. Although Wollstonecraft agreed with many of his educational theories, she strongly disagreed with his belief that young women's education should prepare them to please and support their future husbands.

carried all before it, and given a family character, as it were, to the century. It may then fairly be inferred, that, till society be differently constituted, much cannot be expected from education. It is, however, sufficient for my present purpose to assert, that whatever effect circumstances have on the abilities, every being may become virtuous by the exercise of its own reason; for if but one being was created with vicious inclinations, that is positively bad, what can save us from atheism? or if we worship a God, is not that God a devil?

Consequently, the most perfect education, in my opinion, is such an exercise of the understanding as is best calculated to strengthen the body and form the heart. Or, in other words, to enable the individual to attain such habits of virtue as will render it independent. In fact, it is a farce to call any being virtuous whose virtues do not result from the exercise of its own reason. This was Rousseau's opinion respecting men. I extend it to women, and confidently assert that they have been drawn out of their sphere by false refinement, and not by an endeavour to acquire masculine qualities. Still the regal homage which they receive is so intoxicating, that till the manners of the times are changed, and formed on more reasonable principles, it may be impossible to convince them that the illegitimate power which they obtain, by degrading themselves, is a curse, and that they must return to nature and equality, if they wish to secure the placid satisfaction that unsophisticated affections impart. But for this epoch we must wait—wait, perhaps, till kings and nobles, enlightened by reason, and, preferring the real dignity of man to childish state, throw off their gaudy hereditary trappings: and if then women do not resign the arbitrary power of beauty—they will prove that they have *less* mind than man.

I may be accused of arrogance; still I must declare, what I firmly believe, that all the writers who have written on the subject of female education and manners, from Rousseau to Dr. Gregory,[1] have contributed to render women more artificial, weak characters, than they would otherwise have been; and, consequently, more useless members of society. I might have expressed this conviction in a lower key; but I am afraid it would have been the whine of affectation, and not the faithful expression of my feelings; of the clear result, which experience and reflection have led me to draw.

---

[1]   Dr. John Gregory (1724–73), author of *A Father's Legacy to His Daughters* (see extract above, Appendix D.2).

When I come to that division of the subject, I shall advert to the passages that I more particularly disapprove of, in the works of the authors I have just alluded to; but it is first necessary to observe, that my objection extends to the whole purport of those books, which tend, in my opinion, to degrade one half of the human species, and render women pleasing at the expense of every solid virtue....

... In the present state of society, a little learning is required to support the character of a gentleman; and boys are obliged to submit to a few years of discipline. But in the education of women, the cultivation of the understanding is always subordinate to the acquirement of some corporeal accomplishment; even when enervated by confinement and false notions of modesty, the body is prevented from attaining that grace and beauty which relaxed half-formed limbs never exhibit. Besides, in youth their faculties are not brought forward by emulation; and having no serious scientific study, if they have natural sagacity it is turned too soon on life and manners. They dwell on effects, and modifications, without tracing them back to causes; and complicated rules to adjust behaviour, are a weak substitute for simple principles....

... I respect [Dr. Gregory's] heart; but entirely disapprove of his celebrated Legacy to his Daughters.

He advises them to cultivate a fondness for dress, because a fondness for dress, he asserts, is natural to them. I am unable to comprehend what either he or Rousseau mean, when they frequently use this indefinite term. If they told us that in a pre-existent state the soul was fond of dress, and brought this inclination with it into a new body, I should listen to them with a half smile, as I often do when I hear a rant about innate elegance.—But if he only meant to say that the exercise of the faculties will produce this fondness—I deny it.—It is not natural; but arises, like false ambition in men, from a love of power.

Dr. Gregory goes much further; he actually recommends dissimulation, and advises an innocent girl to give the lie to her feelings, and not dance with spirit, when gaiety of heart would make her feet eloquent without making her gestures immodest. In the name of truth and common sense, why should not one woman acknowledge that she can take more exercise than another? or, in other words, that she has a sound constitution; and why, to damp innocent vivacity, is she darkly to be told that men will draw conclusions which she little thinks of? Let the libertine draw what inference he pleases;

but, I hope, that no sensible mother will restrain the natural frankness of youth by instilling such indecent cautions. Out of the abundance of the heart the mouth speaketh; and a wiser than Solomon hath said, that the heart should be made clean, and not trivial ceremonies observed, which it is not very difficult to fulfil with scrupulous exactness when vice reigns in the heart.

Women ought to endeavour to purify their heart; but can they do so when their uncultivated understandings make them entirely dependent on their senses for employment and amusement, when no noble pursuit sets them above the little vanities of the day, or enables them to curb the wild emotions that agitate a reed over which every passing breeze has power? To gain the affections of a virtuous man is affectation necessary? Nature has given woman a weaker frame than man; but, to ensure her husband's affections, must a wife, who by the exercise of her mind and body whilst she was discharging the duties of a daughter, wife, and mother, has allowed her constitution to retain its natural strength, and her nerves a healthy tone, is she, I say, to condescend to use art and feign a sickly delicacy in order to secure her husband's affection? Weakness may excite tenderness, and gratify the arrogant pride of man; but the lordly caresses of a protector will not gratify a noble mind that pants for, and deserves to be respected. Fondness is a poor substitute for friendship!...

... If all the faculties of woman's mind are only to be cultivated as they respect her dependence on man; if, when she obtains a husband she has arrived at her goal, and meanly proud is satisfied with such a paltry crown, let her grovel contentedly, scarcely raised by her employments above the animal kingdom; but, if she is struggling for the prize of her high calling, let her cultivate her understanding without stopping to consider what character the husband may have whom she is destined to marry. Let her only determine, without being too anxious about present happiness, to acquire the qualities that ennoble a rational being, and a rough inelegant husband may shock her taste without destroying her peace of mind. She will not model her soul to suit the frailties of her companion, but to bear with them: his character may be a trial, but not an impediment to virtue.

If Dr. Gregory confined his remark to romantic expectations of constant love and congenial feelings, he should have recollected that experience will banish what advice can never make us cease to wish for, when the imagination is kept alive at the expense of reason.

I own it frequently happens that women who have fostered a romantic unnatural delicacy of feeling, waste their[1] lives in *imagining* how happy they should have been with a husband who could love them with a fervid increasing affection every day, and all day. But they might as well pine married as single—and would not be a jot more unhappy with a bad husband than longing for a good one. That a proper education; or, to speak with more precision, a well stored mind, would enable a woman to support a single life with dignity, I grant; but that she should avoid cultivating her taste, lest her husband should occasionally shock it, is quitting a substance for a shadow. To say the truth, I do not know of what use is an improved taste, if the individual is not rendered more independent of the casualties of life; if new sources of enjoyment, only dependent on the solitary operations of the mind, are not opened. People of taste, married or single, without distinction, will ever be disgusted by various things that touch not less observing minds. On this conclusion the argument must not be allowed to hinge; but in the whole sum of enjoyment is taste to be denominated a blessing?

The question is, whether it procures most pain or pleasure? The answer will decide the propriety of Dr. Gregory's advice, and shew how absurd and tyrannic it is thus to lay down a system of slavery; or to attempt to educate moral beings by any other rules than those deduced from pure reason, which apply to the whole species.

Gentleness of manners, forbearance and long-suffering, are such amiable Godlike qualities, that in sublime poetic strains the Deity has been invested with them; and, perhaps, no representation of his goodness so strongly fastens on the human affections as those that represent him abundant in mercy and willing to pardon. Gentleness, considered in this point of view, bears on its front all the characteristics of grandeur, combined with the winning graces of condescension; but what a different aspect it assumes when it is the submissive demeanour of dependence, the support of weakness that loves, because it wants protection; and is forbearing, because it must silently endure injuries; smiling under the lash at which it dare not snarl. Abject as this picture appears, it is the portrait of an accomplished woman, according to the received opinion of female excellence, separated by specious reasoners from human excellence. Or,

---

[1]   For example, the herd of novelists. [Wollstonecraft's note.]

they[1] kindly restore the rib, and make one moral being of a man and woman; not forgetting to give her all the 'submissive charms.' How women are to exist in that state where there is to be neither marrying nor giving in marriage, we are not told.—For though moralists have agreed that the tenor of life seems to prove that *man* is prepared by various circumstances for a future state, they constantly concur in advising *woman* only to provide for the present. Gentleness, docility, and a spaniel-like affection are, on this ground, consistently recommended as the cardinal virtues of the sex; and, disregarding the arbitrary economy of nature, one writer has declared that it is masculine for a woman to be melancholy. She was created to be the toy of man, his rattle, and it must jingle in his ears whenever, dismissing reason, he chooses to be amused....

But avoiding, as I have hitherto done, any direct comparison of the two sexes collectively, or frankly acknowledging the inferiority of woman, according to the present appearance of things, I shall only insist that men have increased that inferiority till women are almost sunk below the standard of rational creatures. Let their faculties have room to unfold, and their virtues to gain strength, and then determine where the whole sex must stand in the intellectual scale. Yet let it be remembered, that for a small number of distinguished women I do not ask a place....

If, I say, for I would not impress by declamation when Reason offers her sober light, if [women] are really capable of acting like rational creatures, let them not be treated like slaves; or, like the brutes who are dependent on the reason of man, when they associate with him; but cultivate their minds, give them the salutary, sublime curb of principle, and let them attain conscious dignity by feeling themselves only dependent on God. Teach them, in common with man, to submit to necessity, instead of giving, to render them more pleasing, a sex to morals....

These may be termed Utopian dreams.—Thanks to that Being who impressed them on my soul, and gave me sufficient strength of mind to dare to exert my own reason, till, becoming dependent only on him for the support of my virtue, I view, with indignation, the mistaken notions that enslave my sex....

---

[1] Vide Rousseau, and Swedenborg. [Wollstonecraft's note.] Emanuel Swedenborg (1688–1772) was an influential scientist, philosopher, and theologian who claimed that his 18 books of biblical interpretation were inspired by a direct appeal from Jesus Christ.

7. From Mrs. Sherwood, *The Governess; or, the Little Female Academy*, 1822

[Mary Martha Butt Sherwood (1775-1851) was the daughter of the Reverend George Butt, an Anglican clergyman then serving as rector in Stanford-on-Teme near Worcester. As a young woman, Sherwood became active in local Sunday schools, and along with her sister Lucy, began to write didactic stories for children, including *The History of Susan Gray* (1802). The following year, she married her cousin Henry Sherwood, an officer in the British Army. Sherwood accompanied her husband to India and continued writing children's stories, including the popular *Little Henry and His Bearer* (1814). Perhaps the most famous of her works is the *History of the Fairchild Family*, which was published in 1818. All of Sherwood's works rely heavily on an evangelical tradition that emphasized the sinful nature of humankind, and her reworking of *The Governess* (first published in 1820) is no exception. Sherwood took particular offense at Fielding's inclusion of fairy tales in her novel. As Jill Grey remarks, Sherwood "substituted dull, moral tales for Sarah's fairy-stories and also inserted the gloomiest quotations from the Bible on practically every page" (74). Despite its gloomy tone, Sherwood's text proved popular, going into six editions by 1840.]

Introduction

This little volume [*The Governess*] was published before the middle of the last century, and is said to have been written by a Sister of the celebrated Fielding.

It is remarkable as having been one of the first books of the kind prepared purposely for children: and in this view it may, perhaps, be found not uninteresting to the present generation of children, since it not only contains an exact and lively picture of their Grandmothers and Great-grandmothers, but was probably the favourite companion of their youthful days.

The editor was induced to undertake the revisal of this work by a Parent, who is now no more. It was indeed one of the last tasks allotted her by that dear Parent; and on this account she has been prevailed upon to complete it, although, on a close perusal, she found it necessary to make more alterations in it than she at first intended. Several Fairy-tales were incidentally introduced into the original work; and as it is not unlikely that such compositions formed, at that period, one of the chief amusements of the infant mind, a single tale of this description is admitted into the present edition. But since fanciful productions of this sort can never be rendered generally useful, it has been thought proper to suppress the rest, substituting in their place such appropriate relations as seemed more likely to conduce to juvenile edification.[1]

In the body of the work fewer liberties have been taken. There the original story is preserved nearly throughout; while the old-fashioned manners and modes of speaking have been carefully retained.

An Account of a Fray, *Begun and carried on for the Sake of an Apple: in which are shewn the sad Effects of Dissension and Rage*

The greater part of the first week after the arrival of the little girls was spent in settling and arranging the classes. On the Saturday afternoon, however, it being a fine evening, the children were allowed to divert themselves in the garden; and their governess, who delighted in affording them every reasonable gratification, brought out a little basket of apples, which were intended to be divided equally among them. But Mrs. Teachum being called hastily away, one of her poor neighbours having met with an accident which required her assistance, she left the fruit in the hands of Miss Jenny Peace, with a strict charge to see that every one had her due share of it.

But, alas! the evil of the heart, that deadly evil of which we have every one of us such large experience, turned kind Mrs. Teachum's

---

[1]   The single fairy tale included in Sherwood's text tells the story of the good fairy Serena and Rosalinda. Rosalinda is a spoiled princess whose parents commit her to the care of Serena so that her bad behavior can be corrected. Although this story echoes Fielding's tale of Princess Hebe and the fairy Sybella, none of Sherwood's other additions have any relation to Fielding's fairy stories. For example, Sherwood includes the history of Albert de la Hauteville, who persecuted protestants in France during the reign of the Catholic Louis XIV; in Sherwood's telling, Albert is converted to "true" (i.e., evangelical Protestant) Christianity and stops his persecutions. Sherwood also adds "The History of Miss Fanny; or, the Hard-Hearted Little Girl," in which Fanny is compared to her good cousin Anna. As Sherwood explains, "the difference between the two cousins was not a natural one, but the effect of divine grace operating on the heart" of Anna.

design of giving pleasure, into an occasion of pain and sorrow. There happened to be in the basket one apple something larger than the rest; and upon this the whole company immediately placed their desiring eyes, every one of them crying out at once, "Pray, Miss Jenny, give me that apple." Each hearkening to the suggestions of her own heart, found some reason why she was to be preferred to all her school-fellows, and brought forward this reason with all the vehemence of selfishness: the youngest pleaded her youth, and the eldest her age; one insisted on her goodness; another claimed a title to preference from her rank in the school; and one, in confidence of her superior strength, said positively she would have the large apple; but, all speaking together, it was difficult to distinguish who said *this*, or who said *that*.

Miss Jenny begged them all to be quiet, but in vain, for she could not be heard; they had all set their hearts on the one fine apple looking upon all the rest as not worth having. For this is one sad effect of envy and an eager desire after any thing not within our reach, that it prevents our partaking of those pleasures which are actually offered us, embittering every joy, and poisoning every sweet. And on this account, he who knew the heart of man, said, *Blessed are the meek: for they shall inherit the earth.* (Matt. v. 5.)

In vain Miss Jenny endeavoured to calm the little turbulent spirits of her companions. She spoke to them of the sinfulness of their conduct, and reminded them how greatly they were offending God by their greediness, instead of manifesting that spirit of meekness by which Christian children should ever be distinguished. But they would not hearken to her; and several of them not having been accustomed to be addressed in this manner, seemed not even to comprehend what she meant. She offered next to divide the disputed apple into eight parts, and to give up her own share of the contents of the basket to satisfy them: but she might as well have been silent; for they were all too eagerly talking to attend to her proposal. At last, as a means to quiet the disturbance, she threw the apple which was the cause of their contention, with her utmost force, over a hedge into another garden, where they could not get at it.

At first they were all silent, as if struck dumb with astonishment at the loss of this one poor apple, though at the same time they had a basket full before them. But this failed to effect Miss Jenny's intention: for though the apple was the *obvious* cause of their quarrel, the *latent* cause of all lay in their own evil hearts—the present fray was no more than a breaking forth of those sinful dispositions which exist within the breast of every child of Adam.

Perhaps some of you, my young friends, who peruse this little book, may never have heard the subject of human depravity familiarly explained. In this case, should you be led to suppose that these little Misses of Mrs. Teachum's school were worse than others by nature, I will here endeavour to make plain to you the important doctrine of the depravity of man's heart. And first, I must tell you, that God made man in his own image, pure and free from sin, without one disorderly appetite or improper feeling, but holy, upright, and glorious, like his Maker, requiring no covering for his beautiful and spotless body, nor any imputed righteousness to conceal, as with a garment, the deformity of his soul. But Satan, the enemy of mankind, tempted our first parents to depart from God; in consequence of which, and in a manner not easy to be understood, the whole nature of man received so vitiating a taint, that every feeling and motion of his heart became sinful, and that continually; insomuch, that this strong description of wickedness of man, among many others, is given in Scripture—*And God saw that the wickedness of man was great in the earth, and that every imagination of the thoughts of his heart was only evil continually.* (Gen. vi. 5.)

But although this is universally the case of man upon earth, although we are born children of wrath, and heirs of hell, yet, through the mercy of Christ, a way is opened unto us for escaping these evils. The Lord Jesus Christ, by his death upon the cross, paid the price of our redemption, and procured for us the gift of the Holy Spirit of God; which being received by faith, enters the corrupt heart of man, cleansing and purifying, sanctifying and renewing it in the lost image of God. You are therefore, my dear children, unless you have already received the Holy Spirit by faith into your hearts, in no better a state than these little girls of whom you have just been reading. And if you *have* received that Spirit, you will think humbly of yourselves, and feel a consciousness that, when you are enabled to do better than these little ones, it is not through your own strength, but through the power of the Holy Spirit.

But to return to my story....

Mrs. Teachum on Fairy Tales

Miss Jenny Peace had scarcely finished this little story,[1] when the bell ringing, summoned the young people to their dinner: after which Mrs. Teachum, taking Miss Jenny apart, enquired of her what she had found that day for the amusement of her little companions. Miss Jenny then taking the little book from her pocket, presented it to her governess; who, retiring to her closet,[2] occupied herself in reading it till the bell rang for school.

When school was over, and the little ones were preparing for their evening walk, Mrs. Teachum took the opportunity of returning Miss Jenny's book, saying with a smile, "My dear Miss Jenny, I do not dislike your story, since its tendency is extremely good: but I will give you a reason why fairy-tales and tales of genii, generally speaking, however well written, can scarcely ever be rendered profitable, and therefore should be sparingly used."

Here Miss Jenny coloured, and her eyes filled with tears. Upon which, Mrs. Teachum affectionately taking her hand, said, "I do not intend by this to blame you for what you have done; but I only wish, my dear child, to lead you from these trifles to better things. You are, I know, strongly impressed with the doctrine of the depravity of human nature, the need of a Saviour, and many other important truths taught in Scripture; you know also how necessary it is not to lose any opportunity of inculcating these doctrines on the minds of young people, according to that scriptural direction: *For precept must be upon precept, precept upon precept; line upon line, line upon line; here a little, and there a little.* (Isaiah xxviii. 10.) Now although," continued Mrs. Teachum, "it is not found that very young people are profited by grave discourses or deep discussions of religious subjects, and that instruction when conveyed through the medium of some beautiful story or pleasant tale, more easily insinuates itself into the youthful mind than any thing of a drier nature; yet the greatest care is necessary that the instruction thus conveyed should be perfectly agreeable to the Christian dispensation. Fairy-tales therefore are in general an improper medium of instruction, because it would be absurd in such tales to introduce Christian principles as motives of action: and yet we are assured

---

[1]   The story of Serena and Rosalinda.
[2]   A small, private room, usually attached to the bedroom, often used for reading (*OED*).

from the highest authority, that no one can do well without the help of the Holy Spirit."

Mrs. Teachum here paused a minute, seeing that Miss Jenny Peace looked as if she did not wholly understand her, and then continued—"Children, my dear, should be perpetually reminded of this important truth, that no human being can so much as think a good thought without divine help: all stories, therefore, in which persons are described as acting well without this help, have a most exceedingly evil tendency. But, since it would be wholly absurd to introduce solemn Christian doctrines into fairy-tales; on this account such tales should be very sparingly used, it being extremely difficult, if not impossible, from the reason I have specified, to render them generally useful. I do not, however," added she, "always prohibit fairy-tales, my dear child: but when you next have occasion to read to your companions, apply to me, and I will endeavour to furnish you with some story of a superior tendency to the common run of amusing tales."[1]

Miss Jenny thanked Mrs. Teachum for her instructions and kind indulgence; and promising to give her an exact account of their daily amusements, she took leave, and retired to rest.

---

[1] Compare this explanation to Mrs. Teachum's reasoning in Fielding's version (p. 84–85).

Select Bibliography

Selected Modern Editions of Works by Sarah Fielding

The Adventures of David Simple (1744; 1st ed.) and Volume the Last (1753; 1st ed.). Ed. Peter Sabor. Lexington: UP of Kentucky, 1998.

The Adventures of David Simple. Ed. Linda Bree. London: Penguin, 2002.

The Adventures of David Simple (1744; 2nd ed., revised with preface by Henry Fielding). Ed. Malcolm Kelsall. London: Oxford UP, 1969.

The Correspondence of Henry and Sarah Fielding. Ed. Martin C. Battestin and Clive T. Probyn. Oxford: Clarendon Press, 1993.

The Cry: A New Dramatic Fable. Facsimile ed. Intro. Mary Anne Schofield. Delmar, NY: Scholars' Facsimiles and Reprints, 1986.

The Cry: A New Dramatic Fable. Delmar, NY: Scholars' Facsimiles and Reprints, 1999.

The Governess, or Little Female Academy. Facsimile ed. Intro. Jill E. Grey. London: Oxford UP, 1968.

The Governess, or Little Female Academy. Intro. Mary Cadogan. London: Pandora, 1987.

The History of Ophelia. Ed. Peter Sabor. Peterborough, ON: Broadview Press, 2004.

The History of the Countess of Dellwyn. <http://www.blackmask.com/books64c/countdell.htm>. Blackmask Online: 2002.

The Lives of Cleopatra and Octavia. Ed. Christopher D. Johnson. Lewisburg, PA: Bucknell UP, 1994.

The Lives of Cleopatra and Octavia. Facsimile ed. New York: Garland, 1974.

Remarks on Clarissa. Facsimile ed. Intro. Peter Sabor. Los Angeles: William Andrews Clark Memorial Library, U of California, 1985.

Remarks on Clarissa. Facsimile ed. New York: Garland, 1970.

Selected Secondary Sources

Barchas, Janine. "Sarah Fielding's Dashing Style and Eighteenth-Century Print Culture." ELH 63 (1996): 633–56.

Barker, Gerard A. "David Simple: The Novel of Sensibility in Embryo." Modern Language Studies 12 (1982): 69–80.

Battestin, Martin C. "Henry Fielding, Sarah Fielding, and 'the dreadful Sin of Incest.'" Novel 13 (1979): 6–18.

Bree, Linda. *Sarah Fielding*. Boston: Twayne, 1996.

Burdan, Judith. "Girls Must Be Seen and Heard: Domestic Surveillance in Sarah Fielding's *The Governess*." *Children's Literature Association Quarterly* 19.1 (1994): 8–14.

Burrows, J.F., and A.J. Hassall. "*Anna Boleyn* and the Authenticity of Fielding's Feminine Narratives." *Eighteenth-Century Studies* 21 (1988): 427–53.

Downs-Miers, Deborah. "Springing the Trap: Subtexts and Subversions." *Fetter'd or Free? British Women Novelists, 1670–1815.* Ed. Mary Anne Schofield and Cecilia Macheski. Athens: Ohio UP, 1986: 308–23.

———. "For Betty and the Little Female Academy: A Book of Their Own." *Children's Literature Association Quarterly* 10.1 (1985): 30–33.

Gadeken, Sara. "Gender, Empire, and Nation in Sarah Fielding's *Lives of Cleopatra and Octavia*." *SEL: Studies in English Literature 1500-1900* 39.3 (1999): 523–38.

———. "'A Method of Being Perfectly Happy': Technologies of Self in the Eighteenth-Century Female Community." *Eighteenth-Century Novel* 1 (2001): 217–35.

Gautier, Gary. "Henry and Sarah Fielding on Romance and Sensibility." *Novel: A Forum on Fiction* 31.2 (1998): 195–214.

Nickel, Terri. "'Ingenious Torment': Incest, Family, and the Structure of Community in the Work of Sarah Fielding." *Eighteenth Century: Theory and Interpretation* 36 (1995): 234–47.

Rizzo, Betty. "Satires of Tyrants and Toadeaters: Fielding and Collier." *Companions without Vows: Relationships among Eighteenth-Century British Women.* Athens: U of Georgia P, 1994. 41–60.

Spencer, Jane. "Masculine Approval and Sarah Fielding." *The Rise of the Woman Novelist: From Aphra Behn to Jane Austen.* Oxford: Blackwell, 1986. 91–94.

Spender, Dale. "Sarah Fielding and Misrepresentation." *Mothers of the Novel: 100 Good Women Writers before Jane Austen.* London: Pandora, 1986. 180–93.

Stockstill, Ashley. "Better Homes and Gardens: The Fairy World(s) of Sarah Fielding and Sarah Scott." *Feminist Studies in English Literature* 6.2 (1998): 137–58.

Suzuki, Mika. "The Little Female Academy *and* The Governess." *Women's Writing* 1.3 (1994): 325–39.

Tieken-Boon van Ostade, Ingrid. "Social Network Analysis and the Language of Sarah Fielding." *European Journal of English Studies* 4.3 (2000): 291–301.

Todd, Janet. "Novelists of Sentiment: Sarah Fielding and Frances Sheridan." *The Sign of Angellica: Women, Writing and Fiction, 1660–1800.* New York: Columbia UP, 1992. 161–75.

Wilner, Arelene Fish. "Education and Ideology in Sarah Fielding's *The Governess.*" *Studies in Eighteenth-Century Culture* 24 (1995): 307–27.

Woodward, Carolyn. "'Feminine Virtue, Ladylike Disguise, Women of Community': Sarah Fielding and the Female I Am at Mid-Century." *Transactions of the Samuel Johnson Society of the Northwest* 15 (1984): 57–71.